The Turni

E.M. Phillips

Cover illustration by Julie Hepenstal

This one is for

Will, Tom, Ben, Rosie, Lydia & Beth

May they always

'...fill the unforgiving minute

with sixty seconds' worth of distance run'...

The Turning Point

E.M. Phillips

The Turning Point

Published 2011 by Sagittarius Publications
62 Jacklyns Lane, Alresford, Hampshire SO24 9LH
Tel: 01962 734322

Typeset by John Owen Smith

ISBN 978-0-9555778-7-1

Printed and bound in Great Britain by CPI Antony Rowe, Chippenham and Eastbourne

'LIFE IS ALWAYS AT SOME TURNING POINT'

Irwin Edman

1

Michael Niven parked his Mercedes alongside a small and battered Citroën, checked that he'd left room for passing vehicles and that no crime-hungry traffic warden was in sight, then stepped out onto the roadway and stood for several minutes surveying the rundown terraced house before him. From the ground floor flat came the tuneless rhythmic thump of what, to his sensitive ear, barely passed for music, overlaid by the high-pitched babble of many voices.

Yes, this was the place all right, and pretty much what he'd expected: peeling paint and grimy windows, with slatted blinds hanging askew. A poor return, Michael thought, for the no doubt astronomical rent. As a sudden gust of wind sent empty cans, discarded polystyrene take-away cartons and scraps of paper tumbling along the pavement, he gave a grunt of distaste then shrugged in dour resignation. Oh well, better get it over with. He hoped Simon hadn't sent him on a wild goose chase and that he wouldn't find the girl either pissed out of her mind, or shoving coke up her nose.

The front door was on the latch; opening it he entered a narrow hallway reeking of alcohol overlaid with pot. A normal enough scenario for the last decade of the confused and troubled 20th century. Stepping around a couple, who may or may not have been of opposite sexes, plastered to the wall in a passionate embrace, and circum-navigating a bicycle chained to the newel post, he opened the nearest door.

A blast of music, hot air and smoke hit him. A voluptuous redhead with kohl-rimmed eyes and breath like a lion thrust a can of lager into his hand. 'Dah-ling,' she breathed, 'if you want anything stronger just ask that little tart Julian. He's running a bar in the kitchen,' and drifted away in a cloud of gin and market stall Chanel No.5.

Michael silently cursed Simon. How the hell was he supposed to find a cross between Audrey Hepburn and little orphan Annie is *this* shower of theatrical wannabes?

He let his gaze wander around the overcrowded room until a sudden shift in the gyrating bodies gave him a momentary view straight through to the open French windows, and he knew instinctively that he had run his quarry to earth. Simon, he thought, hadn't been far off target.

Moving with swift determination he shouldered his way across the room and stopped a few paces behind the girl where she sat on the garden steps, her long slim fingers almost absently removing from her bare knee the hand of a young man seated beside her.

At a distance Michael's first impression had been that of a waiflike nineteen-sixty-type model with a tantalising air of innocent sexiness; close up he saw that first snap judgement had probably been right. His faint smile broadened into a grin and setting down his unopened can next to an ashtray overflowing with what appeared to be the remnants of a substantial consignment of South America's finest, leaned against the jamb of the French window and continued at close quarters his silent appraisal of Simon Meyer's protégé.

*   *   *

Oblivious of the music and raised voices in the room beyond, Cassie's thoughts were not on the hot-handed Tony at her side, but of Oliver. She did love him but sometimes he was so bloody insensitive. On the anniversary of Harry's death the very last thing she'd needed was rampant lust...

Her companion squeezed a little higher up her leg; she sighed faintly and removed the encroaching fingers for a second time. Staring moodily at the back of Jono's head she willed him to come to her rescue, but he was too busy with a blonde bimbo currently modelling underwear in a mail-order catalogue to notice her need. She winced as the bimbo tossed her head and whinnied like a horse.

Cassie was very fond of Jono Murray, aka the Honourable Jonathan Murrayfield, since they had met in their first term at Art College; even though halfway through his course he had abandoned art in favour of the theatre. Since then, and on the strength of a few bit parts in the more depressing pub cellars on the London Fringe Theatre circuit, he had begun filling his flat with hoards of partying fellow thespians, most of them "resting" and none instantly recognisable as future star material. On her arrival that evening Cassie had borne stoically with the theatrical shoptalk between Jono and his new flatmate, but drew the line at being quite so blatantly propositioned by the apparently sexually ambivalent Tony.

'Getting a bit homophobic, are you dear? Jono had queried earlier in the evening, 'the boy can't help being bi, you know.'

'He can be gay, bi or whatever floats his boat,' she'd answered crisply, 'I just don't like being touched up by any guy who can't make his mind up one way or the other.'

Now she put another couple of inches between Tony's leg and her own and thought philosophically that she'd just have to stick it out; she couldn't afford to stay elsewhere, even for the next forty-eight hours.

A deep, unfamiliar voice interrupted her reverie. 'Excuse me, but are you Cassandra Chisholm?'

She looked up at the man who had apparently just materialised at her side. Good looking she thought, but...whose grandfather *was* he, for God's sake? At least a couple of decades older than anyone else present and wearing formal evening dress, he looked as out of place as Ian Paisley at a Cardinals' Convention. Cautiously, she said, 'That's me,' and he extended his hand.

'Michael. Michael Niven. Simon, from the Meyer Gallery, said you might be able to help me.'

'Well that rather depends,' she answered, 'on what you want.'

They were suddenly the cynosure of three pairs of curious eyes. The blonde breathed ecstatically, 'Will you get *that*!' Jono said nonchalantly, 'Hi, Michael, long time no see,' while Tony scowled and muttered, 'Old git!'

Cassie took the hand offered by the new arrival and with one smooth movement he drew her up and into the room behind them. 'In here,' he indicated the door to the bathroom, 'I've checked all the comings and goings, and this is probably the only room in the place right now that doesn't have someone either rolling or smoking a joint.'

Cassie blinked, but followed him; once inside he shut the door and leaning broad shoulders against it, said, 'I should introduce myself properly. I am a writer, an old friend of Simon and a distant cousin to Jonathan.' He hesitated a moment. 'I'm also in something of an awkward position. In a few days I leave for my first lecture tour in America. I hadn't realised they were expecting me to provide new publicity pictures. Simon thought you would do a rushed but competent job, and that you could probably do with the money.'

Cassie perched on the edge of the bath and looked him over with a professional eye. 'Well,' she admitted, 'he was right about the last, although portraiture isn't quite my thing.'

He really was very good looking, she thought, with the unmistakable air of someone used to getting what he wanted without the need to bother with any picky arguments. One of those dodgy masterful old geezers, probably a bit of a letch, she judged, but she did need the money, so better grab the opportunity Simon had put her way...

She nodded. 'OK, but I'd rather photograph you outdoors; you know, with a view of good old London in the background, taking a stroll along the Embankment or looking fetching on a bench in St James' Park. The Yanks like that sort of thing.'

He said gravely, 'Something along those lines would be fine.'

'I prefer to work in black and white,' she warned.

'I know. Simon told me.'

'I'm off to Paris on Friday, so if you can manage tomorrow?' She looked up at him questioningly.

He asked, 'What's wrong with now?'

'Everything,' she began to tick off a list on her fingers. 'It's the back end of the day, the shadows are too long, I don't have my camera with me, you aren't exactly dressed for casual poses and it would be *very* rude to walk out of Jono's party; particularly as I'm dossing here for nothing.'

'You didn't look as though you were finding the party particularly exciting. You were daydreaming.'

His voice was very dry. She looked at him closely. 'How would you know that?'

He admitted, 'I've been standing behind you for the past five minutes. You were miles away…that young man was trying so hard to make it and you didn't even notice him.'

'Oh, yes I did; I just chose not to notice, that's different.' She looked at him poker-faced. 'He hopes if he follows me around breathing heavily and looking moody, that I'll sleep with him tonight and make Jono, his latest male fantasy, jealous as hell; as Jono is straight as they come he has no chance there…' she shrugged.

He asked mildly, 'And will you sleep with him?'

'Not if he *paid* me, I wouldn't.'

'Well, as you are not in a party mood, do not lust after that young man, and it won't make the slightest difference to Jonathan whether you are here or not, why don't you come and have dinner with me?'

Again she studied him carefully. She asked 'Why I should want to do that?'

'Well now, if you are hard up and I am willing to write you a cheque for a quite vulgar amount of money – provided you make me look ten years younger and as close to a Richard Gere clone as is humanly possible – it might be politic for you to humour me.'

There was, she decided prudently, only one answer to an offer like that. She sighed. 'OK, you win, but I warn you: I'm *very* hungry.'

'Then we shall dine.' Opening the door and taking her by the arm he steered her through the crowded room. That he was swiftly and expertly checking over her figure beneath her treasured, for-parties-only, knee-high crimson silk dress, the length of her legs and possibly her bra size as well was obvious, but so at odds with his formal speech and manner that she gave a hiccup of laughter. 'I haven't heard anyone talk that naff for...' she hesitated, her voice momentarily unsteady at the sudden remembrance of Harry, then finished rapidly, 'for quite some time.'

He raised his eyebrows slightly, but made no comment as they by-passed the bicycle and the Last Tango in Paris couple in the hall and made it to the street door. When they were outside the flat and standing beside a gleaming black Mercedes, blatantly double-parked beside her Citroën, she put her hand on the roof of her own car and treated him to a sudden grin.

'Your car or mine, Mr Niven?' she asked, mimicking his speech perfectly and he answered without the flicker of a smile, 'I give you one guess, Miss Chisholm.'

*   *   *

'So why are you living in sordid West Ken with my cousin Jonathan when your home is in Cornwall?' Michael Niven pushed aside his plate and leaned to refill her wineglass.

'I don't *live* with Jono; he's my mate.' Rather overwhelmed by the surroundings, which were famous, expensive, and filled with beautiful people, Cassie enunciated carefully, conscious that she'd already drunk rather too much. 'I'm only staying for a few days while I get some work ready for Simon.'

'Myer did say you were at something of a loose end; that's why he thought you might help me out.'

She said honestly, 'Well, he knows I'm broke and that you would be helping *me* out.'

He was silent for a moment then asked unexpectedly, 'Why, if you have no money are you going to Paris?'

'To see my father,' when he again raised an enquiring eyebrow she explained grudgingly, 'he's an artist. Alaric Chisholm. You may have heard of him, he's quite well known.'

'Chisholm? Mmm, yes – I bought a painting off him some years ago; a young girl on a swing.' He gave her another one of his long looks. 'Was it you?'

'Probably, there was a time when he thought I was worth the paint.'

She could have kicked herself when she heard the defensive note in her voice, as he immediately hunched forward in his chair,

11

watching her intently. His dark eyes beneath straight, half-frowning brows were compelling and under their intense gaze something segued slowly and deliciously below her ribcage before glissading down to perform a graceful somersault in the pit of her stomach. She swallowed hard. He asked, 'And your mother – is she in Paris?'

'I haven't a clue where she is; she could be in Paris or Timbuktu for all I know.' A sudden overwhelming urge to take a running kick at all this urbane, old-fashioned formality, made her add loudly enough to be heard at the neighbouring tables, 'I used to tell my school friends I was a love child; it sounded better than bastard.'

He regarded her gravely, 'If I ever decide to forsake Hardy and Trollope and the Brontës to produce my own turgid novel, it might come in useful to have a thumbnail sketch of what is beginning to sound a rather interesting life.'

'You might be disappointed.' She propped her chin on her hand, 'compared with *me*, the Brontës lived it up in a big way.'

'I doubt that,' he said dryly, 'so to use the modern vernacular, shoot!'

She gave him a pitying look. 'Oh, *please*, that is so naff.' She grinned at his pained expression. 'OK, OK...I guess I owe you something for the dinner.' She wrinkled her brow and launched into a rapid, and he suspected, practised and highly coloured version of events.

'My mother, I think, was one of my father's models, although he's always been a bit cagey about that: for all I know she may have been a cleaner he jumped when she came to scrub the floors, or whatever. Anyway, when I was a few weeks old she did a bunk and forgot to take me with her. Actually, for a selfish egomaniac Alaric behaved rather well; he seemed to quite like the idea of being a father, but the novelty must have worn off eventually because when I was about thirteen he suddenly packed me off to boarding school and moved to Paris. There you are – the story of my life so far.'

'Why?'

'Why, what?'

He said patiently, 'Why did your father leave you then go to Paris.'

'Search me – and you do ask one hell of a lot of questions, don't you?'

'One would learn nothing in life without questions; so, why *did* he go to Paris?'

She answered impatiently, 'Like I said, I don't know.' She was suddenly evasive, looking away from him and smoothing her hair.

After a moment or two she added in a carefully neutral tone, 'I spent my vacations from school in Cornwall with his sister Laura, her husband Harry and a wolfhound named Cormack, who thinks he's a human being. We all got on so well that I've been there ever since.' For the first time she gave an unselfconscious smile and her voice softened. 'Harry was a writer too, an art historian, and a clever amateur photographer. He taught me a lot, which is how I ended up doing photography for a living.' For a moment she looked away again then added flatly. 'He died last year.'

'Do you visit your father often?'

'Only when I'm very broke, he's quite generous with his money.'

There was a short silence. She drew patterns on the cloth with her fork then glanced up to find him watching her with a baffled smile. He asked, 'Do you always wear your feelings inside out?'

She said crossly. 'Don't tell me you're a ruddy part-time psychiatrist as well.'

'I'm sorry. That was intrusive.' He spread his hands, palms upward. 'Suppose we close that particular subject; tell me about where you live in Cornwall.'

She relaxed. 'In an old house called Fleetwood in a very small village above a creek on the Helford River.'

'That's an unusual name for a house.'

'Posh, isn't it? My grandfather was the vicar of Treveren. When he retired and a new smaller rectory was built, he bought the old one and re-named it. It's just a rather ordinary Victorian vicarage...you know, high ceilings, smoky chimneys and fuc... Sorry!' she actually blushed, 'I mean, like, its hellish draughty in the winter when the gales blow, but the garden is lovely and as it's high up on the cliffs it has wonderful views. My aunt has lived there since her parents died.'

She gave her sudden wide grin. 'Laura's an amazing person; she did a lot of the research for Harry's books and when he died she carried on where he left off. She's just finishing the one he'd started on a school of nineteenth century Cornish painters.'

'Sounds my sort of person; I should like to meet her.'

'Well, you never know...' She took up her glass and looked at him over the rim. 'Once the book is finished she will probably come up to see Harry's publisher. When she comes to London she usually stays with Simon and Lily, so if you are in the habit of visiting *them* you may get lucky!'

* * *

Michael watched her as she talked and wondered at the odd mixture of naïve and streetwise in her speech and manner. One of Thatcher's children she was not. Something to do with an old-fashioned solid country upbringing overlaid by a thin veneer of the city, he guessed. Simon had said she was twenty-three but she looked about eighteen and exuded a kind of innocent sexiness that was probably nowhere near as innocuous as it seemed. Reason and experience told him to keep his distance, but she was working a particular kind of magic for him that was almost irresistible.

Just who or what he wondered had her mother really been: Italian perhaps, or even Greek? From what he could remember of his brief meeting with her father, Alaric Chisholm was large and ruddy complexioned, with blue eyes and auburn hair; this olive-skinned girl, with eyes like night and hair as dark as his own, would pass as a native of almost any Mediterranean country.

Firmly he disciplined his eyes from continuing their approval of her figure, knowing with a self-mocking awareness that he would like to spend a great many more evenings in her company. But even without the difficulties and disasters of his past, there was still the yawning gap between twenty-three and a man well past the Life Begins at Forty tag.

And there was bound to be another man lurking somewhere in the background of a girl with young Cassandra Chisholm's considerable attributes.

*   *   *

He left her at the flat after making arrangements to meet the following morning. Once inside the door Cassie stepped carefully over the empty glasses, bottles and occasional entwined bodies still sprawled about the sitting-room floor, and went straight to the tiny box room next to Jono's, where, judging by the noises audible through the wall, he was vigorously entertaining the human Barbie Doll. They were, she thought gloomily as she began to undress, all set to make it a very noisy night.

Once away from Michael Niven's charismatic and persuasive presence she was aware that she had told him far too much about herself and where she was at, whilst he had managed to spend the entire evening without revealing anything other than that he was a literary writer and lecturer. Any man that uncommunicative about his life, she reckoned, was either very boring or had something to hide, and boring he was not.

14

Tomorrow she would be polite but professional and keep him at a safe distance. Not that he'd made any attempt to score. Apart from those give-away eyes that at one point in the evening had removed at least the first layer of her clothes, he couldn't have behaved less like an ageing lecher waiting to pounce.

Sleep was a long time coming, but despite the twanging bedsprings and orgasmic yelps and caterwauling from the next room, she did finally drift off, only to find her dreams invaded by visions of her dinner companion's lively gaze and altogether too disturbing mouth.

*   *   *

She met him on the Embankment early the next day. In pale slacks and an open-neck navy silk shirt beneath a cream linen jacket he looked younger and more relaxed than the previous evening. When he greeted her with a smile and a warm handshake, she was again made immediately aware that he had an unfair amount of the kind of charm likely to prove downright lethal at close quarters.

'I don't think we'll do much better than to start here.' She was brisk and professional, determinedly focusing her mind on the technical details of sunlight and shade, at the same time making a swift assessment of his better points, of which there were far too many. 'Then we might move on to Dickens country and the South Bank; there are still a few wonderful old buildings left near the Globe that should suit your style.'

'I didn't know I had a style, and I don't do Dickens.'

'I shouldn't think the Yanks would care if it's Dickens' London, Haworth Parsonage or Hardy's monument, so long as it's old and true blue Brit!' She examined him through narrowed eyes. 'If you'll go closer to the wall there – just a couple of metres – and don't look at me.'

'Why should I not do that?'

'Never mind why, trust me; I know what I'm doing. Just keep talking.'

'What would you like me to talk about?'

'Anything, it doesn't matter,' she grinned, 'your wife and children if you like.'

Momentarily he bent his head and brushed at some invisible speck on his jacket sleeve. 'I don't have either.'

She crouched first on the wall then jumped down, moving around him and shooting quickly. 'I should have known. You don't look that harassed.'

As she lowered her camera and pushed a hand through her short hair, he held her gaze with a quite extraordinarily depth and intensity and she blinked hard, saying breathlessly, 'Don't do that.'

'Don't do what?'

'Stare at me like that: it's freaky. Come along, let's change the scenery.'

He asked, 'Shall we take a taxi?'

'No. I might miss a good shot and we've plenty of time. I'd rather walk. That's if you feel up to it.'

'I'm not that old.' He took her arm and turned to walk back along the Embankment and she lost step for a second as a shock wave travelled straight from her elbow through to the pit of her stomach. *Now let's stop this right here,* she admonished herself silently, twitching her arm away, *he may have sex appeal to die for, but for all you know, he could be a serial killer with a nice line in chat-ups...*

She thought of her return to Cornwall and Oliver's bed, but couldn't help being excited at getting that kind of charge from someone who looked as if he might even be old enough to be her father.

'If we are to get through this morning relatively unscathed, do you think you might uncoil a little?' He was looking down at her, his eyes perceptive and amused. 'If you get any more tense, you might easily break in half.'

'I'm neither coiled nor tense,' she answered shortly, 'just concentrating on my work. I believe in giving value for money.'

'Well don't concentrate quite so hard because I really do hate being photographed, and you are making *me* nervous. If I get the jitters even your best efforts are unlikely to produce anything more attractive than a *doppelganger* for Hannibal Lecter!'

She said tartly, 'I wouldn't have put you down as a nervous type; more the sort to make other people wonder if they might be wearing odd socks.'

He looked her over from head to toe, taking in the narrow cut jeans, the soft cream shirt collar and flame red sweater, all worn over a body that he was willing to bet owed nothing to any cross-your-heart uplift bra. He gave his lazy smile.

'No odd socks, and from where I'm standing everything looks just about one hundred per cent fantastic!' he answered, then watched with undisguised delight as a blush rose from her neck to hairline in one entrancing wave of colour.

This one was, despite an impressively assumed poise, just about the least 'with it' member of her generation he had come across, he thought. Again he wondered what was in her background and up-bringing to make her so vulnerable – and so dangerously attractive.

*   *   *

By eleven-thirty she was finished. 'I'll ring you when the proofs are ready.' She busied herself fitting her Leica back into her bag.

'Where will you be working?'

'At Simon's lab; he lets me have the use of it when I'm in town – and so he should,' she added feelingly, 'he takes a bloody great whack of commission for everything of mine he sells.'

'Ah, but then I daresay that being Simon he gets a good price for them.'

'There is that.' She fastened the straps on her bag and gave him a brief smile. 'I should have the proofs ready by tomorrow.'

She went swiftly, giving him no time to suggest coffee or lunch, and he watched her walk away from him, admiring the way she moved: smoothly from the hips, like a dancer. He turned away in wry disapproval, quoting beneath his breath, '"But it's not going to happen again, my boy, it's *not* going to happen again!"'

*   *   *

When Cassie arrived back at the flat Tony looked up at her with a frown. 'Finished with your old man, have you?' he asked, spooning instant coffee into four mugs. 'He's a smooth old tosser, isn't he?'

'As he's paying me mega bucks for my morning's work, he can be as smooth as he likes.' Cassie pulled a chair from beneath the table and sat down, propping her chin on her knuckles. She nodded at the four mugs. 'Jono got another lodger, has he?'

'No.' Tony stirred milk viciously into the mugs. 'The spare's for his tart – she stayed the night.'

'I know; I heard them.' His scowl deepened and she grinned. 'Temper … I thought it was me you fancied, not Jono!'

He snapped, 'You were bloody late back last night after taking off with that old fart.'

Her grin vanished and she gave him a steely look. 'Whom I am with and what time I come in is nothing to do with you, or any other of the creeps decorating the living room floor last night. I am not a fixture; merely passing through.'

'Bickering again, children?' Jono appeared in the doorway,

17

looking hung-over but well satisfied with his night of unbridled lust. He slumped into a chair beside Cassie, and she eyed him dispassionately, thinking that whoever told him he would look good with bushed-out hair halfway down his back had made a big mistake, because for a basically attractive man it made him look pretty horrible.

'I never bicker.' She sipped her coffee. 'Ugh, Tony!' she grimaced, 'how can even you produce such foul muck from freeze-dried granules?'

Jono said, 'It's a gift he has,' and they both laughed.

'What have you done with the Barbie doll?' she asked, 'Just too shagged to drag herself from beneath the duvet, is she?'

'Bitch,' Jono grinned amiably and nudged her ribs with a bony elbow. 'I saw you and my cousin Michael sloping off – what did he want?'

'Some publicity photographs in a hurry.' She did her best to sound non-committal. 'We discussed them over dinner last night and I met him this morning for a session. When I've finished Tony's homemade paint stripper I'm away to Simon's lab to print a set of proofs.'

'So now you won't need the dosh you borrowed from me to go to Paris and tap your old man.'

She frowned. 'I've already told him I'm coming, and as I've just spent your cash on a 'plane ticket I'd better show up. I don't know how much this job is worth yet, or when your cousin will cough up, but I'll pay you back as soon as I can.'

'He'll cough up all right, and you can pay me back when you're flush again. Meantime stay here as long as you like – anyone's welcome who'll save me from Tony's cooking,' he nudged her again, 'but going back to Michael: how was the family black sheep? Still firing on all cylinders?'

She was instantly alert. 'What do you mean, black sheep?'

Jono chuckled. 'There's been a hell of a rumble between him and his old man for years now – it's one of the family's home grown soap operas. Uncle Archie has been hustling since Michael hit thirty for him to get married and produce the expected brace of little Nivens, otherwise the family name dies out.' He began to butter a piece of dark and brittle toast. 'He, Michael that is, is definitely not the marrying type – I reckon if you laid all his fancy bits end to end, they'd reach from Piccadilly to Oxford Circus. He drives his old man up the wall and they're barely on speaking terms. My ma says he only goes down to the ancestral pile when he gets an attack of conscience,

18

which is about twice a year, if that.'

'You're making it up; no one who talks like a dictionary could possibly pull *that* many women!'

'I'm not making anything up.' He was indignant. 'Mind you, I don't know him all that well; my home being in Yorkshire and his in Suffolk meant we only met at funerals and weddings until I came down here to live. But my ma is a second cousin twice removed and well up on the Niven family news. She and my Aunt Isabel spend hours on the 'phone, filling each other in with all the latest juicy bits.'

He paused to scrape marmalade from the almost empty jar and Cassie prompted impatiently. 'Go on.'

'Oh, a few years ago Michael's supposed to have fallen with a crash for some French bint, and for a while Ma said it appeared like it was the full confetti and rice scene. She said his old man would have thrown a real wobbly if he'd known as he hates the French like poison.'

'Why?'

'How should I know? Reason doesn't come into anything with Uncle Archie.' Jono munched thoughtfully for a moment. 'Anyway, Michael followed this dame back to France and rumour was that he chucked his lectureship at UC and shacked up with her for months at her papa's vineyard. About a year later he popped up back in London, minus his tottie and spitting nails. Since then he's been more or less on his own, apart from the occasional quick shag with an old mistress or two and the odd bit of overnight crumpet.'

Tony interjected sourly, 'If you ask me, he's a scuzzy old tosser.'

'We didn't ask.' Cassandra turned her back on him. She looked enquiringly at Jono. 'What happened to the French bit d'you suppose?'

He shrugged. 'God knows, perhaps he throttled her and buried her in her pa's vineyard. He's an odd bloke, you know, but that's not surprising, his old man is mad as a hatter and the old girl's not far behind.'

He elaborated at some length on Michael's parentage and background, finishing with a warning. 'I wouldn't say he takes after either of them, he's much too stable and brainy for that, but you want to steer clear of him. Ma says he can't help giving women the old 'come on', but when it suits him cousin Michael can put up a dirty great brick wall between himself and any woman who makes like she's after more than dinner and a quick boff.'

Cassie took another mouthful of coffee. 'Well, you don't need to warn *me* off. I like my men uncomplicated and one hell of a lot

19

younger.'

'In that case, just give him his pictures and run, because if you'll pardon me for mentioning it ducky, you were off with him last night like a ferret up a trouser leg.'

'Lose no sleep. It was only the thought of the money.' She gave the hovering Tony an enquiring look. 'Aren't you supposed to be in college by now?'

He glanced at the wall clock and paled. 'O, *God* but you two are a bloody nuisance, gossiping on about that loser. I've got a life class with that swine Benson in fifteen minutes and the model's a guy with a body you wouldn't believe!'

Grabbing his half-eaten piece of toast from his plate he flung himself from the room. Cassie gave a yell of laughter and shouted 'Drama Queen!' Jono listened to the crash of the front door then gave her a reproachful look.

'Now you've upset him good and proper, my girl – and I need his rent. This place costs a bomb and at the moment my pa is cutting up rough about bailing me out. If I don't get some regular work soon, Tony will be the only thing between me and a cardboard box under Waterloo Bridge.'

'I go, I go,' she stood, and putting her hands on his shoulders kissed him. 'Thanks for loaning me the cash and giving me a bed last night. I'm sorry about Tony, but he does rather piss me off. All I want is to get this job over, do my visit to pa then get home to Oliver.'

'Now he really *does* sound a scuzzy old tosser!'

She flushed. 'He's not; and he's only a few years older than me.'

'Ten, to be precise ducky,' he leered. 'Why don't you give Michael a whirl? He may be creaking on a bit, but you wouldn't have to put up with him for long – and I'll bet his sheets are cleaner than Ollie's.'

She walked towards the door enquiring sweetly, 'Hadn't you better go and drag Barbie out of your own sheets, *ducky,* before she takes root?'

He looked moody. 'Yeah, I guess so. I've got a dance class at two-thirty.' He leaned back in his chair and yawned. 'She's all right though…she might look static plastic, but once you've got her started she goes like a train.'

Cassie paused in the doorway to sweep a glance over his appalling hair, baggy sweater and grubby Stars and Stripes boxer shorts. She grinned and turned away. 'I know,' she answered over her shoulder, 'I heard her letting off steam half the night – and don't waste your time worrying about me and your cousin Michael, because I wouldn't get my kit off for *him*, not even if he were twenty years younger and the last guy left in town!'

2

Michael Niven might not love the camera, but the camera certainly loved him. Cassie watched the first print emerging under the developer and felt a quick surge of pleasure and excitement; it was, even to her critical eye, an almost perfect picture.

He wasn't just photogenic, plenty of others were that, but had that extra something the camera would always find and turn into a kind of esoteric love affair between the lens and its subject. When all the proofs hung drying, she studied them carefully. Those taken before he had the chance to become self-conscious were undoubtedly the best.

In the first he stood by the embankment wall, half-turned towards her, one hand in the pocket of his slacks the other by his side, his jacket open with the collar turned up slightly at the back, his hair ruffled by the morning breeze.

Every detail, from the dramatic background of buildings and bridge and river, to the sun lighting the loose waves and half-curls of his dark hair, her camera had caught to perfection. He looked relaxed and as sexy as hell.

Something shifted gear again inside. She examined the line of prints more closely, noting every line and wrinkle. At the very least he must be well past forty, she thought and gave a short laugh. Well, as she was as unlikely to need Michael Niven in her life as he was to need her in his, how old he was, and how many wrinkles he had, shouldn't be a problem, should it?

*　　　*　　　*

'What do you think of Cassandra Chisholm, then?' Simon Meyer handed his visitor a generous measure of whisky in an elegant cut glass tumbler. Michael twitched his shoulders and gave a wry smile.

'I'm trying *not* to think of her too much!'

'Then that's just as well.' Simon was bland. 'Right now she is still struggling for recognition in this cut-throat business, and can do without the likes of *you* popping up to provide her with any further distractions.'

Michael raised his brows.

'Does she have many of those?'

'I think only one at the moment.' Simon made a grimace of distaste. 'Oliver Lingard, a landscape painter: you may have seen his work. He exhibits at Langdons from time to time. He's quite good, but not *my* cup of tea; very modern and abstract – masses of purple and orange angles – all *that* sort of thing. He's undoubtedly talented but a total shit where women are concerned. Unfortunately he lives practically on our little girl's doorstep.'

'How do you know so much about her affairs?'

'I've known her family, or at least Laura and Harry, for years and I've taken a particular interest in Cassie since I went talent spotting and saw her college work. She spent quite a bit of time at home with Lily and the boys when she was in college and had digs up here, but all that *and* the photography went to pot for a while when Harry died.'

He gave a cynical smile. 'That was, until she floated in here one morning on cloud nine; love's young dream was nowhere in it; she just couldn't keep it to herself. Damned shame, because beneath it all she's young and insecure enough to be knocked off course again when the inevitable happens and Lingard moves on to the next one.' He looked at Michael over the top of his spectacles, adding pointedly. 'I hope Lily and I may be around to give some support when that happens. Even with friends at hand, the last thing she'll need then is another no-commitment opportunist waiting in the wings.'

Michael asked placidly, 'Are you warning me off, Simon?'

'Whatever makes you think that?' He gave a thin-lipped smile. 'How's Francine?'

'I wouldn't know; as you are well aware we don't communicate.' Whistling softly between his teeth Michael turned to examine more closely a large framed print of storm-driven seas crashing against towering grey cliffs. 'I see this is one of Cassandra's. She's good, isn't she?'

Simon accepted the change of subject with good grace; no one could be more adept than Michael at sidetracking any subject he wished to avoid.

'Yes, very good indeed, otherwise I wouldn't let her have free range of my darkroom. She could use my studio as well if she wished. She does occasionally, but prefers to work out of doors and on her own home ground.'

Michael drained his glass and set it down on the table. 'As you should know by now, women that young are not my forte. When she brings the proofs to my house this evening I propose only to thank her nicely, pay her well, and send her on her way. She may leave the finished pictures with you and I'll collect them later.'

He smiled grimly to himself as he crossed Kensington High Street. The sooner his business with the disturbing Cassandra was finished the better, and he could certainly do without meeting her again under the gaze of Simon Meyer's satirical eye. They had been friends too long for him not to know that the gallery owner himself had perhaps rather more than just a professional interest in his protégé. Simon may have two young sons and be faithfully married to a wife he adored, but that never stopped any man weaving fantasies about the likes of Miss Chisholm.

What a lecherous lot we are, he thought, as he dodged a speeding taxi. Perhaps there should be a collective noun for the species. He turned towards Chelsea and home, amusing himself as he walked by constructing a few possible definitions…a Posse of Perverts, a Rake of Roués, a Licentiousness of Lechers…a Seduction of Satyrs?

The possibilities were endless.

*   *   *

Cassie stood hesitating on the pavement outside number eleven, Hampden Square that evening. The tall narrow-fronted house was precisely the sort of place she would have expected Michael Niven to own, she thought, the smooth rendered stonework washed in purest white, the graciously proportioned sash windows shining. Curved shallow steps led to a heavy panelled Oxford blue door; over it a leaded half-moon fanlight of alternate petal-shaped pale and dark blue glass. The whole place had an opulent, intimidating air about it, and she thought fleetingly that it was a good job she'd taken the tube and not arrived in her ratty old car.

In her nervousness she gave a longer and louder peal than necessary on the polished brass bell, then waited, pink with embarrassment, as footsteps approached from the other side. Braced to greet Michael Niven she retreated a step when the door swung open to reveal a small, bird-like woman in late middle age, wearing a well below calf-length plain black dress, her sparse grey hair drawn up into a severe bun on top of her head.

She regarded Cassie with unsmiling beady dark eyes and the suspicious air of a nun scenting a possible Jehovah's Witness.

'I'm Cassandra Chisholm.' Annoyed for sounding flustered Cassie added firmly. 'I've come to see Mr Niven.'

'Of course...I'm sorry, but I've been interrupted twice this afternoon, first by a young man trying to sell me dusters then an old one on the knock!' At the broad East Anglian accent, well diluted with cockney, Cassie smothered a grin. The woman stepped back, opening the door wide. 'Mr Michael said you were to wait in the study; he had to go over to Senate House, but he'll be back any time now.'

Cassie followed her into a room to the right of the entrance hall, taking in at a glance the long bench beneath the window, which in stark contrast to the rest of the room's antique furnishing, housed a computer with a large console, printer, scanner and all the other paraphernalia expected of a busy author. She waited until the room door closed behind the housekeeper then gave a low whistle. *Well fancy that; an old retainer in funereal black. Whatever next...*

She began to move about the room, running a finger along the leather-topped mahogany desk; examining the silver tray and inkpots then passing on to study the row of exotic and brightly plumaged porcelain birds on the mantle above the Adam fireplace. 'You're not short of a penny or two are you, Mister Niven?' she murmured, 'I could probably live for a year on what these are worth.'

She began browsing along the bookshelves covering one wall of the room, stopping occasionally to pull out and leaf through a volume at random. He obviously had an eclectic taste in literature: Aldous Huxley and Melvyn Bragg nestled cosily against each other, while Tolstoy fought for space with Ian Fleming, but although she looked carefully she couldn't see anything with the name Michael Niven on the cover.

Spotting a copy of an Encyclopaedia of Erotica just out of reach, she smiled and stepping onto the short library ladder, took down the book and sitting on top of the steps flicked rapidly through the pages. 'Mind you,' she mused aloud, 'from the look in your eye yesterday, mate, I shouldn't have thought there was anything in *this* that you don't already know about.'

'You could be right, but every home should have one,' observed a deep voice from behind her, and she gave a small scream of fright and slid down the steps. He had come in silently and now stood watching her, his back against the closed door. Recovering her balance she shut the book with a bang. 'Don't *do* that!'

'Do what?'

'Creep up on me.' Conscious of the fiery blush rising about her ears, she demanded, 'How long have you been standing there?'

'Long enough,' he came to where she stood and taking the book returned it to the shelf. 'I'm sorry if I startled you.'

She muttered. 'It doesn't matter,' and began to delve into her shoulder bag, 'Here are your proofs.' She drew out the plastic folder and handed it to him. 'I expect you're busy, so if you'd like to choose those you want...'

He took her by both shoulders and guided her to an easy chair.

'Would you just sit down and relax. I don't bite, you know, nor am I going to startle you with some astonishing demonstration of libidinous behaviour culled from the pages of that book! Mrs Harris will be in with tea any moment now and I'd hate her to see you looking quite so wary of me.' Still holding her shoulders he looked down silently for a moment at her flushed face, then gave a dazzling slow-burn smile.

The strength ran like sand from Cassie's legs and she subsided into the luxury of leather worn thin and soft as silk, her lips parting in spontaneous reaction to this devastating and accomplished performance of the masculine art of seduction without words.

'Oh, dear...' He stood very still, gazing in comical dismay at her radiant face. 'I shouldn't do that too often, if I were you; at least, not to any man who has an Encyclopaedia of Erotica on his shelves!'

Cassie's heart went banging about in her chest like so much loose cargo in a ship's hold, only Mrs Harris's timely arrival with the tea tray saving her from making a complete fool of herself.

*   *   *

'I'm glad you chose that one. These three I like almost as well. Would you like some of each? I can do as many as you want, and any size.'

It was an hour since his housekeeper had removed the remains of tea and all trace of the angrily embarrassed young woman he had earlier disturbed had disappeared. When this girl sparkled, Michael thought, she *really* sparkled. She was like a chameleon, reacting to the moment, changing colour with her mood. At their initial meeting she had been first cautious, then deliberately provoking, then endearingly funny. The previous day when working, she'd been concentrated and briskly professional. Open and relaxed as she was now she suddenly seemed terribly young and unguarded.

He smiled at her again for the pure pleasure of seeing her answering smile then pulled back sharply. He really must stop this ridiculous flirtation, because that was what it was, on his side if not hers. He doubted if she knew what flirting was; the young having tossed all that kind of pleasurable verbal foreplay out of the window.

26

He stood beside her as she spread the proofs across his desk, selecting three, letting her guide him in his choice, and knowing she was right.

While she was gathering the prints into the folder and replacing them in her shoulder bag, he walked around the desk and taking a chequebook and fountain pen from the top drawer wrote rapidly before tearing the cheque neatly and handing it to her.

'Here is your well-earned fee, and thank you very much...for your company as well as your work. I really am delighted with the results.' He made his tone carefully neutral and her eyes flickered momentarily over his face. Taking the cheque from him she scanned it then tucked it in the pocket of her jeans.

'Thank *you*.' She gave him a surprisingly shrewd look. 'Would you rather I didn't bring the pictures here?'

Disconcerted by her directness and the fact that she had read his mind so accurately, he hesitated. 'There is a great deal needing attention before I leave for America. I thought perhaps...I was going to ask if you wouldn't mind leaving them at the Gallery; with Simon.'

He stood up, deliberately formal and dismissive, keeping the desk between them. Slinging her bag over one shoulder, she answered with equal formality, 'OK. I'll say goodbye then,' and held out her hand.

He took it, holding it a fraction longer than necessary then asked, 'You don't have to rush off, do you?' He cursed silently as the words left his lips. So much for his resolution...as she stood hesitating he added aloud, 'I thought we might have dinner again.'

'Why?' she asked bluntly, and he knew she was aware that he hadn't intended making the invitation.

'Because you have done me a great favour, and having kept you here so long the very least I can do is to feed you.'

'I'm not dressed for the sort of place we went to the other night.'

'It doesn't have to be Scotts, we could go and spit in the sawdust at Flanagan's, or find a McDonald's if you'd rather.'

For a moment he thought she would refuse then she gave her sudden wide smile. 'Thank you: Flanagan's will be fine. I've been there before: their steak and alc pies make me go weak at the knees.'

He crossed the room to hold open the door. 'While we eat, you must let me know about anything else that does that.'

She gave him a sideways look. 'I told you quite enough about my weaknesses the other night. I reckon this time you can tell me about some of yours...if you have any, of course.'

He muttered, '*Touché!*' under his breath. 'Supposing we get back to where we were a couple of days ago and pretend we've just met – that way we just might manage to have a very pleasant and relaxed farewell meal.'

She gave him a look of suspect docility from beneath her lashes.

'OK, Mister Niven…but if it all ends in tears, remember, you started it.'

*   *   *

Cassie made the journey to Paris with something on her mind other than how her father might be expected to react to her arrival *this* time. Try as she might, she couldn't stop thinking about Michael Niven. It wasn't just his looks; more his air of calm self-assurance that had first drawn her to him. Cursed as she always was by uncertainty and self-doubt, she found this quality very attractive. At the same time she was acutely conscious that beneath the calm and rather overdone mannered formality, there lurked a lethal sexuality. He had charm in spades and in the cold light of day the remembrance that she had actually fallen for it was seriously embarrassing.

She could feel the blood creeping up her face when she remembered how she had raced around to the gallery that morning with the finished photographs, hoping she might find him there, and had to mask her disappointment at Simon's ironic: 'You are out of luck poppet – he is picking them up tomorrow en route for Heathrow. Is there anything I can do for you to make up for his absence?' Blushing, she'd muttered 'Nothing at all,' and left quickly, with Simon's knowing chuckle sounding in her ears.

She stared out of the 'plane window at the clouds below, thinking back over her few meetings with Michael Niven. Had she made a fool of herself because he'd come on to her? Let him know she fancied him? Was that why he'd whipped her out of his house and made the arrangement to collect the pictures from Simon?

But then why had he taken her out again that night? Why spend the whole evening practically taking her to bed with his eyes? She wasn't a complete idiot; she knew when she was being stripped, item by item. Although she might, and did, resent that from others, she had to admit she hadn't minded all that much receiving those attentions from Michael Niven's dark eyes.

The cloud thinned, the heart of France was suddenly spread beneath them and the captain's voice over the speakers informed of their imminent arrival. She dragged her mind back to the present, stretching her cramped muscles and checking her hand luggage before fastening the seat belt. She'd been up since dawn and was tired and hungry and vaguely nauseous.

Now came the part of the journey she hated most: the bank and slow turn before the long, inexorable and stomach-clenching descent onto terra firma. Closing her eyes, she reminded herself that according to statistics, she was far more likely to die under the wheels of a taxi whilst trying to cross Hammersmith Broadway in the rush hour, than by her plane overshooting the runway and ploughing into the Orly control tower.

Not that statistics helped much when you were in a 737 and rushing towards the ground like a greyhound on crack, and with several dozen gallons of unused aviation fuel sloshing around in the tanks.

3

She sat at a pavement table outside the Café de Flore, gazing at the façade of Saint-Germain-des-Prés and letting her coffee grow cold. She had been there for almost an hour since leaving the Métro, delaying the moment when she must make her way towards Quai Malaquais and her father's studio.

As the bored waiter began flicking his napkin around the empty tables she sighed and picked up her cup. If her father was entertaining one of his teenage tarts she would turn around and walk straight out of the studio and return to Cornwall. Better to be broke, she thought, than go again through that embarrassing scenario of her last visit, when she had surprised a pouting Bridget Bardot look-alike, wearing nothing but French knickers and a grubby chef's apron making *crepes* for Alaric while he lounged in the rumpled bed.

Swallowing the rest of her coffee and picking up her airline bag she paid for her lunch then crossed the street as usual, to stick a placatory head inside the church and say, 'Please God, let him be alone!' – but a waft of incense hit her, she sneezed and beat a hasty retreat, thinking morosely that a fat lot of good that ever did anyway. No angel with a drawn sword had ever come to stand between herself and Alaric's latest *poule* over the past ten years.

All the old bitterness and resentment surged through her. She hadn't asked to be left, as it were, on his doorstep, and it was nothing she had done that made him shove her in that bloody convent school and take off. Why the hell should she worry when he didn't give a damn?'

She straightened her shoulders and walked on with her easy swinging step. She was twenty-three, for God's sake; she couldn't keep on living the trauma of waiting to be loved by a father who barely acknowledged her existence. If she couldn't prevent Alaric making her feel one of the great unwashed, then she'd just have to stop showing him it still hurt.

*   *   *

The grey three-storey stone house at the far end of the quay was unnaturally silent. The ground floor and cellar were used as a wine store and her father lived on the two upper floors, the top one given

30

over completely to his studio, with the wall of sloping windows and panoramic view of the area that had once been the haunt of painters and poets. Now only the most successful and wealthy could afford to live and work here.

She pushed open the street door and climbed the stairs quickly, straining her ears for any signs of life, her footsteps sounding hollow on the bare wood. Her father's voice could most often be heard from the bottom of the staircase; either in conversation, uplifted loudly in song, or hurling curses to the heavens when work wasn't going to his satisfaction. Silence most probably meant he was in bed and unlikely to be alone.

As she reached the second floor the opening bars of *La Mer* sounded, then Charles Trenet's light tenor took up the melody and she knew that this time her prayer had been answered; that he was alone and on a nostalgic trip down memory lane, *via* an old Dansette gramophone and a handful of treasured shellac records.

When she pushed open the studio door he was standing at the window, his back to her, humming along softly to the music, his hands in the pockets of the familiar paint-stained smock. Without turning, he observed, 'I notice you didn't do your usual creep up those stairs as though you were Goldilocks expecting to be savaged by a homicidal bear!'

She said spiritedly, 'Well, Hello, how nice to see you, too.'

It came out sounding more derisive than she had intended and he turned, eyebrows lifting in surprise. 'What happened to the air of injured innocence and "*Excusez-moi de vous déranger, papa*"?'

'Well, I suppose I am sorry to disturb you, or I would be if you were working.' She came into the room, shutting the door behind her. 'Somehow I think I've rather given up being afraid of bears.'

'Even when you are here cap in hand, as usual?'

Despite her resolution she was stung. 'Money isn't all I come for.'

'Isn't it? Tell me what else then.'

'As if you'd be interested,' the riposte came sharply and again he raised his brows.

She glanced at several finished canvasses propped against the wall, her lip curling slightly at the half-dozen among them of nubile young females displaying their considerable charms. 'Still at it, I see.'

He gave a short bark of laughter. 'What's got into you today? Growing up at last, are you?'

'I've been *grown-up* for quite some time, but as you haven't been around you wouldn't have noticed, would you?'

'I suppose not.' He stared fixedly at her for a few moments, then

31

shrugged, lifted the play arm from the record and walked to where a brown corduroy jacket hung over a chair. Taking a chequebook from an inside pocket he asked, 'OK, how much do you need?'

She flushed and said defensively. 'You won't have to bail me out much longer. My stuff's selling well at the gallery and I've just earned a fair bit doing some portrait work. I don't want much.'

'I didn't ask how much you want, but what you need. I'm not exactly hard up and I don't want you taking from Laura. The money doesn't matter; God knows you are owed it, if only to make some reparation for my failure as a father,' he gave another bark of laughter at her startled expression before his mouth twisted and he added tauntingly, 'and you must always have enough for these filial visits to papa, mustn't you? Or will those cease when you are famous and financially independent?'

Cassie gritted her teeth and watched in silence as he snapped open the chequebook, remembering Michael Niven doing the same and with a similar air of dismissal.

'Are you proposing to stay for any length of time?' Alaric asked, without looking up from his writing, 'because I need to know. I don't want to offend your sensibilities further by having company call unexpectedly.'

'I was going to stay until Monday; I only got a one-way cheapo. I suppose I can get a flight back tomorrow if I must; I should hate to spoil your fun.'

She stared at the back of his head, noting how the thick, almost mahogany coloured hair was heavily flecked with grey now, his powerful frame sparer than she remembered. She glanced around the studio, looking for the half-eaten food and dirty coffee cups, always an indication that some new piece of work was in progress, but the place was quite remarkably tidy and there was no canvass on the easel. She thought sarcastically that either he had found himself a domesticated floozy, was between commissions, or hadn't yet found another model young enough for his taste.

That there might be another reason didn't occur to her.

She took the cheque he offered and glancing down at it said, 'Thank you. It didn't need to be for that much.'

'It will save you making another trip for a while, won't it?'

'Don't worry. I have to be pretty desperate to bother you any more than I absolutely have to.'

He began pulling the paint smock over his head. 'I have an appointment the other side of the city and shall not be back until late afternoon.' Tossing a hand-full of bank notes onto the table he

32

instructed carelessly, 'Take this and get yourself something to eat, I don't want to add starving you to death to the list of parental sins you already have ranged against me.'

She leaned against the tatty chaise longue and watched as he shrugged himself into his jacket then stooped before a mirror to comb his fingers through his long hair. He turned suddenly to grin at her and ask, 'Do I look respectable?'

'As if...' Cassie returned the grin cautiously. It looked as though for once he might just put himself out to be pleasant. Impulsively she asked, 'Can I come with you; there's nothing much to do here to pass the time.'

He scowled. 'No you bloody can't.'

'I suppose that means you're going to see some minging tart?'

He stood looking down on her and she stared him out. Unexpectedly he gave his sudden rare smile. 'I *can* pass a whole day without getting into a woman's bed, you know.'

Disarmed by the smile she said, 'I'm sorry, look, if you'll be back this evening I could make us dinner here.'

'OK, providing I can trust you to keep your hands off lacing the gravy with rat poison – I'm not ready to meet my maker just yet.'

She turned away, only partially managing to mask the hurt and for a brief moment he lifted his hand as though he would touch her shoulder then let his arm drop again. Ramming his hand into his jacket pocket he said over his shoulder. 'You should wear dark glasses...your thoughts are showing. Dinner would be very nice.'

She listened to his footsteps receding down the stairs then went to the window and for a while stood leaning her head against the glass. Same old scenario, same old bloody-minded Alaric.

She roused herself with an effort. Sod him. If he wanted to throw his money about she would have a bloody good lunch, go to Daudet's for some of their famous and hideously expensive cheeses to take back to Laura, then shop for the evening meal in the Rue de Buci. She enjoyed cooking, and if Alaric gave her grief over the meal she'd give his dinner to Madame Joubert's cat at the corner bar.

Downstairs, in the big old-fashioned kitchen with its odour of herbs and garlic and the lingering miasma left by the stockpots of generations of French housewives, she made a quick inventory of the store cupboards, then after scribbling a shopping list took a rush basket and a linen bag from a hook on the door and went swiftly out into the bright Parisian day.

She lunched off garlic mushrooms, several different kinds of sorbet in a tall glass, and a half carafe of wine at the most expensive restaurant she could find, then spent the next two hours wandering around the market, tasting, squeezing and prodding the produce at every counter until she was satisfied and could return with loaded bags to the house on the quay.

Tipping their contents onto the kitchen table she wrapped herself in an oversize apron and was quickly lost in preparation of the evening meal.

*   *   *

When Alaric returned that evening he was reserved and distant and although he ate with apparent enjoyment, Cassie had a vague sense that it was an effort for him to clear his plate. Finishing, he waved away the proffered cheese and basket of fruit.

'Not for me, thanks; I don't want to get to the stage where I have to undo buttons!' In an automatic gesture she had seen him make hundreds of times he put his plate aside and reached into his pocket, then abruptly withdrew his hand.

She said quickly, 'It's OK. It doesn't bother me if you smoke.'

'That's nice to know, but it doesn't bother me *not* to.'

'You've stopped…and after all these years?' Her face must have mirrored her disbelief and he gave a sarcastic sneer.

'Yes, but I'm glad to say all my other vices remain intact.'

'I'll bet!' she returned with sudden venom and began to clear the table, clashing the plates together and rattling the cutlery. 'I'll wash these up then have an early night, which should give you a nice long evening to screw some silly cow brainless.'

He grinned and tilted back on his chair. 'Temper now! You sound just like you did when you were about six and you called me an old pig. Even after I'd put you over my knee and spanked you, you turned around and told me I was still an old pig.'

*And then you laughed and we went down to the beach and skipped stones over the water…*she remembered, and fighting the sudden angry tears answered bitterly, 'I'm surprised you can recall anything further back than when I was thirteen; I thought everything before that was wiped from your memory.'

He crashed his chair down onto four legs and stood up, his face dark with anger. 'You've got quite a mouth on you all at once, haven't you? If you can't at least make a stab at being civil, you'd damned well better be on that early flight tomorrow!'

He left the room and Cassie listened to him climb to the studio, wincing at the violent slam of the door. Stacking the plates in the sink she began to run the water. That really had torn it; in a sudden explosion of anger she yelled at the top of her voice, 'Just for the record you're *still* an old pig; you always were and you always will be, sod you!'

She began to wash the dishes furiously. She'd be at Orly first thing in the morning for a flight home if she had to wait all day. It wouldn't matter how many times she returned, that cheque in her pocket was as far as he'd ever get to caring about her or showing the slightest interest in her welfare.

Slinging the dishcloth over the taps she wiped her hands, vowing that her apology for a father had seen the last of his daughter for a very long time. In future she would rather starve than ask him for another penny.

*   *   *

Alaric Chisholm sprawled in a chair before the studio window and stared at the vast firmament of stars hanging over the night lights of Paris, hearing his daughter's last defiant yell and listening to the subsequent clatter of savagely washed pans being crashed around in the kitchen below.

'A fucking awful end to a fucking awful day...' he snarled to the unresponsive heavens. 'I had to say it, didn't I? I bloody had to say it.' He shut his ears to the continuing racket clearly audible through the wooden floor. What the hell had got into the girl, anyway? Why hadn't she just come in and made herself invisible as she always had before? That way it was easy to keep her at a distance, thus justifying his continued rejection. Now he questioned what cutting her out of his life had all been for; not that it mattered now anyway. It had all been a complete waste of time and effort. After all these years the danger had passed; it probably, he thought wearily, never would have arisen, but he couldn't have taken that chance.

He sat on, alternately blaming first himself, then her, for the evening's débâcle. After a while the sounds of fury ceased, then after a long interval of ominous silence he heard movement below again; bath water running and the gurgle of water in the pipes as the plug was pulled; then the sound of window shutters being pushed open before silence again descended over the house.

Exhausted, he lay back in the chair, going over the day in his mind, his daughter's arrival after her typically terse and uncommunicative 'phone call a few days before; his own visit to De Witte...he shied away from the humiliation of that encounter: the check on his blood pressure and the stethoscope prowling his chest like a hungry cat, listening, probing; those endless questions…and all to what purpose? He knew, and De Witte knew, that time was running out, that the warnings were becoming more frequent; that if he didn't give up his unsavoury and hugely enjoyable lifestyle in this city he loved, sooner rather than later would come the roaring in his ears and that last massive crushing pain in the chest that would spell finish…

Eventually he roused himself and going quietly down the stairs, walked on silent feet to Cassandra's door. Turning the handle he stepped into the room.

She lay as she had as a child: curled on her side, one hand beneath her pillow, the other held across her breast, clutching her shoulder. The bedside lamp was still burning and a book lay on the floor where it had fallen. He picked it up: *Les Lettres de mon Moulin*, he gave a half smile: an old favourite; she must have found it on the kitchen shelf. As he placed it on the bedside table, he saw in the soft glow of the lamp the smudge of tears on her cheek.

He sat on the edge of the bed and stared down at her sleeping face. *I don't know anything about you, do I? How much you've had to work and struggle for your little bit of success; how hard up you really are, or how much it hurts your pride to ask me for money.* He smoothed a strand of damp hair away from her forehead and she stirred slightly and sighed in her sleep. *Do you have good friends you can turn to in trouble? Is there is a man in your life? I know you only come to me because, much as you love Laura and use Fleetwood as a haven from the world, I suspect you still wouldn't take money from her, even if you didn't have the price of a decent meal. Perhaps you long to be strong and independent, but lack the courage, or the will to go it alone…but by now you should be away from both Laura and Fleetwood, and not mind tapping your father for the odd few quid; that's what fathers are for.*

Drawing the sheet over her shoulders he turned off the lamp and left the room. Soon it wouldn't matter one way or the other, and the less she saw of him until then, the less would be the hurt and anger. He owed her an explanation for all the cold and wasted years; that was one secret he couldn't take to the grave with him. He wasn't lacking in courage, but he dreaded the day he must tell her the truth face-to-face, and watch those dark eyes scour his soul and find him wanting.

*   *   *

Laura welcomed Cassie back with her usual warm hug. 'I thought that

36

must be your heap of scrap-metal grinding up the hill. I'd almost given you up for today. How was London?'

'Perfectly bloody, as usual.'

'And Alaric?'

Cassie shot her a disturbed, uncertain smile. 'Not *quite* as bloody at first, but it didn't last.'

Laura put an arm through hers. 'Well, whatever. You're back now. Come along inside. I've made one of your favourites.'

Cassie carefully deleted from her mind her Paris visit, its explosive end and her early morning bolt to the airport without seeing her father again. She was back again safely at Fleetwood, and that was all that mattered. Cormack leaned against her chair, pressing his great shaggy head against her knee and she caressed his ears and made a fuss of him, before falling upon the fruitcake with an exaggerated cry of joy.

'I'm starving! Honestly, Laura, I don't know how Jono puts up with Tony. He really thinks he can cook, but between the cereal packet and the table he can make even a bowl of corn flakes taste like shi... like nothing on earth,' she amended hastily. 'But it wasn't all bad. I only went to see dad because I'd already booked the flight. Jono threw one of his naff parties and there was this man who treated me to a couple of wickedly expensive dinners and paid me a huge amount of money to take his photograph.'

'He was tall, dark and handsome, I hope.' Laura handed her a mug of tea and wondered what her niece was hiding about her Paris visit, and why she hadn't just cancelled her flight if she didn't need the money.

Cassie gave her husky giggle. 'Umm, yes – like those old movie heartthrobs of yours that Harry used to tease you about; you know, Gregory Peck, Cary Grant...Dirk Bogarde; all darkly enigmatic and sexy...ancient, though.'

Laura chuckled. 'What's ancient to you would probably be Toy Boy to me.'

'Would you like one of those? He might do. He's unattached – I think.'

'No thank you.'

Cassie said abruptly, 'I hate to see you lonely.'

'Loneliness is nothing to do with being alone. Sometimes when I'm working in the study I could swear Harry is there, still breathing down my neck.' Laura's eyes gave a wicked snap, 'although what I really miss most is not having him to go to bed with.'

'Laura, he was *old*!'

'What's that got to do with anything?' She was amused. 'The younger generation always thinks sex stops at fifty. Well, I'm telling you it doesn't, and it's a damned sight more enjoyable when you've spent half a lifetime learning how to get it right.'

Cassie exploded into laughter. 'I can't imagine Harry as one cool sexy dude.'

'Well, he was, and I miss him.' She lifted her cup, holding it in both hands, gazing at Cassie with thoughtful eyes. 'As a matter of fact, I miss him very badly in every way and...well...I've met a man.'

'Who? Where? When? – do I know him?'

'Don't leap on me like that! His name is Miles Trehern and you wouldn't have met him yet. He only left the Navy last year and bought old Victor Treave's bookshop in Keneddy a few months ago. We met when I was doing research for Harry's book.'

Just for a moment, Cassie felt a real ache of jealousy, but it died as swiftly as it had come. She grabbed Laura's hand across the table. 'Oh, you go for it; what will you do; move in with him, or will he come here?'

'Darling, these are early days yet. We do plan to live together eventually, we may even want to get married, but we haven't made any hard and fast plans as to when that will be, or where we shall live, but wherever it is it will always be your home too. You know that, don't you?'

'Your guy may not be so keen to have a third party hanging around.'

'That won't be a problem, I promise you,' Laura said gently, 'and you mustn't think I'm replacing Harry, I couldn't, I'm just moving on. We all have to do that.'

'Yes. We do, don't we?' Clearly, in her mind's eye Cassie saw the door slowly closing on her life at Fleetwood. She said flippantly, 'Anyway, I reckon I'm already past my sell-by date here, don't you?'

'Hardly,' Laura smiled and pressed her hand. 'I think I'll do an hour's work on the book before I turn in, but you look tired; why don't you go to bed?'

'Yeah, I guess.' Cassie yawned and stood up, tousling her hair. 'Simon wants another series of coastal pictures, so I thought I'd try some morning and evening shots around the headland over at Nanwarren. I'll probably make an early start tomorrow. I don't know when I'll be back, so expect me when you see me.'

OK, she thought as she climbed the stairs to her bedroom, as Harry had been so fond of saying: when one door closes, another opens, but when, and if it does, where in hell do I really go from here?

*   *   *

Laura waited until she heard Cassie's door close, then went into the small study that had once been Harry's and was now hers. Sitting before the heavy old-fashioned desk she thought over Cassie's late arrival, pondering again what might have happened in Paris to put that look on her face. Why was it that Alaric couldn't see or, if he saw, didn't care what he was doing to his daughter? She wondered as she had so many times before how Cassie, with such a wonderfully expressive face and those incredible eyes, could manage to miss being beautiful. When she smiled she was almost there, teetering on the brink, but then the wide, troubled mouth always returned to rob her of that final accolade. Perhaps one day, Laura mused silently, the right person will come along who can help lay her particular ghosts and make her truly happy – and then, Hey Presto, it would happen…she sighed then dutifully turned on her PC before reaching for the telephone and dialling a number with quick, impatient fingers.

In his flat above his bookshop in nearby Keneddy, Miles Trehern smiled and reached for the 'phone.

'Hello me queen!' The soft Cornish drawl with its undertones of laughter brought her own mouth into a smiling curve. She leaned her arms on the desk, pushing the fingers of her free hand through her hair.

'How did you know who it was? I might have been one of your customers.'

'My 'phone has a different ring when it's you – and who but you would be calling me at this time of an evening?'

'I thought I might disturb you doing your accounts, or fiddling your tax returns.'

'You never do disturb me, or only in the very nicest possible way,' he leaned back in his chair, asking softly, 'has it been a bad day?'

'Yes, and no.' She gazed at the screen before her, chose 'Books' and clicked the mouse. 'I've just told Cassie about us; she seemed to take it all right, but I can see she thinks she should move out if you move in, and that worries me. In many ways she's still so naïve and immature.'

'Would it help if we were to meet? She might see then that I'm not the type to throw her out on the street.'

Laura smiled and relaxed back into her chair. 'I think it might be a little too soon for a meeting. A slightly longer period to get over the shock of knowing about you might be better.'

'Not having second thoughts, are you?' he teased.

'No, you don't get away that easily.' Absently she clicked on 'Peninsular Painters' and heard him laugh.

'Stop fiddling with that thing; you shouldn't still be working at gone ten o'clock of an evening.'

'I know, but I'm too restless to sleep.'

He said quietly. 'I thought about you all day.' She heard the creak as he settled back into his chair. 'I wish you were here now. I miss you, Laura.'

'I know, and I miss you.'

'And I want you tonight.'

'I know that as well,' she listened to his reply before answering softly, 'me too…goodnight.'

Gently she laid the receiver back on its rest. It took a special kind of man, she thought, to be able to make a fifty-three-year old woman blush in anticipation.

*   *   *

Somewhere on the hill a cock crowed. Cassie woke reluctantly and lay for several minutes with her eyes closed, then with an effort sat and swung her feet to the floor. Heavy-headed and dull from a restless night she yawned widely and glanced at the clock on the bedside table: five-fifteen. Sliding off the bed she crossed the room to open the curtains and look out over the narrow creek.

It was one of those breathless, early spring mornings, the sky palest green, the whole place bathed in the luminous early light of the Cornish coast. 'It's the silver left by the moon that helps the day begin,' Oliver had once observed in an unusually romantic moment. Her pulse quickened at the thought of him as she turned back from the window and began to dress hurriedly in jeans, a long sleeved sweatshirt and trainers.

She might visit Ollie if there were any signs of life at the barn, although unless the creative urge was very strong he seldom rose before noon. She trod quietly along the corridor to the bathroom to splash cold water over her face and clean her teeth, then slinging her camera over one shoulder crept down the stairs, calling softly to Cormack where he slumbered by the stove.

The dew on the glossy leaves of the rhododendron and azalea bushes lining the short drive of the shabby Victorian house sparkled in the strengthening sun, the wet grass crisscrossed by the tracks of small mammals, the clear air filled with birdsong. Suddenly lighthearted, Cassie swung through the low gates onto the shingle track, Cormack bounding down the steep hill ahead of her. Arrived on the tarmac apron before the church she stood for a moment to lean on the stone wall, a wall topped often in winter when the gales blew in from the Atlantic and the spray flew high, stripping paint from the cottage doors and windows and blighting the neat gardens with salt.

A few small rowing dinghies were pulled up on the shingle beach and a half-dozen craft of varying size rode at their mooring buoys. The water moved slowly, the surface only faintly rippled by the rising tide. On the other side of the creek, half hidden in the trees was Oliver's studio, and the large skylight, caught by the strengthening sun winked an erratic semaphore through the branches.

No human life stirred, only a marmalade cat lying stretched on the wall of the chandlers-cum-bait shop watched Cormack with insolent narrowed eyes. When it opened its mouth wide on a soundless insult the wolfhound bristled and sneered, but followed Cassie obediently when she left the wall to mount the half-dozen rough stone steps to the narrow bridge over the creek.

Following the rough path to the point where the estuary began to spread out into the sea, she glanced down in passing at Oliver's ram-shackle converted stone barn. The door was closed and windows shuttered, so she walked on, knowing better than to disturb him at this early hour.

Ten minutes later she reached Nanwarran where, far below, in a wide rocky cove lay her reason for coming to this particular place. She counted quickly: seven, eight...no, ten adults and two pups. Slipping her camera from her shoulder Cassie sank to one knee and focusing swiftly, took several shots of the group of seals as they lay basking in the morning sun.

Finishing, she sat back on her heels and Cormack leaned against her shoulder, breathing heavily into her ear and all at once, the feel of his bony body warm against her, the seals, and the beauty of the morning were too much and tears started to her eyes.

This was where Harry had brought her when she'd first come to Fleetwood. To a hurt, resentful and bewildered thirteen-year-old it had been a magical, seminal moment when she had crouched at the very edge of the cliffs and looked down on the sleek bodies at rest below. And here she had come after Harry's funeral, to be alone and weep for him and for the days of a joyful and loving companionship that had gone, never to return.

Oliver had found her on that grey and desperate morning and

knelt to put his arm around her and say: '"Do not sit by my grave and weep." Come up to my studio instead and I'll make you a coffee!'

She had looked at him with drowned eyes, asking, 'How do you know I was sitting by a grave?'

'I watched you in the churchyard earlier – I have a telescope...' He had taken her hands and heaved her to her feet. 'Come on, it's only a few minutes away. All I'm offering is coffee and a more comfortable place to sit and do your weeping.'

She'd gone with him and sat in a studio as untidy and comfortably cluttered as Harry's study, then in the following weeks had gone back again and again to seek his carelessly given comfort. Inevitably, herself so in need of love and Oliver being Oliver, his change from comforter to lover was swift. Lost and bereft, she had made no resistance to his easy and practised seduction, and in the solace and warmth of his arms discovered a partial substitution for the innocent filial affection she had lost.

But now she was twenty-three and stronger; it really was time to move on and ease the ties that kept her at Fleetwood. Since Harry's death perhaps she and Laura had each in their different ways, become too dependent upon each other. Now Laura had her Miles and she had Oliver, unsatisfactory though he may be from time to time...

She released Cormack and stood brushing the damp earth from her jeans. Well, it would hurt like hell to leave Fleetwood, but she'd go back now, convince Laura that everything was absolutely ace and that she couldn't be more pleased for her and the unknown Miles.

All the same, she couldn't help feeling resentful about the man who had appeared so suddenly in Laura's life, and in doing so had managed to turn her own life upside down.

4

By the time she returned to the house she had her feelings well under control, and when Laura came in from the garden the kitchen was rich with the aroma of freshly brewed coffee.

'Hi!' Cassie turned with a smile from putting out mugs and cream jug on the table. 'I saw you getting in the veggies and guessed you wouldn't be long.'

'I thought we would have a good lunch as I'm going out this evening – you don't mind eating alone tonight, do you?'

'No prob. There should be a good sunset later and I'd like to get some shots along the beach. After that I may do a spot of visiting myself.'

Laura put the trug of vegetables on the dresser and washed her hands at the sink. Picking up her coffee cup she said, 'I'll just take this into the study. I want to go over the last section of the book before I show it to Miles tonight.'

'He knows more than you then, does he?' Cassie was unable to stop a note of sarcasm creeping into her voice. 'You never used to need someone else's approval.'

'Nor do I now, however I am not infallible and it is always helpful to have another to back up one's work.'

Cassie gave her sudden disarming smile. 'Sorry, but you did give me a bit of a smack in the face. I need a little time to sort my head.'

Laura paused. 'I didn't want to tell you until I – until we – were both quite sure. However, as I have a sneaking suspicion that by now half the village has probably guessed, it seemed pointless to even try to go on hiding what was happening. And if you had heard it from someone else you'd have been bound to go off at half-cock, wouldn't you?'

Cassie looked up with a wry grin. 'I daresay!'

'If ten years in this house hasn't taught you that love is neither finite nor rationed and can be shared without fear of loss, then Harry and I wasted an awful lot of time in attempting to show you otherwise!'

'Neither you nor he wasted anything. It's just that I never imagined …you knocked me off course a bit, that's all.'

A smile crinkled Laura's eyes. 'I'll make a bargain with you: if you can forgive this old woman grabbing another chance of happiness with Miles Trehern, I promise not to be rude again about the unspeakable Oliver.'

'I suppose that's the best I can hope for!' Cassie grinned again, but her eyes were shadowed.

Laura squeezed her shoulder and left the room. For a long while Cassie sat, clasping one knee between her hands and staring into space. Even if Miles Trehern turned out to be without fault, she knew she still wouldn't stay around. She couldn't see that either of them, however reasonable and understanding, would want her to be a part of their new life.

It was time she moved out and lived without the backup from Laura or the handouts from her father. Alaric had tried to force independence on her at too early an age, she thought wryly, and she had rebelled against it and settled gratefully for Fleetwood and the undemanding love and affection she had found within its walls.

She thought about Harry: the dishevelled thatch of white hair; the comical lived-in face; the ready wit and easy laughter, especially the laughter. Nobody could laugh quite as wholeheartedly and uproariously as Harry, nor be so acutely understanding and wise.

She finished her coffee and began to clear the table. Leaving Fleetwood did raise one very big problem; if she stayed in Cornwall, where would she live? She wondered what Ollie would say if she asked to move in with him and did she really, deep down, want to do that? She was sure, almost, that she loved him but did he love *her* enough to want her around all the time? She turned the tap and watched the water splash into the bowl. If only there was someone she could turn to and talk over her uncertain future. Not Oliver, he never bothered about his own future, let alone anyone else's; nor Jono who would be brisk and tell her she was a fuck-wit and should move to London and get a life, but someone older and wiser and understanding who might actually *care*...

Someone, she thought, like Michael Niven.

But he was on his way to America by now, and even if available would hardly want some idiot telling him all her troubles. In any case, she wasn't at all sure that it would be a good idea to have any kind of *tête-à-tête* with *him*. He was too sexy by half to stand in as any kind of counsellor or father confessor. Even just thinking about him made her heart skip a beat.

With a decisive bang she upended her cup onto the draining board. She didn't need anyone, least of all Michael Niven to tell her what she should do. Moving in with Ollie made every kind of sense. She was sure he loved her; even if he'd never actually said so.

She leaned her arms on the sink, staring out of the window at the flower filled garden, imagining a future with Ollie in his dilapidated old barn, where they could live together in perfect harmony and she would never have to worry about leaving Cornwall ever again. Resolutely closing her mind against the reality that living with Oliver might not be all she hoped for or imagined; that if she were to chuck away the rose-tinted spectacles of first love he would be revealed as moody and selfish, not all that marvellous a lover and certainly neither wise nor even particularly understanding.

5

Oliver leaned on the stable door, smoking idly and watching the gulls swoop over the cliffs above the barn. It had been a beautifully clear evening with a memorable sunset, but now the shadows were lengthening, sending the birds wheeling off towards the rocky ledges of the cliffs to settle for the night. His peaceful contemplation of nature was interrupted when a flash of colour caught his eye and he swung his gaze around to focus on the tall Bears Britches plants bordering and partially concealing the cliff path.

'*Shit!*'

He leaped back into the studio.

Racing through to the bedroom he plumped the pillows and flung the covers over the disordered bed, scooped from the floor a wine bottle and two glasses – one with a smear of bright lipstick at the rim – then raced into the tiny galley kitchen. Dropping the tell-tale glass into the waste bin and stuffing a handy plastic bag on top he sprinted back to the bathroom, snatched up a Citrus Mist aerosol and sprayed it liberally around the bedroom, hopefully annihilating the lingering traces of the luscious Linda's Jean Paul Gautier perfume.

Smoothing back his lint white hair he grinned at his reflection in the mirror. No sense in chucking what he had with little Cassandra just yet, it was always nice to have her so willing to fall into his arms. Even after a year there was still a refreshing naïveté in the spontaneity of her eager surrender.

It had been surprisingly hard work last night he recalled, to persuade the worldly Linda into his bed, although once there the time taken over the preliminaries had proved to be well spent.

* * *

When Cassie stepped through the door he was back in the studio, sitting relaxed on the couch. He said, 'Hi, kiddo,' and held out his arms.

She went into them with a rush. 'Are you surprised to see me?' she asked, breathless from his kiss. 'I was up on the headland early this morning and wanted to see you so much, but I didn't disturb you then. I know how you need your sleep.'

Remembering how far from sleep he had been while bringing a

46

drowsy Linda to morning arousal, he sent up a prayer of thanks to whatever gods of good fortune had kept Cassie from his door until evening. He kissed her again and unbuttoning her shirt slid his hands over her breasts. 'Umm...I need all the rest I can get if I'm to spend the evening making love to you.'

'Oliver, I need to talk...'

'Later.'

'No not later – now; please Oliver.'

She had come ready to pour out her troubles, have him comfort and reassure her and *then* make love. But he stopped her mouth with his own, his hands already busy with another kind of comfort and she stifled her disappointment, a sudden rush of desire and a need for bodily comfort making her respond with an eager fierceness that almost caught him off guard.

'Hey, hey!' breathing heavily he disengaged himself and stood up, 'steady, my sweet – we don't want any little Lingard's littering the place, now do we?'

She wound her arms about his neck, 'Not that I'd mind having your baby,' she answered recklessly.

'Well, I would.' He pulled her towards the bed, tumbling her onto it. 'It would be such a pity; no, it would be criminal to spoil a body like this,' he murmured, his mouth against hers.

She half sat and stared down on him as he lay beside her. 'Do you love me, Oliver?'

He busied himself with the zip of her jeans. 'Why else would I be doing this?'

'I just don't know if you feel the same as I do. You never say the words.'

'Who needs words? It's deeds that count.'

He stood and began pulling his sweater over his head while she lay back naked, watching him strip, enjoying the sight of his slim, smooth body, so at odds with the lined and worldly face...turning suddenly she sniffed at the pillows and pulled a disgusted face. 'Oliver! What the heck is that stink?'

He lied easily. 'My new after-shave, don't you like it?'

She wrinkled her nose. 'It smells like a tarts boudoir!'

'How would you know.' he grinned. 'I'll give the rest of it to my father. It may help him pull his old bat of a housekeeper at last.'

'You do that, Oliver,' she advised, lifting her body to his as he finished undressing and sliding her hands down his back. 'You don't need it – *you've* pulled already!'

*   *   *

Much later, as she walked back to Fleetwood, she wondered how she had spent so long with him and still not managed to find either the right moment or the words to talk about her plans for their future. Somehow with Oliver there never seemed to be time to talk, or do anything but make love.

If only she had just made him stop and listen to her. The more she thought about it, the more moving in with him was such a simple and obvious solution to her problems. She settled her chin determinedly. She'd give it a few more weeks to see when Laura and her Miles were likely get it together, then if Oliver didn't offer *she* would make the first move. He could only say no.

Her heart gave an uncertain lurch. But he wouldn't do that. He had as good as said he loved her, so why should he refuse?

6

The Boeing made a smooth landing after a tedious flight. Michael peered irritably out of the window as the plane taxied along the runway. The food had been as plastic as the plates it was served on and the film an incomprehensible mish-mash of Kung-fu and sex. Gloomily he surveyed the heavy rain clouds gathering in the murky yellow sky above Heathrow, wishing himself safely back in Chelsea without the actual bore of getting there.

The lecture tour had been a success and he'd had a very pleasant few weeks in America, but now that the whole thing was over and finished with he felt weary and jaded. The thought of returning to his empty house and the cold meal Mrs Harris would have left for him became increasingly unappealing with every passing minute.

Waiting for his luggage to appear on the carousel he passed the time by mentally thumbing through a list of women he would most like to find curled up on the couch in his sitting room, and in the way she had been since their first meeting, Cassandra Chisholm still headed that list.

The fact that she was disgracefully young and entirely unsuitable, even as an occasional companion, made no difference. Tonight he wanted very much to sit in a secluded corner of some candle-lit restaurant and have those dark eyes fixed on his and hear again her low husky laugh. But he had been down that path before and understood his own appetites too well to know it wouldn't stop there. He was too honest for self-deception and while his body told him he wanted her, his brain presented him with the unpalatable fact that he couldn't, or wouldn't take the risk that the having might turn to loving, with all its resultant complications and ultimate misery.

He made his way to the car park where he had arranged for the Mercedes to be delivered and stood by it with his keys in his hand, pulling at his lower lip with thumb and forefinger, feeling more reluctant by the minute to return to his empty house. Even a lone meal in some anonymous hotel would be preferable to that.

It began to rain and he swore and wrenched open the car door. He'd make a detour and call in on Lily and Simon, where he was always welcome. They were a most hospitable pair; Lily's cooking was something to die for and a glass of his old friend's single malt would be a blessing on this wet London night.

With a sudden lifting of his spirits he threw his bag onto the back seat and slipping a CD of Callas into the player, coaxed the Mercedes cold engine into life. As he left Heathrow to join the A4 he was ironically aware that he had chosen the one place to go where he could talk about the girl who had travelled with him in spirit all the long wide highways, from New England to Wyoming and back again.

*   *   *

Oliver lay back against the rumpled pillows and watched Cassie dress. The past months with her had been fun, but since Linda came on the scene some weeks back it had got just too bloody tiring to keep both affairs on the go. On the whole Linda was a better bet; she knew the score and, unlike Cassandra, saw their relationship purely as an enjoyable but short-term affair.

Since that old cow Laura's big fling had come to light Cassie had become something of a problem to him. It wouldn't altogether surprise him, he thought uneasily, if she were on the verge of suggesting she moved in, but he wasn't having that, naïve and pliable she might have been to begin with, but recently she'd developed a disconcerting way of looking in and beyond him as though seeking some missing link, and she was beginning to make him nervous. No, he decided, Linda was most definitely the better bet; she was the sort who liked to have fun while Cassie was the kind of girl who needed more than that – only he wasn't the sort of man to give it.

He began to roll a thin joint. She'd soon get over it, and it was time she stared getting her fun with someone her own age. He lit the joint and drew deeply, reflecting that for a girl with more than the average share of brains she'd been amazingly stupid. Having had the incredible luck to be set free from her old man she'd chosen to tie herself to the dry as dust Penhalligans. *They* were permanently stuck in the fifties and she had stuck there with them…for God's sake, she'd still been a virgin at twenty-one, and that after a couple of years in Art College! No wonder the poor kid was taking it rather hard to find her comfortable life-style threatened by dear Laura having it off with that old goat, Trehern.

He blew a long plume of smoke at the ceiling. Oh, well, better get it over with… He spoke abruptly. 'Cass, we have to get something straight.'

'Get what straight?' she asked, standing on one leg to lace her trainer.

'You have to stop visiting for a while. I shall be too busy for all

50

that; I've a lot of work to get through before the summer exhibition.'

She stopped tying her laces and looked at him over her shoulder. 'What d'you mean, too busy? You never work in the evenings and that's the only time you let me come.'

'I'll still need the extra time.'

'But I'm only here a couple of evenings a week as it is now...a few weeks ago you couldn't wait for me to come every day!' She turned swiftly, challenging him. 'And how can you paint in artificial light?'

Canting the joint between his lips he stared at her through the smoke. 'I can't, but I'll need to work all the hours of daylight and I must have *some* rest!'

'Since when has sleep been more important than getting my knickers off?' Irritably she waved away the smoke. 'Christ, d'you *have* to smoke that stinking stuff while I'm here? I don't want to walk through the village trailing clouds of pot.'

He swung his legs out of bed and began to pull on his trousers. 'Look on the bright side, Cass. I'm sure the eagle-eyed old Laura will be glad to know you'll be seeing less of me – or perhaps not, as she's now busy helping the boyfriend get his leg over.'

She snapped, 'You just keep from shooting your mouth off about Laura.'

'Oh, come *on!* Everyone from here to Lands End must know by now; they haven't exactly tried to hide it, have they? They may be practically in their dotage but even you can't think they spend all those hours shut away in his place just playing Scrabble!'

'Are you trying to get me to pick a fight?'

He shrugged. 'Why should I do that?'

'Easy – I make a scene and give you the excuse to chuck me out.' She forced herself to stay calm and not show her rising panic. 'As for all that crap about working harder and needing more rest...give it a break, will you!''

'Look, darling,' he stood up to administer a patronising pat to her behind. 'I don't know what all the fuss is about. All I'm asking is that we cool it for a while, so just trot along now like a good girl and let me get my supper.'

He turned away and she stared at his back in angry disbelief.

'How long am I supposed to stay away?'

He felt a momentary tug of remorse and said more gently, 'Look, Cass, I don't want to hurt you, but all good things come to an end, don't they? You must have known this couldn't go on.'

'Why can't it? I *love* you, Oliver. I thought you loved me.'

'Nothing lasts forever.' He shrugged himself into his sweater. 'Come on, be a good girl. I'm not exactly saddling my horse and leaving town. I'll see you around – we could have a drink in the Cobb Barn now and again and talk over old times.'

Disbelief and hurt were channelled into a sudden explosion of anger; she moved towards him, fists clenched and eyes blazing. 'Don't you dare patronise *me*, you shit!' He took an instinctive step backwards and sat down hard on the bed. She raged, 'that's right, you bastard – fall back into your natural habitat! I suppose all I've ever meant to you is "good old Cass, always ready for a quick screw!"'

'Now, Cassie: sweetheart. Don't take it like that – '

'Shut up!' Furious, she interrupted him. 'How the bloody hell else did you think I'd take it after all these months?' Dragging on her shirt she buttoned it with shaking fingers. 'Before *I* leave *you,* Oliver the Great,' she said with biting candour, 'you might as well know you're not all that brilliant in bed; all you think about is whether *you're* having a good time – you don't bother to wait for *me*! I used not to think that mattered, but it does, so sod you, Oliver. In future just keep out of my sight or I swear I'll come up here and rip all your fucking awful paintings to shreds!' and she stormed out, slamming the stable door so that both halves crashed back against the wall with the ominous sound of splintering wood. For a moment Oliver sat stunned, listening to the sound of her footsteps racing over the gravel yard. 'Bloody hell!' he wiped his sleeve across his forehead, 'who would have believed it? If I'd known she could be such a little spitfire I might have thought twice about chucking her for Linda!'

*   *   *

Swearing aloud, with tears of fury scalding her eyes, Cassie flew along the headland, heedless of the danger in taking the narrow path at such speed in the failing light.

'Bastard, bastard, *bastard!*'

Reaching the steps above the square she hung onto the rail and half-slid, half-fell down them to lean exhausted and shaken against the sea wall. By now it was dark; lights glowed in the row of cottages by the church and she could hear laughter and raised voices from the open door of the Cobb Barn. It appeared to her distraught mind that the whole village was safe and comfortable while Cassandra Chisholm stood shivering and alone, wondering how the life that had been so safe and secure could be rocked for the second time in only a few short weeks.

She sank down on the bottom step to catch her breath and wait for her legs to stop shaking. What a twat she'd been! How could she have even *thought* that moving permanently into Oliver's bed was going to solve all her problems!

Me – who can't tell the difference between love and a quick screw, she thought, with a half-hysterical gulp of laughter. Well, sod him – the bastard wasn't going to grind *her* down.

Levering herself upright she swung over the wall and splashed her face with water from a rock-pool, welcoming the sting of salt. She ran her wet fingers through her hair before drying them and her face on the front of her shirt. Now what? She glanced at the Cobb Barn and on a sudden impulse marched towards the lighted doorway. A drink or two – or even three, before she returned to Fleetwood might be a very good idea...

''Allo, m'dear!' The landlord greeted her cheerfully, 'You'm not been in 'ere for a while...what'll it be?'

'Cider, please, Will. Out of the cask, not one of those fancy bottles you keep for the grockles!' She put her money on the counter and looked around the sparsely populated bar. 'Judging by all the racket I could hear from over the way I thought you'd be full.'

'That's the dart's team in next room...that lot from over Keneddy been trying to beat us'n again, but they ain't got no 'ope!' he grinned and set down her glass, 'better grab yersel' a stool, for they be a'most through and u'll be in here any minute.' He leaned his arms on the counter, settling for a chat. 'Missus seed you over Helston way the other day...said you was so busy she didn't like to disturb you.'

'I've been doing a series of pictures around the river for the London Gallery.' She raised her glass. 'Cheers, Will –' She broke off as the inner door crashed open, the winning home team flooded into the bar, and she was greeted boisterously by a dozen different voices; old men who had known her since she first came to the village and young men and girls she'd swum and sailed with in the long summer vacations.

I must be doing OK, she thought, after the first few noisy exchanges, nobody has asked what's the matter or if I'm feeling all right! She gulped on a latent sob, straightened her shoulders and sat tall. Looking over the heads of the crowd around the bar for more familiar faces she caught the eye of a bearded stranger standing a few paces away. Thick brown hair curled from under a battered peaked sailing cap and watchful slate-grey eyes crinkled in amusement as their gaze met. He lifted his shoulders and gave a wry grin; she forced a smile and leaned towards him. 'Don't tell me! You're from Keneddy

53

and your team lost!'

'Clever, aren't you,' he moved closer, his glance skimming over her. 'Is it raining then?'

She was puzzled. 'No. Why?'

'I thought it must be: your hair is damp and so is your shirt.'

Under his quizzical gaze her mouth turned up involuntarily. 'No, it isn't raining. I just like bathing in rock pools!'

He said easily, 'It might be better to stay with the bathroom tap. The salt has made your eyes pink.' He took with a word of thanks the drink someone handed him, then turned back, raising his tankard. 'Cheers. What would we Cornishmen do, Cassandra, without cider to drown our sorrows?'

Clasping her own glass in both hands she tilted her head, giving him a look both wary and challenging. 'What sorrows? And how come you know me when I don't know you?'

He took a long pull at his drink before answering.

'I might have asked Will here your name and be trying to pick you up!' he suggested, putting down the tankard. 'Or alternatively I might have heard someone in this crowd use it in the last few minutes.'

Cassie shook her head. 'You might, but you haven't, nobody here calls me that – and I don't like being picked up in bars by men old enough to be my grandfather!'

He gave a shout of laughter, 'I should only qualify for that if both me *and* my old man had been a lot quicker off the mark than we were!'

She said, 'Well ...whatever,' and tried unsuccessfully to stifle a smile.

The crow's feet around his eyes deepened and his weather-beaten face creased into an answering grin. 'I'd better come clean. I know who you are, Cassandra Chisholm, because I've not only seen your photograph but also had you described to me in fascinating detail. I'm Miles Trehern, the man you love to hate!'

She stared at him expressionlessly for a moment. Then putting down her glass walked quickly towards the door. Miles drained his tankard, said, ''Night all!' and snatching up his jacket followed her at a more leisurely pace.

Will swabbed vigorously at the beer stains on the bar counter and dug the nearest customer in the ribs. 'What d'you think, Lenny – should I take bets on which of they two goes skyward first?'

Lenny cackled. 'If you're asking, I reckon t'would be best to get Laura down 'ere quick wi' a bucket of water before either on 'em lights the first rocket!'

*   *   *

Cassie sat on the wall, facing the creek and Miles Trehern sat beside her with his back to the water, gazing in silence at the star-studded sky.

'I shouldn't have sprung it on you,' he said at length. 'I'm sorry. I was just so knocked out to see you there and you looked so....' He hesitated as though seeking the right word, 'so *alone*.'

She shrugged. 'I was just chilling out.'

'Had a bad day, then?'

'An effing awful one...and if you don't mind, I'd rather not talk about it just now.'

'OK.' He took a leather tobacco pouch and pipe from his pocket and began to fill the bowl. Her hands, which had been gripping the wall tightly, relaxed and she half-turned to give him a sideways glance.

'You were wrong, you know. I don't hate you. Just resent you, or I did, but I've been getting over it.'

'Umm, good, but it was understandable you should feel like that.' He struck a match and lit his pipe, eyeing her over the flame. 'Nobody likes having their legs kicked from under them, do they?'

'No-o,' she turned her head away again but not before he'd seen the sudden shine of tears in her eyes.

He really should have kept his mouth shut, he thought remorsefully. He seemed to have blundered into some kind of emotional crisis, but after she had spoken to him in the bar there was nothing else he could have done but come clean. If he'd kept quiet someone in that boisterous crowd would have been bound to call him by name and then the fat would really have been in the fire.

Just what *had* happened before she arrived in the bar tonight to put that look on her face? She gave a sudden shiver and rubbed her bare arms and he said quickly, 'You are cold, here take this,' he placed his reefer jacket around her shoulders, 'you'll get hypothermia if you stay out here any longer in that outfit.'

'Thanks. I'm OK,' she swung her legs over the wall and stood up. 'I'll be warm by the time I've walked up the hill.'

'Keep the coat. I don't need it tonight.' Just in time he managed not to add, *I'll collect it later from Laura.*'

Cassie gave him an ironic glance. 'Thanks again; I can guess I needn't worry about returning it.'

'Quite.' He sketched a salute. 'Goodnight, Cassie.'

'Goodnight, Mr Trehern.'

'Miles will do.'

'Perhaps,' she said and began to walk swiftly up the hill towards Fleetwood, only slowing her steps as she turned the bend and was shielded from his sight.

*   *   *

He wasn't at all what she'd expected; couldn't in fact have been less like Harry. With his lean height, hawkish nose and that grizzled close-clipped beard he looked more like a picture-book smuggler than an ex-naval captain. She slipped her arms into his coat, pulling it tightly around her, her senses immediately assailed by the lingering smell of pipe tobacco and a distinct whiff of fish.

Over the past weeks she had quite deliberately distanced herself from thinking about him, or trying to imagine what kind of man it was who had attracted Laura so much that she was ready to change her life for him. If she thought about him at all she had imagined someone small and old and bookish like Harry.

But Miles Trehern was clearly a convivial sort who played darts for his village, had a bright, discerning eye and the wiry, hard physique of a man who had spent a lifetime in the open air. Even now she reckoned he probably spent as much time out of his bookshop as in it.

When she reached Fleetwood tonight she would tell Laura about her meeting; it would be a whole lot easier to talk about the new man in Laura's life than the one who had just left her own.

7

When Cassie came into the room Laura was instantly aware that something had happened. An almost tangible aura of tension hung about her niece and there were bruised blue shadows beneath the dark eyes, but she answered Laura's greeting with a smile and an amiable. 'Sorry I'm late but I stopped off at the Cob.' She took the chair opposite her, making a good, but not quite good enough attempt to appear relaxed. 'I met your Miles Trehern in the bar; we had a talk.'

'Oh, yes?' Laura rested her head against her chair back and regarded her with interest. 'I hope it was amicable?'

Cassie grinned. 'Doesn't anything ever surprise you?'

'Not much,' she said dryly, 'especially where you are concerned. Things always did tend to happen whenever you were around.'

'Did you know he played darts?'

'Oh, yes, *and* that he has a passion for crime novels and opera and match-fishes with a beach-caster off Carrick Sands.'

'That accounts for the pong on the jacket he loaned me!' Cassie gave a rueful, apologetic shrug. 'I've been a bit naff haven't I? Not asking about him or trying to see him through your eyes? I'm sorry.'

'There is no need for apology. By fifty-odd, one has rather passed the stage of wanting to share every intimate detail of the beloved with the world in general.'

'Ouch!' she winced, 'have I done that?'

'Done it? My dear child, when you first met Oliver you could have won medals for it!'

'Yeah, well...that was a while ago.' She looked down at her hands. 'Laura, is Miles younger than you?'

'Yes. By five years.' She gave a mischievous smile, 'but that doesn't seem to matter these days.'

Cassie grinned. 'It used to be the other way around, didn't it?'

'Mostly, yes.'

'Laura, how old *were* you when you met Harry?'

'Nineteen – and he was forty-two.'

'Wow! How did Gran and Granda take that?'

'Wow, indeed; when they discovered we were already sleeping together your grandmother took to her bed with a migraine and your grandpapa threatened to throw me out!' Her mouth curved into a grin. 'That's what one gets for having an old-fashioned parson for a father;

he was hot on the morals but rather lukewarm on understanding.'

Cassie gaped. 'What did you do?'

'Went to live with Harry of course, and left Alaric to take the flack. It *was* the sixties, after all. We didn't marry until over a year later: it took me that long to convince them both that what we had was too good to lose and that the twenty-odd year's difference in age didn't matter a damn! Once they accepted the *fait accompli,* they eventually came around. Your Grandpa married us, although I don't think he ever really forgave me.'

'So age doesn't matter, is that it?'

Laura gave her a shrewd look. 'I didn't say that. In my case it didn't, but then I was head over heels in love. I wanted Harry as a man, not as a substitute father. I already had a reasonably liveable-with one of those!'

'Is that what you think happened with Oliver and me? That I slept with him because of dad?'

She raised her eyebrows. 'I wouldn't put it quite that crudely, but you did put Harry in place of Alaric, and after Harry died made straight for another man, albeit one considerably younger than Harry but still a good few years older than you. I don't think any psychiatrist would earn his fee working that one out.'

Cassie thought her words over for a few moments then demanded, 'D'you think there's something wrong with me then?'

'No, darling, but I might if you continued to make a habit of it!'

Suddenly, like a poorly-laid-to-rest ghost Michael Niven's face leaped into her mind's eye and her skin flooded with colour. She mumbled, 'I'll take the gypsy's warning then.'

Laura knew when not to press her niece or hand out unwanted advice. Opening a cupboard she took down bottles and glasses. 'That's enough psychoanalysis for one night,' she said firmly, 'you must be hungry. I'll make the Martinis if you make the sandwiches.'

It was past midnight before they went to bed. Pausing outside Cassie's door Laura asked, 'How much older *is* he?'

'Is who?'

'The one who made you blush so prettily tonight!'

Cass said loftily, 'Just some middle-aged stud muffin I met...*en passant*, as it were.' She opened her door and stepped through, closing it quickly behind her, then opening it again to add briefly, 'but, God, Laura, he was sexy, and he couldn't have been less like a father!'

*   *   *

As she lay in bed staring at the ceiling she thought it must have been the combination of rough cider and Laura's famously powerful Martinis loosening her tongue, because stone cold sober she would never have poked her nose quite so far into her aunt's life.

She tried to imagine what the scene with Laura's parents must have been like…if James Chisholm had shouted and her grandmother Sarah wept. They had both died before Cassie was six but she could hazily recollect a plump white-haired woman who wore ample tweed skirts and soft Vyella blouses, had a most accommodating lap and was always ready with a comforting cuddle. Her grandfather she remembered as very tall and upright and bald and not at all cuddly. When they met he would ask if she had said her prayers and give her a sweet when the answer was yes. She had very quickly learned to say yes.

But what had her grandparents really thought? Had they been angry and disappointed in both their children; Alaric, with his careless bohemian life-style, his women, his illegitimate daughter; Laura's childless marriage to her middle-aged gnome of a husband?

Tonight she had discovered more about Laura in one evening than in the previous ten years. The thought struck her that while she may be hyper-quick at spotting and recording on film the hidden potential in an apparently ordinary scene in nature, when it came to getting beneath the surface of her fellow human beings she was something of a non-starter. She had a sudden nasty thought that *she* might in a way be responsible for the ever-widening gap between herself and her father. After all, what did she really know, or had bothered to discover, about *him*?

I am not, she observed sadly to the lampshade, a person who asks questions, which probably means that I'm a self-obsessed retarded loser. I don't even have the faintest idea what makes Oliver tick. If I'd had half a brain when he first made love to me I might have said, Hey, hang on a minute…are you doing this because you care about me or just to get my knickers off? But I never thought beyond the moment; just kidded myself it was all for love.

Cautiously, she examined her feelings about Oliver. A few hours ago she had been devastated, convinced that her heart was broken. Now in this new mood of honest introspection she wasn't able to summon a regretful thought or even squeeze a tear. By any reckoning, she thought, that must make her either a hard-hearted bitch or an emotional cripple. All the same, it had been bloody *marvellous* to let loose like that!

With a groan she reached to turn out the light. *Give me a break, will you* she begged her tired brain. Well, to hell with it all; everything would have to go on hold for tonight. As that irritating silly bitch Scarlett O'Hara comforted herself when Rhett finally took off: Tomorrow is another day.

*   *   *

'Why don't you ask Miles to come here tonight?'

Laura put down the vase she was dusting and turned to her with raised brows. 'Why? Are you going out?'

'No.' Cassie folded the Sunday papers and jammed them into the already overflowing wastepaper basket. 'I have nowhere *to* go.' She bent to pick up the basket then straightened, balancing it on her hip. 'Ollie and I are finished.' She gave an uncertain grin. 'Our affair is like the Python parrot – defunct, deceased, dead; an ex-affair!'

'I see. You finally had the sense to give him the push, then.'

'Not exactly,' she grimaced. 'He was the one doing the pushing. I was so furious that I rather think I may have smashed his door as I left!'

'I should count that as a bonus.' Laura eyed her judiciously. 'Was this the night before last, by any chance?'

'Uh huh, that's why I was in the Cobb Barn.' She leaned against the door, shifting the basket to clasp it in both hands. 'I've been doing a lot of thinking...Laura, I'm going back to London in a few days. Making the break now might be a good move.'

'You don't have to because of Miles. We have no immediate plans to change the status quo.'

'I know, and he is not the reason...well, perhaps he is, just a bit. Really I need to put a distance between Oliver and me. I think he got me out of the way because there's someone else.' Her voice was suddenly unsteady. 'When I was in the stores getting bread early this morning, I saw him driving towards the top road with some blonde piece hanging around his neck. They'd obviously just come from his place and were headed for town. I can cope with being given the heave-ho, but not if he's going to shove the next in line under my nose.'

'Where will you stay? You are no longer a student and the proud possessor of a grant. You'll find it impossibly expensive to live in London now.'

She was vague. 'Oh, Simon still has some cash in hand of mine from gallery sales and I've most of my earnings from that portrait job I did. With that and what Alaric gave me I can manage two or three weeks B&B. That will keep me going while I look around for a job.

60

When the money runs out I can always crash at Jono's for a bit until I find something.'

'Well, don't go short.' Laura smiled. 'I'm not exactly on the bread line, you know!'

'I can't take from you while I can work for what I need.' She was emphatic. 'Don't worry, I shan't go on the game in Soho, I'll pull pints in a pub or wash dishes or something.' She changed the subject abruptly, 'so how about tonight? I think I ought to get to know Miles a bit better before I take off or I shan't get invited to the wedding!'

Laura said blandly. 'You never know, we might not bother with one of those!'

'Why not – is he married?'

'No. His wife died years ago.' She laughed at Cassie's sudden frown. 'Really, my dear – I sometimes wonder at the double standards of your generation. You hop in and out of bed with each other, regardless of whether or not one or the other is married, then start getting up tight if a couple of oldies propose to do the same!'

'*I* do not hop.' She was indignant, 'and married men are definitely out.'

'I'm glad to hear it. Now just go and empty that basket and put the kettle on. If you must talk instead of getting on with the cleaning we can at least sit and do so over a cup of coffee.'

*   *   *

Miles drove through the gates with a deliriously barking Cormack racing alongside his Land Rover. Reaching the house he was relieved to find Laura, not Cassie waiting on the steps to greet him. He had been first amused, then cautious at the latter's sudden and unexpected invitation issued that morning and had spent the remainder of the day wondering if there was a catch somewhere.

Cassie's voice on the 'phone had been amiable, but with a hint of sarcasm.

'As you seem well on the way to being family we should like you to come to dinner this evening.'

'Then I am delighted to accept.'

'Don't get too excited; I'm doing the cooking.'

He'd laughed and enquired, 'Would a bottle of wine be in order?'

'Please...white. We are having *poulet à la Cassandra!* Laura has brandy for later if it's a disaster.' He'd laughed again and she'd said, 'See you tonight,' then rung off, leaving him staring bemusedly at the receiver clasped in his hand and wondering if she was always quite so disturbingly brief with everyone, or only with him.

Laura kissed him, linking her arm in his. 'We are supposed to sit out in the garden and leave the kitchen to Cassie.'

He indicated the bottle of wine. 'Should I take this in first?'

'Oh, yes – there'll just be time for it to be properly chilled. Give it to her and she'll pop it in the 'fridge,' She chuckled at his hesitation. 'Go on, she's a lot more nervous than you are!'

'You're sure about that?'

'Would I lie to you?' She turned him through the open door. 'I'll be in the garden when you've delivered your offering to the cook.'

He made his way through the house to the kitchen and opened the door. From the stove drifted an appetising smell of herbs and garlic. Cassandra sat cross-legged on the table engrossed in the Horoscope page of the local evening paper; she looked up as he placed the bottle beside her. 'White, as requested,' he said, 'and what does that rag predict for Capricorn? I'd like to know my fate for tonight.'

'If I were a Capricorn, I wouldn't ask for trouble by wearing that beard!'

He stroked his chin. 'If *you* were a Capricorn, my girl, it would be a miracle if you managed to grow one!'

'True.' She returned to the paper. 'Let me see...hmm, hmm... *Capricorn should beware a dark woman* – well that lets Laura out, but drops me right in it, doesn't it?' Lowering her voice to Mystic Meg's breathy omniscient tones she continued, '"*You are embarking on uncharted waters but Lady Luck will smile on you. The sun is shining from Uranus bringing good fortune and Poulet à la Cassandra for dinner.*" '

'I knew you were making it up!'

She grinned and picking up the bottle of wine slid off the table. 'I'll chill this, and thank you.' She looked at him over her shoulder. 'Tonight is by way of being a farewell dinner. I'm going back to London at the weekend.'

'Only temporarily, I hope.'

She turned from putting the bottle in the refrigerator. 'I'm not sure about that.'

'Nothing I've done – or am about to do, is it?'

'No, to the first and I don't think you should tell me what you might be *about* to do. There are some things a man shouldn't brag about.' She looked at him in delighted surprise. 'Shit! I didn't think old men could blush like that!'

His eyes glittered dangerously. 'Watch it! I have a daughter quite a few years older than you and she'd know a damned sight better than to sauce me like that.'

'You really are narked, aren't you?' She studied his face carefully before her mouth broke into a smile. 'Sorry – Would you like me to grovel?'

For a moment he wondered if the smile was genuine or a calculated appeal to his male vanity, then decided she was far too impulsively open for that and allowed his own mouth to relax. 'That won't be necessary.'

'Do I get to meet her?'

'That's unlikely, at least for a while. She's married and lives in Seattle.'

'Oh.' She looked disappointed. 'Does she know about Laura?'

'Yes.'

'And?'

'She informs me that she is 'All Charged Up' by the news; I think that is an Americanised version of: 'I'm really pleased for you, dad.'

'So am I, and even more pleased for Laura.'

'Honestly?'

'Honestly. Now you can go and smooch in the garden and know I'm not putting deadly nightshade in your dinner…'

*   *   *

Cassie listened to the sound of the Land-Rover's engine receding into the distance then began stacking crockery into the dishwasher. As Laura entered the kitchen she wrinkled her forehead, asking, 'Do you think he likes me?'

'Oh, yes, he likes you all right.'

'That's good, because I think he's pretty ace. You really ought to marry him, though.'

'Why?'

'Because I think he wants to be married.'

'Why on earth should you think that?'

'Oh, I dunno, just the way he looks at you?'

'Oh, what way is that?'

She flushed. 'The way I'd like someone to look at me someday.'

'I'll think about it.'

'Good. Just don't expect me to be a bridesmaid and dress in something pink and frilly: I don't want to end up looking like Barbara Cartland!'

'You may set your mind at rest on that score,' she promised. 'The second time around it will be very quiet, very informal and probably

63

on the beach.'

'Well whenever, or wherever you decide to do it I'll be there, because I think he is another real cool sexy old dude and you shouldn't let him get away.'

'Wash your mouth out!' Laura snapped a tea towel at her, 'or you quite definitely will *not* be invited.'

Cassie was thoughtful. 'I bet he won't always be a lovey-dovey, though. In fact, I reckon he could definitely be a bit iffy if you really got up his nose.'

'Oh, you've discovered that already, have you? I thought it wouldn't take you long.' Laura gave a perceptive smile. 'But do you really think I'd want to spend the rest of my days with any man who couldn't give as much as he took? After all, *I* don't exactly have the sweetest-nature in Cornwall, do I?'

'Remembering some of the up-and-downers you and Harry used to have maybe I should be saying "poor old Miles!" I hope he knows what he's letting himself in for.'

She joined in Laura's sudden laughter, thinking that if Harry's spirit were still floating around he'd be sitting in a corner somewhere, roaring his head off at the idea that Laura would take on anything, or anyone, that she couldn't handle – or who couldn't handle her. She turned back to stacking dishes, conscious that tonight, for the first time since his death, she had been able to remember without pain that most satisfactory, and irreplaceable substitute father.

8

While Simon was in the office finishing a telephone call, Michael wandered to the far end of the gallery to examine a half-dozen colourful African Wildlife photographs.

It was while he was standing with hands in pockets and thinking of nothing in particular that he heard the discreet *swoosh* of the opening door. Then, at the sound of the swift light footsteps crossing the polished floor behind him, the hairs on the back of his neck prickled with recognition. Turning slowly he faced the owner of the footsteps.

For a long moment the shock of her sudden appearance held him transfixed. Here was the face that for weeks had haunted him and which he had tried in vain to wipe from his memory. The long eyes, straight and dark under winged brows; the small nose and wide mouth with its comical tucked in corners like those of a half-sad, half-wicked clown; the thick black hair that always looked as if she had just run careless fingers through it. In every detail she was just as he remembered.

'Oh!' Cassie stopped, 'Ah!' she said. Colour flooded her face and her eyes widened with surprised delight. Then her gaze took in his grey morning suit and she gave a barely repressed snigger. 'Are you en route for a wedding, or something?'

'Not an unreasonable assumption to make,' he recovered quickly, 'but actually I've just come from taking Jonathan's and my elderly aunt Isabel to a garden party, and will soon be en route for home.'

'It must have been some party!'

'You could say that.' His gaze passed slowly over her white linen trousers, navy striped sweater and white trainers. 'Might I ask why *you* are walking around London dressed like a French sailor? All you need is a flat hat with a pom-pom and one might be forgiven for thinking you were fresh off your *cuirassé*!'

Cassie peered down at herself. 'Yuk – I see what you mean: how gross! I must be more careful when I mix and match from Oxfam.' She grinned. 'Still, for all you know I *might* be planning to spend the weekend on the yacht of some kinky Parisian millionaire with the hots for transvestite sailors!'

'Ah, I hadn't thought of that.'

He stood unmoving, watching her with his dark intense gaze. She was aware of a faint buzzing like that of a trapped bee sounding in her ears and wondered if her thudding heart was audible to the naked ear. *Somebody say something quick* she begged silently then he gave his sudden all-embracing smile and broke the spell.

'I'm neither kinky nor a millionaire and I don't have a yacht, but if you could bear to hang around whilst I slip into something more comfortable, we could go down to Bourne End and cool off in a skiff on the Thames.'

'Why Bourne End? It would be easier to go for a row on the Regent Park Lake.'

Simon came up behind her and placed his hands on her shoulders. 'Darling, the old lecher has a house on the river there and is trying to lure you into his clutches!'

'*Is* he?' She stared at Michael who looked blandly back. 'But then I guess any man who walks about town dressed like an extra from My Fair Lady is probably capable of almost anything!'

Simon laughed. 'He's all done up like that because he's been to see the Queen.'

'Don't be ridiculous.' She looked from Simon's faintly malicious grin to Michael's suddenly drawn brows. Her voice faltered uncertainly. 'You are joking, aren't you?'

'No, I'm not.'

Michael said coldly, 'Stop trying to stir it, Simon.' He turned to Cassie. 'If you must know, I have been dragged to a garden party at Buck House by Isabel, along with God knows how many other idiots. And yes, I do have a house at Bourne End which I chose myself, as opposed to the one in Chelsea that I inherited and only keep because I am too lazy to sell it. I was merely,' he added with sudden asperity, 'inviting you for an afternoon on the river, not luring you to my home in order to have my way with you. So, do you want to come or not?'

She stared at him open-mouthed. 'Do you *always* talk like something out of Jane Austen? Harry used to do that but he had the excuse that he was over eighty! All you had to ask was 'would you like to go for a row on the Thames?' and I'd have said 'yes' straight off.'

Simon wagged an admonitory finger, only half in jest. 'You take your Uncle Simon's advice, my girl and have nothing to do with the lower echelons of the aristocracy!'

'Oh, I *see*...that explains the garden party.' Cassie looked at Michael again. 'I might have known you'd be something like that if you were a relation of Jono's. *That* whole family seems to be crawling with Honourables!'

66

'The one thing Jonathan and I have in common is that we don't care to shout about it from the rooftops.' He gave Simon a tight smile. 'I'd appreciate it, Simon if you'd just stop acting like some self-appointed guardian angel. Can't I issue a perfectly innocent invitation without you trying to blacken my character and make me sound as though I'm about to claim my *droit de signeur?*'

'Of course,' Simon gave way gracefully. 'I think you can trust him, Cassandra – but what brings *you* here today?'

She dragged her eyes away from Michael. 'Oh, I came to see how many of my prints you'd sold. I'll be staying up here for a while and I'll need all the loot I can get.'

Simon moved smoothly and effortlessly into the persona of shrewd businessman. 'All but one of your winter studies have been sold. Come into the office and I'll pay you in cash. Have you brought the river series I suggested?'

'Yes,' she followed him through the office door, 'I left them at the Carrington, which sounds grand but is actually a rather grotty boarding house-come-knocking-shop in Battersea. I only booked in there an hour ago. I'll bring them in the morning when I've got myself sorted.'

*   *   *

Michael stayed in the gallery, listening to the muted voices in the office. Well, he thought, here we go again; so much for any hope of getting her out of my system now. He gave a wry inward smile. Simon was quite right to be protective of her. He *was* attracted but to get too close would be grossly unfair to the girl. And just how did she view him? He suspected that she was interested, but mistrusted the possible reason for that interest. On the other hand the appeal she had for him was perfectly clear and almost certainly a great deal more culpable.

He thought with some exasperation that everything about her, from the way she wore her clothes with that damn-your-eyes air of the born individualist, to her apparent unawareness of the effect she had on men, was either very cleverly contrived or very innocent. That he was sorely tempted to find out for himself only strengthened his original resolve to keep her at a reasonable distance.

When she joined him again she was tucking a bulging envelope into her bag and looking pleased. 'With this and what I already have in the bank I can survive at the Carrington for at least three weeks – or possibly even four if I don't eat too much!' She turned back to the gallery owner. 'Thank you *very* much, Simon. I'll be around in the morning with the other prints.'

'Come to lunch, Lily would love to see you again.' He kissed her cheek. 'Off you go and enjoy yourself with the big bad wolf.'

She looked up at Michael. 'I'm ready now if you are.'

'Fine, it won't take me long to change.' He picked up his top hat from a chair by the door; seeing her barely repressed grin he scowled. 'If you are going to start that again I'll withdraw my invitation.'

'Sorry!' She widened her eyes and for the second time in less than ten minutes he felt the slow insidious stirring of desire. 'It's just that – well, are you really going to walk through town with that on?'

'No. I am not going to walk anywhere with it either on or off; my car is around the corner in the mews.'

'Oh, that's all right then.' She followed him out onto the busy pavement. 'Only I do have my reputation to think of, you know.'

He strode into the cobbled mews to where his car was parked and opened the passenger door. 'In,' he ordered. 'I also have a reputation to maintain and I have a nasty feeling that being seen around with you on tow is likely to do it no good at all!'

*   *   *

She waited again in the study, curled up in the big leather chair, gingerly testing her feelings towards the Michael Niven who went to garden parties at Buckingham Palace and had a house on one of the most prestigious stretches of the Thames. She was confused by him and baffled by his invitation. Had Simon been serious or just teasing when he'd called him an old lecher? Would he try and make a pass once they were alone with no Mrs Harris hovering discreetly in the background? And why had he asked her in the first place?

It was a long time since she had spent the best part of a day with any man other than Oliver, but at least with him she'd known how that time would be spent. She had been sure that her first visit to Chelsea all those weeks ago had been intended to be her last, so what had happened in the meantime to change the mind of the enigmatic Mr Niven?

Above her head she heard a door open and close then the sound of his feet descending the stairs, and her heart gave an involuntary apprehensive thump. She barely knew him, certainly didn't understand him and had no idea how to handle the hours ahead. All her instincts told her that men of Michael Niven's age and background didn't invite hard up young women of no particular importance out for their scintillating conversation – and Jono and Simon had both in their own way warned her off...

Oh, sod it! She thought in sudden irritation, if he did come onto her, well, she could always just run like hell. Couldn't she?

*   *   *

At first she sat stiff and at a distance as they began the drive through London, but when both his hands stayed on the wheel and showed no inclination to wander she began to relax and enjoy the journey. He drove well, calmly and without cursing the occasional suicidal pedestrian darting across the road. Nor did he jump the traffic lights or shake an enraged fist and swear at the lorry driver who cut him up on the Chiswick roundabout; all things that she herself did out of habit when driving around London.

'Are you planning to stay in town for long?' he asked, as he inched the Mercedes through the traffic at Richmond. 'A seedy hotel in Battersea is hardly a home from home for a country girl!'

'I'll probably be here some time.' She was guarded. 'Although unless I go over to Paris and tap Alaric again – and I'd rather cut my own throat than do that – I can only stay there until the money I have runs out, or I've found a job.'

'Doing what?'

'I'm not sure. Simon suggested just now that I try my hand at some serious portraiture. He says I can use his studio if I wish, but I wouldn't know where to get started.'

'He could be right, you know. More than one person has asked who took my publicity shots; if it would help I could drop the word to them you are available for work. Haven't you ever tried that line before?'

'Oh, I've done quite a lot down in Cornwall, but only for myself – fishermen and kids on the beach. Stuff like that. You don't get much call for any serious portrait work in a place like Treveren!'

'It's worth thinking about, though, if you want to earn your living in London.' He gave her a sideways glance. 'Just what *has* brought you up here in quite such a hurry?'

'Oh, things...' She fell silent, watching his strong, capable hands on the wheel. Eventually she began, 'You see, Laura has this guy – '

He winced. 'Oh, *please!*'

'Sorry! Laura has this *gentleman caller.*' She sniffed. 'Is that nineteenth century enough for you?'

The corners of his mouth twitched. 'It will do.'

69

'It looks like the real thing and I just thought I should give them some breathing space, that's all.'

He kept his eyes on the road and asked, his voice non-committal, 'And there was nothing else to keep you in Cornwall?'

There was another silence, longer than the first then he heard her sigh.

'I suppose Simon told you about Oliver. OK, so that didn't work out as planned either and was another reason for leaving.' She gave a strained laugh. 'Suddenly I feel a bit like an unsafe building from which the scaffolding's been nicked; maybe someone up there has got it in for me.'

'Oh, come…none of that Old Testament gloom and doom; there is always the other side of the coin.'

'Like a trip on the Thames?' she asked with faint sarcasm and he turned his head briefly to smile at her.

'It's a start, isn't it? And it beats weeping and wailing hands down.'

She settled back into her seat. 'I'll let you know about that when I've tried it.'

*　　　*　　　*

Set in a backwater, surrounded by well-kept lawns and colourful flowerbeds, the house was a surprise. The smooth, white walls were built in a complete round under a roof of green pantiles, giving it the air of a large but very up-market dovecote. Unsurprisingly, the name on the gate proclaimed that it was The Round House.

Leaving the car in the drive he led the way to the green painted front door and opening it stood back, motioning her into a circular parquet-floored hall. Half a dozen pale oak doors led from this, some standing open and affording a glimpse of the rooms beyond. She stood in the centre, turning around to view the walls painted in softest blue; the delicate wrought iron staircase curving up one wall to a balcony railed in the same wrought iron; in the roof a round glass cupola from which sunlight shafted down to where they stood. She gave an involuntary exclamation of delight and turned to him, her eyes sparkling.

'It's beautiful, absolutely beautiful!'

'Let me show you something rather special – the reason I bought this house.' He began to climb the stairs and opening a door at the top beckoned her through. 'Close your eyes, step in then look up and around,' he said, and without hesitation she did as he asked.

She stood on the threshold, oblivious of the pale oak furniture and wide, white-canopied bed; the white walls and polished floor of blonde wood, aware only of the aspect that made the room breathtakingly and spectacularly unique.

Along one wall a window stretched in a great curve from floor to coving; the river beyond the glass reflected on the ceiling and walls creating an enchanting panorama of endlessly changing movement and light and the illusion that they were under water. For a moment she stood speechless then caught at his arm. 'How can you bear to live in London when you have all this?'

He said dryly, 'I often ask myself the same thing.'

Aware that she was now clutching his arm with both hands, she let go quickly; embarrassed she said, 'Sorry…I didn't mean to grab.'

'No need to apologise; I was enjoying it.' For a moment he watched the colour rise to her hairline before observing, 'You know, I don't think I've ever seen anyone with your colouring blush quite so rosily – or so easily!' then grinned unrepentantly as she moved a step away from him. 'It's all right. I'm not going to make a pass.'

'I didn't think you were.' She turned and left the room, acutely conscious that he was laughing at her. *Serves you right, you silly cow* she told herself crossly as they left the house together and walked over the smooth green turf to where a skiff lay at the water's edge, *that's what you get for going into bedrooms with the likes of Michael Niven!*

'I don't suppose I need ask if you can handle a tiller?' he enquired, taking off his linen jacket and beginning to roll his sleeves.

'I can row, though I'll bet not as well as you, but as it's so hot I'm happy to just sit and steer, which I'm quite capable of doing without ramming any pleasure launches or putting us in the reeds.'

'That figures.' He handed her into the craft and stepping aboard cast off and took up the sculls. 'The first lock is quite a way down river so you've time to get the feel of her before any major obstacle appears.'

He rowed smoothly, his long brown arms sending them swiftly upstream with steady sweeps of the oars. Cassie sat back, a tiller rope under each arm, warning him of oncoming craft; negotiating the skiff through them with ease while viewing with covert appreciation the ripple of muscle beneath the thin white shirt.

He moored at a pleasantly low-key pub where they sat at a table under the trees to eat smoked mackerel and drink cold bitter. She watched a pleasure boat full of camera-happy tourists cruise past and gave a sigh of deep content.

71

'I could get used to all this, you know,' propping her chin on her hands she gave him the sort of smile he was beginning to find increaseingly disturbing, 'but I suppose you take it all for granted.'

He shook his head. 'I take nothing for granted.'

'Hmm,' she looked sceptical. 'You haven't always lived the high life in London though, have you? Jono said your home is in Suffolk.'

'What else did Jonathan say?'

She answered rather too quickly, 'Nothing much,' and he laughed.

'You are a very poor liar. I suppose he told you my father is well on the way to being a lunatic and my mother lives on a different planet from the rest of the human race?'

'Well, yes; something along those lines!' She laughed with him. 'Is it true they live in a crumbling castle and does your father really rush out with a twelve bore and shoot at the local Hunt if it strays onto his land?'

'They do and he does. He also keeps pigs and names them after all the people, mostly dead politicians, he doesn't like or of whom he disapproves. He kills vermin but doesn't allow anyone to hunt on his land, or shoot or fish for anything but the pot. It isn't just old age; he's always preferred animals to people. Believe it or not, he landed in Normandy on D-Day with his favourite ferret stuffed into his battle-dress. He said nobody understood Banjo like he did, and if he was going to be blown to glory then Banjo might as well go with him!'

He finished eating and moved his plate aside, apparently unaware that she was watching him with undisguised fascination. He continued, 'The house is actually structurally sound, but when I last visited about four or five months ago the ceilings in the main rooms were shedding lumps of plaster on the carpets and my parents had retreated into one wing. In contrast the pigs live in comparative splendour and comfort in brick built sties.'

She snapped her mind away from the image of a crumbling castle and a Baronet and his ferret preparing to take on the entire German *Wehrmacht*, to ask reasonably, 'Why on earth don't they repair it? The castle, I mean?'

'It's really only a manor house, not a castle, although it does give that appearance. It was built in the reign of Richard the third and one might say that it's beginning to show its age. My father won't spend the money on repairs and my mother doesn't care; she just picks the plaster out of her hair and says that God will provide. The fact that He doesn't worries her not at all.'

She gazed at him entranced, not sure whether to believe him or not. 'Have you got any brothers?' The unspoken rider: *and are they all batty, too,* hung in the air and she gave a hastily smothered snicker of laughter.

'No.' He looked amused and she had the feeling, not for the first time, that he had a rather uncanny knack of reading her mind.

'Sisters?' she ventured.

'No.'

'Same as me then,' she gave a small sigh. 'I really would have liked to have one or two of each. It must be nice not to be alone.'

He watched her for a few moments in silence before asking, 'Are you happy?' then added swiftly, 'I don't mean just now, but generally?'

She considered his question for a moment. 'No. Not particularly. Is anyone?'

'I imagine most are at twenty-odd. I know I was, with spots and worrying about failing exams and being a virgin well behind me! I can't help wondering what makes you feel otherwise.'

'Well right now I'm a bit bothered about living more or less permanently in London.' She hunched her shoulders. 'I don't fit in, you see. Harry always said I heard a different drummer and he was probably right. I can't get my head around all the things Jono's pals are at; I never could, even at art school. I don't enjoy going to clubs and discos and head-banging the night away. I don't want to sleep around or sniff coke or think it's great to get pissed out of my mind at parties and boff comparative strangers. All that makes me a bit of a misfit, d'you see?'

'Umm, yes, but if what your friends are doing doesn't appeal, where on earth are you going find your night-time pleasure and leisure in London?'

'I suppose I'll just have to try and conform – or take up something like embroidery or bungee-jumping!' She leaned back and closed her eyes against his questioning gaze, uneasily conscious that every minute she spent in his company was bringing an increasing desire to have him sitting a lot closer to her than across a pub table. I don't want all this, she thought, then added honestly, but then again, perhaps I do!

She opened her eyes and found his gaze doing a thoughtful wander over her body again; the look in his eyes telling her he had probably got as far as figuring she wasn't wearing a bra. With sudden asperity she snapped, 'Isn't it time that we made a move? Don't they put you in the Tower or something for running after dark without lights?'

Seemingly oblivious of her irritation he glanced at his watch then up at the deepening blue of the sky. 'Yes, to the first although I'm not sure about the Tower. If we go back now there'll still be time to sit in the garden for a while, have a drink and see the day out before I take you home.'

He spoke little on the way back, but rowed, mostly in silence, his eyes now fixed on the river. Cassie sat in the stern with little to occupy her but to pull on the tiller ropes and attempt to sort out her confused and confusing thoughts about the man seated opposite her in the gently rocking boat.

The attraction he had for her and the feelings he was beginning to arouse were like nothing she'd ever known. All this odd heat and fluttering that she felt inside and the way her heart surged each time he looked at her were sensations of a kind that Oliver Lingard, despite his undoubted charms had never aroused, at least not out of the bedroom and certainly not to the degree that they were now taking over her whole body.

She hunted his face for any sign that he might be feeling the same, but apart from that almost absent-minded mental removal of her clothes he might as well be some kindly uncle giving his niece a day out from school.

Stiffening her original resolve to keep him well at arm's length she decided that she would have just one non-alcoholic drink before asking him politely to take her back to the safety of her small room at the Carrington as soon as possible.

*   *   *

But once back at the house by the river she began to feel that some unseen hand was winding her up slowly and stealthily with a silent and well-oiled key.

They sat on a cushioned swing seat in the quiet garden as night closed about them and thin wraiths of mist from the river began to steal across the lawn. Their bare arms were just touching and the muscles in his thigh moved against hers, as with one foot drawn up with his ankle resting on his knee and the other foot on the ground, he kept the swing moving gently back and forth.

She turned her head and found him watching her again; mesmerised she stared back into his eyes and in the space of a heartbeat fell gently, sweetly and effortlessly into love. In the silence of that moment and without any thought or pause for deliberation she said breathlessly, 'You so much don't want to hear this, but I've simply got to tell you I am in love with you,' and leaning forward she kissed

74

his mouth.

For a long moment he sat still then groaned and swore aloud. 'Oh, hell and damnation, why did you have to say it?' he asked, and taking her face between his hands returned her kiss, exploring her mouth with a concentrated thoroughness that sent the heat of pure desire shooting through her whole body. She gave a smothered moan and linking her hands behind his head gave herself up to quite the most wildly erotic sensations she had ever known. When finally he made to break from her embrace she begged, 'No...please. Don't stop!' and catching both his hands moved them from her face to her breasts.

'For Christ's *sake* Cassie...' He snatched his hands from hers and held her wrists in a vicelike grip. 'What are you *doing*?'

She looked at him with the eyes of a startled faun. 'Making love; what were you doing?'

He said grimly, 'Nothing at all until you kissed me! I'm sorry. Just put what I did down to a sudden rush of youth to the head.' He made an effort to control his breathing and in the light spilling from the house windows she could see his mouth settle into a straight line. 'Let's get something clear right now shall we, because I don't want you to spend the next few minutes, hours, days or weeks wondering when I am going to take you to bed, because I am not, much as I should like to.'

'If you *want* to, then why don't you?'

She leaned towards him again, willing him to repeat the kiss. 'Oh no, you don't get under my guard a second time!' Still holding her by the arms he shook his head. 'I have had a lot more experience than you of this kind of thing, and you are much too young for me to take advantage.' His mouth slackened into a wry smile. 'I also suspect that what you feel for me may have a hidden agenda.' He released her gently. 'I'm sorry I let you take me unawares. At my age I should have known better.'

She asked sharply, 'What hidden agenda?'

'The one which says you need an older man in your life.'

'No,' she shook her head vehemently. 'It isn't like that. Not this time. And I'm not on the rebound, honestly.' She took one of his hands and laid it against her cheek. 'Haven't you ever been in love?'

'Yes, once. She was a lot older than you and that didn't work out either.'

'Jono says you've had a lot of mistresses.'

'Jonathan talks too much.'

She persisted. 'Have you?'

'Yes, though probably not as many as Jonathan imagines!'

'Recently?'

'Quite recently, yes.'

'Then why don't you want me?'

'Did I say that?'

There was a suspicious lump in her throat and suddenly she was afraid she was going to cry. She said hotly, 'Don't treat me like a child; you needn't wrap it up – if you just don't fancy me, say so.'

He felt her curl away on her hurt and said swiftly, 'Darling, I fancy you something rotten, but that isn't love, only lust!'

'I don't mind.' She was stubborn, unwilling to accept the blunt honesty of his reply. 'I love you, I really do; I just want to be with you sometimes. I wouldn't get in the way, or be a nuisance.'

'You are not a nuisance.' He smiled again. 'But you are a menace: to my peace of mind if nothing else.' Again he took both of her hands in his. 'Come along. It's time I took you back to your grotty hotel.'

'Can't we stay here?'

'No.'

She grumbled, 'I hate strong-minded men!'

'I'm not strong-minded. Just a man who cares what happens to you.' His eyes glinted with sudden mischief. 'However I have to admit that were I fifteen, or even ten years younger and without scruples, I'd have jumped you long before this!'

*   *   *

'Can I see you again?' She turned before the hotel door, her voice brittle and controlled.

'If that is what you want.' His eyes were sombre. 'But, darling, we are not going anywhere, you must understand that.'

She winced at the endearment but didn't answer, and he bent to briefly kiss her cheek. 'Enjoy tomorrow evening with Simon and Lily. I'll call for you here at lunchtime on Saturday; we can see a film or have dinner and just talk. Is that all right?'

'I suppose it will have to be.'

He ran down the steps then turned at the bottom to look back and smile. 'Goodnight, Cassie.'

'Goodnight, Michael.' For the first time she used his name, savouring the sound of it as she watched him drive away, holding one hand out of the car window in farewell. She pushed open the door and stepped into the narrow hallway.

Only five days to live through until Saturday.

*   *   *

Waking in the early hours of the morning she lay watching the daylight strengthen against the cheap curtains. 'I'm in love,' she murmured drowsily. 'Oh, Michael, it's no use telling me not to be. I'm in love, I'm in love I'm in *love*!'

*   *   *

Down in Treveren, Miles Trehern also lay awake and watched the moon shinning through the long sash windows. Beside him Laura lay sleeping, her head half buried in the pillow, one arm lying across his chest. He put up a finger to brush the waving auburn tendrils from her temple and at his touch she stirred. 'What is it?'

'Nothing, I'm sorry. I didn't mean to wake you.'

'I never mind you waking me.' She raised herself on one arm, her eyes drowned in sleep. 'What are you thinking about?'

'How much I'd like to be married to you and spend the rest of my life waking you up.'

'Need we be married for you to do that?'

'It would be rather nice…'

Fully awake now she chuckled. 'Cassie thinks we should be.'

'So do I.'

She leaned to switch on the bedside lamp and looked down on him inquiringly. 'At our ages, does it really matter to anyone?'

'It matters to me.'

She smiled. 'It's not every day a young man like you offers to take on an old woman like me, so I'd better agree, hadn't I?'

'Uh huh, but we'll talk about that in the morning.'

'It is morning.'

He put out a long arm and switched the lamp off again 'Don't argue,' he said and pulled her closer into his arms.

9

'Hello Lily.' Michael shifted the receiver to his left ear and twiddled with the pencil on his desk. 'Is Cassandra there?'

'No, not today, she's off somewhere watching Jono rehearse. If she calls in later shall I get her to ring you?'

'No. It's you I want to see. I just wanted to make sure the coast was clear. Can I come around before Simon and the boys get home? I need to talk.'

'Sure. If you can make lunch – say half-an-hour?'

'Thanks. I'll be there.'

He put down the 'phone and sat deep in thought for a moment, then leaving his desk walked to the kitchen to face Elizabeth's disapproval at his last-minute change of plans for lunch.

*   *   *

Lily welcomed him with a kiss on either cheek. 'What have you done, now?' she asked, and when he shrugged and raised both hands, palms upward like a Levantine carpet seller, said, 'My God, not woman trouble again?' then led the way to the kitchen and poured him a cold lager.

Michael drank deeply then sat back in the old wheel-back kitchen chair, rested his elbows on the time-smoothed arms and sniffed appreciatively. 'Coming into your kitchen is like entering an Aladdin's cave of mouth-watering odours; why doesn't my Mrs Harris's cooking smell like yours?'

'Well, for a start she didn't have a Jewish mother.' Lily bent to take a tray of what he knew would be tender and succulent chicken breasts from the oven. 'From the times I've eaten at your house I'd say she probably majored in good, solid nursery dinners with rice pudding for afters if you'd cleaned your plate!'

He gave a smile that didn't reach his eyes and she stood looking down on him, hands on hips, her dark, clever face lively with curiosity. 'O.K. you schmuck – spill the beans.'

He squinted up at her. 'You have a quaint turn of Yiddish/Yankee phrase, darling. Feed me, and I'll tell you my problem.'

'Lend a hand then.' She began to rattle plates and cutlery onto the round wooden table and he left his chair to carry the basket of bread

78

and bowl of salad from the worktop. When they were both seated she gave him another questioning look. 'Come on, you can eat and talk at the same time, can't you?'

He helped himself to salad. 'It is about a woman.'

'When was it not?'

'Oh, come *on*, Lily, I'm not that bad.'

Her shrewd eyes were direct. 'It's Cassandra Chisholm, isn't it?'

He exploded. 'Bloody hell, how did you know?'

'Because Simon told me he has a suspicion that you two are an item – and she's been around here six times in four weeks and hasn't mentioned you once!'

He digested this piece of unfathomable feminine logic slowly, eating in silence for a minute or two before answering with loaded sarcasm. 'You can put your mind at rest; we are *not* an item: and is that last piece of information supposed to be good news or bad?'

'That depends on how you look at it.' Lily cut a piece of chicken, speared it with her fork and waved it in the air. 'When she took up with the Lingard rat she was naïve as hell and completely bowled over. She couldn't stop talking about him because she wanted the whole world to know. But this time...' she took the mouthful of food and chewed in silence for a moment. '*This* time though, she's nothing like so forthcoming. I suspect that instead of hitting her like an express train, it's all kind of snuck up on her and she's much more in control. But one of us only has to mention your name and her eyes kinda give her away.'

He frowned. 'Does Simon realise...'

'No. He's too busy looking at her legs to watch her eyes!' She gave her rich gurgling laugh. 'Not that he'd ever admit it in a million years.'

Absentmindedly Michael took up a piece of bread and began to crumble it onto his plate. 'I'm really stuck, Lily. I don't know what to do.'

'She sure is in love with you, but then are you in love with her?'

He said bitterly, 'I don't know. I want her all right, but I've never been a cradle snatcher. She's young and idealistic and ripe for romance, but I doubt if she'd be so keen if she knew about the debacle of my marriage – how it came about and how it ended.' He turned haunted eyes towards her. 'Don't ask me about love, Lily; I'm not even sure if I know what the word means. I thought I did once, but not anymore.'

'She doesn't know about Francine?'

'Of course not: no one but you and Simon has ever known.'

79

'Shit!' She looked at him thoughtfully. 'Hand on your heart, Michael: have you taken her to bed yet?'

'No. I haven't!' Impatiently, he pushed his plate aside, 'not because I don't want to but because I can't afford to let my feelings get the better of me. She's too young and too bloody trusting – and I'm too old and too bloody shop-soiled to take things further.'

'I don't suppose age matters to her if she loves you.'

'I don't think it does.' He stared down at his hands and shook his head. 'She has a pretty odd kind of background and upbringing. I'm not surprised she doesn't fit in with her contemporaries and is something of an outsider. But by any standards I *am* too old for her and I'm not willing to take the risk, for her sake or mine, of letting her get too close and so start something that can't last.'

'Then stop assing around and get out of the picture!'

'I tried that right at the beginning. I kept well away from her after I returned from the States. Then she walked in on me at the gallery...' He spread his hands. 'I couldn't help it. I despise myself for allowing it to start and I don't know how to end it now without hurting her.'

Lily finished eating and pushed her plate aside.

'Never mind about Cassie – sounds like *you've* got it this time, buster, and just as badly as her.'

'Well, I bloody hope I haven't because I don't think I could bear, as you would put it, to screw up her life. I was totally out of my head over Francine; so besotted that I smothered her and she ended up hating me for it.' He put his head in his hands. 'Look where all *that* ended... God Almighty, Lily, I can't take that kind of risk again.'

'Francine was a first class bitch.' Lily rose to clear the plates. 'I wish to hell I'd never introduced you to her in the first place – and it's a great pity you've spent the last few years blaming yourself for everything that happened and refusing to admit what a neurotic, boozing totally fucking selfish tart she was.'

He stared at her from under lowered brows.

'I know exactly what she was and all about who was to blame, thank you very much, but I'd rather you didn't take it out and give it an airing in quite such a forthright fashion.'

'I'm a nice Jewish girl from the Bronx and over there we call a spade a spade and a bitch a bitch and get on with our lives. We don't chuck it all in Jehovah's lap to sort out, nor dive into the nearest confessional.' She put down the plate she held and placing her arms around him rested her chin on the crown of his head. 'Stop being such a tight-ass and lighten up, Michael. You can't spend your life looking at the past and bewailing your manifold sins. That's the trouble with you Christians: make one bloody balls-up and you start lining up for crucifixion!'

He winced. 'I don't believe you actually said that.' He closed his eyes wearily and leaned his head back against her splendid voluptuous breast. 'But my God, Lily, if I didn't love you and Simon so much I could take *you* to bed right now.'

'And if I didn't love my husband so much, I'd let you!'

He tilted his head to smile into her eyes. 'I wonder what your Jehovah would do about that?'

'Never mind about Jehovah, it's what Simon would do that you'd need to worry about.' She kissed the top of his head. 'Now clear off out of my kitchen. Tomorrow is *Shabos* and I have a lot more cooking to do before my men return.'

At the door she went on her toes to brush her lips across his. 'Give Cassie my love when you see her, and for Pete's sake get your ass into gear, one way or another!'

*   *   *

He walked slowly along the Embankment until he found the place where she had taken his picture over three months before. Leaning his arms on the parapet he thought over the past hour, acknowledging that the perspicacious Lily Meyer probably knew Michael Niven rather better than Michael Niven knew himself.

Tight ass, am I a tight ass? he mused, *probably I am, but what am I supposed to do about it?*

The whole thing was impossible, grotesque. He was over twenty years Cassie's senior; whatever Lily may say he refused to let her make a fool of herself with a middle-aged rake with a mucky divorce and a trail of casual liaisons behind him. He must ease her out of his life and do as he'd always done when living without a woman got to him: return to the no-strings, no-heartache of older and less vulnerable lovers, who asked no questions and expected no commitment.

He watched a line of barges passing, pondering his dilemma and thinking that if he had secrets in his past he wasn't the only one. Just what, he questioned silently, was the reason for the rift between Cassie and her father? However lightly she may have passed over the subject he felt instinctively that the estrangement hurt and was not of her making.

Frowning in concentration he tried to remember their conversation the night they had first met, when she had become so endearingly tipsy and confided those tantalising snippets of her life

81

with Alaric. What was it she had said then? *"He seemed to quite like being a father and I rather liked having him as one."* So what had happened to make that highly successful and respected artist, who had spent his entire life in one place, suddenly dump his only child to whom he "quite liked being a father" in a boarding school, then move himself across the channel? He doubted that a powerful, focused man like Alaric Chisholm would change his life so abruptly without good reason.

He sighed and rubbed a hand over his face. Well, whatever the reason, the man had certainly managed to screw up his daughter's self-esteem along the way; leaving her wide open to all the dangers attendant on an emotionally insecure girl who let her heart rule her head. Abandoned by her father then deprived of Harry, his loving substitute, then seduced and dumped by that Lingard fellow, she'd had more than her share of rejections already. She could do without heading straight into another relationship that could prove equally damaging...

Michael Niven stared across the river with unseeing eyes. He knew all about the love that is blind to the imperfections of the beloved, and the pain it could bring. Impatiently, he shook off the wretched memories of his marriage that Lily had revived and began walking again, his thoughts turning once more to his present dilemma.

The past month had been both a torment and a delight. Against his better judgement he had continued to see the enchanting Cassandra three or four evenings a week. Driving to Hampton Court and Kew with her, a picnic basket in the car boot, or to the theatre and out to dine he had felt young and almost carefree again. One Sunday they had walked through the deserted streets of the city, from Chelsea to St Paul's and back; she had held his hand and walked beside him with her dancer's step and he had known then that he was standing again on the very edge of love.

But it couldn't last. May and December were too far apart and somewhere in the future there would be a younger, less shop-worn lover waiting for her to meet and love.

Now on this July afternoon, three months after he had walked into Jonathan's flat and into Cassie's life, Michael walked alone by the river, knowing that in a few hours he must open his door to that desperately wanted, utterly desirable thorn in his flesh that was Cassandra Chisholm, and do his best to let her go as painlessly, for her, as was possible. Whatever happened, he vowed silently, he must do his utmost to ensure that she didn't see his action as just one more rejection; one more blow to her pride.

Cassie sat in the back row of the little theatre watching the rehearsal, recognising with something of a shock that Jono really was rather good. Wearing a black polo-neck sweater and narrow black jeans, with his long hair shining clean again and tied back into a smooth pony tail, he had the kind of slender, youthful, faintly ravaged good looks that were both attractive and arresting. His voice was clear and well modulated and he possessed that indefinable stage presence which drew the eye, even when he was upstage and with his back turned, doing nothing more riveting than pouring an imaginary drink.

An intense middle-aged man in John Lennon glasses sat at a small table half-way up the central aisle, chain smoking furiously while directing the cast on stage in a lilting Welsh accent and a total disregard for political correctness, or any finer feelings that individually or collectively they might have. Remarkably, even Jono, who was usually ready with a swift comeback only answered with a meek, "OK, Lew, sorry," when the small man thumped the table, urging him, 'You're supposed to want to 'ave 'er on that sofa, boyo, so get yewer focking finger out and give me some fockin' *pa*-shun!' When eventually he called, 'We'll break for loonch now – back 'ere by one-thirty and we'll 'ave another goo!' the group broke, chattering and laughing and Cassie made her way down to the stage.

'How did it look from up there?' Jono grinned and put an arm around her shoulders. 'I know this isn't the Old Vic, but it's a start!'

'It's great. I love this place. Who on earth had the imagination to turn a disused church into a thriving Arts Centre – and in the middle of Blackfriars, too?'

'It's a hoot, isn't it? The bloke's name's Mark Vale. He badgered and hounded every businessman in town to contribute, then managed to wrangle enough Lottery and Arts Council money for the rest. He's a brilliant Artistic Director but a dynamo who works the arse of everyone to make a go of this place...poor old Lew has to do a Saturday morning workshop with about twenty hyped-up semi-delinquent kids to get the theatre space!' Jono chuckled. 'It has another drawback as a theatre: with a train passing every few minutes over the bridge at the end of the road we could put on 'Brief Encounter' or 'the Ghost Train' and have the sound effects for free.' He hustled her backstage. 'Come on, we'll go to the kebab van around the corner; it's brilliantly cheap if you're willing to risk a dose of food poisoning.'

When they were seated in a corner of the old churchyard eating their lunch, he asked peevishly, 'Where have you been hiding – I haven't seen you in weeks and rumour has it you've been running around with my cousin Michael.'

'Well now that depends entirely by what rumour means by "running around,"' she was both defensive and sarcastic. 'I see him almost every other day – I wouldn't still be at the Carrington if I didn't. Only being regularly wined and dined by Michael saves me from getting tarted up and going on the game!'

Jono was startled. 'Is it that bad?'

'Almost, although Simon got me a couple of portrait jobs and sold three of the last batch of Helston prints. Since I've been up here I've done some studies around the river at Greenwich that he likes and thinks will sell.' She shrugged. 'But getting started with no back-up takes time and what I really need *now* is a regular income so I know I'll be able to pay the next week's rent.'

'What about your old man?'

'Absolutely not!'

'Does Michael know you're broke?'

'What do you think?' She gave him an ironic look. 'It's not the sort of thing I'm prepared to discuss over dinner at *Le Caprice*.'

'Are you screwing with him?'

'No, and if I was it wouldn't be any of your business.'

'Huh. That must be a novelty for the old sod.'

'Look.' She began shredding pieces of her kebab and dropping them to the sparrows hopping around their feet. 'This isn't exactly my favourite topic of conversation, you know. I spent a whole year with a man I thought I loved, in a relationship that began and ended in the bedroom. Now I'm stuck with your bloody cousin who's as likely to take me to bed as you are to get your leg over Julia Roberts!'

'Bugger me.' He stared at her open mouthed. 'You've fallen for him, haven't you – and after I'd warned you, you silly cow!'

She hunched her shoulders and stared moodily at a pair of fornicating pigeons. 'I don't know why you're getting so steamed up. I suppose falling in love is a whole foreign concept to you – you're hardly likely to be on the short list for male virgin of the year award are you? What happened to the Barbie Doll, by the way?'

He grinned. 'Dunno, I expect she went back to Ken!'

'Tough.' She bit into her kebab, then swore and wiped grease from her chin with her fingers, 'bloody hell, Jono, why couldn't we have gone somewhere decent for a sandwich?'

'Oh, shut up whinging, will you? I've just had a brilliant idea.'

She clutched her forehead. 'Am I strong enough to cope with one of those?'

'Well, it's like this…' He bolted the last of his lunch and wiped his fingers on his jeans. 'As well as a theatre the Friars Community Centre has just about everything under the roof concerned with the arts: it's full to bursting with all kinds of artists: sculptors, painters, musicians *and* wiz-a-wiz, a photographer. Or rather there was one until the resident snapper went and got pregnant and departed last month looking like Michelin Man and in something of a strop.'

'Why?'

'Why, what?'

She said patiently, 'Why did she depart in a strop?'

'Because *she* claimed it was Llewellyn the Lech got her up the duff and *he* swears it was probably the corporate responsibility of all of the Centre's male members – if you'll pardon the pun!' He added thoughtfully, 'he had a point: she did put it about a bit.'

'Yuk, I'm shocked; shocked I tell you!'

'Yeah, whatever; the point is, do or don't you want to see if Mark Vale will rent Arlene's space to you until she's popped and is ready to return? It wouldn't be for all that long, but better than nothing.'

She regarded him cautiously. 'That would depend what it's worth and whether being screwed by Llewellyn the Lech and the rest of the male members is part of the deal!'

'That's up to you, mate,' he grinned, 'but if you want a reasonably steady income it's not to be sneezed at. Quite a few small professional companies come for front of house and rehearsal stills and Arlene sometimes pulled in as much as a hundred quid for a full day's rehearsal shoot. I'm sure Mark'd let you have the studio cheap if you'd help out generally – run a few classes for him, give a hand now and again with the paper work, that sort of thing. Arlene hated having to give up any time to do that, but she was a lazy cow. You could make a reasonable living – enough to pay the rent and eat anyway – and it would be regular work.'

'What's the set up?'

'There's a pretty scruffy studio and an even scruffier dark room. Arlene left a heap of junk behind and it niffs a bit. I could help you clean it up,' he offered, 'but you'll have to do a deal with Mark quickly; this play goes up in ten days and I'll be well shagged out by then!'

'I could always use Simon's studio for anything I couldn't manage here.' Cassie caught his enthusiasm, her eyes sparkling, 'and you know he always lets me have his lab. Oh, Jono, I love you, I really do!' She flung her arms around his neck and kissed him.

'There, sealed with a nice greasy kiss. Now you go back and "get yewer finger out again, boyo, an' give us a bit more fookin' *pa*-shun" while I see if I can find your Mr Vale and work my womanly wiles on him.'

*   *   *

While Jono returned to the stage Cassie went in search of the Centre's director, eventually running him to earth in the basement, where he was crouched in a cubicle of the Gents busy painting the walls a virulent shade of yellow. When she had explained her mission he studied her over his shoulder for a moment with keen blue eyes, then pushing his straw-coloured hair back from his forehead with a paint-streaked hand resumed his efforts with the wall.

'Hmm, did Jono explain about the classes?'

'Yes.'

'Could you manage a couple of regular evenings with the adults – and Saturday mornings during school holidays?'

'Yes.'

There was a silence. She said conversationally, 'You've missed a bit – left hand side of the bog.'

The paintbrush went *slap-slap* over the offending area and without losing his rhythm he asked, 'Ever taught a teenage Afro-Caribbean guy wanting to be a shit-hot war photographer?'

'No,' she admitted. 'To be honest I've never tried to teach anyone anything. Does that count against me?'

'Not necessarily: this guy would run a mile from a schoolmarm.' He balanced the brush across the paint can then backed out and hitched his behind onto one of the urinals. 'What would you teach him first?'

Cassie thought fleetingly that she was glad she didn't have to wash his jeans but dragged her mind back to give the question serious consideration.

'Probably the same as someone once taught me: Always keep your camera at the ready, know what you're looking for; recognise it when it arrives, then shoot fast and keep on shooting!'

'Sounds good advice to me,' he levered himself off the urinal, his bony face breaking into a smile. 'Come on and I'll show you your work place.'

'What about this?' she gestured at the half-painted walls.

'It can wait.' He strode towards the door. 'I'm not too sure about the colour anyway...I thought perhaps green?'

She shook her head. 'No, yellow's bad enough; green would be disaster!'

He sighed and scratched his head adding a little more colour to his thinning locks. 'You could be right, but what the hell – the yellow was a freebie from the Paint 'n Paste shop around the corner and as my wife would be quick to point out, some joker will only leave his street tag with a spray can the minute it's finished.' He looked back as he led the way up an iron staircase. 'Actually, it will probably look pretty good when a few of them have done that.'

'Yeah,' she grinned. 'Eat your heart out, Jackson Pollack!'

'You've got it,' he said.

They traversed several passages before climbing the stairs to the top floor of what had been the church tower. From behind each door they passed came the sound of music or voices, the sharp rap of tap shoes; a female voice upraised in command: '*One* and *two* and three and *four...*' It was, thought Cassie, like a human beehive, alive with sound and movement.

The studio was small but adequate, the dark room smaller and slightly less adequate. Cassie was thorough, checking the equipment and chemicals. The enlarger was clumsy and old-fashioned and she decided privately that any important enlarging would be done in Simon's studio. However, cleaned up and re-organised these rooms would serve for the proposed students, providing there were not too many. She voiced her reservations and Vale agreed.

'Normally you wouldn't have more than a half dozen adults once a week; same with the kids. I'm not too sure about the school holidays. Arlene didn't have the right touch with kids and it all rather ground to a halt at Easter. The summer vacations begin next week but I don't think you'll be exactly overwhelmed!'

'*I* might not have the right touch,' she admitted, 'but I'll give it my best.'

'I have half-a-dozen basic cameras that can be loaned, but make sure they pay for their own film. Arlene charged five quid per session for adults and a quid for the kids, which seems reasonable, although that shouldn't exclude any kid who is keen and has talent but no cash. She didn't make exceptions but you might feel someone deserves a buckshee place; ask me if you're not sure.' He gave a lop-sided smile. 'You always get the odd crafty bugger pleading poverty...just take a look at their trainers; if they're wearing anything with a designer label I'd tell them they either pay their full whack *and* bring their own cameras, or sod off!'

'Thanks for the tip. I'll remember that.'

He closed the door behind them and locked it securely. 'Come down to the office and I'll give you a set of keys. Always make sure you leave the place secure, even if you only go out for a pee, because if everything isn't either locked up or screwed to the floor they'll have it!' He clattered down the stairs, talking over his shoulder. 'It's a bit of a mess I know, but you can come and go as you like for the next few days, to clean it up a bit and get the feel of the place; see if there's anything you need. Brooms, mops and cleaning stuff are all in the basement. I'll give you a key for that, too.'

'What about rent?' She hurried to keep up with him as he strode along the corridors.

'If you take on the adults and kids and chuck in a spot of office help I'll make it twelve quid a week, but you don't have to pay until you've got it straight and workable, then it's a week in advance on the dot – that OK?'

'Fine.'

He opened a door at the end of a short passageway and motioned her into a room that held two desks, one with the top almost covered by papers spilling from a loaded in-tray. Along the far wall was a rank of filing cabinets and at the second desk a diminutive girl with multiple earrings, a diamond nose stud and long ginger hair caught up in a purple scrunchie, sat before a computer console, eating an apple and poking dispiritedly at the keyboard with one finger. She was so small as to be almost invisible behind the screen. Peering around the console she grinned broadly when she saw Cassie.

'Hi. You joining this effing madhouse?'

Cassie grinned back. 'Looks like it!'

Vale said, 'This is Joy Micklejohn, she sculpts in chicken wire and plaster of Paris. Joy, meet Cassandra Chisholm – she's filling in for Arlene.' He began opening and shutting drawers in the filing cabinets, muttering: 'Now where the sweet Jesus did I put those ruddy keys?'

'Nice to meecha, Cassandra,' Joy waved amiably, 'can you work these effing machines?' she asked.

'Yes.'

'Well thank Gawd for that! You'll be the first one here that can. I'm frightened of losing all the effing files and the boss man there buggers the whole thing up if he effing looks at it.'

Cassie tried not to show her amusement at this diminutive sculptress's gentrification of a word that most used in its plain un-varnished vernacular: also that "giving a hand with the paper work" appeared a euphemism for the fitting of square pegs into round holes.

At this stage she wasn't at all sure just what Jono had let her in for, but when Vale handed her the keys and shook her hand with an enthusiastic bony paw and Joy bent upon her a beaming smile with the benediction of: 'Effing brilliant!' Cassandra's spirits soared.

It wasn't, as Jono had observed, the Old Vic, nor was it Simon's elegant gallery, and in describing her position in this temporary venture into the theatrical world the term general dogsbody sprang most quickly to mind. But the underlying air of energy and excitement that was an integral part of the place had a certain charm and she could, she thought, fit happily into the Friars Arts Centre and do her bit towards its continuing success.

10

That afternoon she waited impatiently for the hours to pass until it was time to go to Hampden Square.

In the weeks following her first visit to The Round House she had been punctilious about not disturbing Michael during the daytime. Disciplined from an early age to treat Alaric's studio as a no-go zone, respecting Michael's working day was no problem, particularly since she had struck up an unlikely friendship with his housekeeper. On most days she would arrive early: creeping quietly down the area steps into the large old fashioned kitchen, where a slatted drying rack hung from the high ceiling above an oversized Aga. There she could sit at the scrubbed wooden table listening with rapt attention to Elizabeth Harris's reminiscences of the boy Michael growing up at Ashenden Hall in far off Suffolk, and of his old lion of a father whose eccentricities and unpredictable outbursts of temper were legendary.

But the past four weeks that had been the most wonderful of her life had also been the most frustrating. Wonderful because she was in love, frustrating because of Michael's continued reserve. At least half the time spent with him was passed in the company of other people, and when they *were* alone his lovemaking never again went beyond a brief kiss on meeting and again when they parted. There had been no return to those few heady moments that first night in the garden by the river, when he had kissed her with such passion. As the weeks passed she realised she'd come up against the implacable brick wall that Jono had warned her about.

But now she had reached the stage in her love where she could see the back of a man's head in a crowd and feel a delicious shaft of joy because the head was covered in crisp dark curls and might possibly belong to Michael. For her that was a new and exhilarating experience, but it wasn't enough. She wanted to know everything about him, to be everything to him. She wasn't promiscuous and she was willing to play the waiting game. She tried hard, and almost succeeded in banishing from her mind his gentle but implacable reminder that their relationship couldn't maintain the status quo forever and that sooner or later it would have to end.

I got it all wrong, she thought as she walked towards Hampden Square that evening. I should never have let him see how I felt so soon. He must have thought I was a silly young airhead who'd just fallen out of one bed and couldn't wait to get into another. But it wasn't, it isn't, like that at all. Why can't he see that I don't mind if he can't love me as I love him; that all I want is to be with him, to be able to make love, to sleep and wake beside him in the morning?

It wasn't, she thought resentfully, as though he had not had other women, there had after all been the numerous mistresses and bits of overnight crumpet that Jono had spoken of so lightly, and that Michael had admitted.

Why did I have to fall for you, she queried silently, *I don't believe you keep me at arm's length because you don't want me, or even because you think you are too old for me, when I can see your eyes giving the lie to all of that. You won't let me get close because of something that's happened in the past – or because you are afraid that someday I'll think I am too young for you. Why can't you understand that I don't care about your age, or your past, that I just love you for what you are now...*

But you won't even give me the chance to prove you wrong, will you, you lousy, secretive bastard!

*　　　*　　　*

Mrs Harris closed the area door. 'He's in the drawing room and brooding about something,' she greeted her. 'He went to lunch with that Mrs Meyer and since then I've taken in two pots of tea and he's touched neither, so you might as well go up now. If you can't get him into a better mood I'll stay at home tomorrow and leave him to get on with it!'

'I'll try.' Cassie smiled, but muttered *'fat chance'* as she climbed the thickly carpeted staircase leading to the cool, blue-painted room on the first floor. If there was one thing she had learned about Michael over the past weeks, it was that when he wanted to keep his thoughts to himself, nothing and no one would make him share them.

The door was open and she went in quietly. He stood at the window gazing down into the garden below. Sensing her presence he looked around, his eyes so dark and opaque that her step faltered. Then swiftly the urbane and unruffled mask was slipped into place and he came towards her saying, 'Sorry. I was miles away...'

He made to take her hands but she said, 'Don't!' and with sudden disquiet put her arms around his waist, leaning her head against his chest. Breathing deeply the warm, male smell of him, she clung to the solid security of his body.

'Don't what?' He cradled her shoulders.

'Don't greet me as though I was one of your blue-rinse fans at some Oldie's Literary Luncheon and didn't really matter.'

He put her from him gently. 'But you do matter, you do.'

'How much?' she looked up into his face.

'Ah, no, you must keep to the rules of the game.'

'Your game; your rules; not mine!'

He ignored the sharp retort and drew her down onto one of the pale grey couches. 'Tell me about your day.'

She gave a little sigh and leaned against his shoulder. 'It was wonderful: so alive and busy; I didn't realise such a place could exist somewhere as grotty and commercial as Blackfriars.'

She described her morning at the Arts Centre while he listened intently and when she finished, gave her shoulders a swift impersonal hug.

'You see? You have spent just a few hours with a crowd of people who have more to occupy them than head-banging, snogging or sniffing coke, and I'd take a bet that you just can't wait for tomorrow when you can return and be with them all again.'

She gave him a long, considering look. 'I know what you're trying to do and you may be right, but it will only work up to a point. I shall still want to come back to you.'

She felt the arm that lay about her shoulders tighten and there was a long silence before he moved. Taking his arm away he leaned forward with his elbows on his knees, frowning down onto the carpet.

'It won't do, darling; it really won't do.'

'Michael, please – not the age thing again!'

'Yes, the age thing again, as you call it,' his mouth set stubbornly, 'I've been doing a great deal of thinking over the past few days and now the time has come when we really must talk.'

'About what?'

'About us. About you. About the future.'

'Why? What's happened?' she asked flippantly, desperate to make him smile, 'has your wife found out?'

'Don't be so bloody ridiculous.' He turned on her a look of such concentrated acrimony that she flinched. Astounded she saw him struggle for composure before he turned his head away and sat pinching his lower lip in silence. Eventually he said quietly. 'Leaving your flights of fancy aside, perhaps you should return to the real world and face some facts.'

'I don't want to face them – I've noticed that when people like you start talking about facing facts, they are invariably about to dump a ruddy great bucket of crap on my head – '

He interrupted her. 'Tell me, Cassie, how old is Miles Treherene?'

'Why?' She was instantly on her guard. 'What's that got to do with us?'

'Quite a lot,' he persisted, his eyes suddenly very straight and steady. 'How old, Cassie?'

'Forty-six or seven, I think.'

'And Laura?'

'Fifty three.'

'Quite. Well, Laura is a mere five or six years older than Miles and you are thirty years younger than her; when you are her age I shall, always providing I live that long, be in my mid-seventies. You must see how impossible it is for us to go on the way we are at present. It is becoming increasingly difficult for me to spend so much time with you without making love...and I can't allow that to happen.' He frowned heavily at her instinctive gesture of denial. 'Understand that I cannot, will not, have an affair with you. You were not made to have affairs; to go from one man to another, nor will I marry you and at some future time have you regret tying yourself to me. You have all your young life before you Cassie, and it's time you started to live it, but not with me.'

Her mouth was dry and her hands shaking, but she played her trump card. 'Harry was almost *thirty* years older than Laura and they had a wonderful marriage!'

He answered quietly, 'And Laura is still full of life and Harry is dead – and Miles or no Miles, she will grieve for him for the rest of her life. If you sit here all night and try to convince me that I am wrong it will make no difference. I will *never* inflict that sort of future on you. I care for you too much for that.'

For a long moment she looked at him with a desperate, deep hurt, then without answering rose to her feet and left the room, going so swiftly that she didn't see his instinctive move to stop her nor hear his despairing, 'Please, darling, *listen* to me...don't just walk away...'

He halted halfway across the room, a sick churning pain in his gut as the door closed behind her; he'd cocked it up, but what else *could* he have said to convince her? He could call her back, but what would that achieve – merely a delay in the inevitable. He heard her cross the tiled hallway, the click of the latch and the street door closing; then counted her footsteps on the stone steps before they faded along the quiet pavements. Dropping into a chair he sat with bowed head and hands covering his face.

'Is everything all right?'

Dragging his fingers down over his eyes he looked up into

Elizabeth Harris's concerned face. 'Not really, in fact I doubt if anything will be all right ever again. I have just,' he said with infinite sadness, 'walked over…no, worse…I have trampled over, someone's dreams.'

'Perhaps you were right. You have to think you were.' She looked with compassion at his ravaged face.

'Yes. Perhaps,' he roused himself and stood up. 'I'm sorry about dinner this evening but I rather think I've had enough of London for a while. I'll pack a case now and go down to The Round House tonight.'

'When will you be back?'

'I've no idea.' He gave a bitter smile. 'Just keep the home fires burning, Elizabeth. I'm not about to emigrate and I shall be back eventually. I just need a little time to adjust to what is likely to seem a long and very painful illness.'

*   *   *

Cassie walked with a blind disregard for traffic or pedestrians, wandering heavy-footed through home-going crowds, crossing the roads heedless of impatient blaring horns or shouted oaths from bus and car windows. She could feel nothing but a numb and terrible emptiness, like a gnawing, aching void in the stomach and chest. Even her thoughts seemed petrified into immobility in the echoing confusion of her brain. Suddenly aware of her surroundings and that she had reached the Cromwell Road, she passed the Oratory and the looming rococo Victorian splendour of the Natural History Museum and began to walk with more determination towards the only place that might offer some shelter and friendly human contact. When she found she had by some roundabout route arrived at Queens Gate and wandered a good two miles off course she leaned against the stone walls and began to weep tears of frustration and exhaustion. It started to rain heavily but heedless of her streaming hair and drenched clothing, and oblivious of the curious stares of passers-by she began walking again.

A wounded animal seeking shelter in a familiar lair, she came at last to Montpellier Gardens as the streetlights sprang into life, turning the smooth rain-soaked roadways into ribbons of gleaming ebony.

Tony opened the door in response to her knock, said 'Christ!' then lifted his voice in a panic stricken shout. 'Jono – come here – quickly!'

Jono came with his swift loping stride and caught her as she stumbled down the hall. 'Bloody hell!' supporting her with one arm he led her down to the warm kitchen. 'Tony, take some cash out of the biscuit barrel and get down to the offy for a half-bottle of Bells,' he ordered, 'and put the kettle on before you go.'

Tony hovered, complaining, 'But Vincent's calling for me in a minute!'

'Bugger Vincent,' Jono rounded on him viciously, 'just get the bloody whisky, you useless turd!'

The door slammed behind Tony's indignant form and Cassie hiccupped on a feeble laugh. 'That told the bastard,' she said then burst into tears.

'First a bath, then a shot of Bells and bed,' Jono hauled her protesting through noisy sobs to her feet, 'shut up and do as you're told before you get pneumonia, you daft cow. You can talk later.'

Blubbering uncontrollably and making only a token protest she let him help her strip off her saturated clothing while the bath filled, then climbed in shivering and lay down, crossing her arms over her breast. 'X marks the spot!' she said and let the water close over her head.

He yanked her upwards by one arm and she surfaced spluttering and coughing. 'You do that again,' he threatened, 'and I'll bloody stay and wash you myself.'

'Go away, you...you flaming *voyeur!*' she yelled in sudden temper and hit him in the chest with the wet sponge.

'Ungrateful bitch!' he pushed her head back under the water then strode to the door, slamming it so hard that a piece of bilious green plaster fell from the cracked ceiling into the bath. Sobbing she fished it out and dropped it over the side.

'Oh, Michael, Michael!' she wailed aloud, her nose and eyes streaming, 'why did you have to do it just when I was so happy? *Why?*'

*   *   *

She came down into the kitchen, shuffling across the room clad in Jono's too-long towelling bathrobe and oversized slippers as he was pouring hot water into two glasses of whisky and lemon. 'Here,' he added sugar to each, stirred vigorously then handed her a glass, 'hot toddy – my Aunt Isabel's answer to everything.'

'Thanks,' she was pale and shaky, her eyes red and swollen but she tried to smile. 'God bless your Aunt Isabel.' She sat down at the table and sipped, looking at him guiltily. 'Sorry about the sponge.'

'That's OK. You were right anyway.'

She looked puzzled and he said laconically. 'I *was* having a good squint; very nice too – great tits!'

She flushed crimson and looked down into her drink. 'Bastard; what happened to my clothes?'

'Drying off over the hot water tank,' he sat down opposite her at the table, nursing his glass in his hands. 'Want to talk about it?'

'Suppose so,' she drooped, lost in the folds of the gown. 'Of course, I might be having a nightmare and wake up any minute, but I don't think so.' She gulped on her drink. 'It's your cousin Michael, and Oh, Jono, I've hit the brick wall and I think I want to die...'

'Well, you're not doing that here – I did warn you.'

'I know, but I couldn't help it; I was in love with him before I knew it had happened and I let him see it. He backed off at once, but I thought if I waited and didn't push it and was patient it would all come right and someday he'd feel the same way about me.'

Jono picked up the whisky bottle and leaned across to add another half inch to her glass. 'Drink up, ducky, tell all then I'll tuck you up in bed.'

She protested. 'You don't have a spare now Tony's stored all his canvasses in the box room, and I can't take yours.'

'It's either that or one of us sleeps with Tony and I'm not volunteering to do *that* – not now he's finally made up his mind and come out of the closet with the winsome Vincent. Three in a bed never was my scene!' He was brisk, topping up his own glass. 'A night on the couch won't kill me, so come along...give, and get it all off your lovely chest.

*   *   *

She lay in Jono's lumpy bed, listening to the sounds of traffic in the street below and wondering if the great raw place in her breast would ever heal. Her retelling of the scene with Michael, healing though it had seemed at the time came back to haunt her, the words going round and round in her brain. She didn't think she could sleep but soon the whisky did its work and she slipped into oblivion, twitching restlessly, the bedclothes pulled over her head.

*   *   *

Jono surfaced slowly from a deep sleep, vaguely aware that something had wakened him. The rain had left a chill in the air and his feet, protruding from the folds of the plaid travelling rug, hung cold and stiff over the end of the couch. He rolled off to sit on the edge, yawning and rubbing one foot against the other to warm them, then stopped to listen as from the next room came the sound of muffled sobs. For a moment he sat undecided until the sounds became even more muffled, indicating that the corner of a pillow or duvet was being used to smother an increasing volume of distress. Muttering, 'Oh, fucky-fuck and bugger you, Michael!' he padded over to the door.

She was lying curled into a ball; her eyes, tear-filled and enormous peered at him over the scrunched duvet. 'Hell,' she mourned, 'I've woken you.'

'Of course you have…bawling like a bloody banshee!' He felt at a disadvantage; girls had cried on him before, but not like this. Indecisive, he jittered from foot to foot. 'D'you want a cup of tea or something?'

'No, I sodding don't! I want to be hugged.'

'OK.' Gingerly he sat beside her and put his arms around her form, made bulky with the swaddling duvet. She said, 'Nice,' then, 'you're cold; get in.'

Only half-joking he asked primly. 'Is that a good idea? I may be the nearest thing you'll ever get to a platonic pal but I'm only flesh and blood, you know.'

She began to weep softly again. 'So am I, but get in, I won't bite!'

He lay beside her, and wresting a portion of the duvet over his shivering form held her gently, saying, 'Poor Cassie,' and smoothing the hair back from her forehead. She wrapped her arms around his thin, wiry body and giving a great sigh, snuggled her face into the hollow of his neck and slowly, gently slipped away into a deep sleep.

*　　　　*　　　　*

The sun was streaming through the window as Jono raised himself on one elbow and blew gently on her closed eyes. She opened them, looking at him without surprise, murmuring sleepily, 'Thanks for not jumping my bones!'

He said almost truthfully, 'I never even gave it a thought.' He slid out of bed. 'I'll get your clothes. Have another nice long soak and take it easy. No need for you to go to the Centre today.'

'But I am going.' She sat up, her mouth settling into a determined line. 'I may snivel and whine to myself whilst I'm scrubbing that disgusting floor and I expect that on and off I'd still like to die, but it isn't that easy is it, because I'd leave too many good things, and

97

people, behind.' Suddenly, there was a glimmer of laughter in her swollen eyes. 'I must say, Jono, you're nothing like as bony as I thought – quite cuddly in fact!'

'Don't imagine I'm going to marry you just because we spent the night together,' he returned. Walking to the door he observed over his shoulder, 'You snored like a pig.'

'Liar!' she threw a pillow then lay back, suddenly bereft again, reliving the trauma of the previous evening...the look on Michael's face before she had turned and walked away from him; the caco-phonous streets and the home-going crowds; the drenching, chilling rain. Then at last the haven of the flat; the warm bath and the night spent in Jono's arms.

She still loved Michael desperately and knew she would ache for him and long to be loved, but if she put a very firm lid on her feelings and didn't let the hurt show, she thought she might fool most people that everything was OK. She might even in time manage to fool herself. Somehow she would cling onto the Carrington and her anonymous, impersonal room, where she could lick her wounds and weep when the black days came, as come they must.

She had the Centre now, and Jono; her mate, her very good friend.

11

Laura checked the contents of the cardboard box once more before handing it to Miles.

'There are his bowls and sufficient food for a week – I'm terribly sorry about that disgusting toy rabbit but he won't sleep without it. Are you sure you don't mind? He really isn't much trouble – except with the postman. He doesn't like him and the feeling's mutual!'

'He'll be fine. Don't worry.' Miles lifted the box over the tailgate of the Land Rover, opened the passenger door and said 'In, hound!' then grinned as Cormack leapt in and immediately settled into the driving seat. Miles shoved him into place then turned to take Laura in his arms. 'Don't fret. He can spend each day in the shop with me and in the evenings we'll walk on the beach and think of you living it up in Paris!'

'I hate leaving you for even a day. I don't know exactly how long I'll be with Alaric but it will not be one minute later than I can help.' She rubbed her head against his cheek. 'Going up today and spending the weekend with Lily and Simon before my flight on Monday means I can see Cassie and find out if everything is as wonderful as she's making out; something very odd is going on there.'

He held her close and kissed her. 'Remind her she must keep the end of September free – tell her I've picked out a frilly salmon pink organza bridesmaid's dress for her and a flowery hat, then watch her face!'

'You are a mischief-making old man,' she stepped into her car as he held the door open. 'Never mind about teasing her over the wedding, just wait until she knows I'm going to see Alaric...that should cause a storm.' Her face clouded suddenly. 'Why can't he use the damned telephone or even come to me? I wouldn't go if he hadn't made it sound so urgent. But that's Alaric all over; he always has thought his baby sister was put on this earth to be his unquestioning slave.'

Miles closed her door and leaned through the open window. 'Somehow I find it difficult to imagine you were ever anybody's slave.'

'I'm willing to be yours – within reason.' She kissed his mouth.

'I'll look forward to that.' He stood back. 'My love to Cassie; drive carefully and don't speak to any strange men!'

Cormack grumbled and moaned as her car turned the corner and was lost to sight. Miles climbed in beside him and fired the engine. 'You and me both pal; what say you we go to the pub and drown our sorrows?' His companion gave forth a full-throated howl and Miles said, 'Shut up you damn' fool or you'll have me at it!' He stamped on the accelerator and shot forward with maximum revs, heading for the Cob Barn, leaving behind a cloud of dust and the smell of burning rubber.

*   *   *

'Come in and make yourself comfortable.' Lily kissed Laura and took her case, stowing it under the hall table. 'Where would you like to have your bracing shot of bourbon – garden or drawing room?'

'Garden please.' Laura followed her into the kitchen where a bottle of Southern Comfort and two glasses stood ready on a tray. She looked around. 'Where are the boys?'

'I sent them off last night to Zeda for a day or two so we could talk in peace: not that they were exactly screaming with joy at going. Aaron carts them off to *Schule* and has them toeing the Orthodox line...so unlike their own dear papa!' Lily picked up the tray and led the way down into the walled garden. 'I love them both dearly but hell, they're a pain in the butt by this stage of the summer vacation!'

'I fully expected to be ambushed as I passed your railings.' Laura answered with feeling. 'The last time I arrived they were lurking under the area steps and came at me like Butch Cassidy and the Sundance Kid!'

'Simon put a stop to all that after they'd done it to old Mrs Bloom at number seventy-four and damn near given her a heart attack. He threw their six-shooters on the bonfire and threatened to paddle their asses! There was a whole lot of muttering about calling Child Line, but I guess they decided not to risk it because they stick to the garden now.'

'Never mind about old Mrs Bloom, they damn near gave *me* a heart attack.' Laura settled gratefully in a long cane chair and put her feet up. 'That's a very long journey to make in this heat and an absence of children at the end of it something of a bonus.'

'What's all this about Alaric then?' Lily put her tray down on the iron table and began to pour. 'I thought you'd more or less given up on him.'

'I had, but his letter was so sparse and intriguingly polite that I couldn't resist.' She took the glass Lily handed her and smiled. 'A

100

few months back I might have told him to get lost, but I have a rather more benign view of life since Miles.'

'Cassie is certainly enchanted by your man, or at least she was when she last visited us.'

Laura looked hard at her companion's blandly innocent expression. 'Oh, when was that?'

'Quite a few weeks back.' Lily stood, slowly swirling the spirit round her glass. 'Quite honestly Laura, I'm beginning to feel I must have raging BO or something. First Michael, then Cassandra, all of a sudden, neither of them are seeing me nor I gather, are they seeing each other.'

Laura put her own glass down on the table. 'Who the hell is Michael?'

'You mean you don't know?'

Laura said patiently. 'Lily, I live in Cornwall, Cassie in London, and she is not the world's best communicator even when in the same room, let alone at a distance. All my instincts tell me something is wrong: her 'phone calls have tailed off over the past month and she never seems to be around when I call *her*. If you know what it is, for God's sake share it with me before I meet with her and put my foot right in it!'

Lily gave an eloquent hunch of the shoulders.

'This is difficult. I didn't realise she hadn't told you about him.' She was silent for a few moments. 'I'd better tread careful here so as not to step on any corns! However, I don't think Michael would mind me putting his point of view *vis-à-vis* Cassie.' She sat down, facing Laura across the table. 'Michael is a very old friend of ours,' she explained. 'His father and mine were in the war together, a pair of equally eccentric Army Captains, who met up in Germany in 'forty-four and then corresponded and met from time to time after they'd returned home. Ten years ago when my father had his heart attack and died on his last visit here, Archie's son drove him down from his home in Suffolk for the funeral. It was the first time Simon and I had met Michael and we all three clicked, as people sometimes do. I guess Simon kinda looks on him as a brother; I wish I could say the same but he's rather too attractive for that!' She gave her mischievous grin. 'Let's just say I find him a real cool cookie and we are great friends. A few weeks back he came to see me, very hot under the collar about his relationship with Cassie which had started shortly after she split with that louse Oliver – '

'Look if Cassie and this friend of yours were having an affair it really isn't either your business or mine to chew it over now, is it?'

101

Laura interrupted.

Lily grinned. 'That's just it, they weren't; Michael was getting his knickers in a twist because the likelihood of them ending up in bed together was getting perilously close and he was fighting it like mad.'

'Why?' Laura was amused. 'He isn't gay, is he?'

'God, *no*,' Lily burst out laughing, 'he's the sexiest thing on two legs since George Clooney and whether he knows it or not, he's as much in love with Cassie as she is with him!'

Puzzled, Laura asked, 'So what's the problem?'

'The problem *is* that he's past his middle forties and had a very brief crap marriage that he's badly hung-up about – Simon and I are the only people who know about that, even his parents haven't a clue. Marriage apart, he really has been rather a bad boy with the dames!' Lily gave her a glance compounded of laughter and despair. 'I suspect that because of his past and Cassie's youth, he's gone all stiff-necked and British and ended the affair before it's properly begun. Now he's gone to ground and she's thrown herself into her work at the Centre. Although she sees Simon at the studio on a regular basis he says she's giving nothing away. I spotted her in Knightsbridge a few days back but I'm pretty sure she saw me coming, dodged into Harrods and I lost her.'

Suddenly Laura saw daylight. 'Did she take this Michael's picture a few months back?'

'That's right. He was off on a lecture tour Stateside. Did she tell you?'

'In a roundabout way,' Laura was thoughtful. 'I'm not so sure it's love though. If he's that much older it's more likely to be to do with her break up with Oliver and a part of her needing a father figure.'

'Oh, no,' Lily shook her head vigorously, 'you can't lay that one on her over Michael; it's love all right.'

'Well, who is he? What does he do?'

'Does the name Michael Niven ring any bells?' Lily smirked at the expression on Laura's face. 'Ah, I see it does!'

'Well, nothing like being forewarned, I've seen his picture in Waterstones' window!' Laura drained her glass then held it out invitingly, 'I think I'd better have another one of those, then while you and Simon have a peaceful evening I shall lure Cassandra out to dinner, lull her into a false sense of security and then pounce!' She laughed. 'I guarantee I'll find out more in ten minutes than you could in ten weeks.'

'I wouldn't count on it, and rather you than me. She's grown up fast over the past few weeks; she's not a naïve kid any longer. I kinda think you can thank Michael for that. He's got that solid Brit public school self-reliance that tends to rub off on others – and it sure has rubbed off on our Cassandra.'

Laura was cryptic. 'I'll be very surprised if she isn't still the same old Cassie underneath.'

Unperturbed, Lily refilled Laura's glass then raised her own in an ironic salute, observing, 'Well then, kid, as some old British prune said in nineteen twenty-somethin', you'll just have to 'Wait and see' won't you!'

*   *   *

'Cassie!' Mark stepped out into the passageway and raised his voice to a stentorian bellow, 'phone for you!'

'Coming,' Cassie's face appeared around the corner of the corridor, 'for God's sake, d'you have to yell like that when I'm only a few feet away from you?' She clutched her temples with both hands. 'After two hours spent with a dozen kids swarming over Battersea Park and scaring the shit out of the wildlife, I've a headache you wouldn't believe! That unspeakable O'Reilly brat actually shoved his camera right up the beak of a particularly nasty-minded swan, and if it hadn't been for some pretty nifty footwork from *moi* we'd all be wearing black armbands and walking behind the hearse.'

'Calm down...you know you love it.' He jerked his head towards the office. 'Someone who sounds like a lady is asking for you. Let's hope she didn't overhear that little lot.'

She grumbled, 'I don't know any ladies, it's probably Tony, he's practising to be a high class tart.' Picking up the receiver she said primly, 'Hello, this is the Blackfriar's home for wayward girls; no old queens allowed! Oh, ah,' she grimaced hideously at Mark, mouthing, '*my gawd.*' 'Sorry Laura, I thought it was someone messing about. What's wrong?'

'Nothing, should there be?'

'No, but why do I get the feeling there will be at any moment now?'

'Perhaps that's just your guilty conscience?'

Cassie gave a snort of laughter. 'I'm much too busy to have one of those.' She made another face at Mark. 'The guy here is a slave-driver!'

Laura chuckled. 'I'm staying with Lily and Simon until Monday and I thought I'd treat you to a decent dinner tonight. That's if you don't have a date.'

'Huh. No chance: these days I'm too exhausted for anything more energetic than a half in the pub with Jono and an evening in front of the telly with my feet up.'

'Well if you can bear to leave the telly and get into something slightly more respectable than tee-shirt and jeans I thought we'd go to Tarentino's in Greenwich.'

'Lovely. Thank you very much. When and where would you like to meet?'

'Seven o'clock at Tower Pier? Then we could go by river bus.'

'OK. I'll see you there.'

Cassie put down the 'phone and looked across at Mark with raised and questioning brows. 'Now what do you suppose has brought my stay-at-home aunt up to the great metropolis without so much as a 'look out, Cassie, here I come?' She stood tapping her teeth with a fingernail. 'Something,' she opined, 'is afoot...'

*   *   *

Back at the Carrington she showered then sat on the bed to pick over her meagre wardrobe with care, finally deciding to play safe with a sleeveless, strawberry-pink cotton dress bought from the charity shop around the corner. Long and slim, it accentuated her slender figure. Gazing in mirrors had never been her preoccupation even before Michael; since their parting she had paid even less attention to her image and was quite unaware of the subtle change in her figure from attractive to drop dead gorgeous. Tonight she enjoyed dressing up for Laura and, when she thought she would pass muster, left for her appointment, walking with her smooth, easy stride and looking, as the Greek waiter at the Acropolis Restaurant on the corner observed to the chef as she passed by their window, as tasty as a dish of ripe figs.

Lily had been right in her assessment Laura mused. In the weeks that she had been away from Cornwall, Cassie had apparently matured and acquired an impressive air of confidence, although how much of that was real and how much a perhaps painfully acquired veneer was difficult to tell. Watching her across the restaurant table, Laura gradually became aware that she was also in a most subtle way steering the conversation in the direction she wished and neatly side-stepping any interest in, or reference to, Lily and Simon or what she might be doing with her leisure time. Intrigued, Laura sat back, listening to the Cassie-edited version of life in London with her friend Jono and her work at the Centre, and awaited her chance to pounce.

The opportunity came almost at the end of their meal when in an unguarded moment her niece gazed appreciatively at a lemon cheese-cake of extreme richness and volunteered: 'I had this before when... ' then paused for a moment before adding quickly, 'when we were having a posh night out!'

Oh, ho, Laura thought, first slip, Cassie! '*We?*' she queried innocently. 'I wouldn't have thought your friend Jono would aspire to anywhere quite so grand on an actor's pay.'

'He couldn't, he didn't...anyway, it's not important.' Cassie turned away from Laura and treated the hovering waiter to a dazzling smile. 'I think that large piece, please.'

When the waiter and his sweet trolley had departed, Laura sighed and leaning across the table lowered her voice. 'Cassie, why don't you stop acting when you are so bad at it? Remember, this is me you are talking to –'

'To whom you are speaking!' Cassie interrupted and Laura smiled.

'That's better. You might as well come clean because Lily's been very informative.'

'What did she tell you?' Cassie was guarded. 'I can't think she knows very much because I haven't said anything to her – or Simon.'

'Michael went to see her weeks ago. She seemed to think he might still be undecided then. Cassie, why on earth didn't you talk to *me* about this man?'

'Oh,' she lifted eloquent shoulders. 'Well, I don't know what he told her but he made it all too clear to me that it was all over.' She hesitated, frowning. 'Something very odd happened that last time we met...I wish I could remember what it was but everything about that evening is so messed up in my mind that I can't put my finger on it. I'd never ever seen him come within a mile of losing his temper but that night he was being a real stuffed shirt and I said something pretty silly because I wanted to make him laugh. Instead he was really angry and after that things just got worse.' She gave a wry smile. 'Just a bad case of "me and my big mouth" I guess! Anyway, there was no point in telling you then. Quite honestly, when it all came apart I didn't want to talk about it to anyone.'

Laura asked gently. 'What was he like before that happened?'

'Kind and balanced and very easy to fall in love with; he made me feel I was *someone*; that what I did and what I was mattered to him. And I think that was true.' She was silent for a moment, then said hesitantly, 'That night, when he said we had to finish and I walked out, he'd talked about you and Harry and I told him how you'd been so happy together. He picked that apart and as good as said Harry had

105

been wrong to tie you in marriage then leave you to grieve – that he would never inflict that sort of future on me. Was he right?'

'Yes and no.' Laura chose her words with care. 'Harry was my husband, lover and friend and I adored him. All the same, I was conscious right from the beginning that he would die when I was relatively young, and as the years passed that became very painful to live with.'

'Do you ever have regrets?'

She smiled and shook her head. 'Not really, at least not enough to matter; looking back now I wouldn't have changed a thing.'

'I wish Michael could hear you say that.'

'Perhaps you gave up too easily. If you had stayed and fought your corner as I did with my parents; you might have won.' Laura suggested. 'It was only *after* I'd done that and failed that I walked out.'

'Ah, but you were fighting your parents, I was fighting Michael, and there's the difference.' She smiled in a way that wrenched Laura's heart. 'I loved him so much that I would have done anything: married him if he'd wanted that, gone to bed with him and no strings attached if he didn't. Just being with him was all that mattered. I didn't *care* if he couldn't commit himself to me. I only wanted to be a part, even a small part of his life. When he turned me down, put up the shutters, I could only turn and run.' She clasped her hands tightly together until the knuckles showed white. 'Why did he pull back like that? He'd had other mistresses, so why not me?'

'Perhaps,' Laura offered, 'it was because you did matter. Perhaps he loves you as much as you love him. Perhaps that was his way of dealing with it: of shielding you from what he saw as the sacrifice of your youth.'

'It's a bit late to try finding that out now.'

Laura persisted. 'Some might say it's never too late. Someone has to start things moving again and perhaps as you did the walking away it may be up to you to make the first move back.'

'No. I'm not offering myself again to a man who doesn't want me, I've already done that once – twice, if you count Michael – and I won't do it again. It hurts too much.' She picked up her fork and dug it into the cheesecake, saying with an air of finality, 'Now if you don't mind, I'd rather not talk about it anymore.'

'If that's what you want…' Laura gave a resigned shrug. 'When you have finished I'd like to find somewhere more private where we can talk. I haven't yet told you my real reason for staying this weekend in London and you may get a little noisy when I do.' At

Cassie's questioning look she added, 'I am going to meet with someone I haven't seen for a very long time and I think you may be able to fill me in on how to avoid some of the more obvious pit-falls of our meeting.'

*   *   *

Laura waited until they were walking along the towpath before she told her about Alaric.

'Of all the bloody nerve...' Cassie exploded violently, 'isn't that just like him!' She stooped to pick up a stone and hurl it in the general direction of the looming Thames Barrier. 'Let him come to you if it's that important, the cheeky bugger!'

Another past taboo demolished by the new Cassandra, Laura thought wryly. The old one had always curbed, in her presence at least, what she had long suspected was a rich vocabulary. 'Those were my thoughts at first,' she admitted, 'but I'm afraid curiosity finally got the better of me. I've never known my brother do anything without a reason.'

Cassie said bitterly, 'Apart from dumping me and doing a bunk.'

'There is that, of course: one of life's greater mysteries. However, I have a feeling this may be something quite different. Alaric is nothing if not proud and it must have taken a great deal of nerve to ask such a favour of me.'

'I'll come with you if you want, although we didn't exactly part on the best of terms; come to think of it, I did a bunk from *him* that time!'

'That seems to be a Chisholm habit.' Laura smiled. 'I thank you for the offer but I think one of you at a time is quite enough.'

'Then promise you'll tell me what it's all about when you get back.'

'Certainly not; I won't break any confidences, even Alaric's; even for you.'

Cassie turned to lean on the railings and gaze down into the water. She said, 'Don't let him give you any money for me; I'm doing all right. Don't forget to tell him that.'

'*Are* you doing all right?'

'I earn sufficient to live on.'

'That wasn't what I meant.'

'I know, but the answer's the same.' Cassie turned, leaning back on her arms. 'I shouldn't have cut you off in the restaurant; you have a right to know what's going on; but you don't have to worry. I shan't

107

pine away or go all loopy with unrequited love. Nobody can touch what I've had. It may not have been much, certainly wasn't all that I wanted, but it was better than anything else that had ever happened to me before and I shall remember it for the rest of my life.'

She gave the sudden upturned grimace that was like a clown's comedic mask over tragedy and pain, before turning her head away and looking down into the water again. 'I can't cut Michael out of my life; that just isn't possible, so now that he has gone I visit his house and talk to his housekeeper, just so that I can imagine him there. I listen for his footsteps and pretend that at any minute he'll come into the room. I remember the feel and the look of him and how long his lashes are and the way his hair curls over the back of his collar,' she looked over her shoulder at Laura, a soft luminous smile replacing the clown's wide grin, 'and I can do all of those things now without falling to pieces or bursting into tears. So you see I really am all right.'

All at once what Laura had looked for over so many years was there. The defensive, awkward, youthful edge had gone. With dignity and maturity and the courage of love, the bloom of beauty had come at last to that troubled and troubling face.

12

Ten days after he had begun his self-imposed exile at The Round House, Michael repacked his case and left without even allowing himself the luxury of a last look at the cool reflections rippling across his bedroom ceiling.

All his wallowing in soulless introspection had achieved nothing. Waking or sleeping – and of the latter he did little – Cassie was still a remembered, wanted presence, her absence a dull ache in heart and mind: engendering a physical turmoil not to be relieved by swimming to excess, or rowing to the point of total exhaustion. Too late he realised he had made a cardinal error in trying to put her out of his life. Losing her had made a hollow mockery of his resolve never to venture again on the path to marriage: least of all with a woman young enough to be his daughter.

After the third sleepless night in a row he decided that in his present foul mood of self-recrimination and despair it was pointless to return to London and attempt to settle to work. Instead he would go up to Suffolk and lose himself in tackling some of the many tasks that always awaited him there. This time, he vowed, he would not allow his father to wind him up, nor let himself become irritated by his mother's over-reliance on the Almighty to provide. But first he must pay at least a flying visit to Chelsea and let Mrs Harris know where to divert any calls or enquiries from Nick Porter, his editor, who was already pressing for another book.

If Nick thought it a good idea, he would drag himself into the twentieth Century; perhaps with a biography of Henry Williamson, that reclusive but most powerful writer, first encountered in his teenage years and admired ever since. Recently he had been re-reading the Flax of Dreams; with roots so firmly planted in the countryside Williamson's stories were evocative of much of his own growing years spent in a similar haunted land of woodland, marsh and river.

Perhaps leaving the corseted, frock-coated and mannered worlds of the Georgians and Victorians for the more gritty and earthy plane of Williamson may not only serve to set his professional feet on a different path, but also give a new perspective to his personal life. An only, lonely childhood leading to a profession that required a dedicated immersion in the lives of those long dead writers, had perhaps made him less than fit to face the problems of a tougher, more realistic and less gentlemanly world. He still winced a little whenever he recalled Lily's brutal: 'Don't be such a tight-ass, Michael...loosen up!'

Well, he'd do his best to 'loosen up' and rid himself of that unflattering image. Out must go Georgians and Victorians...it was time, he decided, to take a step nearer to the present day. If he pursued the twentieth century far enough who knows? Logically he may even end up writing the life and times of some 'nineties chick-lit baby...and how much further could a literary biographer go than that?'

*   *   *

He drove along the Embankment, not because it was the quickest route to Hampden Square, but because every pavement flag and stone balustrade reminded him of Cassie. It was the old childish self-torture; half pleasure and half pain, of picking at the scab on the knee or elbow to uncover the raw hurt beneath.

He knew that he shouldn't be turning his back on certain duties and obligations. He *had* promised Isabel when they were at the garden party Cassie had found so hilarious, that he would keep a fatherly eye on her favourite nephew and godson, but to see Jonathan now would inevitably lead to hearing about, and possibly even meeting, Cassie again, and that he wasn't ready for as yet. And he should call in on Simon, at least ring Lily, but couldn't bring himself to the point where he could make the move. Perhaps when he'd put sufficient distance between them that neither could say, 'Come to dinner,' or 'let's go for a drink,' he would pick up the 'phone and make the call...

*   *   *

Elizabeth Harris opened the door before he had turned the key and after one glance at his face said, 'There is a pot of coffee in the kitchen so if you'll just go on into the study I'll put your case upstairs then bring you a tray.'

'No. I'll have mine with you and I'm not staying so leave the bag,' he smiled at her concerned expression and laid a hand on her shoulder. 'It's all right. I've decided I'll go to Ashenham for a few weeks: possibly right through August. If I leave it until the mists start rolling off the river and creeping under the doors, I shall be even less enchanted with the idea of dealing with collapsing ceilings and falling masonry than I am now!'

'The long range forecast is for plenty of sunshine over the next few weeks, so I'll pack another bag with plenty of cotton shirts…and I daresay you'll need your shorts.' She led the way to the rear kitchen and busied herself setting out mugs for the coffee, 'although looking as you do, if you're going down with the idea of working on that mausoleum through a heat-wave you'll spend more time in bed than putting things to rights!'

'How do I look then?'

'Absolutely dreadful; keep on as you are and you'll be old before your time.'

He said with heavy sarcasm, 'Hardly before my time!'

She pursed disapproving lips before observing caustically, 'We are in the last decade of the twentieth century and thanks to science, both you and I can expect to live well into old age. Discounting the fact that you may be run over by a corporation bus or choke to death on a fish bone, you are very much in the prime of life and have a good few years to run before you take to a Zimmer-frame!'

He took the coffee she offered and smiled. 'Dear Lizzie! What would I do without you to slap my wrist and make me toe the line?'

'Less of the Lizzie – sir,' she sat down opposite, giving him what his father always referred to as "that old witch's evil eye." 'We are all grown up now and Elizabeth, or preferably Mrs Harris, is my name.'

Michael sat back and watched her over the rim of his cup for a moment, then grinned. 'At times like this you make me believe in reincarnation. You don't ever have flashbacks to being a Victorian schoolmarm, do you?'

'No,' she wrapped both hands around her own cup, regarding him composedly, 'but I was fifteen years old when you were born and I came up to the Hall to be a skivvy to that old bitch of a nanny, and *I'm* nowhere near ready yet to drift into old age!'

He reached to place a hand over hers. 'Doesn't a country girl like you still miss the Fens and the forest, the river and that endless sky?'

'Yes I do. But then I also miss the chilblains and hacking coughs I got each winter!'

He laughed. 'When you married that old devil Jack Harris and let him take you off to the smoke, father said you'd be back within the month. How wrong he was.'

'I might have done if that "old devil" hadn't been the best of men,' she squeezed his fingers and smiled, 'and so are you. What would I have done without *you* to pull me out of the doldrums when Jack died?'

'The best thing I ever did – for both of us.' He finished his coffee and stood up. 'I just need to ring Nick Proverbs then I'll be on my way. I can stop off somewhere for lunch en route.'

She smiled to herself at his withdrawal from the discussion of her arrival in this house: a distraught woman, mad with grief, rising up from the past to confront him. When Jack had suddenly dropped dead at the wheel of his cab there was only one person in this huge and still alien city to whom she felt she could turn for help and comfort and Michael Niven had not failed her.

Calmly, compassionately and without question he had taken her into his house, helped piece together her shattered life then, after gradually easing her back into the home she had shared with her husband for almost thirty years, had given her a new reason for living. Since that day and for all of seven years she had come daily from the small terraced house in Pimlico to clean and cook for him, bully him gently, mend his socks and disapprove of his women.

She railed silently at him as she went to sort through his cupboards and pack for him. *You fool; I know what you are doing. You think that by taking yourself away you will free that girl and that she will come to terms, whatever that may mean, with what's happened. Your misplaced sense of honour will wreck your life – and hers too – unless a miracle happens and you come to your senses before it's too late.*

Michael, listening to her forceful footsteps and energetic opening and closing of drawers and cupboards was again assailed by doubts that he had done the right thing all those weeks ago when he had let Cassie walk out of his life. But it was no use wondering if she was as wretched and miserable as he; all he could do was cling to the hope that she had picked herself up and got on with her life rather more successfully than he had to date.

*   *   *

As he approached Bury St Edmunds, unable to shake off the memory of the times Cassie had occupied the seat next to him and sparked the erotic charge against which he had fought so hard, his thoughts turned to an old flame. Jacqui Melrose had over a number of years provided occasional accommodating and discreet companionship, with no questions asked. As baser instincts overrode conscience, and after only a brief tussle between the latter and a rapidly escalating need, he turned off the main road and stopping in a convenient lay-by, punched in a long neglected number on his mobile.

'Well!' The voice that answered his greeting was warm but held an undertone of knowing laughter. 'I wondered how much longer it would be. Where are you?'

'Just your side of Bury; you are still the merry widow I trust, and with time to spare for an old friend?'

'I have no plans for this afternoon but the evening is booked for the theatre.'

'Perfect. I aim to be at Ashenham by six. May I pick you up now for lunch?'

'You may,' the voice was teasing, 'and after?'

'I couldn't possibly say. I always leave such decisions to the lady.'

He turned his mobile off and sat for a few moments making the familiar gesture of pinching his lower lip while communing silently with himself.

Up to your old ways again, you bastard...and after only three months of celibacy; you should be ashamed... 'I am,' he answered aloud, 'but I'm also human and as the old witch pointed out, nowhere near ready yet for a Zimmer frame!'

Despising his weakness he re-started the car and drove on to the next village in the expectation of a quiet lunch followed by an afternoon of experienced and civilised sex.

*   *   *

Not feeling nearly as satisfied and refreshed as he had hoped, he left Jacquie's house with her parting shot: 'Very nice and quite up to standard, but next time darling, a little more enthusiasm would be in order!' sounding accusingly in his ears.

Even before he reached the main road and turned towards Breckland he was regretting his lunch of over-rich *ragu* and the following hours spent between Jacquie's satin sheets. How the hell had he imagined that an afternoon in bed with the merry widow was going to rid him of the aching need to have Cassandra in his arms? Sex, he thought sourly, leaning to rake a hand through the glove compartment for peppermints, should have come before the meal: an *apéritif,* rather than a hard to digest dessert.

*   *   *

He drove slowly along the avenue of horse chestnut trees lining the approach to the house. Crossing the stone bridge over the moat he was filled with a rush of pleasure and affection at the sight of the mellow old building, the tall Tudor chimneys and high leaded windows washed golden by the rays of the afternoon sun; the octagonal turrets on the two forward thrusting wings of the house casting long afternoon shadows over the flagged courtyard. As he stopped the car a flight of white fantails fluttered from the roof to strut importantly around the wheels and he told them severely, 'One day, you are going to miss-time that and it will be pigeon pie for dinner!'

Suddenly the peace was shattered by the roar of a shotgun from the rear of the house. A rook shot skyward in an explosion of feathers then thudded back to earth, accompanied by a jubilant cry of 'Got you, you bastard!' A few seconds later and holding his prize aloft, Archie Niven appeared around the corner accompanied by a trio of Norfolk terriers.

He eyed his son without surprise, then waggled the dead bird. 'Sod's been annoyin' the pigs and Brenda's farrowing any day now!'

'Hello father,' Michael put his hands on his father's shoulders and kissed his smooth-shaven cheek, a waft of bay rum taking him straight back to earliest childhood and memories of an Archie who swung him aloft in strong arms and made him shout with joy.

'Ha!' Archie shook the dead rook again, bringing forth an ear-splitting cacophony of barks from the dogs, 'what d'you think of that? No bad shot for an old man, eh?' Chuckling, he stumped off stiff-legged to the compost heap, leaving a trail of blood and feathers across the flagstones as the terriers leaped and snatched at the unfortunate bird.

'Archie, are you tormenting God's creatures again!' Octavia Niven appeared at the open front door looking cross and holding her hands over both ears, while at her side an ancient pug snorted threateningly. As her gaze fell on Michael she broke into a welcoming smile.

'Oh, it's you, dear. I rather hoped you were the plumber. Your father tried to turn the kitchen tap off the wrong way – you know how rough he is. Now it won't stop and Gerda is so cross and banging the saucepans quite dreadfully. Have a look at it, there's a sweet boy, whilst I go and pick the beans for dinner.'

'What about the plumber?' Michael brushed off the pug, now making a wheezing, asthmatic and half-hearted attempt to shag his shoe.

'Oh,' his mother looked hunted. 'Don't tell your father but I think I forgot to call him. But you can do it, can't you dear?'

He kissed her, said, 'Yes, mother. I expect I can,' and taking his case from the boot of the Mercedes walked up the shallow half-circle of steps to the open door.

For a moment he stood in the cool hall with its faded wall hangings and unsafe minstrel's gallery and looked around, wondering if either of his parents had registered that it was at least six months since his last visit. As a collared dove appeared from somewhere in the rafters and began to fly in circles above his head he swore aloud. 'Oh, bugger, that means the bloody roof needs attention as well!' With a resigned sigh he left his case in the hall and went in search of a spanner and the unstoppable tap.

Later, the flow of water successfully dealt with and the Austrian cook-cum-housekeeper placated, they sat down to their evening meal, but apart from a greeting of 'Good God, are you still here boy?' Archie found little to say to his son, and with Octavia once more lost in her own sweet dream world of untouchable serene faith in the goodness of God and man, the meal was consumed mostly in silence.

They were ageing fast, Michael thought, watching them covertly; both seemed to have shrunk and his mother's hands shook slightly as she lifted her wine glass to him in a shy, silent toast. He smiled back and her lips trembled, her pale eyes filling with sudden tears.

When the meal was finished and Archie pushed back his chair preparatory to leaving the table, Michael braced himself for the inevitable confrontation.

'I see that more of the ceiling mouldings are down in the long gallery, father. Before you disappear again to hold Brenda's trotter I'd like to get your agreement for Mark Bareham to take a look at the Hall in general and the roof in particular.'

'Why?' His father's black eyes snapped beneath lowered brows.

'Because you simply can't keep neglecting the place the way you do. One day a ruddy great chunk of masonry will come away and drop on someone's head.'

'Well it won't be on *my* head, or your mother's! The towers are sound and will do for us when the rest falls down. I've told you before: when you've got yourself a wife and started a family I'll think about it, until then there's no point in spending good money on the place for *you* to rattle around in on your own when we've gone.'

'What were you thinking of doing with your money then – taking it with you?' Michael asked dryly'

'I would if I could!' The angry old eyes challenged him. 'What will *you* do with Ashenham anyway when you've seen me off? Turn it into a hotel or some ruddy conference centre for a load of pin-stripe-suited old farts to play at soldiers and paint-ball each other stupid? Or p'raps you fancy doin' what old Charlie Haverford did over at Lacy de la Hay and havin' a load of chaps in yellow dresses prancin' around and ringing their bloody bells!'

Michael cracked a walnut between his hands. 'It's an idea.'

'Over my dead body it is!'

Resisting the temptation to say that could be arranged Michael shrugged and cracked another nut. His father glowered.

'When are you going to get yourself a woman and settle down? Your mother and me won't live forever, you know. One day you'll arrive and find us both under the sod, with Eva Braun out of the kitchen and filling the place with her Hun relations.'

Michael said patiently, 'If the long-suffering Gerda hears *that* she'll be off and you'll be getting your own dinners in future, for no one else will put up with you.'

Archie wouldn't be deflected. 'You should take a leaf out of my book, m'boy. I saw your mother at a mess dance, knew she was the one, brought her to see my guv'nor the next day and married her within a month. In those days we didn't hang around fiddlin' an' fartin' an' waitin' for the perfect woman; we had a war to fight.'

Octavia nodded vaguely. 'He was very forceful,' her faded eyes became suddenly alert and she glared at him, 'but I don't want to lie under the sod; I've told Father Sebastian; I want to be cremated.'

Archie roared and pounded the table. 'I've told you before 'Tavia, I won't share me grave with a jam-jar of hearth-sweepings!'

'Well, you'll have to get used to the idea,' she was triumphant, immune to his rage. 'It's in my will!'

'Is it? Well it can just come out again. I'll have a word with Father ruddy Sebastian meself; it's disgusting: like a ruddy Hindu walla – an' even they'd stopped puttin' their women on bonfires long before Mountbatten left India!'

Like a naughty child Octavia gleefully stoked the fire she'd started. 'Suttee was different – *you* would have to be the one who was dead and I'd have to be alive – Father Sebastian wouldn't like that at all and neither would I.' She gave a little huff of triumph and started to feed the crust from her apple tart to the pug at her feet. 'Cremation is Christian and hygienic, and in any case until you come to Mass as you should, your opinion doesn't count.'

Michael said 'Jesus!' under his breath and stood up. 'Will you two just leave Father Sebastian and your funeral arrangements and stick to the point?' he asked wearily. 'I shall ask Mark Bareham to make an inventory of all that needs doing in order to at least keep the rain out, then I'll get the damned work done if I have to sell Hampden

Square to pay for it.'

Archie eyes bulged. 'I won't have that jumped-up little weasel over my doorstep! I knew his father when he was a snotty-nosed errand boy helpin' himself to the milk money off the Almshouse steps. If his misbegotten son turns up here I'll pepper his arse with shot.'

'All I want is to have this place made safe and weatherproof. Mark's a good surveyor and can't be held responsible for his father – none of us can. Just humour me will you, pa, and I promise I'll soon leave you in peace again.'

Octavia said wistfully, 'I thought you might stay. I was going to ask Poppy Bingham over so that you could go riding or for some nice walks together. You'd like that, wouldn't you, dear?'

'Not really, mother. It's kind of you to think of it, but she isn't my type.'

He forbore to add that Poppy Bingham, fourteen stone, with a fine moustache and legs like a grand piano, was already happily shacked-up with the local midwife and unlikely to be interested in a nice walk, let alone a ride with any man, either on or off a horse. He helped his mother to rise from the table. 'Let's take a turn about the garden and you can tell me what you'd like me to do out there before I have to go back to town.'

'I'll come too. I've got some crackin' Rhode Island Reds since you were here last and you haven't seen the pigs yet.' Archie's temper subsided as quickly as it had flared, 'but I may have to give Michael Foot the chop; he always was a useless bugger, now he's gettin' slower than a constipated snail…had to practically lift him onto Brenda the last time he served her.' He took his son's other arm and all three walked slowly out into the blue haze of evening.

Michael was hard put to know whether to laugh or howl with despair, questioning again what on earth he thought he might achieve by burying himself here at Ashenden. The delightfully vague indulgent mother, who had been such a soft and safe refuge during his childhood, was now frail and rapidly retreating into a protective dream world, seeing only those things she wished to see and avoiding anything that might upset the warmth and safety of that world. The half-feared, half-loved, once powerful father who had taught him to fish and shoot and beaten him for boyhood scrapes and sins was now an irascible old man, obsessed with his pigs and chickens; only too ready to lash out at the son who had so clearly disappointed him.

What would Cassie say if she could see him on his home ground and wouldn't the short-fused old Archie just love to pit his wits against that acute and lively mind? He had a sudden vivid picture of Cassie walking towards them, that remembered little self-conscious grin on her face, himself saying, 'Mother, Dad, here is the reason I want to keep this place from falling down. Here's the girl I'm going to marry.'

Now what on earth, he thought, had made him imagine anything so utterly unlikely and insane?

*   *   *

'Nearly there, aren't you, Brenda old girl?' Archie leaned over the low wall and scratched the sow's ears with a short piece of stick, while she closed her eyes and grunted, flanks quivering and teats straining. 'At least, me pigs know their duty,' he shot his companion a challenging sideways glance observing, 'you look like hell,' and when Michael kept silence, goaded, 'what's wrong with you? Cat got your blasted tongue?'

'No, father, I'm just trying very hard not to quarrel with you.' Michael propped his elbows on the wall and leaned back, idly swinging his blackthorn stick and watching his mother's slow return to the house.

Archie snorted. 'What's made you change the habit of years? Some woman?' and gave a high cackling laugh at his son's suddenly lowered brows, 'Ho, ho! Scored a bulls-eye, have I?'

Michael said deliberately, 'You are at liberty to think what you like, and I am equally at liberty to tell you to mind your own business.'

'It is my business; at least it would be if you kept a woman for longer than five minutes. I suppose you've backed out again and left another one high and dry rather than do your duty by your mother an' me?'

'I would have been only too delighted to keep this one for the rest of my life.' With his desire and longing for Cassie so dangerously near the surface Michael was stung into incautious admission, adding trenchantly, 'and duty has nothing to do with it!'

His father grunted, scratching harder at Brenda's flank and the sow grunted back. 'I suppose you were bound to get your come-uppance one of these days. Leave you before you left her did she?'

'It wasn't quite like that.' Michael's mouth twisted bitterly. 'I waited too long for the right woman then lost her because I wouldn't admit, even to myself, that she *was* the right one.' He hunched his shoulders, turning his head away. 'Why the hell I've told you that I

118

can't imagine; it will no doubt give you great satisfaction to say, "I told you so."'

'Dunno about that. Depends on the reason you let her go.'

He said tiredly, 'Either I was too old for her or she was too young for me. Whichever way one might look at it, it wouldn't have been right.'

'Bloody fool! What's a man's age ever had to do with marriage?' Archie was contemptuous, 'not past it in bed already, are you?'

'Oh, go to hell!' Michael pushed away from the wall and began walking towards the house. 'I should have known better than to tell you anything, you selfish old bastard. As a father and receiver of confidences you're about as much fucking use as that pig – less, in fact!'

Archie yelled, 'Don't you swear and turn your back on me, boy!' but Michael continued to stalk away from him, fuming and swiping at a bed of nettles with his stick.

Once, he raged silently, *I could have told you anything; once you would have listened and given good advice. Now you are just a useless, bad-tempered old sod who happens to be my father, whom I have still, however much I may try to break free, to love and care for and worry about.*

*   *   *

There now – Archie was shouting again! Octavia's brow creased in a worried frown. If only he would leave the boy alone: all that arguing and pushing he'd been doing for years wouldn't achieve anything. Michael would get married when he met the right woman and not before. She thought wistfully that it would be nice to have a daughter-in-law and some dear little babies. She would have liked a whole nursery full, but there, if God had wanted her to keep producing them like rabbits out of a hat in the way that dear Cousin Janet had, He would no doubt have arranged things differently.

She made her way to the walled garden and sat by the fishpond to watch the slender Golden Orfe dart about between the water lilies. It was all looking very neglected, she thought, gazing around at the overgrown shrubs; the rampaging weeds gradually strangling the bright summer flowers. She really must speak to Milton about it, but these days he never seemed to be around when he was wanted and somehow it had become too difficult for her to manage more than pottering in the greenhouse and sowing the trays with next season's seeds. She stooped to pat the pug.

'We'll ask Michael to go over to have a word with Milton tomorrow, shall we Titus? Then perhaps he'll come soon and help me to make it all pretty again.'

Titus panted and looked up hopefully, his round protuberant eyes moist and his tongue lolling; she patted him again and stood up. 'Come along then and see what nice little tit-bits Gerda has saved for your supper…'

*   *   *

Archie failed to put in a further appearance that evening and while his mother re-read Jayne Eyre for perhaps the fiftieth time, Michael spent the hours after dinner lying back in an armchair and planning a massive attack on the Hall. Archie or no Archie, he determined, something would have to be done about the roof at least; and he'd meant his threat to sell the London house. If that was what it might take to fund the repairs if pa failed to pay up, then that was what must be done.

When the carriage clock on the mantle finished chiming the half-hour after ten Octavia put aside her book saying: 'Time for prayers and bed!' Michael rose to help her from her chair and she leaned against him, looking up into his face and patting his arm. 'You mustn't worry about the house, dear. I've been talking to Our Lord about your father and I'm sure He will help to change his mind. I'm going to the chapel now to ask Him again. Why don't you come with me? If there are two of us He might be able to hear more clearly.'

'I doubt it; I'm a bit out of practice, mother.'

'Never mind, just come to keep me company then.'

He slowed his pace to accommodate her slower step as they walked along the corridor from the main hall to where a wrought iron gate at the top of three shallow steps led into the private chapel. Only the sanctuary lamp glowed red in the dusk and as Octavia instructed 'Just the altar light, dear,' he fumbled with the switches, then finding and pressing the right one, flooded the far end of the small chapel with a soft glow of light.

It was an exquisite little jewel tucked away in this corner of the old house and one that couldn't fail to give pleasure to the eye. Little had been added and nothing removed in the centuries since the Hall had come into being. Even now, after all his years of worldly living, Michael could feel the peace and sanctity of its years closing around him.

It had been built and consecrated in the reign of Richard the Third by one Percival Niven: Lord of the Manor of Ashenham. Unfortunately a few short years later his heir, Sir Howard Niven was forced to de-consecrate it under the orders of Henry the Eighth. When Catholic Mary ascended her father's vacant throne it was re-consecrated for Sir Piers Niven, but after that Queen's untimely demise Sir Piers saw which way the wind was blowing and prudently jettisoned Rome, choosing instead the Anglo-Catholic path to heaven under the more liberal-minded Good Queen Bess. With the addition of a temporary false wall it had remained hidden throughout England's Civil War. Weathering the rise and fall of Oliver Cromwell's East Anglian serial iconoclast, William Dowsing and other less successful bullies, it had quietly and unobtrusively continued to provide the family and a few villagers with an older and, to some, more meaningful form of worship than was to be found elsewhere.

Recently a progressive young born-again cleric from Kings Lyn had arrived in the parish, causing an exodus of the more orthodox villagers to the sanctuary of the little chapel in order to avoid the guitars, tambourines and happy-clappy gospel singing which had rapidly replaced the former organ and choir. This defection provided a half-dozen well trained choirboys and a gratifyingly increased flock for Father Sebastian, who came weekly from the nearby Anglican Abbey to say Mass. It also afforded Archie the opportunity to flog after the Sunday service a few dozen eggs and the odd joint of bacon to those he referred to as The Faithful Departing.

Now Michael knelt beside his mother and listened to her unself-conscious and touching request for the Almighty to do something about Archie and wondered exactly when and how he had lost his own faith. Certainly not as dramatically as his father, who could pinpoint the time of his own defection as the moment he landed on Sword beach on D-Day and saw both of his younger brothers killed beside him.

Whereas mine, his son thought cynically, just seeped away under the twin onslaught of women and work!

He saw his mother into her room and leaving her with a kiss and a 'Sleep well, ma' went to his old room at the rear of the main house.

What am I to do? Leaning his hands on the sill of the open casement he let his gaze rove over the neglected parkland, its imperfections softened but still visible by the light of the full moon. *If I can't persuade him to do something about this place soon it will be too late; I shall find myself facing a horrendous amount in Death Duties and have nothing left to get the place into good repair. It's not even that he hasn't the money, or is mean. He's just digging in his heels and letting me see how much I've disappointed him. In a way the old sod is right when he says I've let them down, and he doesn't even know the half of it. I had my chance with Francine and blew it: then Cassie...Oh, God!* He groaned aloud and beat his hands on the sill.

What had he been thinking of to let her go like that? He wanted her, needed her, and now he'd wrecked everything! No wonder the old man had let rip. He couldn't possibly justify keeping this place up in the future for one person, even if he could get the money together to foot the bill for repairs.

He turned back into the room, seeing with tired eyes all the familiar objects that surrounded him: from the ceiling hung Spitfire and Hurricane and Mosquito, laboriously made from balsa-wood kits on wet afternoons while sitting at the kitchen table chatting to Elizabeth. Battered painted bookshelves packed with Rupert and Just William, Biggles, the Saint and James Bond, D.H. Lawrence and Aldous Huxley, then the sudden switch to Hardy and Austen and George Elliot: a testament to the changing hobbies and taste of boyhood and adolescence. In an alcove stood a wooden chest crammed with Lego and Dinky cars and Action Men; alongside it fishing rods, his first air gun and a ·22 rifle.

In this room he had fought against his tears the night before he went away to school: twelve years old, terrified of the unknown and being labelled a sissy, but Archie had sat him down and given his own gruff but sympathetic maxims for survival: "Have a bloody good bawl; do it now and get it over with while I'm here to hang on to. In the morning it won't seem nearly so bad. All you need to survive school, or anything else, are a few simple rules: Don't lie and don't cheat. Don't go looking for trouble, but if trouble comes looking for you, stand your ground, face it and fight if you have to. That way others will respect you, and what's more important, you'll respect yourself."

Michael picked up the rifle, surprised that it wasn't under lock and key in the gun room; it must have been standing unnoticed in that corner for years, certainly long before it had become the law to keep all guns secured. Probably no one but his mother ever came in here now. He weighed the rifle in his hands, remembering how he had taken it from the gun room without permission one morning when he was thirteen. Aiming at a rook he'd instead shot the head off one of the stone Griffin above the park gate and been knocked almost senseless by the recoil.

Archie had thrashed him for taking the gun, then afterwards

122

hauled him, still smarting, out into the field behind the stables, taught him to shoot properly, then given him the gun.

Silently, he questioned why he had decided to sleep in this room tonight, when over the past thirty years of increasingly infrequent visits he had used one of the guest rooms that were impersonal and less evocative of the past. He gave a sudden involuntary wry smile, thinking that any shrink could tell him the answer to *that* in less than a minute! He sat down in the sagging wicker chair, the gun across his knees, and resting his head back against the wall, faced his problems head on.

I am for the second time in my adult years unsure of myself; no longer master of my emotions and dangerously close to losing control of my life. Partly because I made such a wreck of marriage the first time around but mostly because I've refused to accept that I could be in love again. It comes to something when I've lost it so far that I'll cuss like that at poor old Archie! I'm not only cocking up my own life, but just about everybody else's as well.

Suddenly resolute he rose to his feet and crossing to the chipped washbasin sluiced his head and face with cold water, rubbed his hair dry with a dusty huckaback towel, then went in search of his father.

*   *   *

Archie was sitting up in bed reading; when he saw his visitor he stuffed the book under the bedclothes, but not before Michael had seen it was one of his own biographies.

'What are you doin' wanderin' around at this hour?' His father glared over his reading spectacles. 'Can't a man get a bit of peace in his own bed?'

Michael said dryly, 'I thought you might be sleeping with Brenda!' He held up the ·22. 'I need your keys to the gun cabinet to put this away. If anyone from the police had seen this lying around loose you'd have been in clink.'

'Shove it under the bed.' Archie scowled. 'I'll see to it in the morning.'

Michael looked at him thoughtfully. *You old bugger! You've known it was there all the time, haven't you? I wonder how many times you've been into that room since I left.* He gave a half-grin then sobered and sat down on the edge of the bed. 'Father, I owe you an apology. I shouldn't have sworn at you as I did. I've had a pretty difficult time the past week or two, but that's no excuse for being so downright offensive.'

The old man stared at him, studying the gaunt face and haunted eyes in silence for a moment. It was the first time he had seen such naked misery in his son's face. He knew that something pretty disastrous had happened a few years back with some woman or other, when the boy had dropped out of sight in France for almost a year. Back in England again he had been like the proverbial bear with a sore head. He'd tried then to get the truth out of his stubborn, pig-headed son but when Michael wanted to keep his own counsel he could clam tight and neither he nor Octavia had been made privy to that particular *affaire de cœur*.

But this, thought Archie, was a different kind of silence, a different hurt. In all the years of half-malicious, half-mischievous sparring between them he had never seen his son so disturbed and wretched as now; nor had him lose his temper and turn on him like that. Whoever or whatever this new woman was, her going had touched something in the boy as nothing else ever had.

Archie took off his glasses and placed them carefully on the bedside table. 'I don't have to ask if it's about a woman, that goes without saying, but before you tell me about her, whoever she is, I think you'd best unload all the other things you've been keeping from your mother and me over these past few years. We may be old, but we're not senile yet, not by a long chalk. We both reckoned you'd got up to something pretty stoopid in France a while back and we were right, weren't we?'

Michael raised his head to meet his father's shrewd old eyes. Taking the knuckled fingers in his own strong hand he said quietly. 'Yes, pa, you were both right, but you won't enjoy the hearing of it all, any more than I shall enjoy the telling.'

'Is that so? Well, I'm not sayin' I shan't yell at you if you've been as big a bloody fool as I think you have, but I'll hear what you've got to say before I let loose.'

'Very magnanimous of you, father. At a guess I'd say you'll be doing a fair bit of yelling by the time I'm through...' Michael took a deep steadying breath. 'I think I'd better start with Francine.'

*   *   *

Archie voiced his pithy and unflattering opinion of his son's perfidious and thick-headed behaviour in robust terms. 'You got yourself married to a *Frenchwoman*, for God's sake, and didn't have the guts or even the decency to inform your parents? Then having got out of that apology for a marriage and found the right woman you sent *her* bolting off like a frightened filly! Where the deuce have you been keepin' your brains these past years, boy, in your arse?'

Michael winced; Archie in full cry was spectacular. He could probably, he thought sourly, be heard the length of the county.

'You may write books that people want to read – for all I know you may be as clever as your mother thinks you are – but you've about as much bloody commonsense as a half-witted chicken!'

There was a great deal more in the same vein, Archie finishing his tirade by flinging both arms wide, demanding at the full pitch of his lungs, 'God in Heaven! How did I ever manage to produce such a complete arse hole of a son, just tell me that?'

An uneasy silence descended on the room. Michael's face was set and flushed beneath his tan. Mentally transported back to when he was fourteen and Archie had caught him in the hayloft with his nubile sixteen-year-old cousin Jennifer, he was as deeply embarrassed and at a loss for words as he had been then. Archie, he acknowledged wryly, couldn't be bettered when it came to a no holds barred tongue-lashing. Eventually the old man cleared his throat and said gruffly, 'All the same – sorry about the boy.'

'Yes.' Michael rose and went to the window; for several minutes he stood with his back turned. 'I couldn't have made a bigger mess of things if I'd tried.'

His father's voice was suddenly tired and defeated. 'Your mother's always telling me I shouldn't have hounded you to get married.'

'If you'd left me alone I might have made it earlier and rather better on my own.'

'What makes you so sure you are right this time? What is there about this one that makes her so special and different from all the others?'

'That's like asking what makes the sun shine.' Michael turned, lifting his hands then letting them fall again. 'She has the most wonderful walk...as though she moves to music. She can be more unreasonable and stubborn than any other woman I've known, but...' he hunched his shoulders and smiled, '...she made me laugh; always, in the end, she made me laugh.'

'Sounds like a few bloody good reasons for hanging on to her then.' Abruptly, his father turned out the light and slid beneath the covers. 'I'm going to sleep on it and I advise you to do the same. We'll sort out what's to be done about you *and* the house in the morning – and don't bang the blasted door when you leave!'

Michael crossed the room and stood for a moment with his hand on the latch.

'Pa, you're one awkward old sod!' he said affectionately, then resisting the temptation to bang the door, shut it with extreme care and returned to his own room.

13

While a small army of workmen swarmed over the Hall replacing loose roof tiles, restoring ceilings and cleaning an amazing amount of bird *guano* from the upper floors, Michael rolled up his sleeves and set to work on the grounds. With a couple of youths culled from the Job Centre in Bury, he began the mammoth task of clearing the neglected gardens and repairing broken posts and rails in the parkland. As an exercise in getting super fit it was highly successful but any hope that hard labour and sheer physical exhaustion might lay the ghost of his lost love was doomed to disappointment.

He wanted desperately to return to London, find Cassie wherever she was and use all his powers of persuasion to put things right between them. But his father had counselled caution: 'You must give it time, my boy; with the best of intentions you've made one hell of a mess and it won't be cleared up by chasing back and telling the girl you're sorry an' you've changed your mind. Do that and by the sound of her she'll either tell you to go to hell or do another runner! In my book you've both been damned stoopid. You shouldn't have tried to play God and she shouldn't have bolted like a frightened filly; seems to me you need to get your head together an' she needs a bit of space to finish growing up.'

It was, Michael acknowledged, good advice but hard to take.

So he worked and sweated through the relentless heat of an August when each day brought blistering sunshine and rain began to assume the aspect of a distant, longed-for delight. At evening when he counted the new bruises abrasions and blisters on his arms and hands, he wondered when he would feel able to return home, to lose himself in the work that had been his life before a certain young woman turned his ordered existence not only upside-down, but inside out as well.

Cassie, engaged in a similar attempt to exorcise the recent past was equally unsuccessful. Laura had departed for Paris leaving a friendly but firm suggestion that she should keep in touch with Lily, something she kept putting off, first from day to day then week to week, feeling quite unable to face even one evening in that most hospitable house and run the gauntlet of Lily's shrewd and compassionate gaze. Simon, watching Cassie flit to and from his gallery and studio, ached to comfort her but held back, following his wife's suggestion to wait patiently and be ready to pick up the pieces should that brittle brightness his young *protégé* now wore shatter into a thousand fragments.

But to the surprise of both husband and wife the expected collapse never came. As the weeks passed Cassie grew in confidence, gaining a new maturity in place of her former youthful ambivalence, and with a steely determination to succeed in her work at the centre.

*   *   *

'Something is brewing. I feel it in my bones.' Cassie stared at the ancient headstones leaning drunkenly in the parched grass of the small graveyard. 'Laura has been back from Paris for going on a month and not a word about the visit except that she did a lot of sight-seeing and Alaric sent his love. That alone is enough to make me suspicious.'

Jono threw his apple core into a crowd of strutting pigeons. 'Perhaps it's true: *he's* mellowing and *she* actually only went to do a spot of *haute couture* shopping!'

'Do me a favour!' She was scathing, 'Leopards like my father don't change their spots that fast and Laura wouldn't be seen dead in anything but good English tweed, preferably from Fenwicks.'

Jono yawned. 'You know how it is when people start getting older and think time's running out; they begin to be nice to people they've hated for years!' he leaned back, clasping his hands behind his head. 'My pa's the same. He's hardly spoken to either of his brothers in absolute yonks, now he's talking of having a family Christmas this year. Tell you something: I'll be bloody miles away if he does; I'll go to ground down in Dorset with my aunt Isabel, even if she does hunt out my grass and flush it down the bog.'

'Well, I've no idea what I'll be doing this Christmas, or the next, come to that. I think I may just do a flying visit to Laura and Miles then come back here.'

Jono studied her profile for a few seconds in silence before observing, 'Cass, you really have to get out and get a life. While you're busy with your kids and students, keeping Mark happy and earning enough dosh to live on, there's a thumping great world waiting out there and it's time you got off your ass and joined it.'

'I don't really think I want to join it. There's Miles and Laura's wedding to look forward to and after that – well, I don't have a crystal ball so who knows? Anything could happen.'

'Anything: except Michael coming back.'

She shrugged, watching the pigeons squabble over the apple core.

128

'He won't,' she said flatly, 'and don't rub my nose in it. I'm just hanging on until I can see my way ahead. I'm OK here for a while yet, and when this job finishes I'll find something bigger and better.'

'And that is likely to be when, precisely? And just how long are you staying in that God-awful boarding house that always smells of cat's pee and cabbage?'

'I don't *know* yet. I don't want to live in London permanently; on the other hand I don't particularly want to go back and bury myself in Cornwall.' She posted a fun-size Milky Way into her mouth and continued indistinctly, 'What I'd really like when Arlene returns and I finish here is to teach – not formally in a school or college, but something along the lines of the workshops I run here. I know I swear about them sometimes, but I really enjoy having people come who are enthusiastic and eager to explore and create...'

'Careful, ducky, you're beginning to sound like a glossy brochure for the Arts Council!'

'Don't call me ducky, save that for your fellow lovies!' She began gathering up the plastic bags and empty coke bottles from their lunch and stuffing them in the bin. 'Come on. Time for your rehearsal and my stint on the Mighty Wurlitzer, as Mark calls the PC. No classes tonight, so when I'm through I think I'll pick up a salt beef sandwich from Bernie and take one of my favourite evening walks.'

'Which will lead you nowhere near Chelsea, I hope.' He put his arm around her shoulders as they walked through the graveyard and out onto the City Road. 'Take my advice: hire a rowboat, sit in the middle of Regent Park Lake, smoke a nice big joint and all your troubles will disappear!'

She said, 'Even if that was my style, which it isn't, they still wouldn't, you know.'

'No, I don't suppose they would, but there are better ways to spend your time than hanging around Chelsea. Talking of which...' He grinned and gave her a suggestive nudge with his hip. 'How about a quick shag?'

She gave a splutter of laughter. 'You'd run a mile if I said yes and it would spoil a beautiful memory!' She tucked her arm companionably in his. 'Anyway, if I'm not much mistaken, you're about to lay or get laid by your new leading lady.'

'Have a heart; she's positively ancient. Thirty-five if she's a day and she's already had more nips and tucks than Cher!'

Cassie narrowed her eyes and gave him a dark unfathomable look. 'What's age got to do with it?' she asked. 'You can always shut your eyes and think of England!'

'Just sit yourself down and I'll make you a meal.' Mrs Harris pulled a chair from the kitchen table and Cassie sat, pushing the damp hair from her forehead and sliding the sleeves of her thin cotton tee shirt up to the elbows. She said, 'It's all right, honestly. I've had a sandwich.'

The older woman gave her a sceptical look. 'Indeed? And for lunch?'

Cassie looked guilty. 'A sandwich.'

'Exactly!' she fetched a bowl and began cracking eggs. 'So just do as I say!'

Propping her chin on her hands, Cassie allowed herself a return to the lost cosy nursery world of someone telling her what to do. It was all poignantly reminiscent of childhood and a succession of motherly but transient nanny/housekeepers, whose moral sensibilities alas, were unable to survive for long Alaric's rapid turnover of nubile young scrubbers.

Neither spoke again until Mrs Harris placed an omelette and a plate of thin bread and butter before her. 'Thank you.' Cassie looked up with a smile. 'It is nice to be bullied once in a while; I think that's what I most miss about Laura, she is very good at it and being bullied can be quite comforting!'

'Still in need of comfort, are you then?'

'Umm,' Cassie ate in silence for a minute, then asked tentatively, 'No sign of the boss man coming back yet, I suppose?'

'No. By some miracle he seems to have persuaded his father to let him do the job thoroughly, so I imagine he'll want to stay until the work is complete, just to make sure there's no backsliding!' She was suddenly thoughtful. 'I'd love to know what made Sir Archie give in after all this time.'

'Is he really as barmy as Jono says? He sounds more crafty than loopy.'

Mrs Harris laughed outright. 'He's as sane as you or me; it just suits him to pretend he's a dotty old eccentric in much the same way as it suits Mr Michael to make out he's forever calm and in control.'

'What do you mean?' Cassie paused, her fork halfway to her mouth.

'That it's quite an act!' She sniffed. 'He can't fool *me*; I've known him too long. He can be as unsure and as easily hurt as any woman, *and* he's got a pig of a temper, although he's very good at hiding it!' she sniffed again. 'No morals, either, but I don't think he's ever been deliberately unkind to any woman, whether he's been to bed with her or not.'

Cassie said gloomily, 'But he's the most stubborn and awkward cuss when he lets his principles get in the way.'

'True. So what are you going to do about it?'

She countered, 'What can I do about it – they're his principals, not mine.'

'And you call *him* stubborn and awkward!'

'When it comes to stubborn I'm nowhere in his league.' Cassie was sarcastic. 'If he walked through that door right now I don't think what happened between us that last time we met would count a damn to me, but I bet it would to him; I still love him and nothing is going to change that, but he's made up his mind we don't have a future together and nothing is going to change *that* ... so there's the difference. However,' she gave a down-turned smile. 'I might well do another runner. The fact that he didn't fancy me sufficiently to even want me as a mistress still hurts like hell and I wouldn't want to go through all that again.'

Elizabeth said sharply, 'That's enough of that sort of talk; you're not mistress material!'

'That's what he said.'

'And he was right. Now finish that meal while I make up your bed. If I'm to be up early tomorrow I'll need to be away soon and get my beauty sleep.'

Cassie smiled. 'You'd have made someone an awfully good mum.'

'Either me or Jack didn't have the necessary genes, or whatever they call it these days, to make babies.' She paused, one hand on her hip the other holding the omelette pan aloft, and gave her sudden grin. 'But then I'd been lucky enough to have young Michael dumped in my arms when his old hag of a nanny got up Sir Archie's nose once too often. So you might say life's had its compensations!'

'Hmm.' Cassie looked sceptical. 'I hope you'll still feel the same about him if he ever finds out you're giving me house-room here behind his back!'

*   *   *

Laura stood back to view the main room of the flat over Miles' book-shop, now transformed into a small studio by the addition of a skylight window that ran the length of the sloping roof. Alaric's easels, one upright and one donkey were in place, a table for his paints and brushes nearby, while an easy chair, an old velvet *chaise longue,* a roll-top desk and captain's chair from Fleetwood completed the furnishings. This room, alongside a small kitchen and a bedroom with an adjoining bathroom would become Alaric's home and workplace. A far cry, she acknowledged, from the spacious house in Paris, but sufficient for his now diminished needs.

'I think that's about everything.' She dusted off her hands then ran her fingers through her hair. 'Heavens, but I can do with a bath after all that effort.'

Miles stood behind her his arms around her waist. 'I trust Alaric will appreciate it.'

She turned and taking his face between her hands kissed him. 'Only you would so willingly and generously give up your private space – and to a low-lifer like my brother! Thank you for that and for all that you have given in such measure to me over these past months.'

'Ah, but look what I've acquired in return,' he grinned mischievously, 'Fleetwood and Cormack and you, but in reverse order of importance! Now I think we should return to *our* home, where I shall run *our* bath and join *my* woman for a long and leisurely soak.'

'And forget *my* brother, for a while at least.' She laughed and followed him down the stairs. 'I do hope his singing won't disturb your customers; he can get quite carried away from time to time.'

'I shall charge them extra for the cabaret!'

He locked the side door behind them and they stepped out into the hush of a Sunday afternoon; the small town almost deserted, the summer visitors scattered onto the wide sweeping beaches with buckets and spades and swimsuits, Thermos's of tea, and sandwiches in plastic bags.

It was hot in the Land Rover. Laura leaned back in her seat and closed her eyes, murmuring, 'Before I can truly relax there's one last hurdle to face: what will Cassie think of our part in all this and which way, I wonder, will she jump when Alaric tells her the truth about everything?'

He warned, 'Well, she won't like the *fait accompli* over his homecoming, nor his revelations of the past which I admit stopped *me* dead in my tracks.'

Laura frowned. 'I can't help feeling that it all might have been better coming from us. Then at least she would know we were still on her side and not in league with him against her, but that was his decision and I'm past fighting with him over Cassie.' As they drove back to Fleetwood she fell silent, gradually overcome with an aching sadness, still not quite able to believe that Alaric, always so big and solid and full of life, could be coming home to die.

As children they had fought, Laura throwing herself fruitlessly against his superiority of strength and years, Alaric, irritated and embarrassed by the little sister forever dogging his steps, had treated her with casual cruelty. In more recent years when they had inflicted deep and lasting wounds on each other's souls over his desertion of Cassie, each had become entrenched in their isolation from each other. But in the years between, when they were both grown, they had been loyal to each other and good friends.

When he had turned his back on University and the academic career mapped out for him, and instead embarked on a precarious life as an artist, she had defended him against the anger of their formidable father. Alaric in turn had fought her corner with and for her when she fell in love, standing steadfast and alone to face James Chisholm's truly terrifying wrath after she fled home to live with Harry. Now after ten barren years they faced an adversity greater and more implacable than an angry parent.

In despair that she could ever completely overcome her bitterness and find a way back into warmth and friendship, she had raged at Miles when she returned from Paris. 'He thinks we can turn back the clock – but it's too late – too damned late.'

'It's never too late to make amends,' he'd answered her. 'It is never too late to love.'

And he had been right. Slowly and carefully over these past weeks she and Alaric had begun the journey back towards each other; now at last he was coming home and the breech was almost healed.

She opened her eyes and turned her head to look at the man beside her then put up her hand to touch his face, 'You were right.'

He glanced at her with raised eyebrows asking, 'About what?'

Laura smiled and laid her head against his. 'Oh…just about everything, you aggravating man!'

14

Cassandra finished tidying the darkroom, checked the chemicals were all in the cupboard under the stone sink, locked it then washed her hands, scrubbing hard under her nails, aware of the silent discomfort of the tall black youth who lounged against the half-open door behind her. She finished rinsing her hands under the tap and he handed her a towel, saying gruffly: 'Sorry about all that crap today, but, man, that little shit got to me!'

She confessed, 'He got to me too, Winston, but when you're doing a job, any job, you have to detach yourself from how you feel about people and keep your mind on the business in hand. If you ever make it to being a war correspondent's side kick you'll need to button that big mouth of yours a lot tighter.'

He scowled. 'OK, lady, but he's still a wanker!'

'So he's a wanker; but telling him lost you, and me, a client. Try something like that on the likes of Colonel Gaddafi and you'll more than likely find your camera shoved in a very strange place.'

'It's all that poncing about – an' 'e tried to touch me up!'

His outrage was comical and Cassie bit her lip to hide an involuntary smile. Getting the prickly and defensive Winston a commission to take front-of-house stills for a very new young actor with an inflated ego and a possible identity crisis had been a mistake she wouldn't make again. She said soothingly, 'If it helps any, he tried to touch me up as well,' and watched the youth's handsome face break into a wide grin.

'Oh, man, he sure was climbing the wrong tree there. If you won't let a real dude like me climb it, he ain't got *no* chance!'

They both burst into laughter and still chuckling, Cassie switched off the light and propelled him through the door. 'I'll only forgive you that crack if you bring me one of your ma's ginger cakes next week. Now get to your home and let me get to mine – Ouch!' she yelped as he stopped abruptly and stepped back on her foot. 'Winston, you clot, look where you're going...' she shoved him to one side, then gave an involuntary scream and grabbed his arm with both hands, 'Oh, my *God*!'

'Not quite, but close!' Alaric rose from one of the studio chairs and smiled wolfishly at the startled Winston. 'A charming young lady with purple finger-nails, fourteen earrings and a nose stud directed me here. I've come to take teacher to dinner – that's if you can spare her.'

'I could have a problem with that, man!' The boy turned to Cassie. 'D'you know this old geezer, Cass?'

She said faintly, 'He's my father!'

'Jesus! He's big, in't he?' He looked Alaric up and down then nodded. 'OK, if he's your dad he should be safe enough; 'night then, Cass.'

'Goodnight, Winston.'

She watched the door close then rounded on her father, demanding, 'What the hell are you doing here?'

'Waiting for you,' he stroked his chin, his eyes taking her in from head to foot and back again. 'I must say it's rather disturbing to be confronted by an El Greco! You look as though a bloody good meal wouldn't go amiss...and a rather more filial greeting than "what the hell are you doing here" might be in order!'

'Look.' She recovered rapidly. 'It's a bit much to appear out of the blue like this and expect the dutiful daughter routine.'

'You have point. Now, where can we go to eat that's quiet? I'm a bit out of touch and we need to talk.'

She was wary. 'Talk about what?'

'A number of things, all of them equally important and none of them easy.'

'In that case, I suggest fish and chips and a bench in a quiet graveyard I know.'

'OK.' He opened the door and stood aside for her to pass, adding with heavy sarcasm. 'Don't expect me to call on you again in this eyrie, will you? These stairs are hell to climb.'

'Did I invite you?'

He followed her slowly, leaning on both handrails. 'That's my girl. Now not so fast – my legs are older than yours.'

*　　　*　　　*

She led him to a takeaway where he brought her supper, refusing the fish and chips for himself in favour of fruit from a nearby open-all-hours corner store, before following her to the graveyard in the shadow of the Mary Magdalene church.

'Not many people come here at this time of the day.' Cassie opened her parcel and began to break the fish with her fingers. 'Later on it's full of winos and druggies. Bit of a bore, really; Jono and I have to spend half our lunch breaks chucking bottles and tin-foil and syringes in the bins before its safe to put our arses on a bench.' She glanced sideways at him as he peeled a banana with fastidious fingers. 'Well? What did you want to talk about and why are you not in Paris?'

'One thing at a time: first, tell me what you are doing at that place.' He took a bite of his banana and chewed thoughtfully. 'I thought your advice to that young man was excellent, by the way.'

'Ear-wigging, were you?' She couldn't help a smile. 'He'd had a bad day. We both had. He wants to be a front line war photographer; he also wants to run before he can walk. We can't afford the expense of camcorders and all that stuff here, so I've been pulling strings to get him into college. He's an awkward sod but I shall miss him when he goes next term.'

He prompted, 'And when you are not teaching Winston to keep his big mouth shut?'

She gave him a brief run-down on her work at the Centre, while wondering what had brought him so unexpectedly to London. As she talked she became uneasily aware that this was a different father from the one she had become accustomed to over the past few years. He was still ironic and fairly distant, but now gave every sign of being interested in how she was earning her living and her tentative plans for the future; most particularly her future. All this from a man who had for years treated her with such casual and wounding disregard was positively unnerving. There had to be a catch in it all somewhere.

When she finished speaking he regarded her with curious eyes. 'Somehow I never had you down as a teacher.'

She answered through a mouthful of fish, 'I don't suppose Granda Chisholm had *you* down as an artist!'

'That's true.' He sat in silence for a long minute then slewed sideways on the bench, his blue gaze piercingly direct.

'I have two very important things to tell you and I'm not sure in which order to place them. If I get it wrong you may just take off without waiting to hear them both! I think I have to ask you for your word that you'll stay and hear me out.'

She stared at him for several seconds then gave an affirmative nod. 'You've got it.' Swallowing the last piece of fish she began to attack the chips, inviting, 'OK then – I'm all ears.'

'Ten years ago I made a huge mistake by shoving you into that school and taking off for France,' he began quietly. 'It was a cowardly act, devastating I now realise for you; extremely painful for me, and as it turned out, entirely unnecessary.' He paused for a moment, his mouth down curved and grim. 'While you've not pulled any punches these past few years in letting me know what you thought about all my teen-aged bits on the side, equally you've never been exactly shocked, have you?'

She shrugged, answering flatly, 'No. That was just your bag. It could have been worse.' She only half-repressed a smile and added. 'You might have fancied teenage boys!'

'Ah-h,' He let out a long breath. 'Now if that had been the case I wouldn't have needed to dump you and do quite such a spectacular bunk across the channel!'

Cassie frowned. Where on earth was all this leading? Why the hell couldn't he come out with whatever it was and stop beating around the bush. She looked searchingly into the intent eyes that watched her, a wary, almost pleading expression in their depths. Suddenly she stiffened in outraged disbelief. 'You *can't* mean...' Her face froze in disgust and she rose, ready for flight. 'If you are about to tell me what I think you are, I don't want to hear it.'

He said swiftly, 'Sit down – you said you'd hear me out.'

She sank onto the edge of the bench, backing away from him until she was pressed against the arm. He put out his hand as though he would touch her shoulder and she flinched. 'Don't!' her voice rose. 'I'll stay. Just don't touch me.'

He drew back. 'It wasn't quite as bad as it seems.'

Cassie fought down her mounting hysteria. 'Oh, get real, will you! What could possibly be more disgusting than a man fancying his own daughter – that is what it was all about, isn't it?'

'Sort of: which brings us to the second thing...'

'Christ, there's more?' She gripped her shaking hands together, fighting for control. 'Oh, get on with it, for God's sake, then you can bugger off to your Parisian tarts and I can get back into the company of sane, decent people.'

Suddenly his heart was pounding and his body clammy with sweat. He bent forward gripping his knees, hearing his own voice say distantly, 'I don't think I can do this...' The band began to tighten around his chest and he made a tremendous effort to relax and breathe slowly. This was no moment, he thought with morbid amusement, to hurl himself through the pearly gates.

She insisted, 'I give you just five minutes to say whatever you have to say and then I'm off!' He raised his head and her expression turned from hostile to one of shock to see how the colour had drained from his face. 'If you are going to be sick...' her voice trailed away uncertainly.

'No.' He forced a grin, 'but I could do with a drink of water.'

She said, 'Stay there. I'll get a bottle from the corner shop,' and set off at a run. He fumbled in his pocket for the blister of capsules and slipping one under his tongue leaned back against the bench and waited for the waves of pain to recede. She came back and unscrewing the top of a plastic bottle offered it at arm's length. 'Here,' she said brusquely, 'the one thing I can't stand is puke!' She eyed him dispassionately as he drank in great thirsty gulps. 'Don't think you can get around me by collapsing in a heap. You stirred all this shit: it's your own fault if spilling it gives you the vapours. I certainly didn't want to hear it.'

He said wearily, 'Oh, sit down you brat and save your breath. You're going to need it for part two.'

She opened her mouth then shut it again then sat down, although keeping her shoulder turned and her gaze averted. He gave an audible sigh and hunched forward, resting his arms on his knees, the bottle clasped in his big hands.

'In a minute you'll no doubt want to start effing and blinding like a drunken sailor. All I ask is that you keep your mouth shut until I've finished, at which time I give you full leave to make the dead in this place turn in their graves if you wish. Do we have a bargain?'

'I suppose so.'

'You'll have to do better than that.'

She snapped ungraciously. 'Well all right...yes, then.'

He put the bottle down carefully on the ground and turned towards her. 'Right then, here goes...' he stretched an arm along the back of the bench and took a deep breath. 'Some twenty-four years ago a woman walked into my exhibition in a London gallery and knocked me right off my perch. This was pretty remarkable because we were about the same age and even then I'd never been exactly turned-on by anything over twenty-one. She wore a black mini-skirt over legs that went right up to her shoulders: she had hair like ripe corn and a face like a Hollywood Goddess. She was every Bond girl there'd ever been rolled into one great sexy parcel and you could see every man in the room making a metaphorical beeline for her...' He paused and took up the bottle for another drink. 'But I got there first! The fact that she spoke scarcely a word of English and the only Swedish I knew was *Skål,* seemed at the time to be something of a bonus; at least it meant we never got around to quarrelling.

'A few days later she came back to Cornwall with me and around seven months later she left. I never knew exactly where she came from or where she went afterwards. All I knew was that when we met she was touring with a Continental Ballet company and had just ended an affair with an Italian fellow hoofer. What I *didn't* know for quite a

138

while after we began living together was that she was already pregnant when we met.'

Slowly Cassie turned her head towards him and he looked back at her impassively. There was a very long silence before he spoke again.

'She didn't want a baby, but neither did she want an abortion. She wouldn't return to Sweden, or tell her parents she was pregnant. Her plan, as I discovered subsequently, was to stay in this country for the birth, put the baby in a home, return to Sweden and her family, which was a wealthy and fairly aristocratic one, then take up her career as a dancer again as though nothing had happened. I, of course, had come along at precisely the right moment to serve as prop and provider and a legitimate reason for her getting a work permit and staying here, ostensibly as my housekeeper. Once the baby arrived and my usefulness was at an end I was neatly ditched.'

He stopped and held Cassie's gaze firmly with his own. Reading the agonised question in her eyes he gave a short nod. 'OK – say it.'

'So I wasn't even *your* bastard?' her voice shook. 'I was a bastard unwanted by anyone!'

'Not quite,' he said quietly. '*I* wanted you.'

Her eyes were bright with angry tears. 'You mean you got lumbered with me, but when I got older I began to look like a better bargain than you'd reckoned for until you developed cold feet and had to get shot of me!'

'Wrong again. When I saw you in the hospital a few minutes after you were born, and held you for the first time in my arms I felt you were as much mine as Kristin's. When she admitted she didn't want you and told me her plans for the future I told her she could clear out; that if she didn't want you, I did, and your place was in Cornwall with me, not in some bloody kid's home.

'I fought her tooth and nail for you and in the end, when I threatened to get in touch with her family and let them know their heartless bitch of a daughter had an unwanted child she was about to dump in an orphanage, she packed her bags and left. I registered your birth and the certificate says I am your legitimate father. So far as Laura, my parents and the world in general were concerned, that was exactly what I was and still am. DNA apart, your *are* my daughter and always will be.'

He was silent again, waiting for her to speak, but Cassie shook her head mutely and he asked, 'Do you want me to go on?'

She nodded and turned her head away, and after a few seconds hesitation he took up his story again.

'I like to think you were happy. I hope you were. It wasn't, I know, a very conventional life but you seemed to thrive on it. I couldn't have imagined anything might spoil our relationship. You were my child and I loved you very much: what could possibly go wrong?' He paused to take another drink. 'I'd always liked young women, but after Kristin left, I seemed to have some kind of crisis. I hadn't been in love with her but she was very addictive and she knew all the ways to turn a man on and keep him on the boil. In some strange way that put me off any experienced women and I found myself only fancying anything over the age of consent and under the age of twenty who hadn't yet had time to become a sexual predator.' He rubbed a hand over his face and gave a wry smile. 'Let me put your mind at rest on one point, though, I *didn't* fancy you, I only thought I might. You were such an affectionate little thing: very tactile and loving. You came back from a swim one day when you were about twelve, wearing nothing but a wet bikini and jumped into my arms for a hug. It was then I realised how fast you were growing up and it gave me one hell of a shock. I just panicked...there was I, pulling all those young birds and all of a sudden here was this fledgling right under my nose and maturing day by day.

'It was only then that it really hit me that I *wasn't* your biological father and it was possible, if not very probable, that at some time in the future I might find myself attracted to you.'

Cassie found her voice at last, asking bitterly. 'Why, after all this time have you decided to come over here and stir things up? After all, what difference does it make now? I've had plenty of experience of living without a father for the past ten years so I think you should just bugger off back to Paris: I won't bother you again if you don't bother me.'

He finished the water then got slowly to his feet and crossed to put the empty bottle in the wastebasket. 'I'm not going back to Paris. In a couple of days I'm returning to Cornwall – for good. But the reason for that and why I've chosen to come clean about our relationship, or should I say non-relationship, will have to wait for tomorrow. Right now I'm just too damned tired to give, or take, any more.'

'Wait!' As he turned and began to walk away, Cassie was on her feet. 'What do you mean – returning to Cornwall? Don't tell me you've got around Laura and Miles to have you at Fleetwood!'

He paused, looking back at her over his shoulder. 'No. They both came up with a much better idea!' he answered, then walked away slowly and heavily down the uneven brick pathway, conscious that he was making a bad mistake in not finishing his story. But he simply hadn't the strength or courage this evening to tell her the reason for his return to Cornwall, afraid, that in her anger she would only see it as a play for her sympathy. Alive or dead, it was clear that she would still despise and detest him.

And who, he thought wearily, could blame her for that.

Cassie felt as though she had been reduced to a shell, a mere framework of bones covered by burning skin with nothing inside but a huge aching void more agonising even than the night she had fled from Michael's house. Then as she took in his final words, desolation and despair turned to anger. Laura had known about all this. Known he was coming back, made the arrangements, found him somewhere to live. Without a word of warning or explanation she and Miles had planned and plotted behind her back.

It was the final betrayal.

No father, no mother and now no family worth the name...

Her hurt and fury exploded into a silent scream; one great internal outpouring of invective against all those she had loved and thought had loved her. Well, if that's how they wanted it that's how they could have it. From now on she'd paddle her own canoe and not expect anyone else to paddle it with her.

She sank back onto the bench as the sustaining blaze of fury began to fade. She'd lost Michael and lost her family. In her worst moments she had never felt such despair, never felt so frightened and alone. She couldn't, she really couldn't bear to see Alaric again and hear any more revelations...but where could she go where he wouldn't eventually track her down? Certainly not back to Cornwall – and not to the Carrington or the Centre or Jono's flat, because when he came looking for her tomorrow those were the places he would make for first.

Well, he wouldn't damned well find her at any of them, she'd see to that. She gripped the wooden slats of the bench deliberately hard so that her hands ached, willing the sustaining power of anger to return; refusing to acknowledge yet that nothing would ever wipe from her memory the sight of the man who wasn't her father walking away from her with his shoulders bowed in defeat.

After a while she left the bench and made her way back to the Centre. There was only one thing now to be done.

Ten minutes later she was facing Mark Vale across his paper-strewn desk.

'I'm really sorry; I don't want to drop you in it, but I have to disappear for a few days. It shouldn't make too many waves: my numbers are down to two for the Tuesday and Thursday sessions as the others are still on holiday, and the kids go back to school next week. I'm sure Winston will stand in for me with both lots and he's good with the youngsters.' She paused for breath. 'It's your paperwork that's likely to suffer most.'

He grinned amiably. 'We shall cope. I'll nobble someone else for a bit.'

'Thanks, you're star. Have you heard when Arlene's due back?'

'Two or three weeks, she says,' he was laconic. 'I expect we'll have to put up with her breast-feeding the infant all over the place and moaning about overwork, but we're used to that...the moaning, that is; not the breast bit!'

'I'll be back by the fifteenth and stay until she shows.'

He looked at her, his face pulled into a wry smile. 'We'll miss you, Cass – *I'll* miss you. You've been a breath of fresh air and you've worked bloody hard. You're cut out for this sort of thing, you know. You should go on with it.'

'I'd like to, if I can find a niche.' The top of his desk was dusty and she drew absentminded M's in it with one finger then obliterated them with a sweep of her hand. 'If my father – or anyone else – comes to find me tomorrow, or whenever, I'd rather you just told him I'd left and didn't mention I'll be coming back.'

'As Winston would say, that's no problem, man!'

'Thanks again.' She took the bunch of keys from her pocket and laid them on the desk. 'I'll go over to Waterloo and see Winston on my way back, brief him on what I was going to do with the kids on Saturday, then find myself a bolt-hole for a few days.'

'Sure there's nothing I can do?'

'Nope, just lie through your teeth for me and keep the big bad wolf off my back.' She leaned to plant a kiss on his cheek. 'Goodbye, Mark. See you.'

''Bye, Cass; stay cool.'

She sat in her car in the parking lot behind the Centre for a long time before starting the engine, conscious as she pulled out into the traffic that she was once more running away from a problem that should be faced. 'But I can't take it,' she muttered aloud, 'whatever else it is he wants to tell me he'll just have to stuff it. I've had enough and now I'm for the off....'

15

Michael and his father stood side by side and watched the last work van disappear out of sight down the drive. They gave simultaneous sighs of relief.

'That's it then.' Archie turned to survey the house. 'Now what do we do with the damned place?'

Michael looked up at the long mellow brick frontage of the Hall to where the casements caught the late afternoon sun, the octagonal towers standing like tall sentinels at either end. The air was warm and still, the night-scented stocks along the walls beginning to give off their heavy summer evening fragrance. Tired but wonderfully at peace he thrust his hands into the back pockets of his grubby Levis and smiled at his father.

'Well, letting old George's sheep graze the parkland is a start; at least it saves one hell of a lot of mowing and fertilising! Sometime we shall have to think of how the house itself it can earn its keep, but for now...' he shrugged. 'What else can we do but care for and cherish it. With all the hard graft that's been put into it over the centuries, we can do no less.'

His father said gruffly, 'You've made your mother very happy, she's been out in her garden more these past weeks than she's been for years.' He gave a short bark of laughter. 'I kept telling her it was no use asking the Almighty to sort out the blasted place without some help!'

'Go easy on her, pa. If believing her prayers have been answered brings her contentment, you should just be happy for her; you shouldn't keep sniping at that kind of faith.'

'They haven't been answered without a lot of hard cash – and since when did you start seeing yourself as a visitation from heaven?' Archie began to walk towards the open front door. 'Sun's over the yard-arm now – time for a G 'n' T! When I've got a drink in my hand you can tell me where you'll be heading next.'

*   *   *

Michael bathed and changed and came down the staircase as Gerda began beating the gong in the hall with all the orgasmic Teutonic fervour of a timpanist in the throes of a Wagnerian climax. She always crashed three nerve-shattering warnings at five-minute intervals, in the seldom-realised hope that Archie would respond in time to reach the table before the soup.

'Ach! On time as always, *Gnädige Herr*!' she bellowed over the cacophonous reverberations of her efforts, her round, red face lighting with pleasure as Michael crossed the hall. 'But the *Ladyschaft* I have again lost!'

Michael raised his voice a couple of octaves. 'I'll fetch her. She won't be far away.'

Leaving through the side door he walked alongside the house to Octavia's walled garden, where she was almost always to be found at this time in the evening; dozing on a seat by the long lily pond with the pug Titus snoring at her feet.

She looked up at the sound of his footsteps and smiled invitingly, patting the stone bench beside her.

'Doesn't it look beautiful? I think Milton must have been again. It was very naughty of him to leave it so long.'

Michael sat down at her side, saying gently, 'Old Milton died quite a while back, mother, but those two young chaps you liked so much are going to look after it for you now.'

She sighed, looking round at him with puzzled eyes. 'I forget, you know. I sit out here and doze a little and then when I open my eyes again it all seems just as it used to be, except that the people keep changing. Milton and I used to spend almost every afternoon in the glasshouses – he was always so good with the geranium cuttings you know. Do you think those two nice boys will know about geranium cuttings?'

'You tell them what to do and they'll do it.' He stood, holding out his hands. 'Come in now. Gerda has only just woken the dead with the first gong so you've time to tidy up before dinner. Pa's still upstairs so he'll help you.'

'Do you think your wife will like my garden?' She looked up at him as they walked back, Titus panting and snuffling in their wake. 'I do hope she will.'

'I haven't got a wife, mother.'

'Oh, not yet, I know, but Archie said...' She struggled with her errant memory then smiled delightedly. 'Archie *said,* "the boy's at it again but I think he might have got it right this time!"'

He looked down into the faded blue eyes gazing up into his, silently cursing the garrulous Archie. 'I didn't really want father bothering you until I'd had a chance to sort things out. There was a bit of an upset, you see; I made a mess of things and hurt someone badly.

She walked out on me and like a fool I let her go.'

'Does she have a pretty name? I don't like all these modern ones.' She pursed her mouth in disapproval. 'Kylie and Charlene – what kind of names are those? Father Sebastian said he was asked to baptise some poor child *Jody* the other day; such nonsense!'

'She has a beautiful name: Cassandra.'

'Oh, dear,' she gave a little puff of laughter, 'such a mischievous goddess and if one believes those Greek legends, a very troublesome one!'

He smiled. 'Yes, my Cassandra also has her moments, but I think you will like her. I hope you will because I love her very much.'

'Then so shall I,' for a moment her face clouded and she shook her head reprovingly, 'but I shouldn't at all have liked that French woman; I'm glad you didn't bring *her* here.'

'My God,' he jumped. What the hell else had his father let out of the bag? 'What has Pa been telling you about Francine?'

'Only that you got married to her then got unmarried very quickly.' She was vague again. 'It was very naughty of you to do that behind our backs. Archie was *very* cross with you about it...and French, too!' She gave his arm a little shake. 'We haven't had one of those in the family since your great uncle Milo ran off with that prostitute he met at Saint Tropez in 'thirty-seven.'

He said gravely, 'I promise you she was nothing like the legendary Celeste, but you wouldn't have liked Francine, even though she was, from time to time, what one might call a lady.'

They had reached the hallway; she let go his arm and as she began to climb the stairs delivered a sudden and unexpectedly vigorous parting shot over one shoulder.

'Much better not to get mixed up with the French dear boy; your father never liked them after Dunkirk,' she warned briskly, 'and they use far too much lipstick and perfume and do some *very* unpleasant things in bathrooms!'

It was a good job, Michael reflected as he made his way towards the dining room and a stiff whisky, that he'd be back in London by the end of the week; his mother's occasional forays into the real world were almost as disturbing as his father's increasing reliance upon him to make decisions about the future of Ashenden. The role of parent and child, he acknowledged, was becoming really and truly reversed. Over the past weeks it had become obvious that he was needed here and that in future there could be no more long absences or dereliction of the duty he had shirked for so long. Selling the London house and moving all the machinery of his working environment up to Suffolk was beginning to seem rather more than a distant possibility.

At this precise moment of his life, with his heart in turmoil and his future so uncertain, it was a daunting prospect. He began to view his return to London with something like dread and the successful wooing of a wounded and probably hostile Cassandra as verging on the impossible.

*   *   *

Winston tried hard to mask his elation at being asked to hold the fort for Cassie, while his mother Lou gave her rich laugh and shook her head. 'Lord, but you got more faith in that boy than me, girl! Come Saturday him probably drown all them kids in the Serpentine!'

'I've been tempted to do that a few times myself.' Cassie joined in her laughter. 'Mark will give you the keys, Winston. I'd like you to go in every day, check the work coming in and if you feel you can deal with it, do so. If you're not sure, tell them I'll be back by the end of next week...and watch the kids like a hawk: there's one or two of them will nick the odd roll of film as a matter of course.'

'You got no worries, Cass. I'll watch 'em – and I'll keep my big mouth buttoned!'

'Great. See you next week, Winston. 'Bye mama...keep him on the straight and narrow.' She kissed Lou Brewster's plump cheek and hugged her. 'I'll be looking for that ginger cake when I get back.' She blew Winston a kiss from the doorway, said, 'Good luck!' and was gone before the smile slipped from her face.

Lou stood beside her son on the stone balcony and watched the battered Citroën until it was out of sight. 'That's some nice lady, but she sure got big trouble.' She closed the door of their flat and raised a warning finger at her son. 'You done see you don't let her down, now Winston.'

He poked a playful figure in her ribs, exchanging his native cockney for an exaggerated parody of her Jamaican. 'Now don' you fret none, mama; me gonna be one good man for der fine lady and see her got nuthin' to worry 'bout when she come home agin!'

*   *   *

Leaving Peabody Buildings and the Brewster family behind, Cassie returned through the heavy evening traffic to the Carrington. After pushing a few clothes into a small holdall she paid her next week's rent in advance then drove to Chelsea to clatter with a shaking hand the brass knocker on the blue front door. Mrs Harris took one look at the white faced girl on her threshold and led her to the kitchen, where she brewed a cup of blisteringly hot, strong coffee and listened in silence to the reason for her visitor's flight from Blackfriars.

'I can't go to Jono – my father's bound to get to know about him at the Centre; besides, it's not Jono's problem and I don't want to involve him.' Cassie rubbed distractedly at her hair. 'I don't want to go to Lily either because she's bound to split to Laura. I know Alaric; he isn't the most patient man so he won't wait around for long if I just disappear. You don't mind, do you? No one will think to come here and ask you where I've gone, but I'd feel more comfortable if someone knew where I was just in case of emergencies.'

'And where are you going?'

'I'm not sure yet.' She chewed at her lip. 'I've got just about enough cash left for a week or so in some reasonably cheap room away from London. I have to get away, you see. This may be a big city but it's surprising how often you manage to bump into the people you're trying to avoid.'

'At this time of year you won't find anywhere at a reasonable price, in or out of London,' Elizabeth pointed out. 'But I've got a better idea than hunting some strange town for lodgings: you can stay at The Round House. Not that I think you should be running away, I don't. But you are in no fit state to think clearly at the moment, and I don't want you tumbling head-first into some other kind of trouble.'

'I can't go to *there*,' Cassie was aghast. 'What if Michael –'

She interrupted her brusquely. 'Mr Michael is still in Suffolk and even if he returned unexpectedly is highly unlikely to go down there; he'll have too much work to catch up with in London. Stay here overnight and I'll come over in the morning and travel down with you. There is a good basic store cupboard at the house and you can easily get anything else you need from the village.' She stood up and moved purposefully towards the door. 'You just get to bed now and I'll bring you some supper before I leave.'

'Mrs Harris, I'd love to stay at Bourne End. I'm so tired and muddled that I don't care if he turns up and drives me out with a horse whip!'

She tried to smile, then overwrought, burst into tears. The housekeeper clicked her tongue and picking up the holdall took her arm in firm fingers.

'None of that, now; a warm bath and a night's sleep and you'll be good as new. I'll put you in the back bedroom away from the traffic. If you leave the curtains open the birds will wake you in good time in the morning.'

Emotionally drained and exhausted Cassie allowed herself to be led up the stairs, grateful that her most urgent need for a bath, clean sheets and oblivion was being met with the minimum of fuss and the maximum of efficiency. No wonder, she thought fleetingly, that Michael was such a contented man; he didn't need to burden himself with a wife when he had a treasure like Mrs Harris to hand.

*   *   *

She lay in bed in the silent house, trying to visualise the Swedish mother whose legs went up to her shoulders, and the unknown Italian who had fathered her, each as remote and unheeding of her existence as the turtle that lays its eggs in the sand, leaving its young to hatch alone and fend for themselves.

Except that she hadn't been left alone, she'd had Alaric; at least for a time...

She ruthlessly kicked that consideration aside and scowled into the dark. If he'd come back expecting her gratitude because he'd deigned to notice her again after all the years of neglect he could stuff it; she wasn't having any. Let him bare his bloody soul down in Cornwall. He and Laura could do the putting-it-all-behind-them bit at Fleetwood till the cows came home; *she* wanted none of it.

16

Joy glanced out of the window and, at the sight of Alaric bearing down upon the entrance, squawked a frightened, 'Oh, s*hit,*' and made for the stairs.

All large men alarmed her; at only somewhere around four and a half feet and a bit in her shoes, Alaric's looming and threatening six foot three was more than she could face, particularly as the news of Cassie's departure was likely to be far from welcome.

Mark blinked at her precipitate flight then looked up as Alaric appeared in the doorway. 'Good morning, were you looking for someone?'

Alaric watched the vision in bright green tights and an emerald jersey several sizes too large vanish around the bend in the stairs, then gave his grim smile.

'Yes; my daughter, Cassandra Chisholm.' Advancing into the room he shook Mark's proffered hand, asking laconically, 'Was that *your* little leprechaun doing a runner up the stairs – I didn't scare her, did I?'

'Probably, but so does any man over five-six!'

'That figures. I'd be rather picky if I were that size. However,' he rested a deceptively benign gaze on the director's face, 'I hardly think that could be sufficient reason for quite such a headlong flight. She didn't bolt the first time I came here.'

'Ah, no...' Under cover of the desk Mark crossed the first two fingers of both hands. 'If you are looking for Cassie, I'm afraid she's gone.'

Alaric's brows shot up. 'Gone?'

'Yes. Last night.'

'Gone where?'

'She didn't say.'

'When do you expect her back?'

'Er, I don't. She was only temporary, you know' He added lamely, 'she probably had the offer of a better job.'

Alaric leaned his hands on the desk and gave him the full benefit of his piercing blue gaze. 'Mr Vale,' he said pleasantly, 'Are you an actor?'

'No. That's never been my scene.'

'Then you've saved the theatre-going public a nasty surprise, because you are a lousy one! Like your little leprechaun she's bolted, hasn't she?'

Mark spread his hands. 'She left. I can't tell you any more than that.'

There was a brisk rap on the door and it opened to admit another equally tall but considerably thinner man, at the sight of whom the director covered his eyes with one hand, uttering a heartfelt, 'Oh, my *God,* Niven – not you as well! If you're looking for Cassie she's gone; where, I have no idea and if I had I probably wouldn't tell you.'

He uncovered his eyes and glanced from one to the other. 'Look, as this has all the hallmarks of being the start of some complicated and possibly blood-letting family mini-drama, would you mind awfully going away to play it elsewhere?'

Michael said calmly. 'Keep your hair on.' He turned to Alaric. 'What a pleasant surprise, Mr Chisholm!'

'And who the bloody hell are *you*?' Alaric's face was like thunder.

'Michael Niven. I gather you are looking for Cassandra.'

Mark interspersed sourly. 'Everyone's looking for the wretched girl. I had Jono in here ten minutes ago demanding to know where she was –'

Michael said, 'Ah, yes...my cousin Jonathan: A devious character. Are you sure he wasn't just trying to confuse matters?'

'Don't ask me.' Mark flapped his hands. 'Please; this place doesn't run itself and I have work to do...'

Alaric glared at him then his eyes swivelled back to Michael. 'We could stand here all day and this bugger wouldn't tell us anything.' He shot his cuff to consult his watch. 'It's a mite early but I noticed a pub around the corner which appears to be permanently open.' He showed his teeth. 'Not teetotal are you?'

'Perish the thought.' Michael gave a tight smile. 'You *are* out of touch, aren't you? Most London pubs are open all day now.'

*   *   *

He followed Alaric Chisholm, communing silently with himself. Mini-drama my foot! More likely an Agatha Christie who's-about-to-do-what-to-whom; what on earth had brought the fabled Alaric to London looking for his daughter, and what was all that about her going away? His heart sank. If Cassie wanted to vanish off the face of the earth, for whatever reason, he was sure she was more than capable of doing just that.

Jonathan, he thought grimly as he sat silently, waiting for Alaric to bring their drinks; *that* was the one to tackle. If the young so-and-so did know where she was he'd make damn sure he squeezed it out of him, one way or another.

Alaric put down the brimming glasses of bitter and dropped into a chair opposite, asking with more than a touch of belligerence. 'I know you from somewhere, don't I? And I don't only mean from the dust jackets of your books...bloody awful photograph, by the way!'

'I have a better one now.' Michael said distantly and took a pull at his beer. 'Paris...a few years back: I brought a picture from you: a girl on a swing.'

His companion gave a short bark of laughter. 'I remember. I hope you've kept it. It's worth quite a bit more now than you paid for it!'

'I've kept it.' Michael's face was expressionless as he added, 'in a cupboard.'

'Not very flattering for me, that.'

He answered shortly, 'It was a reminder of a time I wanted to forget.'

Alaric rubbed his chin. 'It was Cass, you know; she was about nine when I painted it. Oddly enough it stirred unwanted memories for me too. That's why I sold it.'

Michael's lip curled. 'Now that shows real paternal feelings, doesn't it?'

'You know,' Alaric's eyes glittered and he hunched forward in his chair, 'I could get to really dislike you. It seems to me you're bit long in the tooth to be hanging around my daughter.'

'There I agree with you.'

'Then what the hell is your reason for chasing after her?'

Michael's tone was glacial. 'Marginally less offensive than I understand yours to have been when pursuing other men's daughters.'

'Ah! I see my fame has preceded me?'

'You could say that. What *I'd* like to know is why she's gone to earth the minute you've shown your face.'

Alaric lounged back in his chair. 'I told her something she didn't want to know then left without telling her the best bit. I guess she decided that she didn't want to hear that either. Pity, it might have persuaded her to stay put: just for the laughs!'

Michael studied him in silence and Alaric looked back at him, the faintest of smiles hovering over his mouth. Eventually he broke the silence to ask: 'You don't like me much, do you?'

Michael shrugged. 'No. Not much, but I could possibly mellow slightly if you come clean about what you actually told your daughter to make her disappear so damn' quick. After all,' he gave his heavy-lidded smile, 'I may, if I'm very lucky, end up as your son-in-law!'

If he had hoped to startle his companion with this revelation he was spectacularly successful, Alaric's expression ranged rapidly through, shock, disbelief and amazement to something like grudging admiration. 'Well, nothing like laying it on the line, is there?' he gave a sarcastic growl of laughter, 'thing is, does Cassie know?'

'Not yet: I have to find her first, don't I? And one way or another you seem to have created a particular problem for me there.'

Alaric finished his beer in one draught; walked to the bar and returned with two more. Setting them down he sat again and folding his arms on the tabletop hunched forward. 'I'll make a bargain with you, Mister Niven – you tell me your story and I'll tell you mine. After that, and depending on whether we like each other any better at the end of it, we might join forces to look for her.'

Michael asked calmly, 'What makes you think I'd do any such thing when she quite obviously doesn't want you within a mile of her?'

'Because you need to find her as much as I do,' Alaric gave his wolfish smile, 'well, are you going to come clean with me or not?'

'Possibly. Within reason.'

'No editing, mister well-known-author!' Alaric's eyes stared intently into his. 'I've got you pegged, now. If memory serves me right, you bought that picture when you were on your honeymoon with old Gustave la Roache's somewhat pregnant daughter. So what have you done with your wife and child, Mr Niven – hidden them away in a cupboard as well?'

Michael finished his first drink then picked up the second. 'As an opening line, that, as my friend Lily Meyer would say, is a real humdinger!'

Alaric clasped his hands in an attitude of prayer and resting his chin on them invited, 'First chapter then, Mr Niven...I am all ears.'

Michael observed without rancour, 'I hope this isn't going to become a habit; I've been through it once already. Perhaps I should cut a disc, because when I *do* find your daughter – and always supposing she stands still long enough to hear me out – I shall undoubtedly have to go through it all again...'

*   *   *

Cassie waited with Mrs Harris on Windsor station platform for the train, which was a predicable ten minutes late. 'Now don't forget: you're here to relax, not fret and worry about the future.' The older woman smiled and gave her a quick peck on the cheek when her train finally pulled into the station. 'I'll ring you tomorrow morning to make sure you are all right then leave you in peace. When you're ready to come back, call me first to make sure the coast is clear.'

'I shall miss you.' Cassie stood by the train door. 'It will seem strange...do you realise this will only be the second time I've ever been alone in a house for more than a night? What an admission from an almost twenty-three year old!'

A porter began walking along the platform, slamming the carriage doors shut. Elizabeth Harris leaned through the window as the train began to move. 'Enjoy it then, it may be a long time before you get another such opportunity to leave the world behind.'

Cassie waved her away then left the station to walk the short distance to where she had left her car. For a moment she was tempted to explore the town, but although it was late afternoon the streets were still crowded with visitors and she was tired. As she negotiated her way through the traffic crowding the unfamiliar streets she reasoned that she had more than week to go before she needed to return to the Centre; there would be plenty more opportunities to sight-see later in her stay.

By the time she reached The Round House and had driven her car into the garage, the sun was going down, casting deep purple shadows over the river banks and setting the tall beech hedges on fire. Standing by the river bank she watched until the last crimson streaks had faded from the sky then returned to the house over the manicured lawn. On their arrival earlier it was being mown by a short-tempered old man, who had grunted a greeting to Mrs Harris before informing Cassie gruffly that he was 'Enry and came every Thursday – and not to pick the bleedin' roses.

Now making a mental rude gesture to 'Enry in particular and men in general, Cassie broke a pale cream bud from a bush by the door. Finding a slender single stem glass in a kitchen cupboard she placed the rose in it and climbed to Michael's room to set it beside the bed Mrs Harris had made up that morning. Her tart observation that there was no sense to Cassie sleeping in the guestroom when there was nobody in the house for her to be a guest *to* was a piece of convoluted logic with which Cassie doubted Michael would agree. However as he was unlikely ever to know this particular Goldilocks had been sleeping in his bed and eating his porridge, she could take a guilty kind of pleasure in the thought of keeping it warm for him.

She decided that the least disturbance made to drawers and cupboards the better and arranged the modest contents of her suitcase on the wooden ottoman at the foot of the bed. Idly she opened the shallow drawer in the bedside table, stared in silence for a moment at the contents then slammed it shut again with a bang.

'A proper little boy Scout, aren't you Michael?' she asked aloud, 'ready for all occasions. It's clear I'm not the first Goldilocks to get into big bear's bed!'

She sat down dejectedly on the edge and stared out of the great curving window to where the evening star hung in the darkening sky. *Where are you, you bastard? And why is it that the first time I sleep here I do so alone, when you quite obviously have expectations of sharing it with others...*

Suddenly she knew she couldn't do it; couldn't possibly sleep in his bed, wake, as he must so often have done to that reflection of sunlit water rippling across the ceiling. The thought that he obviously had on occasions done that with someone else by his side was more than she could bear. Scooping up her clothes she left at a run for the guest room at the other end of the balcony, where the windows looked out onto the trees, the walls were papered white and sprigged with forget-me-nots and the ceiling was a flat unmoving blue.

17

Michael and Alaric walked slowly down to the Embankment and along as far as the Inns of Court before the latter halted. 'This is far enough for me in all this heat.' He passed a hand across his damp forehead. 'God, but I'll be glad to get down to Cornwall again and feel the wind coming off the sea.'

Breathing heavily he leaned his arms on the parapet and looked down in silence for a moment onto the deserted decks of H.M.S. Chrysanthemum. 'It's a bugger,' he admitted, 'I've got used to it in a way, but sometimes it gets to me and I just want to get a gun and finish it all.' He grinned suddenly. 'If I thought it wouldn't be too bloody messy, I might even do it!'

'Bit drastic, that,' Michael was thoughtful. 'How long do you have...if you take care?'

Alaric shrugged. 'I am what is quaintly termed, 'unstable', so nobody is willing to make any guesses. If I change my whole life-style, as Laura is determined I shall, I might manage another year or two. I've had one bad attack that put me in hospital for over a month; I'm told another is likely to by-pass the hospital and put me straight into the morgue. In the meantime the angina is tedious.' He gave his grim smile. 'I was almost run in by a Gendarme last month after falling into the gutter on the Rue de Tivoli. To the average cop there's not a lot of difference between an old fart with angina and one who's dead drunk!'

'Why don't you go down to Cornwall now and get settled in? I can look for Cassandra. I know most of the places she's likely to have gone.'

'Don't you have any work to do?'

Michael said feelingly. 'Yes. But no chance of getting down to it until I find your ruddy daughter! But as I've done little in the past few weeks but work as an unpaid labourer for my father, I can't see a few more days will make things much worse. My agent may be tearing his hair but I can live with that.'

A River Police launch cruised past and set the gulls bobbing in its wake; Alaric followed its progress as it nosed across the water towards Kings Reach, then sighed and turned his back on the river. 'I'll take a taxi now to this boarding house of hers, then pick my bag up from that Arts place and find a hotel for the night. I doubt she'll be at either place but if she is, or the hotel people know where she's gone, I'll let you know. If we both draw a blank and you're willing to continue the search on my behalf...and your own, of course, I'll be glad to go down to Tregedick first thing tomorrow.'

Michael levered himself off the wall. 'No need for a hotel; stay the night with me. I can pick your bag up from the Centre and drop it into the house before I tackle my cousin Jonathan and see what he has to say. It shouldn't take me more than a couple of hours all told...' He took a card from his wallet. 'Here is my address. I'll meet you there around five; any cabbie will know where it is. If you get there before me and after Mrs Harris has left, there's a wine bar just around the corner where you can wait.'

'You're sure? I'd hate to give your housekeeper any trouble: I didn't think such priceless jewels still existed!'

'They don't.' Michael gave his lazy smile. 'Elizabeth is a jewel out of her time.'

Alaric grunted. 'Lucky you, you should have met some of those I employed when Cass was young!'

He glanced down at the address on the card as Michael walked away then stood tapping it against his teeth. *Charisma and money – an almost irresistible combination! I wonder what Cass really thinks about him and if she's as besotted with him as he obviously is with her?'* He sat down on a nearby bench, continuing his silent soliloquy. *I'd take a bet that there's a lot of fire and passion beneath all that laid-back calm – any woman who taps into that is either in for a nasty shock if she's done him wrong, or one hell of a good time if everything's coming up roses!*

*   *   *

Michael walked swiftly to the Centre, catching the unfortunate Joy alone and unawares. She jumped like a startled hare but seeing her alarm he summoned his most reassuring smile. 'It's all right. I only want to pick up the big man's bag and see if Jonathan is still here.'

She relaxed, giving him her puckish grin in return. 'No. He went home in a hurry just after you left – said he had to learn his lines.'

'Ah,' Michael nodded, 'did he now?' Taking Alaric's bag from behind the door he thanked her and left.

He walked along the Blackfriars Road until a taxi travelling in the opposite direction with the 'For Hire' sign up appeared; sprinting across the road he captured it under the nose of a home-bound City worker who, despite the overpowering heat, was in full rig of black jacket, striped trousers, bowler hat and carrying a rolled umbrella.

Sinking back into the stifling confines of the cab and giving the cabby directions, Michael sketched an apologetic salute to the dignified city gent as the taxi moved off; receiving a surprisingly vehement upraised two fingers in return.

The cabby grinned at his fare through the rear view mirror. 'See that, guv'nor? No dignity no more! Fings ain't wot they used ter be' are they?' he asked and Michael laughed.

'No, but I did pinch his cab so I think he's allowed his protest.'

As he let himself into the Chelsea house he was struck at once by the silence, so surmised that Alaric was taking his time in arriving. Calling, 'Elizabeth?' and receiving no answer he went methodically from room to room. Everything was as usual clean and tidy. In the kitchen a faint lingering smell of grilled bacon told him she had been there unusually early in the day. He stood frowning for a moment. He'd telephoned just before leaving Suffolk at nine that morning when he knew she was sure to be there, but had only connected with the answer 'phone.

Returning to the study he saw the light flashing on the answer machine and pressed Play. Hearing only his own disembodied voice repeating his message of that morning he muttered, 'If you are out shopping, Lizzie, it's taking you a bloody long time!' Climbing the stairs again he put his cases in his bedroom then pulling down the blind against the glare of the afternoon sun and snapping the locks on the first case, he began to unpack, all the time turning over in his mind the meeting with Alaric Chisholm.

He couldn't help liking the man; he had been as honest about his past and the reason for his rejection of Cassie's affection as Michael had about his own far-from-blameless past and equally wrong rejection of her love. He thought derisively that with the best intentions they had each managed to make a complete cock-up all round. Whether at this late stage it would be possible to make up for lost years and opportunities remained to be seen.

He had just finished his unpacking when he heard the sound of a key in the lock and went to lean over the banister, calling: 'I'm back, Elizabeth. I'll be down in a minute.'

There was a small shriek of alarm and the clatter of dropped keys; she stooped to retrieve them and turned a startled face up towards him, saying sharply, 'I wish you wouldn't make me jump like that!'

'Sorry,' he began to descend the stairs, 'I did leave a message earlier.'

She recovered herself quickly. 'I thought I should go down to The

Round House and give it an airing. I spent most of the day there…it had become very stuffy in all this heat.'

Michael followed her along the passage to the kitchen, his brow creasing again. It was a perfectly natural thing for her to air the house for an hour or two but unusual and frankly unnecessary to spend a whole day doing so…and there had been a very odd tone to her voice.

With ears fine-tuned to Archie's devious meanings and undertones beneath his most banal remarks, Michael was sure the normally upright and totally honest Elizabeth was being a little economical with the truth. Perhaps, he thought with an inward smile, she had found herself an admirer at Bourne End. Being on the wrong side of sixty was no bar to romance and anything was possible.

He sat at the kitchen table and waited while she filled the kettle for the inevitable pot of tea before asking, 'Would you mind making up the bed in the guest room before you leave?' adding with deliberate nonchalance, 'Cassie's father will be staying here tonight.'

She drew an audible breath but lit the gas with a steady hand. 'I'll see to it, sir. Will you want dinner?'

'No. I'll take him out.' He watched her put on her apron and fetch cups and saucers to the table. 'He's been visiting Cassie and now she seems to have disappeared. I said I'd help him find her.'

'Well as you see, she isn't here.'

'Obviously,' he narrowed his eyes at her bland expression and stirred a little harder. 'You don't seem very concerned, or surprised, that she has apparently gone missing.'

'As you should know by now, sir, nothing much surprises me.'

This, he mused silently, was definitely odd. When Elizabeth started calling him 'Sir' in that particularly distant and disapproving manner he could be sure she was either very annoyed with him, or something was worrying her badly. He said soothingly, 'There is no need for you to do anything other than make up a bed for Mr Chisholm, so please go home when that's done.'

'Thank you, sir; it has been a long day and I can do with the rest.'

Michael gritted his teeth and counted silently to ten. 'Elizabeth, if there is something wrong – something I've done, I wish you would tell me.'

'No, sir, everything is fine.'

'All right, I get the message.' He took the cup she offered, 'I just hope that I'm out of the dog house by tomorrow!'

'I can't think why you imagine you might be in it, sir!'

A blanket of silence descended. She drank her tea standing then waited for him to finish before clearing the table. Washing up and

158

drying the cups quickly she removed her apron. 'Will that be all, sir?'

Without answering Michael pushed back his chair and stalked from the room, inwardly seething. God damn it, but she could be as much of an awkward, close-mouthed bloody-minded East Anglian as Archie when she started. No wonder the knives always came out the moment the pair of them set eyes on each other!

*   *   *

Elizabeth watched him go then sank down into a chair. Now here was a pretty kettle of fish! How on earth had he managed not only to meet, but actually team up with the reprehensible Mr Chisholm? While instinct told her that the quicker Michael found Cassie the better it would be for them both, if he was in cahoots with Alaric Chisholm she couldn't possibly let him know where Cassie was.

For a long time she stood indecisive, then with a worried shake of her head left the kitchen and went to make up a bed for the expected visitor.

When she left the house Michael was still in his own room. Unwilling to face any further questions she called 'Goodnight, sir!' from the hallway then slipped quietly out of the door and walked quickly to the bus stop on Palmerston Street. As soon as she reached home she would telephone Cassie and brief her on this worrying turn of events. It would then be up to her to decide which was the more important of the two options: seeing Michael again or continuing to hide from her father.

The streets were quiet and almost deserted when eventually she arrived at her destination. Leaving the bus to walk towards the small house in Sebastopol Villas and still mulling over her problems, she didn't notice a youth approaching her along the deserted pavements, wearing a sweatshirt with the hood pulled forward to hide his face, only caught a momentary glimpse of an upraised arm before she was struck viciously across the face and her bag snatched from her hand. She fell, her head striking the curb as the mugger sped off, leaving her bleeding and unconscious in the dusty street.

*   *   *

In Montpellier Gardens the plane trees drooped in the heat, even so the windows of Jono's pavement-level flat were closed tight; a sure sign that house-breaking, both planned and casual was as rife in this run down corner of the city as in any of the more affluent areas.

159

Michael gave the heavy knocker a hearty bang, rewarded almost immediately by the appearance of Jono wearing nothing but knee-length Cargo shorts and a pair of fluffy pink bedroom slippers. His hair hung loose and lank about a face covered in a curious mixture of slap and lines of grey grease paint.

At the sight of his visitor he visibly recoiled. 'Jesus! I thought you were still in Suffolk!'

'A mistaken assumption on your part,' Michael looked with disfavour at this apparition and fixing his eyes on the bedroom slippers asked sardonically, 'are you about to transform into a geriatric transvestite?'

Jono recovered himself and leered. 'Yeah, sweetie – come on in and I'll show you my frocks!'

'Watch your mouth.' Michael brushed past him and walked through the hallway of the flat, glancing into each room before stepping out through the French windows to let his gaze rove around the garden.

Jono followed him warily. He didn't take shit from anyone but there was something about Michael that always made him think twice about really getting across him.

'I take it Cassandra isn't here?' his visitor drummed his fingers on the iron balustrade.

'No she isn't.'

'Are you quite sure?'

Biting back the request to see his search warrant Jono snarled, 'Of course I'm sure. What d'you want: a guided tour of the kitchen cupboards?'

'That won't be necessary. I believe you.' Michael treated him to another assessing stare before adding pointedly, 'When you've finished washing and dressing, I'd like to talk to you.'

Jono, who had no plans to either wash or dress, let alone both said, 'It's not very convenient: I'm learning a script and trying out my make-up for a new play.' At his visitor's faint smile he added sulkily, 'and before you ask, I'm not doing a wrinkly drag act; I just have to look forty-five.'

'Much better than actually being it, I can assure you.' Michael turned back into the room and seated himself in an easy chair with the air of a man who had unlimited time at his disposal, 'However, that being the case I fail to see the significance of those slippers.'

'Oh – huh, someone left them behind!'

'Ah,' Michael smiled again, 'so discounting the get up and lingering smell of pot, I can let your Aunt Isabel know that I found you in

160

the pink!'

To his chagrin Jono felt a blush begin to rise about his ears, his discomfort increased by his cousin's encouraging: 'Please: let me not keep you from your ablutions; I don't in the least mind being kept waiting.'

With a silent, 'Up yours, Michael,' Jono conceded defeat and retreated to the bathroom, grudgingly admiring the effortless ease of a put-down that was almost as painless as it was effective. He tried out Michael's faintly raised brows and deceptively amiable smile before the bathroom mirror, but without much success. He'd have to live a lot longer, he decided, before he became quite such a master of the art.

When he returned minus make-up, with his hair tied back, wearing jeans and trainers and a more-or-less clean T-shirt bearing a sketch of Leonardo da Vinci's *David* with the invitation to View My Etchings, Michael was ready with the olive branch of peace. 'Thank you; I apologise for walking in before I was invited, but Cassie seems to have done a very effective vanishing act and I thought you may be doing the gentlemanly thing and covering for her. I'm sorry.'

'It's all right. I would have if she'd asked me.' Jono shrugged. 'Why the sudden interest – I thought you two were all washed up.'

Michael said obliquely, 'Her father saw her yesterday and needs to speak to her again.'

'Oh, so that's it.' He was scathing. 'I might have guessed she wouldn't have done a bunk from *you* if you'd turned up doing your Richard Gere knight-in-shining-armour act!' His voice rose. 'If all you've come for is to try and coerce her into seeing her lousy rotten father I hope she fucking-well stays right away from the pair of you. *I* had to clean up the crap after your last balls-up and I don't want to go down that path again…it's too bloody dangerous!'

'*Is* it?' Michael gave his flushed and angry face a long contemplative look. He said quietly. 'I regret very much what happened between Cassie and myself and I'm sorry if it caused you trouble. However, it is not my business – or yours – to interfere in her relationship with her father, nor assume that it is right for her not to hear what he has to say. In any case, finding her was not my only reason for coming here today. I had intended to see you weeks ago, before I went to Suffolk.' He gave his tight smile. 'However, other matters intervened.'

'What, then?' Jono demanded ungraciously. He reached for the tobacco tin and papers on a cluttered side-table then, at Michael's look, thought better of it. 'Just get on with it, will you…I told you, I've got lines to learn before tomorrow.'

161

'Your Aunt and, heaven help her, godmother asked me to see you. She says your father is hassling again and she's worried about you.'

'Well, she needn't be. I'm O.K.'

'So I'm to tell her that, am I.' Michael sighed wearily and cocked a foot over one knee. 'Look, if you are having money problems she wants to know: it would worry her to death if she thought you weren't eating properly. However, as this place stinks of pot like the Hammersmith Odeon after a Frank Zappa rave you can't be *that* hard up!'

Jono muttered, 'Man, you are so-o not with it!' and Michael gave him a warning glare.

'It doesn't bother *me* but I'd like to be able to look Isobel in the face the next time that we meet and know that drug-wise, that's as far as it goes. Is it?'

'Yeah.' Jono was uncomfortable but he didn't, Michael noted with relief, avoid his eyes. 'I smoke; who doesn't, but I'm no tea-head. I don't use tabs and I'm not stupid enough to start sniffing, or shoving needles in my veins. You can ask Cass…when you find her!'

Michael answered easily, 'I don't need to do that. I'm not just being nosy for the sake of it, or trying to tell you how to live your life, but I'm fond of your Aunt Isabel and you mean a great deal to her you know. She's an old lady now and very lonely since your uncle died.'

'Yeah, yeah, don't pile on the agony!' Jono groaned theatrically, rolling his eyes heavenward. 'I'll call her – I'd thought I'd maybe go down for Christmas anyway.'

'Let's not get carried away.' Michael stood. 'Right, the lecture is over. I'll go home now and leave you to get on with whatever you have to do – but go easy on the wrinkles; forty-five isn't that ancient.'

Jono followed him to the door then stood awkwardly, his hand on the latch. 'Sorry I blew my top. It was bloody rude, but you got up my nose.'

'So long as I'm all that gets up it…' Michael's mouth twitched and Jono grinned.

'If I see Cass, what do I tell her?' he asked.

Michael started to walk down the steps to the street. 'Tell her…' he hesitated then turned around, answering straight-faced, 'Tell her she's a pretty woman and that I'm polishing my armour and thinking of hiring a white horse!' and he walked swiftly away, his young cousin's laughter sounding in his ears.

*   *   *

162

Still chuckling Jono walked back into the living room. Pulling the elastic band from his ponytail and shaking his hair free he picked up the tobacco tin and pressed open the lid.

It was empty except for a folded fifty-pound note and a slip of paper bearing a message written in Michael's neat script. *I thought the former content of this tin surplus to your requirements. The replacement is strictly for groceries, not grass.*

A bientôt...M

For a few moments he stood smoothing the note between his fingers before saying aloud, 'You old bugger, how d'you always manage to leave me feeling a right dick-head!'

He sat for a few minutes, ruminating on the deviousness of Michael Niven and thinking that it really wouldn't hurt him to at least 'phone old Isabel now and again. He owed her a lot; she had been much more than just aunt and godmother to him since he was about twelve.

When his own mother had finally given up the struggle to reconcile her inflexibly disciplinarian soldier husband with her rebellious, artistic son and had a minor breakdown, Jonathan had been sent to spend his vacations from school in his aunt's rambling old colonial bungalow on the Dorset coast. There, where he could take long walks on the shore to declaim poetry to the empty skies, with no father to roar at him and call him a spineless nancy boy, he had been happier and more at peace than at any other time in his life.

Yes, he did owe her a lot; more than he could ever repay. He would call her this evening when he'd finished learning the script that lay abandoned on his bed, but first...

He jumped to his feet, kissed the banknote and tucking it in the back pocket of his jeans left the house. Whistling and trailing a hand along the railings he walked jauntily around the corner to Mr Patel's open-all-hours shop in the High Street and stocked up on sufficient groceries for at least the next two weeks: three even if he could hide the tin opener from Tony. On a last minute whim he added a packet of Cass's favourite Abernethy biscuits.

Just in case she turned up.

18

Cassie woke to the insistent calling of a blackbird outside her window. She lay for a few moments, wondering what she was doing in a strange bed in an unfamiliar room. Memory returned with the feel of her heavy eyes and parched mouth: a sure sign that she had been crying in her sleep. She sat up quickly, hugging her knees and gathering her courage to meet the day.

Jono's right. I have to stop thinking about Michael and wanting him. It's over. I'm never going to know what it would be like to make love, or watch him sleep, or know if he's grumpy when he wakes in the mornings...

Throwing off the covers she crossed to the bathroom and turned on the shower, letting the water pound onto her head as she concentrated her mind on the week ahead. This morning she would stay near the house until Elizabeth rang, then perhaps if it was not too hot she might drive into Windsor and join the crowds of visitors and become a tourist for the day.

It didn't really matter what she did, she thought as she tipped cereal into her bowl. To have put a comforting few miles between herself and Alaric was the important thing.

*   *   *

While an exhausted Alaric slept in the guest room Michael was still awake, unwilling to go to bed and spend yet another sleepless night thinking about Cassie and wondering where she might be.

He had unbuttoned his shirt to the waist and with sleeves rolled to the elbow was slumped in one of the low leather chairs in the study with his bare feet propped on a stool. Yawning over an A4 pad, he was alternately doodling and making desultory notes for the proposed Williams' book, when there was a loud and prolonged peal on the doorbell.

Starting violently he dropped the pencil. Glancing at his watch he saw it was almost one-thirty in the morning and for a wild, improbable moment thought it might be Cassie returning. Leaping from his chair he hurried to the door and flung it wide, his heart racing.

A middle-aged police constable, finger poised above the bell, looked at him enquiringly before stating with ponderous politeness: 'I'm sorry to disturb you so late, sir. Are you Mr Michael Niven?'

'I am, but why the hell are you ringing my bell at this hour? I hope it isn't just to tell me my parking permit's fallen off the windscreen again!'

'No. I'm not aware of that possibility, sir.' He held up a creased oblong of paper. 'An elderly lady was attacked and robbed of her handbag some hours ago in Pimlico. A nurse at St Catherine's Hospital found this parcel delivery receipt bearing your name and address in the lady's coat pocket. As she hasn't yet recovered consciousness we had no idea of her identity or where she lives. We hoped you might be able to tell us.' The walkie-talkie on his shoulder crackled, and he listened for a moment then glanced at Michael's shocked expression. 'Yes, sergeant; I'm at the house now and I think I've found the right gentleman, if you'd let them know at the hospital.'

Michael fingered the slip of paper the constable handed to him. Elizabeth had telephoned him less than a week ago to say a book had arrived by recorded delivery and asking if she should post it on. His face drained of colour. 'I think she must be my housekeeper, Elizabeth Harris. I'll come right away.'

'Are you sure you're all right to drive, sir?' The constable looked pointedly at the tie hanging loose from his collar, passed his gaze slowly over Michael's disordered shirt and brought it to rest finally on his bare feet. Michael could hear him thinking: *Looks like the old bugger's been at the bottle all evening...*

He calculated rapidly in his head: A pint at mid-day, one glass of wine at dinner, a small whisky at least three hours ago...He answered crisply, 'Perfectly all right, thank you. If I wasn't I'd call a taxi. You may let the hospital know I'll be there in about fifteen minutes.'

'Very well, sir, if you're sure...'

'I'm quite sure. Thank you.'

Michael closed the door firmly on his doubting face and returned to the study. Locating and replacing his socks, shoes and jacket he went swiftly up the stairs to look in on his guest.

Alaric slept soundly; even in sleep the lines of illness were deeply carved and Michael felt a rush of understanding and compassion. It must have been devastating to be faced so suddenly and unexpectedly with the imminence of death, then so violently rejected by the young woman he had always loved and thought of as his daughter. But then, he thought with cynical detachment, what else could the man have expected of his shattering revelations to Cassandra? He couldn't have known her very well to leave her without finishing what he'd started. That at least might have gained him a few sympathy points! As it was he'd have one hell of a job now to find her and once found, pin her down long enough to hear him out and benefit from any compassion she might then be feeling.

The unpalatable fact that he had in his own way made pretty much the same mistake and handled Cassie just as disastrously was no comfort at all.

In the event that Alaric might wake before his return he took the evening's restaurant bill from his pocket, wrote a brief explanation on the back and propping it against the bedside lamp went downstairs and out into the heat of the night.

*   *   *

When he returned hours later a yellow haze lay over the parched city, presaging another sun-drenched day. Recalling the comfort of America's air-conditioned shops and offices he pitied the clerks and store workers in this city, whose only escape from stifling workplaces would be into the parks and dusty squares for a brief and airless hour at noon.

'We are unused to this,' he mused, sweat prickling his back as he let himself into the house, thinking longingly of Bourne End and the whirring ceiling fans in the cool rooms of The Round House. Why on earth hadn't he had them fitted here, where there was no cool sparkling river and windows must be kept tightly closed against the city's lethal cocktail of diesel and petrol fumes?

He found Alaric already in the kitchen, bathed and shaved, a freshly brewed carafe of coffee sending a powerful message to Michael's tired brain and body.

'Caffeine!' he smiled wearily, 'a miracle – and at five-thirty in the morning!'

'I woke and found your note. You must have had one hell of a shock. How is she?'

'Sleeping soundly when I left her twenty minutes ago,' he dropped into a chair. 'Her skull isn't fractured, thank God, but she's badly bruised about the face. She's sedated of course: although she knew I was there and was trying to tell me something; I couldn't make sense of any of it...' He gave a perplexed frown. 'It was all just a jumble about The Round House and needing to telephone someone. Perhaps when I go back later she'll be rather more *compos mentis* and I'll discover what's worrying her.'

166

Alaric handed him a mug of coffee and Michael took it, waving away the proffered milk jug. 'No thank you, I'll need all the caffeine I can get this morning. After I've driven you to Paddington I must visit Lily and Simon to see if they've any news of Cassie.'

Alaric shook his head. 'I can make my own way to Paddington and chasing after my errant daughter can wait for today. You look as though you need a few hours sleep before you go anywhere or see anyone.'

Aware of the bone-weary malaise beginning to creep over him, Michael grimaced but capitulated. 'Perhaps you are right. I'll think I'll have that milk after all.' He topped up his coffee with a generous hand. 'What train do you want to take?'

'The earliest possible: there's one due to leave at nine-twenty, I'll try for that.'

'Call a taxi when you're ready – there's a number pinned on the board over there.' Michael yawned prodigiously. 'And call your sister or her chap to meet you at Penzance.'

'Christ! You sound like my old Nanny!' Alaric gave his rumbling laugh. 'Shut up and sod off up to bed will you, and leave me to organise myself. I've been doing it a damned sight longer than you!'

'OK, OK!' Michael stood, raising peaceable hands. 'I'll call you this evening if I have any news. Don't worry; unless she's fled the country, I'll find her.'

Waving a tired hand in farewell he picked up his coffee and staggering slightly left the room muttering aloud: 'And when I do, God help you, Cassandra Chisholm, you crafty, aggravating abso-bloody-lutely *fantastic* woman, because it'll be a close run thing between kissing you senseless or wringing your blasted neck!'

Alaric studied his retreating figure and gave another growl of laughter.

'And God help you too, because after the cock-ups we've both made you're certainly going to need all the help you can get!'

*   *   *

When Mrs Harris hadn't rung by noon on the following day, Cassie wasn't overly worried, deciding it must just have slipped her mind. The novelty of being cut off from everyone for a few days was highly conducive to just lying around and doing nothing at all, so she spent the remainder of that morning swimming in the river and lazing on the cushioned swing seat in the garden.

She made a sandwich at lunchtime and carried it, together with a glass of wine, into the garden. Sitting at a small table on the lawn she made a resolute attempt to take a long serious look at her future, realising rather belatedly that she had arrived at an important, perhaps *the* most important, turning point in her life.

She couldn't go back to her life in Cornwall, where photographing the wildlife and scenery on her own doorstep now seemed rather more than a little self-indulgent. Since moving to work in London she had been moderately successful with the theatre work, but that wasn't her preferred métier, although the workshops, particularly with the adult students, were. She could work comfortably with them and had found in the relaxed atmosphere of her small studio that she had quite a flair for teaching and an apparent ability to pass on her enthusiasm for her craft to others. Although quite how she was to put the experience gained at Blackfriars to provide her with a sufficient income to remain independent of Alaric was not yet clear.

Such an enterprise would mean renting premises, and for someone who was only just managing to keep her head above water financially, going it alone was a daunting prospect.

Money and her father being largely synonymous, she found the memory of that last confrontation with him intruding on her thoughts and stirring an uncomfortable mixture of guilt and unease. From the moment when he had appeared so suddenly in the studio he had seemed uncharacteristically quiet and subdued, dispirited even. Remembering how ill he had looked in the churchyard and her instinctive dash to fetch water, she found herself wishing she had been more patient instead of losing it so completely and driving him away.

It still hurt desperately to think of Laura and Miles' betrayal; whatever the reasons for her father's return to live in Cornwall, Laura should not gone over to the enemy and delivered her into his hands without warning. *But if you hadn't cleared off so fast,* argued her conscience, *had waited for him to finish what he had come to say, you'd have known why he wanted to return home, wouldn't you?*

It could be anything; he might be broke, or reached a phase where he couldn't paint…or lying low because some tottie's father was after him with a shotgun! She gave an explosive giggle at the thought, but the uneasy feelings persisted and, as the hours passed, she began to wonder more and more about the things that had been left unsaid.

But however important they may seem to him, if the revelations about the past he'd already made were anything to go by, she really didn't think she wanted to hear any more home truths…

By evening the heat had become almost unbearable, and after a last swim in the river she went indoors to shower and change before preparing a salad for her evening meal, which she carried with her into the book-lined study. Turning on the ceiling fan she began to browse along the shelves. Anything, even one of the leather-bound works of long-dead writers that filled the shelves in this house, would be better than an evening spent asking questions of herself that she couldn't answer.

Then right at the far end by the window and on the top shelf she found Michael's books: six dauntingly thick volumes in sober dust jackets. Putting her plate on the desk she pushed the library steps into place and climbed to take the books down two at a time: Thomas Hardy and Anthony Trolope first, then Charlotte Brontë, a very thick Jane Austen and finally R.D. Blackmore and John Galsworthy. On the back of each cover an unsmiling Michael gazed up at her, correct and formal in a white shirt, dark suit and an incongruous bow tie. With a break in her voice she said, 'Oh Michael, no wonder the Yanks needed something new for your tour. The Daughter's of the Revolution who filled that hall in Maine wouldn't have gone a bundle on this one!'

Stacking the books on the corner of the desk she selected the Galsworthy as being rather more twentieth than nineteenth century, propped it open against the others beside her plate and began to read.

She read through the evening, only moving to clear her finished meal aside and later switch on the lamp. It was, she thought as she closed the book at last and rubbed her tired eyes, a far cry from the dull as ditch-water stuff she'd had to plough through at school. Michael wrote with wit and passion, bringing alive to an extraordinary degree not only Galsworthy the man and writer, but also the full flavour of his life and times.

Eventually she rose and flexing her cramped shoulders returned her plate to the kitchen, but before she could begin to make her way to bed the 'phone rang. She hesitated, one hand on the banister rail. Now who on earth would be calling her at this hour?

*   *   *

Miles was waiting for Alaric outside Penzance station, Cormac in the open back of the Land-Rover, his great head lolling over the side and tail beating a thunderous tattoo against the side of the vehicle.

'I hope you don't mind if we go to Fleetwood first.' Miles swung Alaric's bag alongside Cormac and held open the passenger door. 'Laura thought you'd need a good meal and a rest after your journey. Tomorrow I've arranged for you to have a look at a few decent runarounds; so you can take your choice of a car and be independent of me in the future.'

'What a man!' Alaric grinned and climbed in, relaxing back against Cormac who had ingratiated the whole front part of his body over the back of the seat. He gave the dog's ears an affectionate rub. 'Hello, pal, you stay right there, you make a great pillow!'

Miles glanced briefly at his companion's drawn face as he turned the engine. 'How was it? No luck finding Cassie, I gather.'

'No. I tried the Arts Centre and her hotel, if that's what you call it, but they hadn't any idea – or so they said.' He stared straight ahead. 'Some chap called Michael Niven turned up looking for her at the same time. D'you know him?'

Miles answered cautiously, 'Not personally,' and received a doubting sideways glance.

'He's not exactly in the first flush of youth but to give him his due he made no secret about that – or about his feelings for Cass. He's a bloody cool customer though; I'd hardly met him when he told me he intended to marry her then had the gall to admit a past that would make even Laura's hair curl!'

Miles' only comment was a muffled grunt of laughter and his companion gave a rueful grin. 'Yes, I know: I'm a nice one to talk! He's a useful bloke to have around though. He was all set to start the great Cassie hunt today until the police arrived on his doorstep in the early hours of this morning. His housekeeper had been mugged and was in hospital so he spent most of the night with her and I left him sleeping it off. I think he's going to be pretty tied up with visiting and keeping a general eye on her to do much for a day or two, although he said he'd visit a couple of mutual friends called Lily and Simon and see if they could help.'

'That figures; Simon buys a lot of Cassandra's prints and Lily and Laura are old pals.' Miles put his foot down as they left the town and joined the dual carriageway. 'It sounds as though your lass is all set to lead you quite a dance. I'll say one thing, she's showing some spirit!'

'She's a damned sight more of a firebrand than she ever used to be; yesterday she bloody nearly blasted my ears off!' Alaric was silent for a few minutes, then asked: 'This Niven character – how much does Laura know about him?'

Miles laughed. 'They've never met so she only has the Lily Meyer version.'

'Which is?'

'Calm, controlled and sexy as hell!'

'Sounds about right!' he gave an unwilling smile. 'He seems

genuine about his feelings for Cassie, but I gather that, like me, he rather messed things up in that department; now he's not at all sure how she's feeling about *him*!'

'Well, if I may offer a spot of advice: keep out of it now and just leave him to find her. If he's successful and she's still speaking to him he may be able to persuade her down here, and that has to be a better option than you wearing yourself out looking for her. Keep on like that and you won't get much use out of that studio Laura's created for you!'

'I'm all right; just a bit tired, that's all.' He raked his fingers through his thick mane of hair. 'I feel I owe you a huge apology...if I know my sister she will have caused one hell of an upheaval at your place!'

'Think nothing of it. Since I've moved into Fleetwood the flat has been just so much wasted space...and let's face it, there's nothing Laura enjoys more than the odd spot of organising!'

'Yes,' Alaric agreed, adding: 'She's good at doing that; given half a chance she'll do it with any unwary man as well – she kept Harry in order, I can tell you, despite being young enough to be his daughter!'

'Maybe,' Miles gave a derisive snort, 'but she's too damned smart to try organising the likes of you – or me!' He drove in silence for several minutes before glancing around to find his companion had fallen asleep with his head resting against Cormack's hairy neck, continuing to sleep soundly until they turned through the gates and onto the gravelled drive at Fleetwood. Then, as if at some intuitive signal his eyes opened and he bent his satirical gaze upon his old home, observing succinctly:

'Thank God that's Laura I see on the steps and not my old man waiting for me to get near enough for him to smell the dram I had on the train!'

Climbing stiffly from the Land-Rover and swaying slightly with fatigue, he kissed his sister on both cheeks before putting his arms around her saying: '"Home is the sailor, home from the sea and the hunter home from the hill..."'

She held him tightly for a moment then stood back to cast a quizzical eye over a face as lined and wearily creased as his linen suit. 'More like "Double, double, toil and trouble" by the look of you! Just come in off the steps, you fool, before you fall down! You have time for a bath or shower before we eat – I've put out some clean towels – then you'd better have an early night here and go to Tregedick in the morning.'

Alaric looked at Miles over Laura's tawny head and gave a slow wink before enquiring innocently, '*What* was that you were saying Miles…about who wouldn't try to organise whom?'

19

In her bed in a small side room of Nightingale ward Elizabeth Harris lay with closed eyes, slowly gathering her returning wits. Moving each limb in turn she found with relief that nothing seemed to be broken, although she was aware that one side of her face was swollen and painful and that she had, as her late husband would have said: 'The bleedin' father and mother of an 'eadache!'

She started and her eyes flew open as she felt a hand on her wrist; the young nurse who had come in so quietly gave a broad encouraging smile.

'Awake at last! I thought the sedative should be wearing off about now. How are we feeling?'

Wincing, she struggled to sit up answering tartly, 'Mad as a wet hen at whoever put me in here and *we* could do with a cup of tea!'

'You shall have one as soon as I've checked your pulse and blood pressure.'

Elizabeth contained her impatience until the rituals were complete and her chart filled in, then fixed the nurse with a determined eye.

'Before you flit off for that tea, I'd like to know who hit me.'

The nurse smiled again, putting up the backrest and arranging her pillows to help her sit upright. 'So would we, but I'm afraid the lout who attacked you got clean away. The gentleman who came and stayed with you most of last night had quite a lot to say to the police on that subject.'

Her patient's gaze softened perceptibly. 'I bet he did! Stayed all night, did he?'

'I believe so. Sister must have been very taken with him because I'm told you were moved from the ward to this room within minutes of his arrival, and that's something she doesn't do at the drop of a hat for any old Tom, Dick or Harry.'

Elizabeth arranged the bedcover to her satisfaction and allowed a faint note of pride to creep into her voice. 'Oh, yes...he can be very persuasive, especially with women.' She looked up at the clock on the wall. 'Is that morning or evening?'

'Evening.'

Her heart gave a thump. 'You mean I've been out all this time?'

'You did come round but doctor gave you a pretty powerful sedative once we knew all your brains were still in place!'

Elizabeth thought rapidly and clearly despite her aching head. 'Can you do me a favour, please?'

'I'll try. What is it?'

'I need someone to get me to a telephone: can you do that?'

'We-ell...' She looked doubtful. 'You should really be going back to sleep.'

'It's very urgent. Oh –' she broke off, suddenly distressed, 'my bag – I haven't any money!'

The nurse was quick to assure her. 'You don't have to worry about *that*. Your Mr Niven left ten pounds with sister for anything you might need before his return.' She lowered her voice conspiratorially, 'Now if you promise to keep it short I'll get an orderly to bring the 'phone and some small change.'

When she had left the room Elizabeth lay back on her pillows. The talk and movement had tired her and she felt helpless and close to tears. What a thing to happen! Cassie would be wondering why she hadn't telephoned as promised and Michael could come at any time.

Caught off guard the previous evening by his unexpected return, she'd hardly been convincing about her day in Berkshire. Airing the house had never before taken her more than an hour or two and she didn't want to face any questions about why she had spent the day there, nor why she had left the Chelsea house last night without saying goodbye.

In her present weakened state she was afraid she might easily be lured into saying something that would send him driving straight down to Bourne End. She was torn, part of her knowing that the sooner those two got together the better for them both, while realising that she couldn't possibly allow Michael to walk in on Cassie unless she was first made aware of his alliance with her father.

When the orderly arrived wheeling the mobile pay phone, she waited for him to leave, then fed the coins he'd handed her into the box before dialling the number with trembling fingers.

It seemed to ring for an age before the receiver was lifted. When she heard Cassie's voice utter a cautious: 'Hello. Who is it?' she gave a great sigh of relief. 'Elizabeth Harris o' coorse – who else were you expecting?' Stress brought her almost eradicated Norfolk burr to life and there was a reassuring gurgle of laughter from Cassie.

'Not the Archbishop of Canterbury with that accent, that's for sure!'

'You might rather it was when you've heard the news I've got for you.'

'Oh...' There was a pause. 'Good or bad?'

174

She said cryptically, 'Now that rather depends on whether you view it from your point of view or mine!'

*   *   *

Cassie put the 'phone down then stood staring at it for a minute, letting the full import of Elizabeth's words sink in.

Her first reaction to the news that Elizabeth was in hospital had been to say: 'I'm coming now,' then rush straight there, but Elizabeth's emphatic 'Don't!' followed by her hurried explanations made Cassie realise that her own presence at the bedside would take one hell of a lot of explaining away should Michael find her there. She couldn't possibly risk causing any kind of trouble between him and the woman who was so clearly devoted to him and had shown her such kindness. Distractedly she rumpled her hair. But what if he suddenly decided to come down to The Round House and discovered her making free of his belongings? Cassie shuddered. After the way they had parted all those weeks ago what on earth could she say if he arrived unheralded on the doorstep?

Her stomach lurched and she was swept suddenly with such a longing to see him again; such a sheer physical need of him that she had to lean against a chair, gripping the back hard to keep from crumpling to the floor. Taking several deep, steadying breaths she sat down by the 'phone table and propping her chin on her hand began to marshal her thoughts into some kind of order.

So long as Mrs Harris kept her nerve there was no need for Michael to know his housekeeper had been helping her. Mrs Harris had been kindness itself and it wasn't fair that she should bear any kind of blame. If someone's head was about to roll, Cassie thought glumly, it had better be hers. After all, if she hadn't been running from Alaric, she wouldn't now be sitting here wondering what to do next.

But Michael was looking for her; her heart began to race. If she called him now he could be in this room in less than an hour.

Impulsively she put out her hand to take up the receiver again then snatched it back. She must be crazy to even think of calling him. Oh, he'd come all right, she thought bitterly, but not, as Mrs Harris seemed to think, because he wanted to or needed her, he'd come not for himself or by himself. Like Laura and Miles, he had gone over to the enemy: to Alaric, who had appeared from his Parisian eyrie like a bad genie and was now refusing to go away and leave her in peace.

The thought of seeing the two of them together was more than she could bear and she beat her hands against the table exclaiming aloud, 'I won't – I *can't* see you; not when you are trying to trap me into meeting again with Alaric. I've had, enough. I'm not his daughter; I never was and I don't want to hear any more of his disgusting confessions just so that he can feel better about himself.'

For long minutes she sat immobile, staring out of the window to where the evening shadows were creeping across the lawn, her outburst of anger slowly replaced by despair at the thought of leaving this peaceful house which had welcomed her so warmly and drawn her into Michael's world. Playing his music and reading his books, walking in his garden and spending just one night under his roof had made it a place where, in the absence of his physical presence, she could feel close to him again.

She returned to the study and touched the books she had taken from the shelves, the second still lying open at the first page as she had left it. It seemed too cruel a stroke of Fate to have in just a few short seconds shattered the peace and tranquillity of this quiet place.

Giving one convulsive sob she straightened her shoulders. 'Right!' she admonished aloud. 'Get a grip on yourself. Back to the Carrington tomorrow to collect the rest of your gear, then a quick visit to Jono and then…and then?' She started for the door, 'and then, you take off somewhere, anywhere that will provide a bolt hole from the hunters!'

20

Michael drove automatically through the evening traffic, his thoughts returning again and again to the discovery he had made less than an hour ago; wondering anew how on earth one of Cassie's lipsticks had come to be nestling in the pocket of his bathrobe. He had intended going straight to the Meyer's before visiting Elizabeth again, but after his long sleep he had rapidly revised his plans. Now, brows knit into a frown, he drove towards the hospital. One thing was certain, he thought grimly as he turned into the forecourt of St Catherine's, following the arrows to the car park, his bathrobe had never been wrapped around Casie's inviting form whilst *he* had been in the house! With an effort he tore his errant imagination away from the picture that evoked. Time enough for that when he caught up with her again...he corrected himself morosely, *if* he caught up with her again.

Armed with a large sheaf of flowers and the ward sister's assurances that the patient was, despite her cuts and bruises remarkably recovered, he walked swiftly down the corridor to the small side room before the main ward.

Elizabeth looked up at his entrance and gave a faintly wary, and because of her injuries, very lop-sided smile. 'You look like a what's-its-name – a Greek bearing gifts,' she said as he leaned to kiss her undamaged cheek.

'What makes you think a sinister motive lurks beneath this bouquet?' Laying the flowers on the end of the bed he pulled up the plastic chair and seated himself by her side. 'I must say you've still got a wonderful shiner there!'

'So they tell me; I haven't looked yet.'

'Don't, at least not for another day or two,' he advised. 'Simon and Lily send their love by the way. I called them before I left home.'

His tone was light but he crossed his arms on the coverlet and leaned forward, staring at her intently and she looked back unblinking for a few moments before giving a faint resigned sigh. 'All right; say what you came to say; I'm too old to play games and I never could do with you asking questions with your eyes instead of your tongue!'

He asked: 'Has Cassie been visiting Hampden Square while I've been away?'

She answered him promptly. 'Yes. She came to talk about you. For some reason I can't fathom she seemed to like doing that.'

'And exactly when did she sleep there?'

Masking her surprise and buying time she narrowed her eyes as though in thought. Now just what had put him onto that? 'Wednesday night,' she answered eventually, 'after she'd met with her father.'

'And then?'

Her eyes flickered briefly before she answered.

'Then she went, sir!'

He sighed. 'Lizzie, if you start that again I'll black the other eye!' He stood up. 'I'll find her, you know. If I have to turn the whole bloody country upside down, I'll find her.'

'Then better you get on with looking before she gets too far, because right now she thinks every man's hand is against her, including yours…and she's right, isn't she?'

'I suppose that's how it must seem, but I'm looking for her for *me*. Not Alaric; just me.' He gave a bleak smile. 'If I get lucky, so may he, but she doesn't know about that and it's by no means at the top of my list of priorities.'

It was on the tip of her tongue to say that Cassie certainly did know about his meeting and joining forces with her erstwhile father because she had told her. Instead she answered him briskly saying, 'Well don't stand back and wait to see how she feels about you; first let her know how you feel about *her* and if you have to grab her and hang on while you tell her, then that's what you have to do.' She sniffed disparagingly. 'Try to remember that with this particular woman being a gentleman and saying 'Ladies first' just won't wash.'

'Pa's right when he calls you an old witch!' He stood looking down on her. 'Where is she now, Lizzie?'

'That I'm not sure; I really am not.' She shook her head as weak tears suddenly filled her eyes. 'I'm so sorry.'

'It's all right. Please don't cry.' He bent and kissed her forehead. 'I'll come back in the morning. Just rest now and don't worry about anything. I'm not angry; I'm glad she came to you.'

She watched him go then turned her head into the pillow and closed her eyes. It hadn't really been a lie. Cassie might have left The Round House by now, although she hadn't said she would leave at once. It was all a gamble; perhaps her reluctance to see her father wouldn't over-ride her need to be with Michael again, on the other hand it might. Either way there was nothing that she could do about it other than pray.

Clinging to this thought she slipped back into a restless sleep

*   *   *

In response to Michael's impatient knock the door opened and Lily stood on the threshold drawling, 'Wa-al, you took your time!'

She looked cool in a thin tee shirt that hid little of her spectacular figure and a micro skirt that concealed even less. 'My God,' he averted his eyes. 'Must you?'

She raised her eyebrows almost to her hairline.

'Simon likes it!'

'I'll bet he does!'

'I'm celebrating the end of *Shabos*. You want I should dress up decent again for a goy like you?'

Michael's eyes glinted. 'Just pack in the Yiddisha Momma act, Lily. I needed to get my head down for a while and I had to visit Elizabeth again. I won't stay long, Where's Simon?'

'Getting the boys cleaned up and into bed.' As she led the way through the house she asked, 'How's your Mrs Harris? I couldn't believe it when you 'phoned this morning. London gets more like downtown New York every day. It sure isn't safe anymore for little old ladies to be in the streets after dark.'

'She's better, but much shaken and I agree with you about London; I'd like to see her back in Suffolk, that's if she would go. Stable Cottage has stood empty since ma's old gardener died last Christmas and Elizabeth could be very comfortable there. But you know how she is: proud and stubborn as hell.'

'Persuade her.' She grinned and turned to go back into the house. 'After all, that's what you're good at, buddy!'

The paved terrace was a cool haven after the heat of the day and he sank gratefully into one of the cushioned chairs set about the round wooden table. Despite his long exhausted sleep after he'd been called to the hospital, he was still weary. He settled deeper into the chair, closed his eyes and began to slide over the edge of consciousness and was on the very edge of sleep when Lily returned a few minutes later bearing a tray with three long glasses and a jug of coffee clinking with ice cubes, she looked knowingly at his sleepy expression.

'Better wake up. Simon wants to talk to you and he'll be down any minute.'

'Talk to me? About what?'

'About Cassie.'

Michael sat upright demanding, 'Why? Has she been here?'

'No, but Simon sees her from time to time.' She began to pour the coffee, 'I warn you, buddy, he's megga pissed-off with you!'

'Why should he be that?'

179

'He'll soon let you know –' She broke off as her husband appeared on the steps into the garden wearing knee length green shorts and a tee shirt in a shade of shocking pink that hurt the eyes. He kissed her, said 'Bloody kids,' and slapped her rear. 'Be a pal and go tell them goodnight while I talk to this snake in the grass.'

She winked, ran her fingers down his chest then picked up her glass and walked up the steps. Pausing at the top she twitched her long fingers in farewell. 'Bless you my children, and mind: no blood on the paving.'

Michael watched her departing derrière appreciatively. 'That's quite a woman you've got there, Simon!'

'Yes, I have and if I didn't know her so well I wouldn't let *you* within a mile of this house!' Helping himself to coffee he sat down and went straight into the attack. 'Michael, we've been friends a long time, but I have to say this: you are an absolute *shite*, and if you don't get this business with Cassie cleared up we really are going to fall out in a big way.'

Michael scowled. 'Well I'm not chasing all over London looking for her so that I can screw things up even further. I had hoped you might be able to tell me where she's hiding out.'

'If I knew that we wouldn't be having this conversation…' Simon took off his glasses, polished them on his shirt then put them back on his nose, 'she'd be here with us and you wouldn't have even got past the door! I told you right at the beginning to be careful; that she needed any kind of involvement with you like a rabbi needs a bacon sandwich, but I might have saved my breath, mightn't I?' He sat down, glaring at him across the table. 'These weeks since you buggered off she's grown up, been managing her life just fine, now she's apparently all over the place again and it just isn't on. It's bad enough that she was so hard up that she had to squander her talents at that bloody Centre: if you start stirring things up again the work she does for me will very likely go to cock and she'll be back not knowing where the hell she's heading.'

'I didn't know she was short of money; she never said…' Michael stood up and paced across the courtyard, turned, then paced slowly back; he sat down again and rubbed a hand over his hair. 'You're a bit off the beam but in a way you're right, although I disagree with you about the Centre. According to her father she seems to be making quite a success of it.' He hunched forward in his chair and held Simon's gaze earnestly. 'I swear to you that I really did my very best not to let all this happen, although that was as much for my sake as hers: the last thing I wanted was any kind of deep involvement with another woman. I had no intention of having an affair with Cassie, although believe me, keeping her at a distance wasn't easy. The last time we met I tried to reason with her but she walked out on me before I'd finished...which is a bad habit she has!' He spread his hands helplessly. 'It was only later I realised that in letting her go I'd made if not the first, certainly the second most disastrous mistake of my life so far.'

'If that's true why the hell didn't you go after her instead of skulking in Suffolk all these weeks?'

Michael answered patiently, 'Because it was better not to hound her but give her time to think things out; I can only hope it's been successful. I need to find her now to tell her I was wrong and she was right; that I can't even begin to imagine living the rest of my life without her...and if she walks out on me again I'll follow her and keep telling it until she gives in and marries me. If that sounds selfish and greedy to you it's just too bad.'

Simon asked dryly, 'Are you thinking of doing all that before or after you've told her about Francine?'

Michael winced. 'That's a bit below the belt isn't it, even from you? I don't know. I haven't got that far.'

'Rather you than me however you tell it: but you'd better be quite sure that if you bring it all out into the open, you can *both* put it all behind you.'

'I wasn't sure *I* could do that before I went home, but I am now. Cassie's reaction I'll have to take a chance on.' He took up his glass and sat nursing it in both hands. 'I told Pa everything: about Francine, the marriage...Gervaise. I had to. After *that*, telling Cassandra can only be a minor descent into hell.'

'Ah, but I'd like to have been a fly on the wall to hear what Archie had to say to all your revelations!'

'Um.' Michael gave a reluctant grin. 'He did make me feel rather as though I was back in short trousers and had just kicked a football through the greenhouse roof.' He drained his glass and set it down on the table. 'Now I must go. I need a bath and something to eat before I try to get some sleep. Tomorrow looks like being another long day.'

'Going so soon?' Lily slipped her arm through Michael's as they re-entered the house. 'How about coming to lunch tomorrow?'

'Thanks, but I'm not sure where I'll be. First I must call in at the hospital and find out when Elizabeth can come home. I'll insist she comes to Hampden Square for a few days then perhaps I can persuade her back to Suffolk; for a holiday if nothing more.'

Lily wrinkled her forehead. 'Cassie told Simon that she visited your place while you were away. Are you sure the old girl doesn't know where she is now?'

'I don't *think* so.'

'I bet she's got some idea, but she's the sort you'd have to beat it out of with a baseball bat!'

Simon laughed. 'Unlike you, my sweet; you couldn't keep a secret for five minutes,' he kissed her and she said 'Umm. Nice...more please!'

Michael pressed her arm. 'I'm going. All this domestic bliss is giving me indigestion...pure envy really.'

'Poor old Michael,' she gave him a quick hug. 'If Cassie turns up here we'll sit on her until you come to claim her.'

'Bless you. Goodnight.'

Simon walked with him to the door.

'When you find her, see you do make her happy or you'll have me to reckon with.' He softened his words with a smile and added, 'you jammy bastard!'

'I don't feel very jammy right now.' Michael looked at him with troubled eyes. 'Simon, I just don't know where to start looking. She won't stay in London – or go anywhere near Cornwall, because she won't be sure of where Alaric is, but so far as I know she doesn't have any friends she could go to out of town. The only really close friend here she might stay with is my cousin Jonathan, and I've already checked up on him.'

Simon eyed him shrewdly then suggested, 'If I was in your place and she's up to it, *I'd* push a little harder with your Mrs Harris. She may be very fond of Cassie but she's a lot fonder of you. Find out just how close they've become over these past weeks and exactly what's been happening since Cassie saw her father. You might then be on your way to finding her.'

For a moment Michael stood lost in thought then looked at his friend with dawning comprehension. 'Elizabeth told me Cassie slept at Hampden Square that night – and the old witch spent all Thursday at the Round House. You don't think...?'

'Oh, but I do! And if that's the lie of the land I'll eat my hat if she isn't worrying herself stiff over whether to tell you or not – hey, wait a minute!'

But Michael was already down the steps and halfway into his car before Simon reached him and clapped a restraining hand on his shoulder.

'Wait! You can't go charging down there on spec...'

'Can't I? You bloody watch me!' Michael slid into his seat and leaned out of the door. 'Thanks for the tip. I'll tackle Elizabeth now then if your hunch is right, I'll get a good night's sleep and gather strength for the Round House tomorrow morning.' He slammed the door, the engine roared into life and within seconds the Mercedes was out of sight.

Simon sat down on the bottom step as Lily appeared in the doorway above him.

'What's going on, hon? You look bletch.'

'Oh shit!' He groaned and put his head in his hands. 'I think I've just dropped the old witch in the gazpacho!'

'Like she doesn't have troubles enough without some flat-foot opens his big mouth and sets that lunatic after her ass…'

He snarled, 'Oh, get off my back and sod off, smart arse!'

She came down the steps and stirred him with her foot.

'You can't take all the blame; the trouble with laid-back guys like Michael is that when they blow, they *really* blow; but don't you worry about old Elizabeth, she's one hell of a lot tougher than he is.' She sat down beside him and ran a coaxing hand through his hair. 'C'mon, cheer up; the boys u'll be asleep pretty soon now. What d'ya want to do then, honey?'

He said grumpily, 'Go to bed and try and get a bit of peace from you.'

She slid a hand up the back of his shirt. 'The bed I can guarantee – and you can have whichever piece of me that takes your fancy.'

Simon eyed her mistrustfully. 'Why are you getting ideas like that so early in the evening?'

She looked at him limp eyed. 'It's Michael's fault. He always makes me feel sexy.'

'Trollop!'

Nathan pressed his nose against the window then turned to his brother, busy acquiring Repetitive Strain Injury courtesy of the latest Play Station. 'Psst!' he called in a hoarse stage whisper, 'come and look, dick-head – the wrinklies are snogging again…and on the front step, too! I can see Mrs Harper looking from behind her curtains.'

'Ugh! Who wants to watch,' his brother didn't look up. 'Mrs Harper's wasting her time, they won't do anything much 'till they think we're asleep…*then* they'll be up the stairs and at it like rabbits. Sex, sex, sex,' he said, 'that's all they ever think about. Mrs Goldbaum at the paper shop blames it on the permissive society; she says it's the sixties lot that started all the porno movies and shag mags and that they get right on her tits…' He jammed his finger on the control button and splattered an Alien across the screen. 'If I had any, they'd get on mine too!'

*   *   *

Michael stood with his back against the door and fixed Elizabeth with a glittering eye.

'Lizzie Harris, if you don't tell me the truth, the whole truth and nothing but the truth right now, I swear I'll never eat another one of your treacle puddings again as long as I live...

*   *   *

Early on a bright Sunday morning near Hammersmith Broadway, Cassie and Michael passed within a few hundred yards of each other; the Mercedes driven at speed to the Round House, the Citroën more circumspectly to Montpellier Gardens; the occupant of each on the same merry-go-round only riding on opposite sides of the carousel, each hearing a different tune.

21

Jono eyed Cassie bleakly as they sat cross-legged on the grass at Montpellier Gardens. 'You can hide away here for as long as you like, but the thing is...' he removed the ring-pull from his can of beer and took a long swallow then wiped his mouth with the back of his hand. 'I think you should see Michael; I really think you should.'

'*Et tu, Brutus!*' She parodied, rolling her eyes and making stabbing motions at her chest. 'Don't be such a twat; if I see him, then *ergo*, I also see Alaric!'

'I don't know about that. What I do know is that he really cares about you – God knows why because you're just about the most bloody-minded and awkward cow under the sun!'

'Thanks for the vote of confidence.' Cassie opened her own can and squinted down into its contents enquiring, 'You quite sure Tony hasn't managed to do anything to make this undrinkable?'

'Don't change the subject.'

'All right...' she waved the can at him, 'tell me why I should believe your two-faced, bed-shy cousin has had a change of heart since he gave me the bums rush.'

Jono repeated Michael's parting words to him and she looked down, tightening her hands on the can. 'Words are easy. When it's all boys together and keeping up appearances most blokes will say anything. The fact still remains that he wasn't looking very hard for me until Alaric turned up.'

Jono sighed. 'OK. I suppose you have a point although I still think you're wrong. But Michael's a persistent bastard and I'd take a bet on him coming here again when he's drawn a blank everywhere else.' He was thoughtful, rolling the can between his hands. 'Look, this is just an idea; I've five clear days before rehearsals start on the new play – even Llewellyn the Letch needs the occasional break. I've this old aunt down in Dorset: we could both spend a few days there. It would give me a break and you space to get your head together without worrying about Michael appearing at any moment.'

She demurred. 'You can't just arrive on even the most understanding aunt's doorstep with some strange female on tow – '

'Isabel isn't your average aunt.' He was impatient. 'I tell you, whether you come or not, *I'm* not sitting here and waiting for Michael to come and kick my arse.'

'Don't be stupid. He isn't like that.'

'Isn't he? That's all you know!' He blew rudely through pursed lips. 'That nice quiet gentleman can get a look in his eye that would have stopped Ghengis Khan in his tracks. He doesn't have to yell to let you know when he's mad – frankly, he frightens the shit out of me when he really gets going.' He finished his beer and crumpled the can. 'Well, are you coming to Dorset or not?'

She said ungraciously, 'I suppose I'll have to, but only if you call your aunt first and warn her. I refuse to turn up unannounced on anyone's doorstep.'

'OK. I'll 'phone now – you sure that old banger of yours will get us there?'

'If it can get me to Cornwall and back I should think it could manage Dorset without collapsing by the roadside.'

'Right; I'll have to wait until Tony comes in because the silly sod went out this morning and left his keys, but he'll be here before lunch. We could leave then and get a sandwich somewhere on the way down.'

Cassie leaned back on her hands as he went into the flat. Tilting her head to watch the sunlight dappling through the branches of the plane tree above, she could feel her insides swoosh about like so much poorly set jelly. If only she could believe Michael wanted to be her knight in shining armour she'd be the happiest woman on earth; but she'd given up believing in miracles a long time ago. She thought with more than a little apprehension that after the dance she was leading him he would be highly unlikely to be overflowing with *bonhomie.* If Jono was so wary of his cousin's disapproval, that didn't say much for her own chances of remaining unscathed when they met, as meet they surely must at some time. But on her terms, she thought firmly, and at her time and place.

Within a few minutes Jono returned. 'Everything's arranged. She says she'd love to have company for a few days and will expect us when she sees us.' He sat down again and gave vent to a satisfied sigh. 'That should fox the old bugger; he'll never in a million years guess you'd be there – but I warn you: you ever let him know I took you there and I'll shut you naked in the broom cupboard all night with Llewellyn the Letch!'

'Promises, promises,' she sat up and leaned forward to take his face between her hands and kiss him. 'I love you to bits!'

'No you don't; you love Michael, you daft cow.' Unceremoniously he shoved her away. 'So for God's sake do something about it soon and let me enjoy my dirty weekends again instead of traipsing about the country with you on tow.'

'Oh, sod you Jono...I'm not in this for my health!' She flung herself back on the grass; her breast heaved and tears trickled from the corners of her eyes, while he sat and watched helplessly, not knowing whether they were tears of laughter or pain, or both.

For a brief moment he allowed himself to remember the night she had wept and he had comforted her before she fell asleep in his arms. Seeing now the outline of her body beneath the thin silk of her dress, the tilt of the short nose above the long mouth, the tears spilling from those unbelievable eyes, he thought almost that he could love her.

He scowled and threw his handkerchief over her face.

'Shut up, will you and use this – your nose is running!'

*   *   *

With a road map propped on his knees Jono directed her through the prim towns and past the manicured hills of Surrey and the cornfields and narrow rivers of Hampshire. Coming at last into the winding Dorset lanes where low hills dipped suddenly to reveal stone houses roofed with slate or thatch in small villages with unfamiliar soft sounding names.

Driving on through wooded valleys and grey stone towns they at last joined the smugglers' road that ran, dipping and curving from Tassingham down to where Wytchwood lay in the crease of a hill within sight and sound of the sea.

It was a low, rambling one-story Colonial bungalow, built on wooden piles with a long covered veranda facing the sea. The garden was an untamed riot of colour and at the rear grew a small wood of pines, acting as a break to the wind that in winter would funnel down the long valley. As the Citroën came to a halt before the rickety picket fence three dignified cats strolled nonchalantly out to meet them.

Jono leaned out of the car window and greeted them affably.

'Hi, Ghandi, Nehru, Jinnah – where's the memsahib?'

Cassie chuckled. 'Are they really called that?'

'Amongst other things...watch out for Ghandi; he likes to play with your ankles.' He stepped out of the car, stretching and easing his back, explaining, 'Isabel was born in India, and apart from school spent most of her life there until Partition. She used to go back from time to time visiting old friends, but not since Nikhil died – and bye the way, she likes to be called Isabel, not Aunt or Mrs Singh!'

'*Singh?*' She looked at him over the roof of the car. 'She married an Indian?' He nodded and her eyes widened. 'That must have taken

187

one hell of a lot of courage for them to marry in those days.'

'It did. There were a lot of cold-shoulders turned, but they were very happy. He was a lovely man.'

She said dryly, 'You have a very *interesting* family.'

He grinned, 'Not half as interesting as yours, mate!'

A tall, spare, grey-haired woman came towards them along the brick path, both hands outstretched in welcome.

'Jonathan – and Cassie – that's right, isn't it? Come along in. The kettle is on the range and I made a special trip into the village for some absolutely delicious cake from the W.I. market!' She took Cassie's hands in hers, confiding; 'I'm hopeless at cakes!'

'But brilliant at curries,' Jono interjected and she aimed a mock slap at his cheek. 'Neither curries nor cakes for you, my dear, unless your pockets are clean.'

'Clean as a whistle; Michael relieved me of all I had...a bit of a cheek really when you consider he can afford to buy his own.' He laughed and added, 'You don't have to bother about Cassandra; she's as po-faced as Michael about my wacky-baccy!'

'I'm glad to hear it.' With the cats wreathing around her feet and making sudden leaps and pounces at her flowing skirt she led the way into the house, walking slowly but with an easy grace that belied her years. Cassie followed, wholly captivated by this most extraordinary woman. Ethnic hardly described her clothing, comprising as it did a multi-coloured cotton skirt and red silk blouse, over this a sleeveless jacket of deep blue velvet shimmering with tiny mirrors. Though not conventionally beautiful the lined, high cheek-boned face framed by shoulder length silver-grey hair was arrestingly attractive.

They sat on the veranda at a long metal table to drink tea poured from a silver teapot and eat cake off plates decorated with exotic birds and flowers. The whole house was filled with an eclectic collection of objects that told of an Eastern past: statuettes of Hindu deities jostled for space with images of Buddha. Indian rugs were scattered on the polished wood floors and the walls hung with silk tapestries, while on a round brass table were displayed silver ornaments and tiny delicate musical boxes of wood and ivory inlaid with mother-of-pearl.

In the long sitting room with its unbleached calico curtains and low furniture covered with rich coloured cloths hung a large oil painting of a handsome middle-aged man, with waving black hair and the darkest of brown eyes looking out from the canvas with the secret smile of a lover.

Cassie sat back, letting the talk and family gossip flow between aunt and nephew: seeing a new side to Jono. One of relaxed humour and the kind of speech and manners not exhibited within the environs of Montpellier Gardens, at least, none that she had ever seen or heard.

From time to time Isabel glanced in her direction, giving a comfortably inclusive smile without pressing her to take part in the conversation. Only when Jono left to fetch their bags from the car did she say guilelessly, 'As Jonathan told me you were Michael's girl I have made two rooms ready; I hope this meets with your approval, if not his!'

'Both of us actually,' Cassie smiled, 'we really are just good friends!'

'I thought so when I first saw you together. Young men do look so predatory don't they, when they have nothing but sex on their minds?'

'Umm, I had noticed.' Cassie placed her plate carefully to one side and met the blue eyes directly. 'I don't know what Jono has told you about Michael and me, but I don't want to be here under false pretences. I should hate something awful to blow up and cause trouble when you are being so kind.'

'He said only that Michael was looking for you and you weren't yet ready to see him.' Isobel smiled. 'If that is all you want me to know, then that is quite all right.'

For a few moments Cassie struggled. Michael had spoken with great warmth of this woman; little as Cassie wanted to air her problems to a stranger she knew that she couldn't be less than honest with Isabel Singh.

She said cautiously, 'It's a little more complicated than that! It isn't so much that I don't want to meet Michael, as not being at all sure that Michael actually wants to meet *me*. I think it more likely that my father has managed to con him into helping him find me.'

'I'll be very surprised if anyone could con Michael into doing anything he didn't want to do.' her companion observed dryly.

Cassie stared moodily into space. 'Jono says he still cares about me, but as I walked out on him some weeks ago and have spent the past few days giving him the run around, I should think I've probably finished anything there ever might have been between us – not that there was ever much; Michael saw to that!' She gave a wan smile. 'It's all a bit of a mess, isn't it? I don't know what I'd have done if you hadn't allowed me to come here with Jono. At least I'll have a few days peace to think things over.'

'And when you've done that?'

'I don't know.' She shook her head. 'I left Michael because he made it quite clear I didn't have a future with him. Now if Jono's to be believed he's changed his mind. Quite honestly, if he's put himself on my father's side and against me, I don't think I could ever trust him again. Either way it doesn't make a difference where I'm concerned. I don't want to hear what Alaric has to say, nor risk another rebuff from Michael; all of that hurt too much.'

Isabel said obliquely, 'Love is seldom perfect and often hurts. It is all part of the price we pay for loving.'

'That must be why I'm bankrupt then,' Jono had returned from the car and now stood on the veranda steps, a bag in each hand. 'Tell me where to put these, Isabel, before my arms reach my ankles!'

'The blue bedroom for Cassandra and you are at the end of the corridor. Now run along both of you and unpack, then feel free to do as you wish while I have my siesta.' She touched Cassie's hand briefly. 'We can talk later if you wish.'

Jono swung the bags and looked inquiringly at Cassie. 'What about a swim...you did bring a cozzy, I hope?'

She forced a smile. 'Never travel without one.'

'Great! Come on...five minutes to change and I'll see you on the beach.'

'A quid I'm there before you.'

'Done!'

Solemnly they spat on their palms and shook hands before jostling each other along the passageway. Isabel looked after them with a smile, commenting beneath her breath, 'Let *that* one slip through your fingers, Michael Niven, and you are not the man I think you are!'

*   *   *

A long hot summer was all right, Michael thought, but this particular one seemed to be going on forever. He drove through the city with the car windows down and the roof open but still the sweat trickled down from his hairline so that he had to keep taking a hand off the wheel to wipe it away. Cutting across country the air became cleaner and the heat less intense and he eased back in his seat, letting the car cruise at a comfortable speed while luxuriating in the breeze from the open windows.

When the gates of The Round House came into sight he cut the engine to glide the last few yards in silence. Drawing up across the entrance as a precaution against the precipitant flight by any possible occupant he stepped out, then pushing gently on the gate, and avoiding the gravelled drive walked over the grass to the front door.

For a full minute he stood quite still head cocked to one side,

190

listening to the silence, then sliding his key into the lock pushed open the door and stepped inside. As he crossed the hallway, his footsteps sounding unnaturally loud on the polished floor, he was aware of a complete absence of sound in any part of the house. Abandoning all further attempts at stealth he mounted the stairs quickly, knowing as he did so that he was too late and the bird had once more flown.

The door to his bedroom was open and he stood looking around the immaculate room, his gaze coming finally to rest on a full-blown rose in a vase by the bed.

'Ah-ha!' he let out a long breath and moved to take the rose from the vase, then stood smiling and twisting it in his fingers for a moment before turning to continue along the landing. Opening and shutting doors to give each interior a swift glance, he came to the fourth and last and found what he was looking for: a stripped bed with the used sheets and pillowcases neatly folded at the foot.

He said aloud, 'So Lizzy needn't have confessed that little sin; you didn't sleep in my bed after all! But she didn't believe you'd leave quite so soon, did she? So where my dear infuriating Cassandra, will you be laying your head tonight?'

Still holding the rose he went back down the stairs and continued his tour of the house, finding everything as clean and tidy as though Elizabeth herself had just that morning run her eagle eye over it and cleared every sign of occupancy from the place. It was only when he reached the small study that he detected signs of a recent visitor. In the morning rush Cassie had forgotten to replace his books on the shelves; the one she had begun reading when the telephone rang still lay open on the desk.

Michael raised his brows. 'Well, well; you have been a busy girl haven't you?' he glanced at the music centre where the standby light glowed and gave a satirical smile. 'What did you choose from my sadly dated collection – Domingo or Lennon, Callas or Alison Moyet?' He pushed the play button on the CD and the unmistakable beat and unmatchable voice of Sinatra filled the room.

"Just in time, I found you just in time
Just when I thought my time was running low..."

He dropped into a chair and resting his head against the back stared bleakly at the machine. 'My sentiments exactly, but are they yours Cassie, or was that just a random choice? And if you will keep running from me, how the hell am I supposed to find out?'

Now there was nowhere left to look and no clue to her where-abouts: only one forlorn hope, one person to visit who may know the answer to that last question.

22

Vincent looked up at the sharp rat-tat on the flat door.

'Who the hell's that?' he demanded. 'You said they'd gone for the rest of the week and we'd have the place to ourselves!'

Tony swore and dumped the pan of baked beans back on the stove. 'They have, but it's just like that tart Cassie to have forgotten a lipstick or something!'

Grumbling under his breath he yanked open the door then stared nonplussed at the man facing him. Hell! It was that old geezer Cassie had gone off with months ago from Jono's party! What could *he* want?

Michael cast an eye over Tony and recognised the youth who had been laying claim to Cassie's attention the night he'd first met her. He searched his memory...Terry? Tim? It was something like that. He summoned a smile.

'I'm looking for Jonathan; is he in?'

'No. You've just missed them.'

Michael raised an eyebrow. 'Them?'

'Yeah, Jono and his tottie...they've gone away for the week to shack up in some country love nest!'

'Ah, I see. Well in that case perhaps you can help. Would you know if Cassandra Chisholm has been here recently?'

'Yeah – like I said; you've just missed them.'

Michael frowned. 'Let me get this straight; are you telling me that Jonathan and Cassie have gone away together?'

'That's right.'

Michael allowed himself a brief smile. 'And you assume because of that they are "shacking up"?'

Tony scowled. This old geezer was beginning to get up his nose. As if he didn't have enough to put up with from Jono and that stuck up little bitch, here was this smooth bastard laughing at him. 'I don't assume anything mate, when they don't even bother to shut the door here when they're having a shag I wouldn't think they've gone off to pick daffodils all week, would you?'

Controlling his immediate urge to hit the little bastard where it would hurt him most Michael asked coldly. 'Quite sure of your facts, are you?'

'You bet!' Tony leered. 'Saw 'em at it with my own eyes months ago when I got up one night for a pee.'

Michael masked his shock by commenting frostily, 'No doubt if you'd had a camera you would have made a video of the event!' and turning on his heel walked back down the steps.

Tony called blithely, 'Any message for when they get back?'

'No. No message.'

Tony watched him get into the car before closing the door. He returned to the kitchen, metaphorically rubbing his hands. That had sorted *him* out. He didn't know what the old geezer had wanted with either Jono or Cassie but he'd looked pretty miffed to hear the good news!

Of course, he'd only spotted them in bed together that once when Cassie had turned up looking like a drowned rat and bawling her eyes out, and that had been weeks, not months ago, but it stood to reason they'd probably been at it ever since...

Vincent asked, 'Anything important?'

Tony picked up the saucepan and began ladling beans onto two plates.

'Nah, just some toffee-nosed old wanker looking for Jono, but I've sorted him out. *He* won't be disturbing us again in a hurry!'

*   *   *

Michael turned into the square, slotted the car into his parking bay and went into the house. Going swiftly up the stairs to the drawing room he poured a large whisky, slumped down onto one of the twin couches and let the anger build inside him.

Cassie and Jonathan! He had never for a moment imagined...for months they'd been sleeping together, that little rat had said! Why on earth, he raged, had she bothered with a middle-aged old fool like himself if she was sleeping with Jonathan – unless the lure of free meals and a wealthier swain on tow had been the reason. Perhaps they'd laughed about him when they were in bed together...He downed the drink in one draught and stood to pour another.

And Lily and poor old Elizabeth! How could *they* have got it all so wrong? He pressed his fingers against his eyes. Well, that really had finished things. No chance now of letting her know how much he loved...*had*, loved her, he amended furiously; no chance either of getting her down to Cornwall and Alaric. He began to walk about the room, swearing aloud; every low-down disgusting word he could dredge from the depths poured from his lips until spent and exhausted he stopped to lean his burning forehead against the window glass,

193

staring down into the street below. He would have to call Archie. He'd promised to do that as soon as he had news of Cassie. Well, he had news now all right, but none that would cause that old fox's heart to swell with joy.

Half an hour and several whiskies later he levered himself from the couch and swaying visibly, picked up the 'phone, fumbling as he dialled the familiar number.

Archie barked, 'It's a hell of a time to call, whoever you are – can't a man even *lunch* in peace?'

Michael winced and closed his eyes. Holding the receiver away from his ear he wondered dimly how he could possibly have acquired a hangover that quickly...

'Hello, pa,' he tried to hit the right tone for imparting his unwelcome tidings. 'Whish news d'you want firsht? The bad, or the shimply fucking awful?'

Archie's jaw slackened as he listened to his son's succinct if somewhat slurred explanations and when Michael's voice ceased gazed at the receiver for a moment in disbelief then raised his voice in a roar, ''Tavia – your son's on the 'phone and drunk as a fiddler's bitch!'

Michael started to laugh. He laughed until the tears ran down his face while the molten lake of pain inside just got deeper and deeper until he thought he might drown in it.

*   *   *

Archie dropped the 'phone back on the rest and turned bewildered eyes on Octavia. 'I don't know what to make of it. A few days ago I'd have staked my life that he wouldn't stop 'till he'd found her. Now he says he's given up.' He shook his head. 'He says his woman's gone off somewhere with Sholto Murrayfield's boy!'

Octavia pursed her lips and put her head on one side, giving the matter thought. 'Jonathan!' she announced after a few moments, 'he used to tease Sholto's dogs until one bit him. Margery said he got his own back by feeding the animal Ex-Lax. The poor creatures ruined Sholto's study carpet!' She sniffed. 'He's not the sort to run off anywhere.'

Archie struggled to find the connection between these two observations and failed. 'Well he just has...to some love nest he's got in the country, Michael says.'

She huffed meaningfully. 'Love nest, rubbish – he's an actor; they can't afford love nests; if he's anywhere in the country it'll be with

Isabel.'

Archie looked as astounded as though Brenda had suddenly sprouted wings and flown through the hallway singing the Hallelujah Chorus. '*Isabel*? What – go there with a tottie on tow?'

Octavia said patiently, 'Of course; where else?' She bent to pick up Titus and gave a vague smile, her brief inspirational flash vanishing as swiftly as it had come. 'Isabel has cats but she won't let him tease those…come along Titus: din-dins!'

Archie watched her retreating back with a kind of exasperated admiration. 'I wonder…' He pounced on the address book by the telephone and began to thumb through it muttering; 'No use calling the boy, not when he's still drunk as a skunk – Ah, ha!' he stabbed a finger on the book. 'Here we are…' He picked up the receiver again and began to dial.

*   *   *

Isabel sighed and sat down on the edge of her bed. 'It's very sweet of you to call, Archie, but I'm just about to have my noonday nap.'

'What? Should have thought you'd been back here long enough to have done with that heathenish habit.' Archie's voice was loud and querulous.

Smiling faintly she settled back against the pillows and put her feet up.

'Call it my way of trying to grow old gracefully. Now what can I do for you?'

'Have you got Sholto's boy there?'

'Yes, do you want to speak to him?'

'No, I just want to know if he's alone.'

Isabel thought rapidly. Now what on earth was old Archie Niven up to coming so hard on the heels of her guests like this? She asked mildly, 'Were you expecting him to be?'

'Don't you lark with me Izzy – I know that tone of voice. I remember when you were at school and playing merry hell with all us chaps in the holidays; he's down there with Michael's girl, isn't he?'

'He has a friend with him, yes.'

'For immoral purposes?'

She gave a shout of laughter. 'Oh, Archie…*really*, what a sweet old-fashioned thing you are, but I'm sorry to disappoint you; it's nothing like that…not even the whiff of an affair. They have separate rooms.'

'Doesn't mean they're going to stay in them, does it?'

'I think in this case it does…Now come on, Archie; either say what's on your mind or hang up and let me get on with my afternoon zizz.'

Suddenly his voice sounded old and defeated. 'It's our boy, Isabel. He's in love with that girl you have there. She keeps running away from him for all sorts of stoopid reasons. He was trying to find her until some little snot told him she's rompin' in the hay with young Jonathan – now he's given up and got completely rat-arsed and I don't know what to do!'

She sat bolt upright. 'Don't be silly, Archie. Michael *never* drinks to excess.'

'I tell you he's pissed as a newt!'

She sighed again and settled herself back against the pillows. 'All right, if you say so…fire away: You tell me all you know and I'll see what I can do. But I warn you; if Cassandra is really adamant that she won't see him, I won't connive with you or anyone else to bring about a meeting.'

She listened in silence to Archie's outpourings. Really, she thought with rare impatience, how on earth could two such intelligent beings who quite clearly loved each other to distraction, have made such a monumental mess of their lives? And poor old Archie; she stifled a gurgle of laughter. Just as he thought his errant and obstinate son was about to settle down and provide the heir he craved, up had popped Cassandra's big bad daddy and thrown a spanner in the works. That explained why the girl was on the run. Parents, she mused, were frequently more hindrance than help.

It seemed crystal clear to her that without a third party to administer a few pretty hefty nudges in the right places, Michael Niven and Cassandra Chisholm would continue on their separate and lonely paths.

She had a great affection and admiration for Michael, whom she considered to be a most parfit gentil knight, and on what was admittedly a very short acquaintance had found his Cassie to be an obvious, albeit spirited, damsel in distress. But as a newcomer to this particular game of happy families she felt disinclined to be the one doing the nudging.

The old war-horse Archie, she determined, was just the one for that little job.

Accordingly she waited for him to finish then suggested sweetly: 'Just supposing that you were to come down on a surprise visit? Then you could judge for yourself if Michael's girl is just another trollop or a woman worth fighting for!'

Like Michael before her she held the receiver away from her ear for several seconds, before interrupting briskly: 'Don't you use that language to me Archie Niven; I know quite well that the police asked you to stop driving after you took that man off his bicycle! Get someone who isn't senile to drive your damned car and you could do it in a day. I always have my nap from two until four so you know when you can talk without disturbing me.'

*   *   *

Wayne was washing his hands under the tap by the greenhouse and looked up warily at Archie's approach, wondering uneasily why the old boy was bearing down on him showing all of his teeth like that. Normally he passed by with only a brief anonymous grunt, which might have been either greeting or some ancient curse.

'Ah – hum – thought I'd missed you!' Archie came to a halt before him. 'Have you got much to do here tomorrow?'

Wayne eyed him mistrustfully.

'I've got the cuttings to do for 'er Ladyship, sor, an' then there's all the watering, but nothin' that Ginger can't do as well.'

'How would you like to earn an extra fifty quid?'

Wayne blinked. He'd already had one brush with the Law over a little matter of a thousand cigarettes that had fallen off the back of a lorry.

Archie gave a brief hoot of laughter.

'It's all legal an' above board if you've a valid licence! Get me down to the Dorset coast and back tomorrow and I'll make it cash in hand.'

'Not in that there ole van of moin oi can't, sor; gearbox 'ud never stand it.'

'Neither would mine!' Archie crooked a bony finger. 'Come with me...'

Minutes later Wayne was gazing awestruck at a dark green Alvis, thirty years old at least, but with gleaming paintwork, polished wooden dashboard and white leather seats. 'Shit!' his eyes gleamed. 'Oi get to drive this *and* fifty quid? Wick-*ed*!'

'Only if I bloody arrive back in one piece; crash the thing and you pay *me* the fifty quid and work the next ten years for nothing!'

'Doan' you worry, sor,' Wayne passed his hands lovingly over the bonnet 'Oi'll treat 'er loik a babby!'

'Right, nine o'clock in the morning sharp – and mind, no boozing tonight, I don't want to sit next to a fartin' beer barrel all the way to

197

Dorset!'

Archie locked the barn door and stumped off to commune with Brenda's twelve thriving offspring and her new *amour*, Stafford-Cripps, an altogether more satisfactory replacement for the useless Michael Foot. *He* was now in the freezer in handy family-sized packages. That was sorted then! Archie began to sing "Somewhere I'll Find You" in a high cracked tenor. Brenda heard him coming and squealed an ecstatic accompaniment.

When Sir Archibald Niven sang then God really was in His heaven and all was well in a pig's world.

*   *   *

Isabel and Cassie relaxed on the veranda, a pitcher of home made lemonade clinking with ice on the low table between them: Cassie lying back on an old-fashioned wood-slatted steamer chair, Isabel very upright in a cane basket chair with a high rounded back. The hush of evening was all about them, broken only by the wind rustling the coarse grass of the dunes and the slow susurration of waves over the sands beyond. Jono had borrowed his late uncle's beach-caster to join a handful of fishermen on the shore and in the thirty minutes since his departure neither woman had spoken. When at last Isabel broke the silence it was to ask a direct question:

'It isn't in my nature to pry, but why are you running so hard from your father and why do you find it so difficult to accept that Michael has struck some kind of rapport with him? Parents can be hell, I know, but Michael is a most discerning man and not one to willingly help anyone whom he didn't think straight and above board.'

'If you knew my father you wouldn't need to ask.' Cassie turned her head and met Isabel's gaze. 'But as you've been so kind and not at all censorious, if you want I'll give you a brief résumé of life with Alaric so far.'

Looking out over the dunes and keeping her voice deliberately unemotional, Cassie gave a swift but clear and honest explanation of her relationship with her father, her non-affair with Michael and the events following her last encounter with each of them. Isabel heard her in silence then gave a barely audible sigh.

'Leaving Michael aside for the moment; why was it so impossible for you to meet your father again and hear what else he had to say?'

Cassie chewed at her lip for a moment then shrugged. 'Cowardice, I suppose. After I'd really taken in what he *had* told me I just couldn't face hearing any more.'

'Have you given any thought to what might have been so important that he would be willing to put himself through another such encounter? The first must have been equally as traumatic and unpleasant for him as for you.'

She answered shortly, 'I haven't let myself think,' then gave another small shrug. 'Why should I speculate on what other nasty shocks he may have up his sleeve? After all, he isn't really my father, is he?'

'That depends what you mean by that title.' The older woman's voice was gentle and without censure. 'One might say that any man who willingly takes on another's child; cares for, protects and loves it, feeds, clothes and educates it and then is courageous enough to tell that child the truth about her parentage and honest enough to admit his own shortcomings, might have earned his status as a father.' She smiled. 'But then I'm only an outsider looking in.'

Cassie was silent, testing her feelings. Somewhere deep down there was a swift spark of anger against Isabel for prodding at her own doubts. A feeling almost immediately overlaid by a creeping guilt as all the memories she had wilfully suppressed for ten years struggled to the surface: Alaric's easy laughter and the safety of his big arms when she was a child. The freedom he had allowed her to roam and explore; his unfailing interest in even the least exciting shell, or ragged piece of seaweed, or fish skeleton she brought proudly back for his inspection. An unconventional childhood certainly, she acknowledged silently, but a very happy one; his eye for a pretty girl and all the changing bedfellows had been accepted, indeed barely noticed by the contented and cherished child she once had been.

Eventually she stirred and one side of her mouth went down in a wry smile.

'I know I must at some time see Alaric; hear whatever else it is he needs to tell me, but not if Michael's around; he was the one who decided I was too young for him, not me: now I couldn't bear to meet him then have to let go again. I could never just be a friend...I love him too much for that.'

While they had been talking night had closed in; now the only light came from the crescent quarter moon and a lamp in the room behind them. Isabel's face was in shadow so that Cassie couldn't read her expression but her voice when she spoke was gentle and compassionate.

'Well, perhaps you should sleep on it, my dear. All things are possible if one wants them sufficiently and is patient enough to wait.' She smiled into the darkness and quoted softly:

"To wake at dawn with a winged heart and
give thanks for another day of loving"
'No bad thought to take to bed alone, is it?'

Cassie stood up and as she passed Isabel's chair, took the hand she held up and squeezed it lightly. 'Not bad at all. Thank you.'

Isabel leaned back and looked out to where the fishermen's lights threw a soft glow at the edge of the dunes.

Well, I've put in my plea for her poor beleaguered father, now all it needs is some little chore to take Jonathan away whilst I am having my nap tomorrow!

She waited for a while before following her visitor into the house, finishing her silent communing with the observation: *If Cassie won't and Michael can't, then Archie dear, I rather think it's all up to you!* Pausing before the portrait in the sitting room she put her fingers first to her lips then laid them lightly on the subject's forehead. *Goodnight, sweet dreams, darling Niki...and don't look at me like that! I know I'm meddling but with a little push in the right direction, who knows? They may even be as happy as we two, if that were possible.'*

23

Michael lay supine for several minutes, testing his hangover, cautiously probing at his temples and moving his eyes from side to side. He winced, God in heaven – that was the first and certainly the last time he would ever attempt to drink himself into oblivion! The telephone began a shrill insistent ringing and groaning aloud he rolled over on the bed, fumbling for the receiver.

'Mr Niven?' The voice was female and polite, but with intimidating undertones.

His tongue felt as though someone had laid asphalt in it while he slept; holding onto the top of his head with his free hand he cleared his throat painfully. 'Yes.'

'This is Sister on Nightingale at St Catherine's. We have been trying to contact you all afternoon.' The voice was cool with reproof. 'You asked to be called when Mrs Harris was due for discharge. As we are very short of beds we were hoping you might take her home today.'

'Right, thank you. I'll be there by...' he glanced at the bedside clock then continued faintly, 'by eight o'clock?'

'That *is* a little late but I'm sure Mrs Harris will be pleased not to spend another night in hospital. I shall tell her to expect you then.'

Oh, God! He sat on the edge of the bed, surveying in the long cheval glass by the window his crumpled clothes and ravaged face. He'd been out for the count for almost six hours! Moving with extreme caution he walked to his bathroom, stripped off his clothes and stood under the shower. He must have at least five minutes of mindless peace beneath the soothing benediction of warm water before facing the prospect of getting shaved, changed and sufficiently recovered in the next half hour to meet the old witch's beady eye with confidence.

But visions of Cassie with Jonathan crowded his brain until it throbbed and jumped like a live thing inside his skull. He shampooed his hair with vicious fingers. The two-timing, deceitful little bitch; how could she do this...keep him hanging on, knowing he was trying to find her...and for what? To pay him back for that far off day when he'd rejected all her arguments and she'd escaped from his house? At the core of his anger was utter bewilderment that she could change from the frank and open girl he had known to such a duplicitous, mendacious liar. At least, he though with rare self-righteousness, I was honest; I never pretended to be something I wasn't and I didn't sleep with anyone else behind *her* back...Here the memory of his afternoon spent in the Merry Widow's bed rose to rebuke him but he swept it aside.

That had been after Cassie left. No one could count *that* against him.

*   *   *

When he reached the hospital Elizabeth was waiting in the empty, echoing hallway. Seated on an upright chair, clutching the holdall with the few belongings he had brought in to her, she looked pathetically small and defenceless and his heart contracted with pity at the sight of her thin, anxious face. But the moment she saw him she drew herself up, the old light returned to her eye and greeted him tartly.

'They didn't have to drag you out – I could have been home hours ago if that fool of a staff nurse had let me call a taxi!'

'Of course you couldn't leave on your own. I'm sorry I didn't hear the 'phone and they were unable to get hold of me earlier, but it's too late for you to go home tonight – you're coming back to Chelsea with me now, then I think The Round House for a few days would be an excellent idea. I have to catch up with some work and it's cooler there.'

'I'm not helpless you know. You don't need me around all the time and I can manage for myself.'

'Now don't start playing me up. Just for once do as I ask, will you?' He took the bag and put a firm hand under her elbow. 'What would you like for supper? I haven't had any and I daresay you could do with a change from hospital food.'

Slyly she attempted to establish the old order. 'I could do some scrambled eggs, sir –'

'You'll do nothing of the sort – and if you start that 'sir' business again I'll take you to the Savoy and order you a plate of squid!'

She gave him a prim disapproving look.

'If you must make yourself responsible for my welfare, then fish and chips would be nice – but eaten properly and off a plate.'

He held the car door open then stood looking down at her, his voice softening, 'I've missed you and needed your hard, wise old head, Lizzie Harris more than you'll ever know.'

For a moment she stared at him intently. 'Hmm, I see...well when we've eaten perhaps you'll tell me what's made you look as though you've been to hell and back – and why you are still alone.'

*   *   *

'So you've given up?' she was scornful. 'Not putting up much of a fight, are you?'

His eyes were steely. 'What's the point? I have no one but myself to blame. However, I was fortunate to discover when I did how little I must have meant to her over these past months. Had I actually found her before I discovered the truth it would have been much more hurtful.' His mouth twisted sarcastically. 'If I have regrets they will pass; everything does, eventually.'

They were in the study, Elizabeth lost in the depths of one of the leather club chairs while Michael perched on the edge of his desk, his arms folded across his chest as though to ward off any concern or pity she might be tempted to express.

'Oh, does it? I don't believe a word of what that young man told you. Cassie is the very last person to have been leading a double life! She may still be refusing to see you – you hurt her badly, you know, and to find you'd allied yourself with her father was the last straw! But whatever you say or believe *I* know that she is incapable of that sort of deceit; anyone with eyes in their head could see that.' She sat back and clasped her hands across her stomach. 'There now, I've said my piece – and much good may it do me. You'll still go your own way and cut her out of your life, won't you?'

'Do I have a choice?'

'Of course you do. Instead of rabbiting about the past you should be thinking of the future – and you might try a charitable thought for Cassie instead of damning her out of hand. Doesn't she at least get the chance to defend herself?'

He said coldly, 'She doesn't need to defend herself to me; I am no longer interested. That boy was *not* lying, damn him! He saw them together all right. Tomorrow we'll go down to Bourne End, then later when you are quite recovered we'll try to put all this behind us and get back into the old routine.'

'Whatever you say,' she was suspiciously docile and he gave her a speculative look.

'I hope you are not thinking of doing any more conniving behind my back. I want neither to see nor hear from Cassandra again. It's over. Understand that.'

'Very well, I won't say any more. I'll just let you go on sneakily

203

steering me away from going back to Pimlico…as if you ever fooled me for more than a minute at a time!' She got heavily to her feet. 'Well, we shall see; "the best laid plans of mice and men…"' momentarily her face puckered into a mischievous grin. 'I wouldn't even put it past you to try getting me back to Ashenham again!'

He rose and looked down on her asking blandly, 'Whatever gave you that idea?'

'You did – I can see your mind working; I always could.'

'Getting back in your stride again, aren't you?' He took her arm to lead her from the room. 'One day, Lizzie, I'll pension you off – but not just yet because I rather think I'm going to need you around for quite some time!'

*   *   *

After Isabel had gone for her nap, Jono departed obediently if reluctantly to the nearest town, with an inordinately lengthy shopping list, leaving Cassie stretched out on the long chair on the veranda with a book. But she wasn't in the mood to read and her attention kept wandering from the printed page. After a few minutes she sighed and lay the book down on her lap, then lulled by the combination of heat and the hum of bees foraging for pollen in the buddleia shrubs she let the book slide to the floor and drifted into a shallow sleep.

She came back to consciousness slowly, aware even before she opened her eyes that she was no longer alone. Peering cautiously between half-closed eyes she saw a very thin, very upright old man was now seated in Isabel's chair. Both hands clasped the handle of an old-fashioned rattan walking stick and the steady dark eyes set deep beneath shaggy grey brows were fixed unblinking on her face. To her startled eyes he looked like an apparition straight out of the Lord of the Rings but without the inevitable beard, although no Gandalf worthy of the name, she thought hazily, would be seen dead in that crumpled linen suit and yellowing Panama hat.

She opened her eyes wider and stared back at him in silence, then suddenly aware that she was showing a great deal of leg in very brief shorts sat up. Hastily doing up the top buttons of her shirt she said crossly: 'I don't know how long you've been there but you might have coughed or something! If you've come to see Isabel she's having a nap and hates to be disturbed.'

'I know. But I didn't come to see her; I came to see you.' He extended a long bony hand. 'My name is Archie Niven. I believe you know my son.'

If he had announced he was a terrorist and had Semtex oozing from every pore she couldn't have been more horrified, but with commendable presence of mind managed to refrain from screaming aloud. Taking the proffered hand she answered shakily, 'How do you do. I'm Cassandra Chisholm.'

'I know who you are,' he said, with a gruff but familiar dryness, 'I've had you described in such detail that I couldn't miss!'

As there really was no answer to this she decided to shut up and leave the ball firmly on his side of the net. He watched her in silence again for a long minute and she raised her chin, staring him out. Eventually he took off his hat and fanned vigorously at his face.

'Can't keep boltin' around the countryside, y'know – bad for morale – yours and his…God knows what he was doing runnin' around with a stubborn little cuss like you – or you with him, for that matter. But as they don't come any more bloody-minded and difficult than my son it seems to me you might have been made for each other; why you don't just get on with it beats me!'

She said heatedly, 'It's not that simple –'

'Neither am I,' he interrupted sharply; 'if I was I'd still be in the comfort of me own home – not botherin' my head over either of you!' He gazed at her severely. 'That spotty little tyke at young Murryfield's place told him you and Sholto's boy have been at it like Jack rabbits for months. Now m'boy is rampaging and hollering around Chelsea like a pig with the squits because thinks the pair of you are shacked-up in a secluded love nest for a week of unbridled lust!'

Silently she cursed that malicious lying little rat Tony before the thought of the calm and controlled Michael acting so completely out of character made her give an involuntary and hastily suppressed snort of laughter. This was ridiculous. The Michael she knew couldn't rampage if he tried!

Then all at once she was hit by the awful realisation that perhaps she didn't really know him at all. It seemed he had the knack of changing his personality to suit his company: where she saw him as sexy and predatory beneath all that control, to Elizabeth he was clearly a man with flawed morals but always a gentleman. Lily accepted him as a physically attractive and forgivable rogue, Simon treated him with the wary caution of a duellist and Jono with extreme caution, as a force to be reckoned with – and how about this old man now watching her so intently? He apparently saw Michael as the prodigal son returned and was prepared to go to any amount of trouble and inconvenience on his behalf.

Cassie thought morosely that rather like the iceberg that sunk the Titanic, only one tenth of Michael Niven showed above the water, and not always the same tenth! All at once the idea of a turbulent and possibly contumacious Michael heading her way was becoming more frightening by the minute.

Something of what she was thinking must have shown on her face because the old man volunteered testily, 'Don't panic woman; he's no idea the pair of you are with Isabel, and if he did I doubt he'd come here after you. Not when he thinks you are playing lovebirds with Jonathan.' He gave a disparaging sniff so reminiscent of Elizabeth Harris that Cassie almost smiled until he added: 'By all accounts *that* young man's no better than his father before him – at least where women are concerned!'

Cassie was nettled at this slight, even though true, on Jono. 'You can leave Jono out of this. He's a *friend* and there aren't a lot of those in my life right now.' She sat with hunched shoulders, gazing at him narrow-eyed. 'I'm not, as you put it, shacked-up with him or anyone else. If Michael chooses to believe whatever that revolting little creep Tony says, what d'you expect *me* to do about it? It seems to me,' she began warming to the task of putting Michael's old man in his place, 'that anyone who's spent as much time jumping between the sheets as your son has a bloody nerve sending his pa down to check up on *me*!'

'He didn't send me.' He rested his chin on the hands clasped over his stick, cocking his head slightly to one side. 'I came quite of my own accord. In fact if the boy knew I was here and talking to you like this he'd blow a ruddy gasket!'

Suddenly in the tilt of his head and dark contemplative stare she could see Michael. Her heart turned and all her high-minded resolve never to see this man's son again left her. All the painfully suppressed feelings of longing and loving returned in one enormous rush that for a moment left her breathless.

She didn't care if Michael was angry, didn't, as Laura would say, give a tinker's cuss if he booted her out of his life with both feet. She just had to see him again and explain if she could, and if he would let her, all the muddled and painful thoughts and feelings that had sent her hurtling off on one disastrous journey after another other since the night they had parted.

She moistened her dry lips with her tongue; shaking her head slightly to clear it, while Archie continued to hold her gaze with his own. Stubbornly she kept the tidal wave of feelings at bay.

'I'm sorry, but the boy, as you call him, gave me one hell of a hard time; I might have believed he really wanted to see me again if I hadn't found he was trailing my father along with him. That was a dirty trick because he knew how I felt about Alaric.'

He gave an emphatic bang on the wooden floor with his stick, 'My son never does anything without a good reason...an' the pair of you have got to clear it up, with or without your bloody father, d'ye hear – 'Tavia and me can't be doin' with it.'

Despite his words his voice was suddenly tired and querulous and he seemed to shrink into his chair. Cassie was horrified: this frail old man had made a long and tiring journey with only one purpose in mind: to plead with her in his own irascible way to help untangle the web that she and Michael had woven between them. She had been rude and thoughtless and if he died on her right here and now it would be all her fault...

Impulsively she leaned forward to lay a hand on his arm. 'It's all right. Please don't worry; if it will help you I'll go to see him. Honestly: I promise. Do you know where he is?'

With a struggle he pulled himself upright again. 'Not sure – The Round House I think...said he was takin' old Lizzie there.' He grasped her hand, asking urgently. 'You're not really rompin' in the hay with Sholto's lad, are you?'

'No, of course I'm not.'

'Ha! I told him that bugger was lying!'

'It's all a bit complicated.' Cassie met the suddenly sharp old eyes and said rashly. 'I'll tell Michael about how Tony got the idea...if he'll listen!'

'Hmm,' he was still holding her hand and gave it a hard squeeze. 'You'll manage, and when the dust has settled you must come and see m'pigs...and 'Tavia of course.' He grinned, 'Amazin' woman my wife. She knew where you were.'

'How?'

'No idea,' he was vague. 'Somethin' to do with lateral thinking. She does a lot of that, my wife. At least, I think that's what it is.'

Cassie was saved from having to reply by the sudden appearance of Jono on the other side of the picket fence. He was carrying two bulging plastic supermarket bags in one hand and struggling to open the gate with the other.

'Cass, give a hand – my frigging arms are dropping off! I couldn't get your car down the track because someone's left a bloody great old relic from the London to Brighton run stuck halfway across it'

Archie said loudly and irascibly, 'I knew that apology for a chauffeur would be off to find a pub as soon as my back was turned!'

Jono froze. 'Uncle Archie!' He dropped both bags and looked

around in panic. 'Where's Michael?' he demanded.

Cassie went swiftly to meet him. 'At least a couple of hour's driving time away from here, so don't get your knickers in a twist. Here, I'll give you a hand.' Taking one of the bags she added in a fierce whisper, 'Whatever you do don't let that old man get one word out of you about that night we once spent in the same bed, or I'll bloody well throttle you!'

'Are you crazy?' Jono rolled his eyes. 'I'd rather have all my teeth pulled.' Summoning his professional actor's smile he approached Archie with outstretched hand.

'Hello, Uncle, I didn't expect to see you here.'

'I daresay. Come and have a chat before your aunt wakes up an' starts askin' questions.' Archie released Jono's hand from a crushing grip and settled himself back in his chair. 'Sit down and let me tell you all about me sow Brenda.'

Jono sniggered. 'Brenda? I didn't know you read Private Eye, uncle!'

'There are a lot of things you don't know about me.'

Cassie said quickly, 'I'll make some tea.' Taking the bags into the kitchen she put the contents away in the cupboards. Jono, she thought with a stab of guilt, would have to hold the fort with the unnerving Archie until she gathered her courage to go out there again.

She swung the kettle from the back of the Aga onto the hotplate then fetched a tray and began taking cups and saucers from the dresser. What a mess; what a simply awful effing bloody mess! She stood clasping the teapot in her hands, staring out of the window to where a Mediterranean-blue sea shimmered in the afternoon heat, her heart racing as she faced up to the fact that her impulsive promise to talk to Michael would have to be carried through.

'What the hell am I to say to him when I get there?' she wondered aloud. '"Sorry Michael if I've cocked-up on the last few months; subverted your housekeeper and made myself free of both your houses," that would be a great opening line wouldn't it? Or perhaps "Because I was out of my mind at losing you I invited Jono into my bed."' She shuddered. 'No, not that, I couldn't say that to a nice, cool, calm Michael, let alone one who, mad as it may seem, thinks I've been making it with Jono for months and is now apparently about as restrained and forgiving as an enraged bull elephant with a bullet in its bum!'

The door opened and Isabel entered the kitchen fresh from her siesta; Cassie blushed, wondering if she had been overheard. She asked hastily, 'Hello – we have a visitor, did you know?'

'Yes.' Isabel smiled. 'He woke me up extolling the virtues and merits of his pigs and chickens to Jonathan.'

Cassie gulped. 'Oh, God, Isabel, we were having a bit of a ding-dong and I was all set to demolish him when he went all frail and upset. I felt so guilty that he was old and tired and miserable that I said I'd see Michael.' Still clutching the teapot she sat down suddenly at the table, her face white. 'What am I going to *do*?'

'Do? See Michael of course.' Taking the teapot from her nerveless fingers Isabel finished preparing the tray, moving with unhurried efficiency from worktop to table, setting out milk jug, sugar bowl and biscuit barrel. Cassie watched her silently whilst her stomach performed complicated gyrations and her knees jittered as though someone was pulling strings in her feet. It wasn't so much fear of Michael's anger that was causing her turmoil, because she couldn't really believe in that; rather it was the greater dread of cold rejection, or polite indifference and a courteous showing her the door.

As Isabel lifted the tray she blurted, 'I don't think I can go out there again and make small talk to his father.'

'Yes you can.' Isabel handed her the tray and for a moment held her hands clasped over Cassie's. 'Anyone can do anything if they try, and anyway, Archie wouldn't know how to make small talk. Now carry that outside and we'll all have a civilised cup of tea.' She smiled and held open the door. 'Spending another hour with his crafty old father is a small price to pay for being pushed into being able to tell Michael that you love him, isn't it?'

'You don't know the half of it yet or you wouldn't say that!' Cassie retorted. 'I doubt very much that I shall get nearer than the front door – and what do you mean, pushed? – I wasn't *pushed* into anything!'

'Were you not?' She smiled again. 'If that is so, then Archie must have lost his touch. Think about it, and you'll see what I mean.' Leaving her words to sink in she made her way out onto the veranda and Cassie followed slowly.

Reluctantly she had to acknowledge that Isabel was right: the old man had played her like a fish, and was intent on landing her just where he wanted her – at Michael's feet!

*   *   *

Tired as he was, Archie enjoyed his return journey. He was pleased with himself; he may be old, he thought, but he knew how to handle a filly, and that girl of Michael's was some filly. He let go a throaty

209

chuckle that ended in a cough and had Wayne looking nervously at him in the rear-view mirror. Archie poked his stick at the boy's shoulder. 'Keep your eyes on the road – I ain't about to croak yet!' he informed him tersely. He stretched his legs, folded his hands over his barely discernable old man's paunch and closing his eyes thought about that young filly's lovely legs. He'd always admired a good pair of legs on a woman. A little sigh of contentment puffed his lips. He hoped they'd get on with the baby business pdq...his head nodded forward; 'Tavia would like that: he smiled in his sleep.

Wayne glanced in the rear view mirror again and grinned. He put his foot down on the accelerator and the Alvis gathered speed. Just wait until they hit the motorway, he thought, keeping a wary eye on the slumbering Archie, then if the old geezer stayed asleep he'd *really* let her go.

24

On reaching The Round House, Michael gave up trying to make Elizabeth take a rest from her housekeeping duties. When she had pointedly addressed him as 'sir' three times in succession he took the hint and retreated to the study. Seating himself at his desk and pulling the 'phone towards him he thumbed through his diary until he found the telephone number in Cornwall that Alaric had left.

Better to break the bad news now rather than later.

*   *   *

'Alaric? It's Michael Niven. I'm not disturbing your work, am I?'

'No.' Alaric stood back from his easel, brush in one hand and telephone in the other. 'Glad to hear from you; your friend Simon 'phoned Laura yesterday to tell her Mrs Harris was out of hospital. Is she all right now?'

'Yes, and driving me spare.' Michael's voice was laconic. 'I don't know what else Simon told your sister...?' he left the question open.

Alaric was silent for a moment. 'Still no luck, then?'

'No, not yet...Look, I'm sorry about this but I have to tell you there is no point in *my* continuing to look for Cassandra. I don't want to go into details but as things now stand I imagine either you or your sister will have more chance of getting her down to Cornwall than I. That is,' he added astringently, 'if you can find her!'

'Why? What's changed?' Alaric put down his brush and seated himself in a chair, weariness invading his mind and body at the certainty that the news he was about to hear would be anything but welcome.

'Quite a lot,' beneath the apparently unemotional tone Alaric could hear the hurt. 'She is, to use the modern idiom, happily shacked up with my young cousin and apparently has been for months. That being so I have no intention of pursuing her further –'

'Are you sure about this?' Alaric interrupted him. 'She certainly gave Laura the impression that she had a bad case of unrequited love – for you.'

Michael answered tautly, 'Laura is not alone in thinking that. I could name you at least three other people who would swear the same on a stack of Bibles, or possibly the Torah. Just to clinch matters, the pair of them are at present on holiday together; where, I have no idea, but as Jonathan is apparently due back at the theatre this weekend and Cassandra still needs to earn her living, I imagine she will return with him.'

'Right,' Alaric in turn tried to mask his weariness and disappointment. 'If you'll let me have the boyfriend's address I'll give them time to get back and settle down, then either Laura or myself will do our best to persuade her to come back here – at least for the wedding. She can hardly refuse to attend that.'

Michael's reply was caustic. 'Don't count on it. Your daughter is a law unto herself.'

'Yes, she is isn't she; all the same, I would have sworn she was too honest and up-front to live the sort of a lie you think her capable of.' He was silent a moment, then asked tentatively, 'Are you saying you *won't* see her again?'

'Not willingly or voluntarily, I won't.'

'I'm sorry.'

Michael said abruptly. 'Keep in touch with me. I'd like to know how things work out for you.'

'Sure. You never know: I may get lucky. I'll call if and when I have any news of her.'

Alaric put the handset down and sat for some moments deep in thought; then stood again and picking up his brush addressed the canvass set on his easel.

'You'd better turn up again before it's too late, my girl, because I've never yet left a painting unfinished...but I can't get you; I just can't get you now without seeing you again.'

Cassie's face looked back at him: unsubstantial, cloudy and unfinished; as it would remain unless, or until, she returned.

*   *   *

'She will be back.' Laura poured him a small brandy and gave it to him neat. 'I know her. Cassie is neither spiteful nor uncaring, but she's been through a lot over these past few months.' Her lips tightened angrily. 'She was just getting back on her feet after the Lingard disaster when along comes Mr Niven and tips her world upside down again – it's his fault entirely that she left him, and if she's changed her mind and gone for her friend Jono, he's only himself to blame.'

Alaric said heatedly. 'Defend her all you like, but clearing off like that and leaving the poor bloke to chase around the countryside after

212

her…I thought better of her than that.'

'You seem to forget: initially it wasn't him she was running from, it was you.' Laura was dangerously close to losing patience with her brother. 'After all, you turned up out of the blue and told her things she didn't want to know then chickened-out of finishing the job. Now because you wouldn't let *me* tell her you were returning home for good, she thinks Miles and I let her down as well – which we did in a way.'

Miles put in quietly, 'For God's sake you two, stop picking it over. I doubt very much that she's having an affair with anyone, but until she can stop running long enough to think things through herself, or alternatively stand still while someone gives her a helping hand in the right direction, we'll never know, will we?'

They both turned startled eyes on him where he sat drawing on his pipe and he gazed back unperturbed. 'No need to look as though the sky's fallen in; it's true: I don't wonder she buggered off. Laura, *you* should stop apportioning blame and behaving as though she's still in need of your protection. Alaric, *you* should have levelled with her long before you did, but rather less dramatically; as for Michael Niven, he should have come down off bloody Mount Olympus and treated her as an equal instead of an immature teenager.' He stood up. 'She's not a pathetic child, but a lovely intelligent young woman doing her best to stay afloat in other people's mucky waters. Now I think I'll take a turn in the garden before either or both of you drive me completely nuts!'

Turning, he made a dignified exit through the French windows; Laura stared after him then gave her brother a rueful smile. 'He's right, you know.'

'Of course he is, but I'd rather he hadn't said it.' Alaric scowled. 'This country appears to be infested with laid-back men several years my junior who are exceedingly good at getting under my skin – much more of it and I'll begin to wish I'd stayed in Paris.'

Laura linked her arm with his, mocking, 'That's more like the Alaric we all know and love!' She was suddenly thoughtful. 'It's quite true that the onlooker, in this case Miles, sees most of the game. I *have* continued to treat her as a child and you have been trying to get in too close, too soon. Now we must both stand back and wait for her.'

He grimaced then laughed with her. 'OK – but what happened to the old Laura, who would have let fly at any man who as good as told her to shut up? Harry wouldn't have got away with that.'

She smiled and pressed his arm. 'Oh, like Cassie, I guess the old

Laura just fell in love again!'

*   *   *

Cassie stood and watched Archie's car out of sight then turned to Isobel. 'I have to go now – as soon as I've packed,' she was apologetic. 'I'm really sorry if I seem ungrateful Isabel – and Jono, I hate leaving you in the lurch but if I wait until morning I'll feel even less like going. You do understand, don't you?'

'Of course, but you won't be there until quite late – not, perhaps the best time of the day to beard the lion in his den!' Isabel was concerned.

Cassie gave an uncertain laugh. 'But much easier to make my escape under cover of darkness if he cuts up rough.'

'I'll come with you, if you like,' Jono volunteered. 'The two of us together should be able to convince him that shit-for-brains Tony got it wrong; besides, I can't wait to get back and chuck him out of my flat – that's after I've blacked the little scumbag's eye for him.'

She shook her head. 'No, you stay here and I'll come back for you as soon as I've got it over and done with – you need your break and I daresay I'll need a couple of days to recuperate before I start work again.' She grinned suddenly. 'Then we can both go find Tony and black an eye each!'

Isabel looked disapproving but her eyes sparkled with laughter as she admonished, 'Not both eyes at once my dears; that would be just too unkind.'

*   *   *

By the time Cassie passed Reading it was almost dark. Leaden clouds began to obscure a pale moon and there was a hushed and heavy feel to the air that presaged thunder. The long hot summer, she thought glumly, was about to break and once she had kept her promise to Archie to meet Michael again, her journey on to the Carrington afterwards was likely to be as stormy as the confrontation now coming inexorably closer.

She drove fast and with every mile her anxiety heightened, so that by the time the Round House finally came into sight her nerve had almost deserted her. Stopping well short of the gates she sat for a moment gathering whatever shreds of courage remained. Leaving the car parked close against a hedge she covered the last twenty yards on foot.

Cautiously pushing open the gate she saw the Mercedes was parked in the drive and there were lights in the hall and study. Avoiding the gravelled path that ran past the curtained windows of the latter she walked on the grass round to the back of the house. When she saw light streaming across the lawn from the kitchen window she gave little sigh of relief and holding her breath, reached to steady herself against the sill and peer inside.

A quick glance showed her there was no sign of Michael: only Elizabeth Harris stood by the stove, pouring water from a steaming kettle into a teapot. Waiting until the housekeeper had returned the kettle to the hob Cassie tapped gently on the window and Elizabeth looked up her eyes widening with alarm. Quickly Cassie put her finger to her lips then pointed towards the back door.

Elizabeth hurried to open it, drawing her in and kissing her cheek.

'You gave me a fright!' she pulled out a chair and sat down. 'Where on earth have you *been*? I was so worried about you.'

'In Dorset with Jono and his aunt Isabel...and I was so worried about *you*.' Cassie held both of her hands in her own. 'Are you really recovered?' She smiled. 'You don't look any different, except for that colourful eye!'

'Oh, *that*,' Elizabeth gave a dismissive sniff. 'I'd forgotten all about that – you didn't think I'd let some little toe-rag put me off my feet for long, did you?'

'No. Not really.' Cassie kept hold of her hands, feeling warmth and courage seeping through her from their firm and steady grip. 'I've come to talk to Michael, but I'm so glad I could see you first because I've got the most awful attack of cold feet.'

'Well, my dear, from the mood he's been in this past day or two you'll not find it an easy meeting.' Elizabeth gave her a long look, her eyes shrewd and assessing. '*I* don't believe you've been sleeping with that young man all this time, but he does and he's made up his mind that he won't see or speak to you again. That lodger must have been very convincing.'

'I'm sure he was.' Cassie wasn't to be drawn. 'I see the study light is on. Is he in there?'

'Yes.'

'Then I'd better go and get it over with. I promised his father, you see.'

'You've seen *him*?' Elizabeth's expression was a wonderful mixture of dismay and a kind of wicked mirth. 'I'll bet that set the fur flying!'

'Almost, but I liked him and I think he liked me – and it's nice to

215

know there's one member of the Niven family who doesn't want to cut my throat.' Cassie stooped to give her a swift kiss. 'Wish me luck,' she said and left quickly, shoulders well back, head held high but with her stomach gyrating with apprehension and something like fear.

Then with her fingers on the handle of the study door she had a sudden resurrection of fighting spirit; there was no way she was going into that room to grovel and beg for forgiveness. So she'd deliberately avoided Michael and her father and led them a bit of dance over these past few days; what was so awful about that? She had got out of Michael's life as he had wanted her to – how had she been supposed to know he would come looking for her again, and with Alaric on tow?

The small matter of having spent a night, however innocent, with Jono though, was quite a different kettle of fish. Thanks to Tony's exaggerated flights of fancy that might prove to be a very hairy topic indeed.

Pressing down on the brass handle she pushed open the door and stepped quietly but determinedly into the room.

25

Michael sat at his desk, staring at a page of doodles and turning a pencil between his fingers. At the sound of the opening door he looked up and for a few moments time hung suspended. Thinking about it later, he was convinced that he'd felt an actual physical blow around the region of his heart and that for a long minute had ceased to draw a single breath.

Every detail of her appearance: her face, form, even the way her eyes first narrowed, then widened again was startlingly clear. Like an image caught in the click of a camera lens she stood unmoving, her back against the door and with both hands behind her.

He let his gaze pass slowly over the soft ankle length dress that moulded her body; drawn to her full height she stood poised and tall and he realised with sudden shock that this wasn't the young girl who had fled his house all those weeks ago. This was a grown woman with a new certainty and determination showing clearly in the way she was regarding him with her challenging level gaze.

Ruthlessly he suppressed his immediate shock of desire, aware that she had come not as a bewildered and wounded child, expecting to be first scolded, then perhaps forgiven but as an equal with parity and strength, ready to fight if necessary. Then out of the corner of his eye he saw the door move fractionally and knew the old uncertain Cassie was there still, just beneath the surface.

'You can drop the façade and let go the door handle now,' he observed with heavy sarcasm, 'I promise you don't need to keep that avenue of escape open!'

She flushed, letting her hands drop, but stayed by the door and kept her dark eyes steady on his face.

'Hello, Michael.'

His grip on the pencil tightened until it snapped between his fingers. 'Hello, Cassandra.'

He forced himself to stay seated when his heart told him to cross the space between them and take her in his arms. But that wouldn't solve anything, nor alter the fact that she had lied to and deceived him. In this contest between the head and the heart, he couldn't afford to let the heart win. He asked coldly, 'What do you want?'

Her back stiffened and she thought with sudden belligerence: *To have a bloody good row with you, you supercilious bastard!*

He saw the flash of anger in her eyes and felt his own temper begin to rise dangerously. When she remained silent he demanded harshly, 'Where and with whom have you been for this past week?'

'*That* is none of your business. In any case I'm sure you know exactly where I've been.'

'Not during recent days I don't.'

'I'm surprised you didn't get straight on the 'phone to God and find out!' she snapped, 'but to put you out of your misery, I've been in Dorset with Isabel.'

'Why?'

'Why not? You don't have a monopoly on *all* your family members, do you?' She gave an indifferent shrug. 'At the time it seemed a good idea and I was enjoying myself, but that was before your mother apparently got the second sight and sent your father visiting.' Her eyes didn't waver from his intimidating stare but there was a sudden catch in her voice. 'You should have warned me about him.'

'I might have, had you given me the chance, though I can't imagine why my father should think it any business of his to travel from Norfolk to Dorset to see someone that he knows quite well I don't want to meet again. Particularly since that someone had taken such pains to ensure that they didn't meet with *me*.'

For the first time she looked away. 'You set the ball rolling when you told him I was sleeping with Jono; he came to see for himself if that was true.'

'Ah,' he was caustic. 'No doubt he gave you a hard time.'

'No. He knew you were wrong.'

With dangerous quiet he asked, 'Was I?'

'Yes, you bloody-well were...' She hesitated for a split second before adding, 'in a way!'

He jumped to his feet and came around the desk positively oozing menace, but she stood her ground. Putting up a hand she said, 'That's near enough; come any closer and I'm off!'

She was pale beneath her tan and her voice shook. He stopped, his face dark with anger, 'All right, but I want to hear the truth even if it's what I think it is,' he spoke through teeth clenched so hard that his jaw ached. Struggling to banish from his head the images of her with Jono that had haunted him for these past days he repeated with ominous calm: 'I want to hear the truth and I want to hear it *now* – and no more prevarication.'

Cassie measured the stretch of carpet between them and prudently moved several steps sideways and behind a chair. Steadying herself with a hand on the back she said icily, 'In case you had forgotten, it was *you* who told me to get out of your life and find one of my own …' she faltered slightly, then drawing a deep breath went on with a rush, 'I don't remember where I went or what I did after I left you that evening, but I must have walked around for hours in the pouring rain because it was dark when I fetched up at Jono's place…'

Watching her face as she related the bald facts of that night Michael realised that in seeking to do what he had thought was the right thing, he might quite literally have pushed her straight into another man's arms. The anger he had directed against her was now turned against himself as he heard her out in a savage, ashamed silence.

She stood gripping the chair with both hands, keeping it between them, trying to read his face. She said quietly. 'Whatever you may think, I was only looking for comfort and Jono happened to be there. Yes, we spent the night together but we didn't make love. He didn't get into bed with the intention of having sex with me and I didn't invite him in for that reason.'

He admitted with bitter irony, 'Well I think you should know that shortly afterwards I *did* get into bed with precisely that intention. It wasn't, you may be interested to know, at all satisfactory.'

'Really?' she mocked, 'that must have been a first!' He moved a step nearer and she cast a fleeting glance back at the door.

Christ, he thought, you take one step towards that door and I really will break your bloody neck! Controlling himself with an effort he said, 'If you are expecting an apology for treating you the way I did, you've got it. If you want another for my thinking you capable of carrying on any kind of affair beneath my nose for months on end, you've got that, too. Anything else you'll have to grovel for –'

'*Months?*' she interrupted him. 'Are you saying that you actually thought me capable of making it with Jono while you and I were still meeting?'

'The information I was given certainly had the ring of truth about it,' he said stiffly. Slowly under her outraged gaze he actually felt a blush beginning to rise about his ears. He closed his eyes. 'Oh, God, that little bastard said you'd been at it for months and I just…I just…' he foundered.

'Jumped the gun and thought I'd prefer a stud-muffin like Jono to you?' she asked with withering sarcasm. 'No wonder your father said you were rampaging around and hollering like a pig with the squits!'

He took another step towards her and she could almost see the heat begin to simmer around him. Unsure whether it came from lust or fury she decided that either way she'd be safer out of it. Controlling an urge to run screaming from the room she half turned to go, saying dismissively, 'As beneath your usual mightily impressive and stoical calm you are probably still spitting nails, I might as well shove off.'

'You'll do nothing of the kind!' His roar would have equalled Archie's. 'I want this sorted out right now, and if you so much as try to do another runner so help me, I'll brain you.' He slapped his open hand onto the desk, shouting belligerently, 'Why the bloody hell did you bolt like that you goddamned, irritating, idiotic bitch?'

She yelled, 'Because you told me to go you stupid, arrogant, bloody-minded moron!'

They stood facing each other for what seemed to be an eternity: in the silence Michael could hear her breathing de-escalate in a series of painful gulps. Light-headed and breathless he had no defence left now against the desire that had began to flood through him from the moment he'd looked up and seen her standing at the doorway. Waiting until his own chest had ceased heaving and without taking his eyes from hers he leaned to push the play button on the CD. As music filled the room he enquired with all the exquisite formality of a duke at a soiree, 'Can you dance without head-banging?'

She said with shaky defiance, 'Yes... but you can't dance to this.'

'You can the way I do it,' he said, and with a shaft of pure delight saw the corners of that long mouth tuck in on a familiar smile as he took her hand and spun her into his arms, then wrapping them around her began to move to the music.

*   *   *

Now miraculously she was where she had longed to be, but still she held back from complete surrender, a small insidious voice warning: *You know this man even less than you knew Oliver and he's already hurt you once; don't give him the chance to do it again.*

Michael felt her withdrawal and held her even closer. 'Relax, let go...trust me, darling Cass.'

Now you're here and I know just where I'm going
No more doubts or fears, I'm on my way...

Beneath the twin assault on her senses of Ol' Blue Eye's provocative, sexy tones and Michael's body hard against her own she lost the battle with the voice of reason. Surrendering to a languid arousal she couldn't have halted if she'd tried, she let him do as he wished. This could hardly be called dancing she thought dreamily, winding her arms about his neck as his hands moved from the small of her back to caress her hips and the base of her spine; seduction to music perhaps, but not dancing.

The track ended; they remained close and swaying gently to and fro. 'Yes?' he asked with his mouth close against hers and when she answered, 'Absolutely, yes!' put an arm about her shoulders and walked her slowly from the study and up the long curving staircase to his room.

Once inside he shut the door with his foot, his fingers found the long zip at her back and her dress slid to the floor. Unresisting she stood smiling up into his eyes; every man's fantasy: wispy white lace against smooth olive brown skin. She murmured, 'What will Elizabeth think?'

'That it's about fucking time!' he answered and closed his mouth hard on hers.

*   *   *

For a man who presented such a calm and impregnable image to the world Michael Niven was a breathtakingly unconstrained and uninhibited lover. First astonished then exhilarated, Cassie responded to the unleashing of this unexpectedly erotic onslaught with a degree of wanton abandonment that surprised her and delighted Michael.

'*Wow*!' She gave a muted shriek as he sent her spiralling to reach for and capture the ultimate prize, and, '*Wow*!' she crowed again as a nanosecond later he reached for and captured it with her. As he collapsed into her arms she gasped weakly, 'Where does a man learn to do all *that*?' and felt his chest heave with laughter.

'It might just be,' he answered, 'that *this* man has an Encyclopaedia of Erotica on his shelves.'

'And it might just be that this man has had a lot of practice!' she observed, surprised to find that now she didn't mind about all the others, who had undoubtedly contributed to such expertise while sharing the favours and the sexual charisma of Michael Niven; after all she was the one reaping the final reward.

For a while she watched the reflected water wavering across the ceiling then murmured meditatively, 'It was never like that with Oliver.'

'Do you mind – I don't want *him* in bed with us!'

'Can we do it again?'

'Why not...give me another ten minutes...ahhh...' She wound her arms and legs around him. He opened his eyes wide. 'On second thoughts, if you are going to do *that*, perhaps a five will suffice!'

221

*   *   *

There was a roll of thunder and then the rain came, drumming on the tiles and cascading from the beleaguered gutters; Cassie, torn rudely from a deep sleep awoke and for a confused moment struggled against the arm lying across her body. Then Michael's voice spoke in her ear. 'It's all right. Just a storm,' and she relaxed back against his warm nakedness. Seconds later lightning stabbed the heavens and she shivered, pulling the sheet to cover them. He asked: 'Are you afraid?'

'No, just cold,' she ran her hand across his chest and down over his taut stomach, remembering and relishing the night. 'You see, I was right and you were wrong: you weren't too old for me and I wasn't too young for you!'

He demurred. 'All the same, I'm no Keanu Reeves – after all that I feel rather more on a par with Michael Douglas!'

She gave her husky laugh. 'I've always fancied Michael Douglas! Anyway, he's loads older than you but it didn't stop him pulling KZJ did it?'

'True.' He curved a hand around her breast, caressing her with his thumb. 'I knew I was right. You didn't need lycra and an uplift bra.'

'Umm, I noticed you working that one out the second time we met.'

'Was I that obvious?' He leaned on one elbow and looked down on her. 'I've spent so much time these past months thinking about your body that I can't believe it's actually lying here next to mine.' He traced a finger over her face. 'You look and feel,' he said, 'like a woman who's been thoroughly made love to.'

'That's because I have.'

He reached to turn on the bedside lamp then lay back, cradling her head against his shoulder.

'As neither of us are likely to get to sleep again while this storm lasts, I think I ought to tell you something I was saving until the morning.'

Cassie watched the rain cascading down the great window, turning it into a giant waterfall. She said, *'Ce n'est pas le moment!'*

'What makes you say that?'

'You've got that old stuffy, anal-retentive note in your voice, that's why.'

'Excuse me? That's a disgusting thing to say to a man who's spent half the night giving you his all!'

She twisted her head to stare into his eyes. 'It's about you, isn't it

– it's something you've done? I'm not stupid, you know. I knew right from the beginning that you were hiding something; that it wasn't only the age thing that made you hold back.'

'You are not an easy woman to fool, are you?' He pushed the hair away from her forehead with a gentle hand. 'But, darling, you've grown a great deal over the past five months...you really did have your blinkers on about me then, didn't you?'

'Yes, I suppose I did,' she gave an embarrassed grin, 'I think I shocked myself, never mind you, that night I told you I was falling in love with you.'

His mouth twitched. 'You did rather take the wind out of my sails.' He was silent for a few moments. 'There is something very important that you must know about me; something you might find it hard to accept, but before I tell you, I want you to understand and believe how much I love you and everything about you...'

'*Everything,* are you sure about that?'

'Everything; I love the way you look and move and laugh. I love the way you stick your chin in the air when you are going to be stroppy and unreasonable, and I love the way your eyes give you away when you are about to tell a whopping great lie! I love the way you make love and what your body does to mine. I love *you*.'

He paused and she caught at his hand and held it tightly, feeling a small shiver of apprehension. 'Whatever it is you don't have to tell me; I won't ever pry or try to make you.'

He looked soberly back at her then kissed her eyes. 'I must.' He took a deep breath. 'Now, here begineth the sordid confessions of Michael Howard Gervaise Archibald Niven...' he peered suspiciously at her mouth, 'and if that infinitesimal grin I can see beginning gets any wider, I shall slap you!'

*   *   *

He propped himself against the pillows, holding her so that she couldn't see his face.

'A little over ten years ago I was at a party with Simon and Lily when one of Simon's best clients, a wine-grower from Provence, arrived with his daughter Francine.' He made a wry face. 'My first meeting with her had pretty much the same impact as I imagine Alaric's with your mother. Lily says she introduced us but I didn't hear her; I was too busy falling like the proverbial ton of bricks. Francine was quite unbelievably beautiful but also, as I was to discover much too late, an unstable nymphomaniac lush. I'd just had

223

my first book published and was still lecturing at the University, but as her visit to this country coincided with the long summer vacation, I had time on my hands and the money to give her a good time around the London clubs and night-spots.

'When she and her father were due to return home she suggested I went back with them. By then too blinded by love and lust to take in the fact that she was a spoilt, massively overindulged only child of a doting widowed father, who since infancy had let her have her own way in almost everything, I was off like a shot. However, I was brought down to earth with a crash a month later when I was about to return home for the new University term and she announced over breakfast one morning that she was pregnant. Papa la Roache was overjoyed, and I suspect relieved, that his darling daughter's extravagances could now be transferred to someone else's bank balance. I only wished I could have been so happy. She was on the pill, but it was sheer stupidity on my part not to have realised that given the amount of wine she managed to down each day, she would be unreliable about taking it. I couldn't, in all conscience back out of my responsibilities, and in less time than it took to say "American Express" we were well and truly married. Papa settled us in our own cosy little love nest close by the vineyard and that seemed to be that.'

He stopped as though waiting for her to comment, but when she remained silent continued, 'I admit that the very last thing I wanted at that time in my life was a child. I hadn't even got around to telling my parents about my marriage, never mind springing on them a prospective grandson: my father might be desperate for me to provide an heir but he loathed France and everything French. I just couldn't see him accepting Francine and she had no intention of doing the dutiful daughter-in-law bit by living with me at Ashenham. I knew that sometime I would have to face my parents with the whole ghastly mess, but later rather than sooner. Anyway, even that prospect rapidly receded into the background when within a few weeks things started to go badly wrong.

'I was still totally besotted with Francine and I suppose I went way over the top. She was my wife and carrying my child and I wanted to protect her and keep her close, which was a big mistake. She'd always been free to do as she wished and I was, I admit, a jealous husband who resented the habit she had of suddenly disappearing for hours – on occasions, all night – and refusing to say where she'd been. The rows were tremendous. She could be paranoid, accusing *me* of having affairs and of being the worst kind of chauvinist pig in expecting her to behave like a *bourgeois* British housewife. After a few weeks of this the interior walls of our love nest had collected some very impressive dents and we'd hardly a decent piece of crockery left!'

He paused again and made his characteristic gesture of pinching his lower lip while a pulse in his temple began to jump. 'Being pregnant didn't seem to be a bar to enjoying herself,' he continued, 'and it wasn't long before someone was kind enough to tell me I was sharing my new wife with a local teenage Lothario. We fought – God, how we fought! If it hadn't been for the child I think I might have killed her, but somehow I kept my hands off her and we jogged along until Gervaise was born.

'He was a small sickly baby who cried a lot and Francine took no more interest in him than she did in me. I didn't cope very well with a crying baby and a faithless and increasingly alcoholic wife, so I engaged a local girl to look after him while I spent a few hours each day trying to write another book. By then I was getting desperate. I'd had to give up my University post and my advance from the book was running out. Papa la Roache was keeping a tight hold on *his* purse strings and Francine was going through my capital like a forest fire. In addition to all this I was living a totally unnatural life. Rowing and fighting was meat and drink to Francine but anathema to me. I'm a peaceable kind of man and in normal circumstances it takes a lot to make me lose my temper, but circumstances weren't normal and I knew that sooner or later something, or someone, would have to give.

'One night when Gervaise was about three months old I had to go to Paris, to the library of the Sorbonne for some books I needed for reference. The baby wasn't well and I asked Francine to be sure and stay with him and to call the doctor if he didn't improve. When I came back the following evening he was in his cot, vomiting and running a high fever and obviously very ill. The girl from the village who was supposed to be looking after him was in our bedroom shagging her boyfriend and Francine nowhere in sight.

'I think I went a little mad then. I kicked the boyfriend out – quite literally – down the steps and into the road, and sent the girl to find Francine, threatening I'd break her neck if she didn't come back with her pdq. Meantime I cleaned Gervaise up, wrapped him in blankets and put him in his Moses basket.

'It was only some six kilometres to the nearest hospital but it had been snowing heavily and the roads were treacherous, with deep drifts on the lanes and hard packed snow and ice on the main roads. I decided to take the old Land Rover that was used mainly for running around the vineyard. Although it only had a soft top there was a good heater and I felt it would be safer and hold the road better than my own car. There weren't any seat belts so I got some cord and secured the Moses basket on the back seat, making sure neither it nor the baby would shift if there was a skid or we hit a patch of deep snow.

'Francine arrived just as I was about to leave. She'd been drinking as usual and immediately demanded I should take Gervaise back into the house, insisting that there was nothing wrong with him the local doctor couldn't put right in the morning. I didn't stop to argue. I stuffed her in the back and told her to keep hold of the Moses basket. I drove as fast as I dared; Francine started cursing me and hanging over my shoulder and I could smell not only the wine on her breath but the unmistakable odour of stale sex and knew she'd been with a man. I called her a whore and swung my arm back to hit her. She began clawing her way over into the front seat, wrenching at the wheel and tearing at my hair and face. I lost control and we went into a massive skid; there was a tremendous crash and the car began turning over and over down a bank towards the river.

'Francine and I were thrown clear and both ended up in hospital: she with a fractured collarbone, me with concussion and a fractured femur. Gervaise was still in the car when it went through the ice and into the river...'

For the first time Cassie turned her head to look at him. His face was grey and his eyes closed. The pulse jumping in his temple seemed like a live thing beneath the tightened skin and his whole body was clammy with sweat. After a long silence he roused himself and shook his head. 'Give me a moment...'

Sitting up she turned to face him, putting both hands over his and clasping them tightly. 'Go on.'

He drew a long shuddering breath. 'I remember lying halfway down the bank, watching the vehicle sink and being unable to move...I think that memory will be with me until the day I die. He is buried in the graveyard of a little church near the vineyard and I go sometimes. Francine still lives nearby. Her father fetched her from the hospital the day after the crash and we have never met since. I'd rather keep it that way. I came back to this country leaving Francine to get a mercifully quick divorce.'

He stopped speaking and sat for a moment in silence, weighing her hands in his. 'Now you know that the Michael you thought so safe and controlled was just a sham. I'm human and, as you saw when you first arrived here last night, with the potential to be as nasty and brutish and cowardly and out of control as the next man. I didn't even have the courage to tell my parents about my marriage until a few weeks ago. Only Lily and Simon knew, because of their connection with Francine's family. Simon tells me she has recently re-married, but there are, thank God, no children. I am not proud of any part of my marriage and I shall feel guilt for my son's death for the rest of my life. It was I who made the decision to take the Land Rover and who made sure he didn't have the chance to be thrown clear like us.'

Still holding his hands she asked, 'Why didn't you tell me about this ages ago? Why did you keep the wall between us?'

He frowned, puzzled. 'What wall?'

'The one you built in there.' She touched his forehead.

He shrugged, 'Perhaps because I was already half-way towards being in love again and I thought you would leave me if you knew.'

She said with a touching honesty that made him smile, 'I might have, then.'

'Ah, but what will you do now?'

She put her arms about him, for a moment she laid her head against his then sat back, her eyes searching his drawn face.

'What else but say thank you for telling me; thank you for being brave and honest; thank you for letting me past the wall,' she took his head between her hands and kissed him then reaching past him turned out the light and drew him down into her embrace. 'I didn't think it was possible to feel any more love for you than I already had, but it is, it is.'

He was still, his head heavy against her shoulder. 'Until tonight I couldn't mourn for my son...I could feel anger and guilt and grief, but I couldn't mourn...'

His voice broke and after a few moments he began to weep; great tearing sobs that shook his whole body, and she stroked his hair and rocked him gently until eventually, still clasped in her arms he fell into an exhausted sleep.

She lay awake for a long time listening to the dying rumble of the storm as it moved away, leaving only the occasional flash of distant lightning and the sound of rain pattering gently on the roof. Michael's face was turned onto her breast and she could feel the occasional flutter of his eyelashes and his breath warm against her skin.

In years to come, when she looked back on that night it wasn't their lovemaking, the joyous exploration and the passionate fusion of their bodies that she remembered most clearly. It was the deep, almost mystical experience of holding the sleeping Michael in her arms, knowing that he had turned to her in his pain and sorrow, and that she had not failed him.

*   *   *

When Cassie awoke she was alone. Putting out her hand she found the still warm imprint of Michael's body on the sheet and with a sigh of pleasure rolled to cover it with her own. Watching the flow of reflected water over the ceiling she played over in her mind the hours since she had walked into this house. In the pale morning sun the moving patterns were wavering and insubstantial and she could feel the first chill of autumn spicing the air. It had been right, she thought, that the first time they made love it should be in this room which had so enchanted her when she had seen it all those months before.

Michael appeared from the adjacent bathroom, vigorously towelling his wet hair and wearing a dark blue silk brocade dressing gown. She sat up smiling as he came towards her. 'How very Oscar Wilde you look in that!'

'There the resemblance ends.' He sat down on the bed and taking her in his arms kissed her long and deep. When he released her she leaned back a little and examined his face carefully. He was pale but this morning his eyes were clear and unclouded. She put up her hand to caress the damp curls. 'Are you always so wide-awake first thing?'

'No, not always; my euphoria now is the result of making love with the loveliest woman in the world…' his voice softened, 'and because last night that same lovely and loving woman rocked me to sleep against her breast.'

She hugged her knees, questioning, 'Are you all right now; really all right?'

'More or less,' he looked at her intently, 'Are *you* all right? I'm so sorry to have spoilt our first night together.'

'I'm fine; and you spoiled nothing. Now we can talk about it or not; whichever makes it easier for you to bear.'

'Not, I think; at least for a time if that's all right by you.' He smiled and nodded at the bedside table. 'I see Elizabeth has brought our morning tea – would you like yours now?'

'Holy *shit!*' she sat bolt upright, clutching the sheet to her chin. 'You mean you let her see me like this?'

'I couldn't stop her, darling, I was in the shower – and isn't it a bit late for the maidenly modesty?' He was unperturbed. 'Anyway, I can't imagine the sight of you lying there starkers would worry her; mine can't be the only naked body she's seen in her sixty-odd years.'

Picking up quickly on his need for levity she snickered, 'Don't tell me you're a closet nudist?'

'No-o,' he began to pour the tea. 'The last time she saw me in the

228

buff I was about six years old; after that I insisted on bathing myself. Now if you'll be a good girl and drink your tea, I'll run a bath and scrub your back for you – *now* what are you laughing at?'

'You, because you are sweet and funny and not at all like snooty old Michael Howard Gervaise Archibald Niven who wouldn't make love to me...' letting the sheet fall she raised her arms to him. 'Oh, I do love you so much!'

Putting the cup he held back on the tray he took her by the shoulders, pressing her back against the pillows. Pushing the brocaded gown from his shoulders she whispered, '*To wake at dawn with a winged heart and give thanks for another day of loving...*'

He looked down on her upturned face. 'Where did you hear that?'

Placing her hands behind his head she drew him down onto her. 'Isabel told it to me.'

'Ah, wise, wise Isabel,' he murmured against her mouth.

*   *   *

When eventually they made an appearance downstairs there was no sign of Elizabeth, but Michael tracked unerringly across the hall murmuring, 'Just follow the smell of crisply grilled bacon, darling!' as he pushed open the door to the dining room.

At the head of the long polished table two places were set with crested mats, napkins and heavy silver cutlery. A covered dish sat on a hotplate on a side table while a basket of warm rolls lay swaddled in a cloth beside a freshly made *cafetière* of coffee.

Cassie's eyes widened as she gazed at all this splendour: 'How did she manage to time all this so accurately and why all the ceremony?'

'Elizabeth has ears like a fox; I daresay she counted down the minutes from when she heard the shower stop running for the second time!' Michael pulled out her chair. 'It's all right to eat around the kitchen table with her when you are *à deux*, but while you and I are here together, protocol must be observed!'

She gave a horrified shriek. 'That's positively feudal!'

'Yes, it is, isn't it!' He gave her an amused glance before he took the cover from the dish and cast an eye over the contents, 'but don't blame me, blame Elizabeth; she is a woman who trails the manners and foibles of a lost age wherever she goes. She's always been like that and nothing will change her now, so you must not hurt her feelings by letting her see you disapprove, nor snigger when, afflicted by a periodic need to put me in my place, she calls me Sir!'

He began to fill their plates with bacon and mushrooms and scrambled eggs while Cassie fingered the fine linen of the napkin and wondered what she had let herself in for. This was all a far cry from the easy informality of Fleetwood, or supper with Elizabeth round the kitchen table in Chelsea, or the kebabs and fish and chips eaten with Jono in the old graveyard. Still, if this was how it had to be she supposed she'd soon get used to it. She watched Michael's muscles moving beneath his silk shirt, remembering how his back had felt under her hands less than an hour ago and conceded that for him she could adapt to anything; even breakfast served à la Brideshead Revisited.

He sat down opposite her with his own plate and gave his slow, perceptive smile. 'Don't worry,' he said, 'I may be an old man who lets his nanny still call the tune but the advantages of marrying me will far outweigh the disadvantages, I promise you!'

She looked at him narrow-eyed. 'Who's worried – and when did you mention marriage? It isn't exactly the sort of thing a girl would miss, is it?'

'Oh, my God,' He clapped his hand to his forehead, 'did I forget to ask?' He put down his knife and fork then pushed back his chair to walk around the table and drop to one knee beside her.

'Cassandra…' he stopped and regarded her with raised brows. 'Do you have another name, darling?'

'Yes.'

Her face pinked and he prompted encouragingly. 'So?'

'If you laugh I'll never speak to you again.'

'I won't laugh; cross my heart!'

'Alaric had a poetic turn when I was born…it's Ariadne.'

He said poker-faced, 'Then you had one hell of a cheek to snigger at mine, didn't you? However, to the matter in hand…Cassandra Ariadne Chisholm will you marry me?'

She said solemnly, 'Yes, please!'

'Are you sure you wouldn't like to think it over?'

'Quite sure.'

'In that case,' he kissed her hands then said 'Ouch!' and stood to massage his knee. 'I think when I have finished breakfast you should find the old family retainer and tell her you are going to make an honest man of me at last.'

*   *   *

Cassie found Elizabeth alone in the kitchen and gave her a hug, demanding, 'You aren't going to go all stuffy now and start calling me madam are you? Because if you are I shall get very stroppy and not invite you to my wedding!'

Elizabeth sat down hard on a chair and struggled to look disapproving. 'Once the knot is tied, young lady, I shall call you madam in company, whether you like it or not; although what I call you out of it could be anybody's guess if you don't behave yourself and stay put with that man!'

'If I promise I will never, ever, leave him will you let me make another pot of coffee and natter with me over the kitchen table?' Cassie hugged her again. 'You don't know how happy I am this morning, Elizabeth. I just wish we could stay here with you forever.'

'You can't hide any longer, my lass. There are still people to face and problems to solve and you can't do that without going back out into the world.'

'I know: Alaric and Laura and Miles for a start.' Cassie made a face. 'I don't know why it seems to be my lot in life to keep coming up against people who know me better than I know myself; Laura was bad enough, but you and Sir Archie just about take the biscuit!' She spooned coffee into the percolator then took two mugs from the cupboard. 'I reckon Alaric will come as a positive relief. No one could ever accuse him of having had the slightest idea of who I am for at least ten years!'

'Nor you of him, I daresay' returned Elizabeth tartly.

Cassie gave her a peevish look.

'Did anyone ever tell you,' she asked pointedly, 'that you have a nasty habit of always being right?'

She answered cheerfully, 'If you can't have a few nasty habits at sixty, when can you have 'em, eh?'

Cassie laughed, and bending kissed her cheek, 'Sir Archie is right; you are an old witch!' she said.

26

The storm had gone, leaving in its wake a newly-washed world smelling fresh and clean. 'A day for the river,' Michael said and together they turned the skiff into the water and putting cushions on the damp thwarts and heaping them in the well of the boat, pushed off into a morning bright with wet shimmering banks and trees loud with birdsong.

He sent the skiff swiftly downstream: through the locks and the jostling yachts and motor launches, out to where the river widened into a breath-taking vista of unbroken water, lined on either side with great bushes of rhododendrons and trees whose roots spread to the very edge of the water.

Cassie was so entranced watching a vole plop out of a hole beneath one of these and startle a flotilla of ducks into sudden flight, that she gave a yelp of alarm and dropped the tiller ropes when Michael called, 'Hey – wake up! I said into the bank there – underneath those willows, not straight into the path of that yacht!' Grabbing the ropes again she steered the skiff where he directed, wondering as they secured it fore and aft to wooden post, how he had known there was a narrow landing stage beneath the trees.

'Now,' he spread the cushions and took her in his arms. 'No people, no telephone, and no outside world! Today is just for us; to talk to plan...' he gave his lazy smile, 'and to rest and recoup our energies for later!'

She looked over his shoulder. 'But perhaps not here: that board says "Private Mooring. No Trespassers!"'

'We're not trespassing,' he answered negligently. 'It's my cousin Dickie's land and he's away in Hong Kong making lots of dollars!'

She groaned softly. 'God, how many more useful relatives do you have lurking in the woodwork?'

'Dozens, and given time you'll meet them all!' He drew her head down onto his shoulder. 'Now just relax, and as Isabel would say, "Have a little zizz before we find somewhere to lunch. You've had a busy night –'

'And morning,' she murmured.

'Exactly,' he said, 'so do as you are told!'

Without protest she sighed and tucking her head under his chin closed her eyes. When she had drifted into sleep he shifted her into the crook of his arm and for a long time watched her quiet face before touching his lips to her eyes and winding a lock of her hair about his fingers. Stretching out beside her he closed his own eyes and let the sound of the river lull him to sleep.

*   *   *

'Where shall we live?' she asked, leaning over the stern, dipping her fingers in the water and patting them on her face, 'in London, I suppose?'

He lay back, watching her with lazy eyes. 'Where would you like to live?'

'Anywhere you are.' She looked at him over her shoulder. 'Don't you need to be in town for your work?'

'Not necessarily; I can write anywhere. At least I can when I'm not careering around the countryside looking for you!'

'Ouch,' she winced. 'That's a bit mean of you.'

'But true, none the less.' He chuckled at her pained expression. 'However, while you were busy making your mark on the London scene I was thinking about selling Hampden Square and moving permanently to Ashenden.' He looked at her enquiringly. 'How would you feel about leaving the great Metropolis for Suffolk?'

'Sounds all right to me; you forget – I'm a country girl, born and bred.'

'So you are, but Ashenden is quite a way inland, could you live without the sea?'

'A river nearby would help.'

'There is one of those about a half-mile away, and we do have a moat!'

She grinned. 'I'll settle for that: I don't know about your pa, though, he's a bit frightening, and your mother might just hate having to put up with another female about the place.'

'It's possible she may not notice!' She looked alarmed and he grinned. 'Don't worry, darling, she is nowhere near senile – just one of those eccentric Englishwomen who spend more time and thought on their dogs, gardens and the Almighty than they do on their husbands and children – they tend to get even more vague and forgetful with age. She can tell you the common and Latin names of every flower and shrub on the estate and the correct collect for the day; but would be hard put to say what month it is. As for Archie...' he gave a sudden hoot of laughter, 'you don't have to worry about him. He is, as our old gardener used to say, "full of piss and vinegar

233

but soft as pig shit underneath!'"

She howled at this vulgarity, uttered as it was in Michael's precise and euphonious tones and he laughed with her. Wiping her eyes she said, 'I'm not sure how long I'll survive your family, or they me, but I'm willing to give it a try; just so long as I can go on working as usual!'

He asked indulgently, 'What will you do in deepest Suffolk?'

'I'm not sure. Continue supplying Simon with prints...branch out on my own perhaps...I'd like to go on doing the sort of thing they do at the Centre; not the theatrical bit, but the teaching and workshops.'

'I don't see why you shouldn't if it's what you want, and if you have any great ideas that might help fill the coffers of Ashenden in time for the next face-lift I would be eternally grateful!'

'Gawd,' she said inelegantly, 'are you that hard up?'

'No, but I have to think of a way to capitalise on the place before long: quite how I don't know. It's too small and too far off the motorways to be used as anything like a conference centre or health farm, and not opulent or well enough known for a stately home. In any case, anything like that would be unthinkable while the parents are still managing to keep out of the obituary column in the Times!'

She was thoughtful, giving him a speculative look that immediately put him on his guard. 'I can think of something you *could* do.'

He said cautiously, 'Before you say it, the answer is probably, No.'

She grinned. 'Defeatist! How many bedrooms are there?'

'Twelve – sixteen I suppose if you count the old servant's quarters in the attics, but they haven't been occupied for years. Why?'

'Discounting – what? Two for your parents and one for us, leaving thirteen...'

'Leaving twelve,' he interrupted, straight-faced. 'You left out a nursery!'

'Hmm,' she cast him an uncertain eye. 'Twelve then – that's enough to make a start. I'm talking about students; visitors...summer schools and courses: spring and autumn ones as well if we could stand the pace...' She sat up, narrowing her eyes in concentrated thought. 'We could start with workshops for writers – that's you, and photography students – that's me, then bring in artists and potters and drama as well in time. It wouldn't be all year round and you could always get seasonal staff to cope with the housekeeping side of things.'

'Hang on a minute!' Michael held up an imploring hand. 'I know

234

absolutely nothing about such things and don't have the time to find out. You forget: I actually had a career as a writer and lecturer before I met you! I can't chuck all that out of the window to run courses for gaggles of students; never mind about flooding Ashenden with outside staff and having Gerda throttling anyone who set foot in her kitchen...' he waved his arms. 'Just the thought of pa loosing off at the rooks with his twelve-bore at regular intervals with the house full of middle-aged lady novelists makes my blood run cold –'

She interrupted him scornfully. 'You can't afford to be a literary snob if you want to make money. Not when women *writers* can put the jam on your bread!'

He said loftily. 'I don't talk about money, it's vulgar.'

'So is letting a load of tourists pay their whack to see where the Earl of Leicester might have got his leg over Queen Elizabeth, but plenty of your lot do it!'

He began to laugh. 'Don't forget that this morning you agreed to join my lot.'

'So I did.' She leaned to put her arms around his neck; kissing his mouth and letting him draw her down again onto the cushions. 'But don't you see? You won't have to do it all yourself – what do you think badly paid teachers and students and hard-up graduates *do* in the holidays?'

'I've no idea, but you're going to tell me, aren't you?'

'Not just yet.' She settled into his arms and ran an experimental finger down his back, 'as you said: today is just for us.'

'Oh, no you don't!' He stood and pulled her to her feet, making the boat rock. 'I'm taking you to the Mucky Duck for cheese and pickles. We'll talk more about your crazy plans over a pint of decent ale, and in a public place where you can't proposition me!'

Sighing audibly she stepped onto the wooden planking. 'Have it your own way; you usually do.'

'I don't mind having *you* any way!'

She stuck her nose in the air. 'That's a very obvious *double entendre* – and I don't think you should talk about sex – it's vulgar.'

'I suppose I asked for that,' he took her hand and began to walk her along a path that wound through the woodland, 'but, by God, Cassandra Chisholm, if you imagine you can fool me that I've had it all my own way so far you must think I'm wearing blinkers. *You* are just about the most deviously determined getter-of-your-own-way that I have ever come across in my life, you aggravating woman.'

She simpered and fluttered her eyelashes. 'Flatterer,' she said

*   *   *

When they were settled with their ploughman's and beer at a table by
the water's edge Michael eyed her carefully. 'Now, if you promise to
keep both feet on the ground and not take off on quite such
frightening flights of fancy, I'm willing to listen and co-operate –
within reason.'

'I'm sorry.' She laid her hand over his where it rested on the table.
'It's just that it seemed such a good idea: you know so much and write
so beautifully.'

'But I'm not a writer *per se*. I'm an historian who writes within a
specific field, not a novelist or journalist and that's what people would
be expecting.'

'I hadn't thought of that.' She was downcast. 'So you don't think
it's a good idea?'

'I think it's a great idea, but not necessarily for me.' He was silent
for a minute, looking out across the river with thoughtful eyes. 'How
would it be,' he asked, 'if we began slowly? If we turned part of the
old stables into a studio and work room for you to process your own
pictures and have, say, a half-dozen would-be photographers next
summer to begin with?'

'I'd love that, but it would cost quite a lot to do and we wouldn't
make a fortune out of just a half-dozen, would we?'

He smiled. 'I don't expect you to fill the coffers single-handed,
darling. It isn't such a vast project to convert the stables; they are not
wooden shacks, you know, but four lovely old fashioned loose boxes
in a large brick built stable block.' He gave her hand an encouraging
squeeze. 'If it is anything like a success, then I promise you I'll think
very seriously about expanding and see if we can recruit enough
competent professionals to run more courses by the following summer
– I think I know sufficient people in the right places to do that and I'm
happy to do the organising, find the extra staff and take the flack
when Pa hears what you are up to!'

'Oh, *God,*' she groaned, 'you're going to tell me he'll create hell
at the thought of having strangers swarming around the place, aren't
you?'

'At first and without a doubt, but my mother will love the idea
and once he realises it will make her happy he'll stop chewing the
carpet!'

'Do you think so?' She was doubtful. 'I should hate to get off on
the wrong foot with *him.*'

He gave her a quizzical look. 'I would take a bet that you've already got off on the right one.'

She asked tentatively. 'He won't expect me to start producing absolutely hoards of babies in double-quick time, will he?' She stopped suddenly and gave a little scream of alarm. '*You* don't honestly want me to right away, do you?'

He gave her a long, meaningful look. 'Not particularly, but after last night I shouldn't be at all surprised!'

'Oh!' she caught her lower lip between her teeth. 'Will you mind? I didn't think…'

'Neither did I, it didn't seem to be the sort of occasion for thinking, did it?' He leaned across the table to touch her face with gentle fingers. 'The thing is, my love, would *you* mind.'

She stared into his eyes, then caught his hand and held it against her heart. 'Only if it's triplets,' she said.

*   *   *

After supper that evening they went out into the garden. Cassie leaned back against the cushions of the seat and set it swinging gently, stroking Michael's hair as he lay with his head in her lap; thinking that this was an almost identical setting as that first evening they had spent in this same garden, with daylight fading around them and lamplight from the windows bathing them in a golden glow.

'What is going to happen to Elizabeth if you sell the London house?' she asked quietly. 'It would be awful to just go and leave her alone.'

'She's had to face the fact that London is not the safest place for her now and I'm pretty sure she's ready to leave. I'd *like* her to come to Ashenden, but I'm not sure she'd do that. Alternatively she could stay here but it's rather lonely for one person.' He twisted his head to look up into her eyes. 'What do we do about this place, anyway?'

'It would be lovely to know it was here to come back to from time to time, but you shouldn't ask me. All this – you and I – is still a bit too new for me to feel comfortable about making those kinds of decisions.'

'Of course,' he was thoughtful. 'Isabel comes regularly to town so it would be convenient for her to have somewhere to stay and be looked after.' He gave a sudden laugh. 'I'd suggest Jonathan left that awful flat for which he struggles to pay the rent and made this his base, if I didn't think he'd have the place stinking of pot and fill it with that shower of hangers-on – not to mention all the overnight crumpet.'

She asked indulgently, 'Where did you entertain all *your* overnight crumpet when you were Jono's age?'

'Never you mind, anyway it's too far out of town for him.'

She coaxed, 'No it isn't, and Elizabeth would keep Jono in order wouldn't she – and it would be a welcome place at the week-ends for us occasionally, and for Isobel.'

'Maybe.'

'Think about it?' she asked.

'I'll think about it.'

They relapsed into a companionable silence but after a time she could feel the tightening of his jaw that told her he was about to put whatever he was thinking into speech. After enduring the uncertainty for several minutes she pre-empted him, asking: 'Whatever it is you are thinking, would you mind saying it now because I can't bear the suspense much longer!'

He twisted his head up again. 'A couple of hundred years ago you'd have been burned at the stake for that kind of thought reading.' He sighed. 'I was thinking about your father.'

She said resignedly, 'When do you think we should leave?'

He took her hand, 'Soon, very soon.'

'We have to go tomorrow, don't we? I can feel you thinking it, but why? On Friday, Jono and I have to be back in London. It would be lovely if you and I could spend the time here until we fetch him from Dorset. In only a week or so I shall be finished at the Centre; by then it will be almost time for Laura and Miles' wedding. Couldn't we wait and go then?'

'I think it is important that you see him sooner than that.'

'Why should it be more important than for us to have these few days together?'

He said gently, 'He will tell you.'

'You know what he's going to say, don't you?'

'Yes, I know.'

'But you won't tell me?'

'No. It has to come from your father – and Cassie however you may feel about him, he *is* your father.'

'I shan't want to stay if it all goes horribly wrong,' she warned.

'It won't,' he stroked her cheek. 'How do you really feel about him now?'

'I'm not sure. It's been years since we actually *talked* to each other.' She gave him a sideways glance. 'Yours wasn't the first brick wall I've come up against, you know.'

'Well, if you could breach mine, his should be a pushover.' he said dryly.

She gave a small sigh: 'OK, you win. I'm ready.'

He kissed her then stood up. 'If I let him know we'll be starting after lunch tomorrow, will that be all right?'

She nodded and watched him walk away and felt a quick surge of resentment that something as precious as their time together should be spoiled in order to meet Alaric's wishes. Almost immediately she stifled the thought, curbing the impulse to call Michael back. If she'd learned anything at all over these past months it was that if one didn't seize the day it could be gone before one could enjoy, or accomplish anything in it.

What she and Michael had found was too rare to let slip away; they were bound to each other now and would love, and fight, and make up and love again for as many years as they might have together. When there was that to look forward to then finding time for Alaric and Laura, good, caring Miles, irascible old Archie and his so far unknown laterally-thinking 'Tavia, was a small price to pay for such happiness.

When Michael returned a few minutes later she left the swing and went across the lawn to meet him. For a moment she looked up into his eyes, then smiled and put her hands on his shoulders. 'You really care about him, don't you?'

He asked, 'How did you know?' and she answered, 'Because now the wall has come right down and I can read your eyes.'

*   *   *

It was early the following evening when they reached Tregedick. Stopping the car short of the town Michael put an arm about her shoulders. 'I know how your father wants this meeting to be, but are *you* sure you want to do it alone?'

'I have to. It's our mess, not yours or Laura's or Miles'. Just leave me at the door then take cover!' She gave a tentative grin. 'If it all blows up in my face I'll hang out of the window and scream for you. Now just drive, will you, before I lose my nerve.'

He re-started the car and drove down the hill and she directed him through the evening traffic of the small town to where Miles' bookshop nestled cosily between The Tregedick Arms and Martha's Bakery.

As they sat for a few moments looking at the bow-fronted shop with its sagging lintel and weathered grey Cornish stone, Cassie said, 'Miles reckons he has the best of both worlds here: booze on one side

239

and the staff of life on the other.' She smiled. 'You'll like Miles; the pair of you can sit around being calm and reasonable while the rest of us jump about tearing our hair and screaming!'

'I look forward to it.' He kissed her at length, holding her close. 'Come back to me soon. Good luck and God love you...'

She raised a sceptical eyebrow. 'Since when did God have anything to do with Alaric or me?'

He said gravely, 'According to my mother, nothing is ever done without the personal approval or disapproval of the Almighty.'

'Oh, well then, I shall know who's to blame if it all goes pear-shaped shan't I?'

He leaned to open her door. 'Better face the music, darling: I'll be waiting with the posse!'

She kissed him swiftly and sliding from the car crossed the road without a backward glance. Michael watched her knock on the door beside the shop; saw it open and ached for her momentary hesitation before she stepped in. As the door closed behind her he let out a long breath.

You'd better be right, ma, because right now there's an awful lot riding on the efficacy of the Almighty's all-seeing and hopefully, benevolent eye!

*   *   *

'Would you like a drink?' Alaric gestured towards the bottle on the table. 'Only whisky, I'm afraid: I meant to dodge next door and wangle some wine only I ran out of time.'

'Whisky will do fine.' She watched him pour the drink then took it with a cautious smile. 'How did you manage to wind Michael round your little finger?'

'I didn't even try; strange though it may seem to you, we speak the same language.' He eyed her speculatively over his glass, observing her for so long that she shifted uncomfortably.

'If I'm getting a boil on my nose please tell me...'

'Sorry. I have been trying to fix you in my mind but without success. It's been quite a time and you've changed so much.' His mouth twisted. 'You look like a woman in love and I've never seen that before.'

She said obliquely, 'Perhaps you've never looked before.'

'Perhaps,' he leaned forward in his chair and watched her as she sat on the couch, turning her glass in her hands. 'I know this is difficult for you because I feel pretty awkward about it too. I wish I'd told you everything that day in London; I should have faced the whole thing then and not walked away.' He paused and for a few moments watched her impassive face.

She looked, he thought, like a wary cat that found itself faced with a very large dog but was prepared to stand its ground and spit and scratch if necessary. He hunched his shoulders and ran a hand though his hair. 'Before I go any further I want you to know that what I'm going to tell you won't be a play for your sympathy. I don't expect you to fall on my neck weeping and say that all is forgiven. I just want you to know the reason I came back here and why I didn't want Laura to say anything before I was able to tell you myself.'

She put down her glass. 'I promise I won't fall on your neck. I'm listening, and I give you my word that I won't do another bunk.'

'That's enough for me.' He sat back and contemplated her with sober eyes then gave a rueful shrug.

'I've come home,' he said, 'because I thought Harry might be glad of some company…'

*　　　*　　　*

He talked and Cassie listened, grateful for the close of day that brought the concealing dusk creeping into a room that was deadly quiet apart from his voice and the muffled sound of traffic beyond the closed windows. She felt tears begin to build at the back of her eyes, but with a savage determination kept them at bay. They had been virtual strangers for so long that she couldn't even begin to guess what he may be thinking or feeling. She only knew that one wrong word or gesture from her might shatter the precarious calm of that quiet room.

But I don't know how *I* feel either, she thought, only that I am unbearably sad and that I will miss him…but we don't know each other any more. Supposing he doesn't want my compassion, suppose I say the wrong thing and drive him back into sarcasm or ridicule?

Overwhelmed by a sudden rush of conflicting emotions she groped for an answer. A few months ago she might not have felt like this: might not have been able even to want to begin building a bridge over ten years of rejection and hurt. Now she didn't know if it was possible to cross the awful distance between them.

She looked across the room to where he sat in silence now, his face in shadow, and her heart thudded unevenly at the thought of making that first momentous step towards him. Then she remembered her feelings of the previous day, when she had sat on the swing and watched Michael walk away from her…now indeed was the chance to seize the day.

She crossed the distance between them and sat on the arm of his chair. 'You never did have any finesse dad,' her voice was unsteady, 'that's one hell of a thing to tell a girl who's just had her father turn up on her doorstep.'

'I suppose so, but then you're one hell of a girl for a father to come back to.'

He studied her face for a moment then put his hand over hers and held it there. Rubbing his thumb over her fingers he said, 'I think it's OK for you to cry if you must, but do it quietly – I don't want that man of yours pounding up the stairs to the rescue!'

So she did it quietly while Alaric continued to hold her hand and think that dying might be faced with rather more equanimity than he had afforded it so far, if getting his daughter back again was part of the deal.

*   *   *

When it was time for her to leave he walked down the stairs with her then stood for a moment in the hallway. Holding her shoulders between his big hands he asked, 'Do you want me to try and find your mother – or your father? I will if that's what you want.'

'No, I already have all I need in that line.'

'What about later?'

She shook her head. 'I want nothing from the past but the memories I already have.'

'OK, then we'll close that subject for good, shall we?'

She acknowledged this with a nod and he continued, 'I know you have only a few days before you go back, but will you come for an hour tomorrow and sit for me?' He smiled at her smothered grin. 'No, I'm not looking for a nymphet; those days are now behind me; I would just like to find you on canvass once more.'

'I'll come tomorrow and every day until we leave.'

He bent and kissed her cheek. 'It won't be easy: the way back, but we've made a start, haven't we? If we don't try too hard I think we may make it, don't you?'

'Yes. I think we may.' She opened the door. 'Goodnight dad.'

'Goodnight, Cass.'

*   *   *

He had done what he had set out to do. The bridge they had begun to build may be a trifle shaky as yet, but with a little luck and a lot of care it would surely strengthen. No use pretending he wouldn't miss a companion in his bed, nor wish himself back in Paris, painting Nicole or Aimee or Bernadette, but now he wanted to preserve and prolong the life he had for as long as his uncertain heart allowed. He might, he thought with a sudden grin quite enjoy trying his hand at painting some jolly Beryl Cook-type women as a complete contrast to the nymphets – but only when such ample curves were quite definitely fully clothed.

He waited by the widow until his daughter had crossed the road towards the car where Michael stood and watched as the tall figure saluted him with upraised hand. Alaric returned the salute then, as Cassie ran the last few yards into Michael's waiting arms, stepped back and closed the door.

*   *   *

He climbed again to the studio and stood for a long time gazing at the unfinished portrait. Tomorrow, or the day after, or the day after that he would finally capture and keep his daughter; keep her for all time, on canvas and in his heart.

By the same author

A Year Out of Time

A Year Out of Time is the story of one twelve year old girl from a "nice" middle-class background and a "nice" private school (where her mother hoped she might learn to be a lady) who, in the Autumn of 1940, finds herself pitched into the totally foreign environment of a small Worcestershire hamlet.

For the space of one year her life revolves around the village school and its manic headmaster; the friends she makes, notably Georgie Little the "bad influence"; the twee but useful fellow evacuees, Mavis and Mickey Harper, whose possession of an old pigsty proves the springboard to some surprising and sometimes hilarious happenings; and Mrs 'Arris, the vast and formidable landlady of The Green Dragon Inn.

In the company of Georgie Little she awakens to the joys of a new and exhilarating world: a secret world which excludes most adults and frequently verges on the lawless.

The year comes to an explosive end and she returns unwillingly to her former life – but the joyous, anarchic influence of the Forest and Georgie remains, and sixty years on is remembered with gratitude and love.

ISBN 978-0-9555778-0-2

Available from Sagittarius Publications
62 Jacklyns Lane, Alresford, Hampshire SO24 9LH

By the same author

And All Shall Be Well

And All Shall Be Well begins Francis Lindsey's journey through childhood to middle age; from a suddenly orphaned ten year old to a carefree adolescent; through the harsh expectations of becoming a man in a world caught in war.

Set mainly against the dramatic background of the Cornish Coast, it is a story about friendships and relationships, courage and weakness, guilt and reparation. — *The first book in a Cornish trilogy.*

ISBN 978-0-9555778-1-9

**Chosen as the runner-up
to the Society of Authors 2003 Sagittarius Prize**

"The author has succeeded to an extraordinary degree in bringing Francis to full masculine life. The storyline is always interesting and keeps the reader turning the pages. All in all it is a good novel that can be warmly recommended to anyone who enjoys a good read."
– Michael Legat

"Seldom do I get a book that simply cannot be put down. The settings and characters are so believable, the shy falling in love for the first time and the passion of forbidden liaisons written with feeling. Many of the sequences left me with a smile on my face, others to wipe a tear from my eye." – Jenny Davidson, The Society of Women Writers and Journalists Book Review

"A beautifully written novel. Eve Phillips' writing is a pure joy to read and her wonderfully graphic descriptions of the Penzance area of the Cornish Coast made me yearn to be there."
– Erica James, Author

Available from Sagittarius Publications
62 Jacklyns Lane, Alresford, Hampshire SO24 9LH

By the same author

Matthew's Daughter

Matthew's Daughter is the second book in a Cornish Trilogy and follows Caroline Penrose, as she returns from her wartime service in the WAAF to her father's flower farm in Cornwall. But once home she finds a number of obstacles and family conspiracies impeding her path to peace...

ISBN 978-0-9555778-2-6

The Changing Day

The Changing Day the final book in a Cornish Trilogy, begins in 1940, when a meeting between WREN Joanna Dunne and Navy Lieutenant Mark Eden is the start of a love affair that at first seems unlikely to stand the test of time. She is 22, single and an Oxford graduate; he is 36, married and in civilian life a country vet. She is attracted but not looking for romance, he is attracted but not looking for commitment and, as Joanna soon discovers, he is the black sheep of his family and has a very murky past.

ISBN 978-0-9555778-3-3

Available from Sagittarius Publications
62 Jacklyns Lane, Alresford, Hampshire SO24 9LH

By the same author

A Very Private Arrangement

When in the spring of 1934, fourteen year old orphan Anna Farrell is transported from a life of drab, penny-pinching, genteel poverty with her cousin Ruth, to the elegant, affluent Bloomsbury household of distant cousin Patrick Farrell, and his manservant, Charlie Caulter, she is at first blissfully unaware of the well hidden secret kept by the two men, until a meeting with the quasi-charming Madame Gallimard and her sons becomes the catalyst that threatens to tear her world apart.

Against the backcloth of WW2 and a diversity of places and people, with her beloved Patrick and Charlie to smooth her path through the inevitable pitfalls of first, second and last love, Anna matures from naïve young girl to confident young woman, well able to cope with the men in her life – and some of the women in theirs.

ISBN 978-0-9555778-4-0

Return to Falcon Field

Ryan Petersen, a professor of European Literature at a New England University, accepts a year's exchange lectureship in London. But in coming to England the cynical, detached Ryan has a hidden agenda: to find the woman with whom he had a passionate wartime love affair over twenty years before.

He returns to the now derelict airbase of Falcon Field and the nearby Hampshire village of Hawksley, to begin a journey into the past; one that proves both painful and inspiring as he re-discovers the man he once was, and perhaps could be again.

ISBN 978-0-9555778-5-7

Available from Sagittarius Publications
62 Jacklyns Lane, Alresford, Hampshire SO24 9LH

By the same author

A Very Artistic Affair

The year is nineteen sixty-five. After twenty years of marriage Olivia, a forty-five year old wife and mother, discovers that her husband, Giles, has fallen in love with a young actress half his age.

Already feeling the first stirrings of discontent as the conventional and dutiful wife of her far from faithful husband, and conscious that the Swinging Sixties is rapidly passing her by, a humiliated and angry Olivia leaves the family home, moves from Hampshire to Devonshire, discards her twin-set and pearls image, resumes her earlier career as an artist, acquires her own occasional lover and copes successfully with her teenage son's burgeoning affair with a sculptor's daughter.

But as the months pass neither Olivia nor Giles find the separate paths they have chosen free from difficulty. There is confrontation, conflict and pain as events take many unexpected, sometimes tragic, and sometimes farcical twists and turns, before either can leave the past behind them and move forward into a new, and hopefully more peaceful, future.

ISBN 978-0-9555778-6-4

Available from Sagittarius Publications
62 Jacklyns Lane, Alresford, Hampshire SO24 9LH